Written in their Stars
The Lydiard Chronicles | 1649-1664

ELIZABETH ST.JOHN

Published by Falcon Historical Press 2019
ISBN: 978-0-9993944-6-5

Other books by Elizabeth St.John
The Lydiard Chronicles

The Lady of the Tower
A Novel
By Love Divided
A Novel

Counterpoint: Theo, Earl of Suffolk
A Novelette
Counterpoint: Barbara, Lady Villiers
A Novelette

"Her world and characters are so real I wanted to remain there. The Lydiard
Chronicles are now on my list of all-time favorite historical novels.
A fantastic read."
- Historical Novel Society -

Acknowledgements

The quotes featured at each chapter heading for Luce are extracts from Lucy Apsley Hutchinson's own work, *Memoirs of the Life of Colonel Hutchinson*, edited by N.H. Keeble; her extraordinary writing served as the inspiration for The Lydiard Chronicles.

In addition to solitary reading, the best research takes place in the field, and throughout the years I have had the pleasure of spending time with the custodians of my character's histories. My heartfelt thanks to the Earl and Countess of Bathurst for generously sharing their home and beautiful family portraits with me; to Mike Montagu, Bursar at Ditchley Park. who encouraged me to endlessly explore the house and grounds; the staff at Historic Royal Palaces who kindly opened private doors and hidden rooms at the Tower of London; the staff at Lydiard Park who always greet me with such a warm welcome; and Sarah Finch-Crisp and the Trustees of The Friends of Lydiard Park who have provided such bountiful resources and unfailing support.

My special appreciation to Professor David Norbrook, whose seminal work on Lucy Hutchinson has been my North Star, and his willingness to explore obscure genealogy and lost fishponds with equal enthusiasm brightened so many days.

My sincere thanks to the kindest of friends who read multiple drafts and answered incessant questions. This includes the online writing community at Scribophile.com, Deborah, Sally, Cryssa, RJ and Barry for fine beta draft insights, and librarians the world over.

Huge thanks to my extraordinary editors Jenny Quinlan and Emma Craft, who rescued me from plotholes and cried in all the right places.

Finally, my heartfelt gratitude to my family and friends who have traveled with me through time and place and always brought me down to earth.

A word on Lydiard
The St.John family home of Lydiard Park and House, along with St. Mary's Church, is located just west of Swindon, England. Set in more than 200 acres of beautiful parkland, the house is open to the public, and contains many portraits of the St.John family featured in The Lydiard Chronicles. St. Mary's Church, one of the finest small churches in England, is full of extraordinary monuments to the seventeenth century St.Johns.

The Friends of Lydiard Park is an independent charity dedicated to supporting the conservation and continued enhancement of Lydiard House and Park. As Ambassador of The Friends, I hope you will visit Lydiard one day and enjoy my "special place."

www.FriendsofLydiardPark.org.uk
www.stmaryslydiardtregoze.co.uk

Selected Family Tree

Lucy St.John m. Sir Allen Apsley
-         Allen Apsley b. 1616 m. **Frances Petre** b. 1624
           Isabella, Peter, Franny
-         **Luce Apsley** b. 1620 m. Colonel John Hutchinson
           Tom, Bee

John St.John m. Anne Leighton
-         **Nan St.John** b. 1614 m. (1) Francis Lee
        m. (2) Henry Wilmot
          Harry and Frank Lee
          Johnny Wilmot

Barbara St.John m. Edward Villiers
-         William Villiers b. 1614 m. Mary Bayning
          Barbary Villiers
-         Ned Villiers b. 1620

PART ONE

1649
DEPARTURES

1

Luce

. . . he, upon serious debate, both privately and in his addresses to God, and in conferences with conscientious, upright, unbiassed persons, proceeded to sign the sentence against the king.

Luce Hutchinson
Winter 1649

A dying candle flame trembled and smoked, casting distracting shadows across her journal. Luce cupped the wax stub as she scratched thoughts from her drying quill. A draft upon the creaking of the chamber door extinguished the light.

Rex debet mori

Her final words were scrawled by blood-red firelight.

The king must die.

Luce arose as her husband slipped into their bedroom. The flames threw his shadow onto the wall tapestry of the Last Supper.

"John? Who dared break curfew and row you to Battersey?" Her words tumbled forth. "Cromwell threatened to lock the judges inside Westminster all night. Why did he release you so soon?"

John scraped a flint, and a lantern flickered and flared. His hair fell forward, eclipsing his face.

"It is done."

She ran to him, heart hammering. This moment, his words, two years in the making.

"You signed?"

John held her as she trembled, whether from cold limbs or cold heart she knew not. His lips caressed her forehead.

"My Luce, my light, your destiny is fulfilled." His voice was measured, serene. "Today, your birthday, we realize your mother's prophecy."

She nodded, anxiety muzzling her.

Speak, John, speak of the deed you have committed tonight. For saying aloud makes it true.

1

John's arms tightened. "Upon your birth, your parents predicted their daughter would achieve eminence—"

Her heart quickened. His beat strong, resolute beneath her palm. The chilled wool of his coat still carried the tang of London's sea coal smoke.

"—and tonight we have attained the destiny foretold by the stars." John held her at arm's length, and a knife-blade of cold air sliced between them. "I signed the warrant to execute Charles Stuart, once King of England."

His eyes shone.

Luce acknowledged his victory. "It is done."

Even as others who judged with John lost courage and stole away like thieves in the night. If there were not enough signatories, all would be lost. If she could have snatched a quill and signed herself, she would.

"And now?"

He kissed her. "Now rest, for what is done cannot be undone. Tomorrow he dies."

"And the republic is born. A small sacrifice to liberate an entire nation."

John lit candles and added logs to the fire. The room grew golden and warm as he shrugged his thick winter coat to the bench and pulled off his fine embroidered waistcoat and dark breeches. His body was long-muscled, lean and graceful. Abruptly, she put aside her thinking and yielded to the urge to make love, to validate life, to banish the horror of seven years of the king's war.

"Remember our wedding night," he whispered as he drew her close again. His voice softened to the mellow timbre she loved. "Remember the rose petals strewn in our bed, how frightened you were I would think you hideous?"

She nodded. "Even the pox marks could not scare you from me."

John stroked the hair from her face and kissed her lips, softly and then deeply, sweetly. "And now you have healed, and the scars have faded from memory. Just as the years of fighting and war and death are behind us. Our wedding night reminds us not to fear the future. We are in a new world, my love, a world where we create our destiny." He drew her to the bed, caressing her, trailing his fingers on a familiar path, and she responded by pulling him to her, opening herself to his touch. "As you are my fate, I pledge you my soul and my eternal future."

How instinctive, the human need to affirm life in the face of death, no matter how deep the sorrow, how great the shock. On her wedding night,

John had kissed away the deadly smallpox blemishes and restored her body to life. Now, as his passion rose and was spent with a gasp, her mind flew to the approaching execution that would restore life to England's people.

Later, much later, she lay sleepless next to him, the weight of covers holding her captive in the posted bed. A single candle remained on the sill, weak flame quivering in the opaque glass. As John's breathing steadied and deepened, she carefully slid from under the fur mantle and, pulling her robe tight, trod quietly to the window seat. A familiar view, for she knew this house of old. Her family's home had remained a refuge to all of them over the years. And now they gathered to seek comfort here again.

Faint lights gleamed across the Thames on the Chelsea shore, a watchman's fire or two, but mostly the river ran as dark as the Styx. Apt, for tonight was the border between worlds, the old once ruled by a king, the new by the people. Starlight glistened in the face of the night sky, and as she examined the firmament for another sign, wonder crept into her heart.

John was a good man, a fair man. But just as he had taken six weeks to declare for king or Parliament at the beginning of the wars, so wavered his resolve as Oliver Cromwell commanded him to end the conflict.

Do not hesitate now, Husband. She had urged him ever forward, served him up logic and rhetoric, debated his principles late into the nights until the candles drowned in their wax puddles.

And so John had signed.

She became Salome. And her demand granted. The king's head.

Revenge.

Luce searched the heavens again. No shooting star seared the black midwinter night. But no need to watch more, for the omen had arrived on the morning she was born in the Tower of London in the year of our Lord 1620. She'd carried her purpose within these past nine and twenty years.

It is done.

And what of her brother and his wife, asleep in the adjacent room? Allen would be distraught, betrayed by John's decision. He'd recognize her part in it, perhaps find her role unforgiveable. But Frances would surely help him come to terms with the outcome of the king's war. They knew no alternative existed but execution for this dishonourable Stuart.

For Luce had avenged the untimely death of their father, the terrible casualties of their beloved cousins and John's loyal troop of Nottingham men slaughtered in battle.

And ended the terrible conflict between herself and Allen.

Already, words formed for the pamphlet she would write and circulate among their trusted friends. Her theme? The birth of liberty. Undoubtedly, the execution of the Catholic king made way for their true Calvinist worship. Ultimately, words succeeded where men failed.

Luce wrapped her arms around herself and pressed her forehead against the icy windowpane. She welcomed the numbing cold as she waited for the sun to rise and deliver light to the new dawn.

2

Frances

Frances shifted under the fine Rennes linen sheets, thoughts skittering in all directions, sleep running from her. A door closing, whispered voices and then a muffled cry murmured beyond the partition wall told of John and Luce's triumph. She unclenched her fists and slowly opened her fingers, flexing her stiff hands.

"Frances?" Allen drowsily reached for her.

"Hush. Go back to sleep, my love."

It is done.

John had signed the warrant this night. Death would be immediate. Parliament would not permit time for the exiled prince to return at the head of a Catholic army, rallying the Royalists.

She touched her neck. Crossed herself.

Mother of God.

Allen's breathing deepened, the brandy pulling him back into its warm embrace.

She fidgeted again. After John's decree, would her sister-in-law make love so passionately, so that moans and exclamations kept Frances awake?

Yes.

For had not Allen fallen in love with Frances herself in the shadow of war's surrender? Ardor healed where words failed.

Will tomorrow's execution toss Allen back into his mind's abyss?

A small hiccup next to her, the sound the baby made just before she cried. Frances held her breath, willing Isabella not to wake. Surprising she slept at all, given her parents' anguish. A few minutes, and she quietened.

Frances slid her arm from between Allen's head and the bolster. He mumbled and reached for her, but she inched from his grip. Let this troubled husband of hers rest, for he bore the burden of a hundred deaths, of those he knew and loved and those by the numbers only.

Mother Mary, grant these men eternal rest.

Allen's beloved cousins. Luce's too. And yet her sister-in-law's religion forbade prayers for the dead. What hope for salvation if God did not guide them from purgatory?

Frances rolled over to face Allen. Exhaustion and brandy had loosened his expression, a sweetness playing around his full lips and long lashes. She tucked a lock of curling dark hair from his forehead. A frown flitted across his face and disappeared as quickly as it had arrived.

How she loved this man and his mercurial passion. Tonight, as he drank steadily, Allen had recounted a boyhood story of his cousins at this manor house. They'd stolen their uncle's wine, raided the kitchens of a fine feast, and drank themselves silly as they teased and talked about the university years ahead. He'd laughed heartily at the memory. And then wept bitterly for his loss.

Only he remained.

And tomorrow, because of John's signature, the divinely appointed king whose life they had defended with their own, whose beliefs were the very essence of England's soul, would join Allen's soldier-cousins in death.

"Is it done?"

While she reflected, Allen's smoke-grey eyes had opened.

"Yes."

"John has signed the death warrant?" The familiar blankness shuttered his face.

"I believe so." John would not have come home with the business unfinished.

"My best friend. My sister. Traitors to the king." Allen's bitter whisper travelled to her ears alone.

Frances remained silent.

"These past two years John and I negotiated England's solution. We carried the messages back and forth from king to Parliament. We talked, we found common ground." He sat up abruptly, as if to march to John now, continue their parley. "A way to govern England, give voice again to Parliament. And yet, tomorrow, the axe severing the king's life finishes ours as we know it too." Allen rubbed his eyes wearily. "John betrayed our agreements. Luce encouraged the king's death. And now you and I are doomed by their decisions."

"You never gave up, neither of you. Perhaps in the end the king could not accept the advice of anyone but God," replied Frances. Scant comfort,

6

but anything to shift the blame from Allen's conscience. "Perhaps you and John can still find your brotherhood."

Allen ran his fingers through his hair. Such fine hands, the sword scar on his forearm glinting white in the dim light. Frances studied him, cheek pillowed in her hand.

"Not at the price of the king's death," he said. "I go tomorrow. Nan too."

"Your cousin told me this evening she must attend."

"Naturally. To honour my cousins, her brothers who died in the king's service. Don't come if you do not wish to."

"Of course I will." Frances sat up, the velvet covers falling from her, the night cold descending upon her shoulders. "Why would you think otherwise?"

Allen shrugged. "It is not a scene for a woman to observe."

"Nan attends."

And had made a point of telling Frances within minutes of their meeting this evening.

"She has her reasons."

Frances's temper flashed. "And I don't? I cared for the king's infant daughter, Queen Henrietta, her ladies. I held the prince by the hand and comforted him when he lost all hope of seeing his father again. When the court sought refuge with us, I risked everything to aid them."

Isabella stirred, disturbed by Frances's anger. She whimpered.

Allen rolled from the bed, leaned over the crib and picked her up. The little girl immediately settled, snuggling into his arms.

"You're right. I'm sorry. You were as a sister to Prince Charles. Of course. We will go together with Nan."

"Are you sure you should be there?" Allen's condition lay between them, unspoken but present.

"He is my king. He is dying for me."

Floorboards creaked from the next chamber. Someone had arisen. Allen climbed back into bed, tucked Isabella between them. The fire died and darkness flowed over them, except for a bead of light trickling from the adjoining room.

"And Luce? What words for her? She will attend too."

"Luce is lost to me." Allen's words were muffled in the softness of Isabella's hair.

7

Frances curled under the covers and turned to face the window. Candlelight flickered through the partition. Today's judgment gave John and Luce victory. But tonight one of them could not find peace.

Allen's words lingered. The world they knew ended tomorrow. She must think past the moment of death to life beyond. Mary, Mother of God, guide her well, for survival lay in her hands, not her husband's.

3

Nan

Nan Wilmot stood at Allen's side, charged by her husband to witness the king's execution, pinned to the barrier by the silent crowd, frozen in place by London's stunned citizens and the bitter January weather. No matter she wore her favourite sables, for no luxury could thaw her heart.

"Do not flinch, darling Nan, do not turn your head when the axe falls, for fall it doubtless will," Henry had written in cypher from his exile with Prince Charles in Paris. "Even at this late date, the prince denies to himself they will dare to execute his father. You must stand strong and capture every moment. What he says, when he kneels, how he lays his head on the block. Listen for his words and look into his eyes. And when the deed is done, dip your handkerchief in his gore, for his is the blood of a martyr. One day, my dearest wife, you will travel here and tell us how the prince's father died."

So upon Henry Wilmot's encrypted orders, Nan fixed her eyes on this hellish scene.

Parliament's troops stood ten deep in front of the scaffold, crowding the entrance to King Street—how ironic the name—facing them down, horses skittish, men taut. To walk against this sullen horde was nigh impossible.

She would not move. Not even if Oliver Cromwell himself commanded. And Lord knew she'd challenged him a few times, whether he recognized her defiance or not.

She sniffed.

He may consider her a simpering lady of the manor, a grieving widow, a distracted bride marrying his greatest enemy. The Protector's God would not credit a woman the brain to think beyond planning the next dinner. Let him be content with that ruse all day long.

As before in these difficult war years, her cousin stood by her, as handsome as ever, his shoulders broad under his leather overcoat, his dark hair curling over the collar. But no light in his cloud-grey eyes for her today. This morning Allen had brought his pretty wife, turned out in her fur-trimmed crimson wool. No sad Puritan colours for this beauty, casting aside even a linen cap in favour of a demure little hat tipped fashionably over her forehead. Frances Petre, of Devon. A family of the old religion, favourites at the court of King Charles the First of England and the Catholic Queen Henrietta.

"What's keeping them?" Nan hissed at Allen. "Where is the king? Where is the executioner? Where is John? Is he standing on the roof with the other commissioners?"

Allen remained silent. As he had been all morning. His wife opened her mouth to speak for him. Nan turned away.

London's citizens surrounded them, the brittle morning laden with sorrow and disbelief. She could not turn, pressed as she was, but the back of Nan's neck ached with the burden of a hundred thousand eyes fixed in her direction. Never had she witnessed such a pouring of humanity from the alleys and streets. A steady tramp of footsteps, but no words, no talk. Dark clothes against a granite sky, snow threatening again. Ice hid treacherously between the cobbles, frost bruising her feet despite her elegant calfskin boots and warm silk stockings.

She looked up at Allen, his fine profile chiseled against the lowering clouds. "You've seen executions before. God knows when you and Luce grew up in the Tower of London, your father's governance made you no stranger to the scaffold."

He turned to her, his eyes blank.

She read his thoughts, as only she could.

Today was different. Today, their king was to be slaughtered.

Nan dragged her eyes from Allen to the face of the Banqueting House. A curious location. Here their family had made merry with the court. Enjoyed the masques so beloved by the king and queen. The name of the last one Nan performed in? The Triumph of Peace? How ironic. And here Aunt Barbara Villiers had encouraged their carousing under the masterpiece ceiling of Rubens, glorifying the king's father, James Stuart, the Sixth of Scotland, First of England, First of Great Britain.

How the ghosts mocked their mood today.

The king's cause lost. God save the army and the Parliament.

Did Allen remember those times?

"Do you recall the winter we danced here every night in the queen's entertainments, when John courted Luce?" Surely, he remembered. He must, for Allen and her brother Edward were inseparable then, and Whitehall had been their palace.

He faced forward still. "And Edward is dead and the king-killers compel Charles to walk his last under his painted ceiling." His voice broke. "Where his father looks down as the guard escorts him to heaven."

God Almighty. Was there no end to this commission's cruelty that they made each last moment on earth a sword-thrust in itself?

And now death, the ultimate Lord of Misrule, commanded her to change partners in the masque. Nan would take his bony hand and dance his volta. She cared not who she cavorted with, simply that she survive to the dance's end.

King. Parliament. King. Parliament. Turn.

Before the Banqueting House, in the direction of Charing, a wooden stage jutted from a tall open window. Nan forced herself to look to the platform, draped in black cloth so at his last the king would have his privacy. Only God and those who leaned on high from the windows and roofs would witness his final breath.

"The executioner. The executioner." A whisper shivered through the crowd, buoyed by shuffling as the people stepped forward as one.

There appeared the axe-man, with felt hat pulled over his masked eyes. Nan could not see the block. Thank God, for they must have built it low. At least death would come quick, the king prone, neck exposed for the axe's blow.

And there, crowded at the windows, were the murderers, the men who had signed, whose stroke of a pen was the stroke of an axe, the stroke of death.

There, somewhere, stood Colonel John Hutchinson. With the other king-killers.

And behind him, high in the spectator's balcony under the painted ceiling, watching with eager eyes, his wife, Allen's sister, her beloved cousin Luce.

Did she realize at this moment how John's signature was about to change the world?

Of course she did. Luce had written of the necessity for England's liberty from the god-king for years.

Nan's eyes met Frances's, who stared back at her and gathered Allen tightly to her side. His mouth formed a silent prayer. Was it for the king's soul, or John's? Nan could not surmise.

"The king. The king comes." Next to her a woman sobbed. Nan bit back her own tears.

And now appeared the king, dignified and delicate of stature, with his attendant bishop, and the star of George twinkling on his doublet. The anonymous crowd reduced to the mourners around her. A soldier with silent tears running ragged down his battle-scarred face. A woman clutching a child, holding him aloft to witness. A baby crying, and yet such silence.

The king's lips moved, and Nan strained to hear the words.

He turned to the man standing by him.

"Colonel Hacker," murmured Frances.

Nan nodded at the detail. "My husband commands I observe every moment."

Frances stared ahead. "Queen Henrietta waits with Prince Charles in Paris. I promised her myself we would never desert the king. Their son must know how his father died."

Nan turned her eyes back to the scaffold. "This is why we are here, is it not?"

The king spoke again. His voice carried unnaturally loud through the thin and bitter air.

"Take care they do not put me to pain." He flinched as another soldier approached. "Take heed of the axe, pray, take heed!"

Nan caught her breath at the anguished words. These were not to be repeated. The prince would want to hear of his father's bravery and compassion, even at his dreadful end.

The king continued. She attended to every word.

"I shall say but very short prayers, and when I stretch forth my arms—"

A moan from Allen. Nan fixed on the scaffold. Frances could comfort him.

"I go from a corruptible to an incorruptible crown, where no disturbance can be, no disturbance in the world."

Now the crowd wept aloud, and the king's words were drowning in London's anguish. He tucked his own hair into a white nightcap. He removed his George garter from his chest and handed it to the bishop at his side. He uttered just one phrase.

"Remember."

Nan consumed every word, every gesture to share with the prince. Edgehill, Newbury, Cropredy Bridge—once, her husband and her brothers and Allen had ridden to war for the king, prepared to sacrifice all for the Royalist cause. And most did, never returning home from those terrible battles. Thank God her own sons were safe at home, too young to soldier.

And now their king died for them. God's anointed no more. Sovereignty would next dwell with the people. Luce and John had won.

King Charles took a step forward and hesitated.

He asked one question. "Can this be higher?"

No.

Nan's heart twisted as she imagined her king lying horizontal behind the black-hung railings, flat on the rough wooden boards, vulnerable as a child.

Get this over with, get this done. You would kill a horse injured at Naseby more quickly. Get this done.

The crowd stood silent, one breath held by all.

The executioner raised his axe.

The steel vanished against the sombre clouds. Perhaps it did not exist.

The blade descended.

A thud. And beyond the dark cloth, a spray of crimson, the colour of Frances's cloak, of the Cross of St. George, of England's life blood.

It is done.

Allen's groan mingled with the groan of the crowd, the world, the heavens. Such a sound Nan had never known in birth or death.

The executioner held the king's head aloft, blood dripping, hair no longer tucked in his fine linen bedcap, eyes closed.

He slept the absolute and infinite rest of martyrs.

Allen staggered, steadied by Frances. The man beside Nan vomited, the rancid stench overpowering the iron reek of blood. The hangings were tugged aside, revealing the corpse, ragged neck pumping crimson.

One more responsibility she must carry out. Nan moved forward, observed her own detachment, people melting into the grey.

She pushed her way through the troops. Paying her shilling to the executioner, she stood on tiptoe to dip the lacy fragment of her kerchief in the royal blood.

She returned to Allen and spoke clearly, for his head remained bowed. "This is for Prince Charles. I will tell him myself, in Paris, of the day his father died. Of the day he became King Charles the Second. Of how in the face of great loss, survival is the victor."

"According to Luce, the monarchy is finished." Frances spoke practically of the nature of the deed, as Allen's sister would see it. This woman did not flinch from truth.

Allen lifted his eyes, haunted, hollowed. "There will always be a monarchy. Our king is dead. Long live the king."

"And one day we shall restore Charles to England," continued Frances. "Home to England, where he belongs."

She looked up at the Banqueting House windows, and Nan followed her gaze to the figure of John, framed by the tall window. He lifted his hand, almost a benediction.

"We must go home ourselves," Frances continued, ignoring John's gesture. "Home to Battersey, Owthorpe, Lydiard, to start our lives again. The war is over."

Nan shook her head. "It has just begun."

4

Frances

"Your pass?" The soldier eased forward from the cluster of Roundheads blocking the alley to Scotland Yard. A fire heaped high with hefty tree limbs and a broken gate belched an acrid yellow smoke that hung in the chill afternoon air. Through the haze, Frances glimpsed the river, leaden under the oppressive cold. At the passage end stood a wall of guards, pikes forming a barrier ten feet high. She took Allen's arm.

He cautiously pulled his credentials from inside his cloak, and Frances glanced at Nan.

John had ensured Oliver Cromwell's seal ratified them. The remnants of when he and Allen worked for peace. These days, no telling where loyalties lay, but at least the commander's stamp secured safe passage.

"You're not London militia." Allen assessed the man's uniform. "Did Parliament expect an uprising and bring in its own troops?"

The soldier grunted. A livid red scar snaked across his mangled face, puckering an empty eye socket. "Where you heading?"

"Home. Battersey Manor."

"Where you been?" Thrusting Allen's pass at him, the soldier beckoned a couple of his men.

"Isn't it obvious? Or have you forgotten already what just happened?" Allen snapped, his educated accent to the fore.

Frances's heart jumped.

The men stank, their leather jackets sweat stained, their britches filthy from living rough for months. "Turn back. You ain't got no right to go through Whitehall today."

A protest rose in Frances's throat. She must return to Battersey, hold Isabella in her arms, the reassurance of life on this day of death. This guard would not stop her. She stepped forward, but Nan grabbed her elbow, pinching her flesh hard.

"I travel under Cromwell's protection." Allen glared at the leader, who met his gaze quite insolently.

"How nice, my friend." The man hawked and spat, the yellow glob narrowly missing Frances's boot. "And I enforce Cromwell's orders."

Laughter exploded about the burly men. One of them kicked a glowing timber back on the fire, and sparks exploded into the darkening sky. Nan tightened her grip, and Frances tried to dislodge her hand.

The leader took a step closer to Allen.

"You think an expired pass with Cromwell's signature is getting you anywhere? Turn back, fine sir. Whitehall is not your palace and never will be again for you and your fancy Catholic friends. Today we took care of England's future"—triumph coloured the captain's words—"and you have no business abroad."

The soldier drew his sword and let it hang at his side, glistening menace in the firelight. The streets had swiftly emptied. An echoing thump of a marching patrol rattled behind them. White-faced, a woman seated at an upstairs casement stared down, expressionless. A twitch of a curtain. A shutter slamming shut. And the incessant, overly loud crackling of the blaze.

Frances reached out to Allen to turn back when Nan's low tone broke through the tension. "My cousin will hear of this. And he will not be pleased."

"Your cuzzin?" The soldier mimicked Nan's refined accent. "And who might he be, when he's home? Turn back, the lot of you, before I throw you all in the Fleet for disobeying the army." He looked pointedly at Allen. "Or worse."

Allen's forearm braced under Frances's grip. Nan stood her ground. "Colonel John Hutchinson."

The man stopped and turned. "Got anything to prove it, Coz?"

Nan pulled her own papers from her purse and thrust them at the soldier. He looked at them briefly, nodding his head a few times. He whistled through yellowed teeth.

"Signed by Colonel John Hutchinson indeed. May I extend the thanks of myself, my men and England, Lady Lee." The man bowed. Frances held her breath. Was this sarcasm or genuine? And Lady Lee—not Wilmot? "Delighted to make the acquaintance of the relative of a king-killer. Proceed."

Nan retrieved her papers and took Frances's arm again, turning towards the river and a barge to Battersey. The soldier thrust forward his sword and

16

stayed Allen. He raised the blade higher, the tip of it cutting the tape on Allen's linen shirt.

"You was lucky this time. Had a nice helping, and from a lady. Don't try it again."

At his words, Nan whirled around. She stared at the soldier, stared him down until he dropped his sword to Allen's chest.

"Bugger off," he yelled, to the laughter of his men. "Bugger off, Lord Muck. Before you lose your head too."

Nan grabbed Allen, jerking him so sharply he stumbled, and then stalked ahead.

"Lady Lee?" Frances asked, hurrying to keep apace. "You are Lady Wilmot."

"I awoke so this morning. This afternoon it is not favourable to be a Royalist and married to the king's best friend. This afternoon, I am still widowed Nan Lee, married into a respected Puritan family."

"False papers? You are well prepared." Frances conceded Nan's quick thinking. There appeared more to Allen's cousin than fine airs and graces.

"The past years have taught me much in the art of survival," Nan said drily. "As they have you, I suspect."

Away from the blaze, the rancid London air enfolded them, easterly cold and river dank. The chill crept into Frances's bones. Already, the light dwindled, and if they were to be safe at Battersey before the watch patrolled, they must hurry. The streets belonged to the fanatics of Cromwell's army, and they needed no further encounters with the enemy.

The river tide ran in their favour, thanks be to St. Christopher. As they settled into the barge, images of the day flooded her mind. Frances worried at the humour that now subdued Allen. If she had not held him as he sagged against her when the axe fell, he would have collapsed. Even now sweat glistened on his brow on this freezing day. The encounter with the guards had briefly revived him, a reaction from years of warfare. Now he sank back into his memories.

As Frances balanced on the planked bench, Allen's leg pressed against hers, snatches of the day's events kept tumbling before her eyes.

And now this newly met cousin of Allen's, Nan Wilmot, commanding Allen to stay steady, soaking her handkerchief in the king's blood, pulling him away from the soldiers and flourishing false papers.

Nan's low-pitched voice broke her thoughts. "Allen, it is good we return to Battersey. My brother waits for us with your mother. We shall confer as a family and plan our future."

Was this woman intentionally excluding her with her know-all and uppity ways? "We need no counsel from them. Allen and I have considered our situation—"

"I'm sure you have." Nan leaned across Allen, making Frances tilt forward to hear better. "But there's a difference between considering and acting." She lowered her voice. "And at this moment, Allen isn't capable of either. My brother Walter will give us sound advice."

The only surviving St. John heir. Doling out Roundhead guidance.

Nan lapsed into silence, and in the hour the barge took to return to Battersey, Frances's plan formed.

The crumpled parchment concealed in her purse's inner pocket held hope, a letter to Allen secreted through Sir Edward Hyde's network. And yes, she was right to intercept it, for as long as Allen remained lost in his darkness, she must be responsible for both of them.

Frances recalled the letter from their Villiers cousin, read so often she'd memorized the words.

> *Come to court, Allen, for although penniless, we are among friends. And when the monarchy is restored, never again will England suffer under Parliament's army. Your place is here. Family is vital in this unknown future. Take advice from Nan. Come to court. Come to Paris. With my dearest love and affection.*
>
> *Anne Villiers*
> *Countess of Morton*

A shout from the boatman heralded the lights of Battersey, flaming torches illuminating the jetty and casting a ragged icy path across the black water. Safe for now from the army. Safe for a night, enough time to draw breath.

Frances stepped out of the boat before Nan, and, taking Allen's arm, she marched up the landing stage to their future.

"Lady Francke." Frances curtseyed to Allen's mother, who was waiting for them in the hall. A relief to be in her gentle presence, her quiet strength

18

soothing Frances immediately. No sign of John yet. No doubt he remained at Whitehall, drinking the health of the Commonwealth.

"Frances." Lucy clasped her hands and glanced at Allen. Frances shook her head slightly. Silent on the journey from Whitehall, he did not speak now. Her husband teetered on the edge of the abyss.

"He is exhausted, Lady Francke, and just needs rest." She must conceal his indisposition from the family, for his pride would not stand for their sympathy. Nan's curious eyes were already upon him.

Lucy nodded. "You know what is best for my son, Frances. Sit with him by the fire until the chill lifts." She paused and, embracing Frances, whispered, "I have placed a posset on the hearth. Please be sure he drinks it all."

Thanks be to God she had the wisdom not to question Frances in front of the others. Ignoring Nan's inquisitive stare, Frances guided Allen to the fireplace, where he slumped, head in his hands. She handed the curative to him and waited until he drank deep. He leaned back in the chair and closed his eyes.

No time to see Isabella yet. Should she join Nan, where she stood with her Parliamentarian brother Walter and his new bride? Or return to Lady Francke's side and relive the execution over and over?

"Allen is not well?" Nan called across the hall, her voice full of concern.

Frances walked to her side to stem her questions. "You witnessed the horror of the king's execution. And he's exhausted from the months leading up to this day." Frances paused. Nan was firmly Royalist, God knew. "It's been a deep shock. Even until the moment of death, he expected a reprieve."

Nan shot a quick glance at Walter before answering. "We all hoped for justice. You saw for yourself. Even General Fairfax distanced himself from the trial, unwilling to be condemned as a king-killer."

"Condemned?"

Nan lowered her voice, her lips hardly moving, forcing Frances to incline her head. "Revenge will be foremost on Prince Charles's mind. His father slaughtered by an illegal Parliament with no authority? Pah. Henry forecasted if this happened, Scotland would declare him king within the week."

Frances's eyes rested on Walter and his pretty young wife, Johanna. Nan's brother, the future hope of the St. John family, could be taken for any Royalist trooper in a fine lace collar, hand on hip, wine in hand, head thrown

19

back in laughter. But Walter embraced Parliament's cause. And Johanna St.John was a favourite cousin of Oliver Cromwell. How complex this family, loyalties divided and yet united in their devotion to each other.

All drinking the health of the new republic. And all related to Luce and John Hutchinson, king-killer.

"Yes," murmured Nan. "Look around. For this is Allen's future. Can he pretend to support Cromwell while crushed under the heel of the Parliamentarian regime? He'll die or be hanged rather than give in to this governance." Her voice became intimate, sympathetic. "Allen's brother, James, left with the prince. I'm surprised your husband remained."

"You understand his character." Allen had spoken little of this woman, and yet Nan recognised much about him.

Allen's cousin shrugged slightly and lifted a delicate eyebrow, her flawless complexion a fine asset she did not hesitate to reveal. The exquisitely cut blue silk gown under her sable wrap enhanced her figure.

"My husband is with the prince in Paris, guests of the French court," Nan continued. "They are building an army to return to England and restore the prince—the king—to the throne." She laid her hand on Frances's arm, inviting intimacy. "Already, many who fought for the king have joined the prince. Henry admires Allen for both his experience and his courage. How simple to join the prince's household, especially as a cousin of one so well respected—"

"We are leaving England." Frances snatched her arm away.

Nan smiled, tilting her head.

"We travel to Paris to join Queen Henrietta's court at Saint-Germain. The Countess of Morton invited us. Your words convince me this is the only solution."

A shadow chased across Nan's face, gone so quickly Frances could not be sure it even appeared.

"Our cousin Anne Villiers? I would not be hasty to reveal your friendship to Luce and Aunt Lucy. That wound will never heal."

"I don't understand." Frances shook her head. Really, there were so many hidden layers in this family. "Surely that rift is long forgotten?"

"Anne's mother, Barbara, deceived Lucy and nearly ruined her life. Even today the poverty this caused lingers. Luce carries a daughter's grudge." Nan flicked a glance over Frances's shoulder and raised her voice.

"Still, a Villiers's invitation is worth much, even from the offspring of an enemy. And you will tell Allen when?"

"Tell Allen what?"

Allen stood behind them. The firelight caught the hollows under his cheekbones and shone in his clear eyes. He had returned from his nightmare.

"Tell Allen what?" he repeated.

The rest of the family moved closer. Frances swallowed, her mouth suddenly dry.

Nan kissed his cheek. "I am glad to see you recovered, Allen," she said smoothly. "Frances was explaining that you both are travelling to France to join the household of our cousin Anne Villiers, the Countess of Morton. I simply advised if she needed any help, Henry would be willing to assist."

"Frances?" He looked from her to Nan and back again. "What does Nan mean? What have you committed us to?"

"Just a thought, Husband," she replied quickly. "Anne Villiers sent a letter of invitation, and I spoke to Nan—"

"—about joining the royal family in exile," Nan finished. "If France is where your heart lies, Allen, then you must go. And quickly, before Cromwell demands more reparation of you than he has already."

"Anne Villiers? You would join Barbara's daughter instead of remaining here?" Lucy's eyes fixed on her son. Frances could have kicked herself for taking Nan into her confidence.

Nan's brother broke the heavy silence. "You will be branded a traitor and forbidden legal return to this country. Allen, for God's sake, man, ponder on this before you act. Where you go, John and I cannot help you."

"Walter, I do not ask for your help, nor do I need your patronage," Allen replied. "I am not of this regime."

"Allen, we understand your dilemma. But my brother is right," said Nan. "Only those who are prepared to bow to Cromwell and his Parliament flourish. Those who don't will be cast out, hunted and vilified. Think well before you commit. But know my husband and Prince—soon to be crowned king, no doubt—Prince Charles will reward you greatly for your loyalty."

Walter shook his head. "You continue to play a dangerous game, Sister."

A log cracked with the resonance of a gunshot, and outside the wind picked up, moaning about the eaves of the house and rattling the windows.

Frances shivered. Surely ghosts walked abroad tonight, the whole firmament in mourning, aghast at receiving the soul of the king?

Lucy clasped Allen's hands, her eyes filled with tears. "There is a life to be lived here in England, my son, if you conform to the requests of Parliament and pay the fines. John has negotiated a reduction; they can be paid in time. He has power, influence." A drop spilled down her cheek, and she quickly brushed it away. "John will find a place for you in this new world. Look how well Nan has thrived, through her widowhood and even a Royalist marriage. The Lee land at Ditchley, her wealth, her boys' inheritance intact, making allies out of enemies where she must to survive. She is proof there is a life to be lived here." Lucy appeared frail. "Do not leave, my son, do not, I beg you."

Frances's heart twisted. A year ago she would not have felt Lucy's anguish so deeply. Now she realized the pain of a mother's love.

Allen looked from Nan to Frances and back to Nan again.

"Frances is right," he said.

Lucy's hands flew to her face.

Frances took a deep, shuddering breath. This man she had fallen in love with, lucid, decisive and true to his conscience. She reached for his hand, his familiar warm clasp united with hers.

"There is no life here for me, for my family. I cannot kneel to Cromwell's control nor live gagged for the rest of my life. John and Luce have done much for me these past years, providing a home, reducing my fines. But still I am almost destitute; sequestration is an enormous burden." Allen looked directly at his mother now. "And I will not mimic my father's life, existing on credit, living on hope, starving in debt. I would rather be in exile with the King of England, than live a life of deception with the riches of Cromwell's Commonwealth heaped upon me."

"And so you leave all that is dear, your family, your homeland—to join the Villiers," Lucy broke off, speechless through her weeping.

Frances stood forlorn before her mother-in-law's torment. Her idea had taken a devastating turn.

Shaking his head, Allen gently blotted another tear from his mother's cheek with his thumb.

"And so Frances and I will take our daughter and leave for Paris to serve the king." He turned to Nan. "Sweet coz, send a messenger on to

Henry. I will gladly join him. And in our hearts, although we may leave England, England will never leave us."

Those words. Frances closed her eyes for a moment, back in the garrison at Barnstaple, bidding good-bye to the brave young prince fleeing for his life. Those were Prince Charles's farewell words to his followers. And now Allen repeated them to give their own lives purpose. She caressed his hand, and he lifted hers to his lips, lingering on her ring finger as he always did, their own secret message of love. So be it. If another new start must be made, she would walk to the ends of the earth with this man.

The door banged open, and she jumped. On a rush of cold air, John and Luce entered the hall, shaking a light dusting of snow from their cloaks. Allen turned away with a curse and tightened his grip.

"I cannot see them now," he muttered. "For my mother's sake, help me leave before I forget myself."

"Come." Frances urged Allen towards the grand staircase. "Come and say good night to Isabella."

Nan stepped in front of them, clasping Frances's elbow. "Join me at Ditchley Park," she murmured. "Allen will recover his health at my home, and we can prepare for your departure. I leave this week, for nothing keeps me in London. And besides, Henry will be arriving as soon as news of the king's death reaches him."

Frances paused. "Your husband's a fugitive with a price on his head."

Nan smiled. "That won't stop him. He'll be in England within the month. Henry has no fear of Cromwell's thugs."

"We will join you at Ditchley." Allen kissed Nan's cheek. "And await Henry."

Frances pushed away a sense of uneasiness. "Perhaps we should travel to Lydiard, my love? It is far from the strife of London, and you can enjoy the peace there."

"Lydiard?" Nan and Allen spoke simultaneously.

"I don't think so," Allen said. "Walter's stewardship of the deer park has been sorely lacking. There is no recreation to be had there."

"That dull place?" Nan laughed. "No, Ditchley is much more suited to Allen's humour."

Frances refused to smile. "But I do not—"

Cheers and the clinking of glasses drowned her words.

23

"Allen!" Luce called across the hall. "Allen, join us, we talk of the future."

Allen turned away from his sister's voice. "I follow my own fate. And my future does not include yours."

"Allen, wait." John stepped forward. "We must talk, Brother—"

"I have no brother," Allen shot back, "except James, in France. And I go to join him and the king."

Luce ran across the hall and stopped in front of them. "Allen, you must accept our new world—"

"Accept? Accept?" Allen turned on his sister. "I accept nothing. I do not accept your brutal revolution, I do not accept your murderous politics, and I certainly do not accept your right to tell me where my loyalty lies."

Luce recoiled as if slapped. "I do not ask for your loyalty, Brother. Simply your acceptance."

"Never!" Allen's anger erupted and silenced everyone.

Frances held her breath. The grave quarrel between brother and sister lay exposed again.

"Our country is at peace, Allen," Luce pleaded. "Healing can begin. Please, I implore you, open your heart to your family who loves you; join us in rebuilding England. Our world is fair and open, where men can speak their minds."

"And execute a divinely appointed king because of his beliefs?" Allen turned from his sister. "Your conscience cannot be as clear as you state, Luce. And one day, when you stand before the God you claim you love so well, you will confront the terrible deed you and John have committed today. You may be able to reject the heart and soul of England, but for me, the monarchy lives on."

He bowed to his mother, every inch of him taut with dignity and pride. He held out his arm to Frances, and as she guided Allen upstairs, steadying him through his rage, only she knew the trembling that convulsed him.

From the gallery, Frances looked down as Nan took John to one side. She paused, for what business would Nan have with a king-killer? She could not hear their words, but it was apparent that Nan talked seriously with John. Leaning forward, laughing, her conversation carried force. And John nodded his head in agreement.

5

Nan

Ditchley Park proved to be Allen's salvation. Nan's ministrations brought him back to life. At Battersey, Allen's ill health troubled her despite Frances's inadequate attempts to conceal his plight. After four months at Ditchley, he made a fine recovery. She encouraged him to speak of the war years, of their common love for her beloved brother Edward, his dearest cousin, his lost brother-in-arms. And with their intimate conversations and long walks came healing, as talking of the dead so often did.

Now she had thoroughly instructed Frances in his care, Nan worried less about him relapsing.

Along with a satisfactory yield of new lambs, spring heralded renewal, and her cousin spent his days on horseback, hunting in the great park. 'Struth, if he continued this way, Nan's sons would have no deer herd left to inherit. Already, Allen's trophies crowded the great hall, sitting proudly between mounted antlers from stags killed by King James and Prince Henry. Nan adored her ancient house, its grand history of royal patronage and pleasure. She kept it a refuge for her beloved husband, the king's most loyal follower.

And out of Parliament's thieving hands.

For now.

The magnificent upper gallery at Ditchley House exceeded twenty paces in length, and as Nan strode from the hall stairs to the northern corner, she ignored the cluster of Lee family paintings crowding the paneling. Yes, they were her sons' ancestors, favoured courtiers, great landholders, lords of the manor, useful Puritans. But she had no interest in these prideful men today.

The still figure at the end of the gallery called to her. Framed in gold, a tall woman, her white gown iridescent in the shadowed alcove, moonlight at her shoulder, waiting to greet the lady of the manor. As Nan approached, holding her candle higher, the woman's familiar red hair and beautiful long-fingered hands emerged, the priceless jewels and long ropes of pearls adorning her gown proclaiming her royal status. Magnificently positioned on a map of England, the toe of her shoe delicately pointed to Oxfordshire—and Ditchley Park.

"Elizabeth," murmured Nan, bowing her head slightly. Years of discussion with this portrait permitted the intimacy of first names, but she must still acknowledge the sovereign before her. "Majesty, your guidance is my North Star, for in God's Truth, without your inspiration I would collapse from the strain." Only with Elizabeth could she share her inner fears. "These long months since the king's death have been a terrible ordeal, and I fear daily Parliament will demand more than I can possibly give. The future of Ditchley depends on me."

Queen Elizabeth's eyes, a rich tawny brown, gazed upon her with empathy.

"And now Allen will join my husband in The Hague, and I fear I have encouraged his exile to the sorrow of my family," Nan continued. "But there are choices to be made, and if I can support the prince while saving Ditchley, then I must use all the ammunition I have."

The woman stared at her impassively.

"I must now play both sides. For if I do not comply with Cromwell, my sons will be the target of his retaliation. Sequestration will bite deep. The demands will be exorbitant. And I refuse to be the woman who loses Ditchley. As you did not lose England to the Spanish heretics."

Nan lowered her candle, illuminating the map, seeking reassurance the queen's touch guarded Ditchley. Once, Elizabeth had walked this gallery, danced a galliard in the great hall below, shone her radiance upon this home and bestowed eminence upon the Lee family. She looked up again at the calm eyes, lucid in the perfect oval face.

"I will not be the woman who loses Ditchley." In repetition came truth. "Like you, I will work from the shadows to find the light."

A commotion from the great hall as the entrance door slammed and the ring of spurs clanged over the flagstone floor. A scraping of chairs from the dais, a scurrying of footsteps, exclamations of surprise and joy.

Henry. Her love. Her mercurial man.

"I must go," Nan whispered. "My husband returns."

In God's truth, we love the adventurers, the explorers, the soldiers and courtiers who charm us, worship us, and inspire us to be fearless.

Each time Henry returned home, Nan noticed a small change in him: a new crease on his forehead, silver at his temples. Yet still his rugged demeanour captivated her, and the scar puckering the corner of his sensual mouth charmed her. Nan touched the tender place on her smooth neck, the love blemish left by a man's rough beard and sweet lips. How delicious to have her husband in her bed again after so long apart. And yet she could not keep him, for he would arise one morning and leave, the call of his king and his troops transcending her love.

"You realise we fight on multiple fronts." Henry turned to Allen and Frances, motioning with the wine flagon he'd clasped since they'd first strolled into Ditchley's pleasure garden. Frances gestured her refusal; Allen waved his glass for more.

Nan's favourite arbour beckoned, and they sat close in the June dusk, the rosy light turning the garden a radiant pink and the plaster of the house a mellow gold. The sudden shrill piping of a blackbird stirred the peacefulness. Nan wanted to hold this moment forever.

"What mean you?" asked Allen. "Surely those who declare for the king have all made their way to the Continent by now. You must have formed a sizable army."

Henry nodded. "True. And we have men, supplies, arms, ships at our call. But there is still much to be done to coordinate our efforts on both sides of the Narrow Sea. King Charles now seeks the queen's official support to invade. We are readying ourselves." He stood suddenly and paced in front of them. Nan recognised his restlessness; her man despised sitting still.

"You are well-organised. What more do you need? We have no money." As was her way, Allen's wife came directly to the point.

"Henry, my love, tell them the truth." Nan caught her husband's hand, caressed the familiar calluses on his palm. "Allen and Frances can be trusted."

Allen turned to Nan. "Trusted with what?"

Henry poured another glass of wine for himself, frowning slightly as he realised he'd drained the flagon.

"Our fight does not begin with swords," he replied. "The great need is for information. Intelligence. Numbers, locations, attitudes. Security and defence. Where we might be exposed. Where Cromwell is vulnerable. And, God help us, where England's safe houses are hidden in the midst of our enemies. When we return with our army, we can afford no mistakes."

Nan removed his glass. She needed his mind clear. "Ditchley Park is central to the effort of restoring our rightful king," she continued. "Allen, when I gave you shelter after Edgehill, and supplied powder and horses to Henry and our cousin Sir Edward Hyde, I committed to the cause. As the widow Lee, I was free of suspicion, and even as the Lady Wilmot, I keep a neutral house. I have spent the war years cultivating allies on both sides, friends who support us and family who have no idea the information they share with me is filtered back to the king."

Allen crossed to Nan's side, knelt beside her. "What allies?"

She smoothed his hair, letting her hand drop to his cheek for a moment. He tilted his head to her touch. "Networks of people I trust. And who trust me. Recruited by Sir Edward Hyde and others placed strategically within the king's inner circle." She glanced at Frances. Allen's wife paid close attention. Good. Let her be curious, a vital trait for sure. "Whatever I can learn I send back to Sir Edward through trusted messengers, travellers, even nuns fleeing persecution."

Understanding dawned on Allen. Would he respond the way Nan had forecasted?

"And family? Luce? John?" he demanded. "What do they tell you?"

"Nothing to compromise them," she reassured him. "Yet the company they keep, the military men who now rule the country, all have something to say once the wine flows."

"You betray my sister's trust to spy on their allies?" Shadows masked Allen's face in the deepening twilight. "And you play both sides?"

"Are you really surprised, Allen?" Nan asked. She gestured at her house, her deer park, the rolling Lee land flowing into the dusk-dark forest. "How else do you think I managed to keep this safe during the war, when all around me fell? My sons deserve their inheritance. The more I align to the Lee family—for their grandmother is a model Puritan—the better for all of us. Yes, I may encourage loose lips at John's table. But he urges me to dine with them, advocates open discussion. And with every revelation, we are one step closer to the rightful return of our king Do you think this a hard decision?"

Nan reached for Allen's familiar hand, connecting him to Henry through her. These men she loved fiercely.

She continued drawing him in. "When I sheltered Henry after Edgehill and fell in love with him and married him, I also committed to his loyalty to the king and his cause. And you are part of that life now. You made your

28

choice. In front of your family, you pledged to join the king in exile. You've lived with me at Ditchley these past months. You met with Henry tonight. You belong in our network, Allen, you and your clever wife, Frances." Nan glanced at her cousin's lady, no reluctance showing in her pretty face. She kissed first Allen's hand and then her husband's. "Are you ready to serve your king and restore the monarchy to England? While you and Henry wage war with armies, Frances will be my covert liaison in Paris, safeguarding our cause with my intelligence."

By silent agreement, no further words of spying were spoken between them that evening. Henry loved her again and slipped away in the silvery dawn, leaving Nan to hug his cooling pillow and cry her secret tears before summoning Frances to walk with her to the arbour.

No prying eyes would find them in the garden. She trusted her servants completely, but still the wartime habits lingered. Best to take no risks. And what looked like a simple stroll with their young children would conceal their real conversation. Without the distraction of Allen between them.

Frances kept her own counsel, did not rush to speak. Johnny and Isabella toddled along the gravel path.

"They adore each other's company," Nan remarked. "For young cousins who have only just met, they are remarkably similar."

The children's heads bent over a clump of lavender, intently watching the bees, golden curls mingling in the summer sunshine. The air hummed with the droning of insects over a distant cooing from the doves in the cote. Her maid watched over the children, close enough to mind, far enough away not to overhear Nan's words.

"This beautiful garden, this birdsong, reminds me of my childhood," replied Frances. She had the look of a sensual country wench about her today, her golden hair entwined in a thick braid, curling tendrils framing her pretty face. Little wonder Allen had lost his heart to her. "I wonder if my daughter will ever know the tranquility of home and the certainty of days stretching before her uninterrupted."

"Do not feel guilt that you are taking Isabella into the unknown," replied Nan. "My two oldest boys have known little but war and yet still sport with the innocence of childhood. I have preserved their inheritance to ensure their future someday. And even now Henry is outlawed, our son,

Johnny, will always be close to the entire family, as he is with Isabella today. They share much in temperament."

"The family resemblance is strong," Frances agreed. "They both have Lucy's eyes."

Nan laughed. "The St.John eyes are unmistakable, and Johnny has inherited them. Allen too. We were often mistaken for brother and sister when we were young."

"And you still are devoted." Frances stretched catlike, lids half-closed in the late afternoon sun. Nan sensed a sharper truth-seeking beneath her languid tone. "He relies upon you and your counsel. Anne Villiers instructed him in her letter to pay heed to you. Others know how attached you are."

"Anne lived close to us growing up. She remembers." Nan spoke quietly under the echoing birdsong. "Allen and I are bred of the same stock. We feel the same happiness . . . and despair."

Allen's wife opened her eyes at Nan's tone. "You do not show your sadness."

The children clasped hands and ran towards the fishpond, where soon their excited squeals affirmed carp hid under the lily pads. They pulled off their shoes and stockings and dipped their toes in the green water.

"I gave up the indulgence of self-pity a long while ago, when my first husband died, leaving me a widow with two boys." Nan brushed from her skirts mauve wisteria blossoms that had drifted from the vine above them. She stood. "This war allowed me no time to feel sorry for myself nor to waste in mourning. Survival is all that matters."

"And you have survived, and thrived, Nan." Frances stood too. Purple clouds crowded the western sky, and a chill wind had sprung up, whipping her blond hair across her face. "You have walked a fine line between the two sides in this war. You conceal your ambitions admirably. I am not sure I can deceive as well as you."

Nan searched her expression. Did indecision colour her words? "Are you having second thoughts, Frances? Do you fear what lies ahead for you and Allen? There is no room for doubt in this world you are entering."

"No," Frances retorted. "No doubts." Allen's pretty young wife shook her own skirts and turned towards the house.

"Wait." Nan stayed Frances and bid the maid to take the children inside. "I must be sure you understand exactly what is being asked of you. You ride tomorrow to say good-bye to Lucy and Luce. You still may change your heart."

"And Allen's too?"

"And Allen's," Nan confirmed. "I heard of your role in Barnstaple's surrender in the last days of the war. You helped Allen negotiate the terms. If not for you, there would have been bloodshed instead of peace."

"Who told you details of the siege? Allen was ill, drinking to drown his pain. The time was difficult." Frances bit off her words.

"Why, he did, of course."

"When? When did he tell you?"

"He visited me at Ditchley shortly after the king's surrender, after you both returned to Owthorpe. Maybe three years ago, just before I fell pregnant with Johnny."

Frances could keep a blank face, she'd give her that. But the involuntary clenching of her fingers revealed her surprise. She'd be a good secret-keeper. Better than Allen, who wore every emotion on his sleeve.

Nan continued. "Frances, you kept him from making a terrible decision at Barnstaple. Hundreds would have been slaughtered as the Roundheads stormed the city. When he reached me, I despaired of his health. But Ditchley worked its magic. The war damaged him, yet still he craves to fight again."

"This is his desire." Frances drew her shawl closer. An invisible breeze rippled the surface of the lily pond. "He would die staying here, subservient to Cromwell's rule, eking out an existence on John Hutchinson's charity."

"And yet he welcomed John's intervention when it came to negotiating down his fines."

"He's not stupid."

Nan lifted her eyebrow. "But he is biddable. To women like us."

"Is that why you married Henry? He shares much of Allen's character, it seems. Fond of his drink, of soldiering, both restless in their own way. Your husband and your cousin are cut of the same cloth."

"You notice much in a short time. I thought your eyes only for Allen."

Frances ignored the jibe. "What exactly is being asked of me?" She sat on the bench overlooking the pond, half turning her back to Nan, her eyes on the rippling water. "Last night you explained your part in this—eavesdropping at dinners, gathering information, playing the innocent while those around you talk with unguarded tongues. It seems you plan to spend much time with Allen's sister and her husband."

Nan came to Frances's side but did not sit. "They are my dear family. Time with them will not be questioned. My role assigned is vital in acquiring information." She paused. "And yours crucial in distributing it."

"Go on."

They were as two she-cats, staking territory, claiming hierarchy.

"Before you leave for Paris, I will teach you a cypher to memorise, inks to use and paper-folding techniques, so you may read the information I send to you. Letters will come a number of different ways, primarily through the abbess at the convent on Rue Christine."

Frances remained silent. Another point in her favour. This was not the time for Allen's wife to show her familiarity with the Catholic ways. Nan surmised Frances's family had recently converted from the old religion, and the fines and persecution inflicted on recusants probably still stung. She continued, intentionally keeping her face in shadow against the darkening sky.

"You will meet with messengers, mostly displaced nuns, when you get to court. Or you will pay your respects at the convent and visit the abbess. The notes they give you are of critical importance to the king and Prince Rupert as they plan their army's return to England."

"Who should I give this information to?"

"Sir Edward Hyde." Now Nan paced. Enough cat and mouse.

"Allen's cousin? You mentioned him yesterday. He sends us letters from the family, but surely he is too occupied with the king's business to trouble with domestic tattle dribbling out of England." Frances turned away from Nan, dismissing her.

Laughing, Nan reached down and clasped Frances's hands, drawing her to her feet so they were eye to eye. "Dearest Frances, our cousin Sir Edward Hyde oversees the entire intelligence network. He is the king's spymaster. And you have more than proven your nerve to serve the cause from your new home in Paris."

6

Luce

After the death of the king, it was debated and resolved to change the form of government from monarchical into a commonwealth.

Luce Hutchinson
Summer 1649

In the narrow Holborn town house, once her father-in-law's London residence, Luce completed the last lines of her manuscript with a flourish. Seated at a small inlaid writing desk positioned to catch the sunlight as it squeezed into the square outside, she carefully reread her essay. Her patron had promised this one would receive a wider circulation than any of her previous treatises. To enjoy any credence as a writer, she must not allow one error in her rhetoric or logic, for the public discounted a female mind.

She frowned. This prejudice prevailed across all Parliament. Dinner last night with John Milton had been a refreshing change in perspective, for once engaged in discussion, his respect had grown for her revolutionary thoughts on freedom of speech. Her father had provided her an exceptional education, and she would not waste it on mere women's duties. She adored her children, but privately she loved her studies equally.

Luce stood and stretched, cramped by writing since dawn. Midsummer's Day. Dappled shadows from the chestnut tree reminded her the morning had disappeared. When writing, she forgot the hours, and now she must hurry. Today, for the first time since leaving the scaffold site in January, she returned to Whitehall.

"Are you ready?" Lucy appeared in the passage, her light mauve gown accented by a lace shawl woven by the skilled Huguenot women of Blackfriars. As always, her mother dressed fashionably and yet maintained her reserve.

"Yes, I suppose so."

Her mother pulled a face. "You too? My heart dreads returning to the palace, but John insists."

Luce pushed her manuscript under a pile of papers. Best not to have this thinking in open sight after she left. "You and Father were among the favoured few admitted to the king's privy chambers to view his paintings. John says it's a collection unrivalled anywhere in Christendom."

Lucy nodded. "All so long ago, Luce. I cannot imagine what further wealth the king acquired after I left court."

"We'll see today as they dismantle the collection." Luce picked up her purse and tucked her hand in her mother's arm. "Our bags have been sent on to Battersey. Now to Whitehall to view the king's hoard, for his treasure now belongs to the people of England. Our blood funded his obsession."

"You speak with such vehemence. Allen would say the king's divinely inspired benevolence extends to his people regardless of his riches. That is what my boy defended and is prepared to die for." Her mother's voice cracked, and Luce's heart relented.

"Allen will always be his father's son." She kissed Lucy's cheek, fragrant with her familiar scent of rosewater. "Tonight we bid him good-bye. And although it pains our hearts, you can be proud of the virtues you and father instilled in him. He and I are fiercely opposed, but he is no empty-headed courtier. My brother is an ethical man who lives by his beliefs."

"As is John." Lucy sighed. "I see no reconciliation, Luce, and I am desperately saddened you and Allen will never dwell in harmony."

Luce swallowed the lump in her throat that threatened her own voice and shook her head to dismiss the quick tears. Allen's parting words on the day of the execution had made his feelings clear. And she could not compromise her own.

The years since Luce last walked the Long Gallery had not been kind to Whitehall. Abandoned when the king fled to Oxford in the early years of the war, the warren of rooms, apartments and galleries were left deserted, occupied only by army guards. Furniture, books, precious objects lay discarded in place, as if the court had been mysteriously whisked away by demons. Only ghosts wandered the empty halls, memories of the living and dead mingling and blending until the very air itself threatened those who dared trespass. Where once had resounded music and laughter, now echoed crow caws and a window banging in the breeze.

Luce shivered. "I did not expect to find it still inhabited," she murmured. "The spirits are close, no matter the king has been cast out."

Life-size portraits of individuals and families, architectural drawings, pastoral scenes, great landscapes, classical allegories—if the courtiers' ghosts walked abroad, here remained their earthly abodes.

"These walls have seen much," replied Lucy. "Once, younger than you, I promenaded this gallery with your aunts." She paused, her gaze drifting. "We thought life began and ended with the king and the court. Simple times."

"Father was an ardent Royalist," Luce commented.

"No great divide existed then. The king and George Villiers, the Duke of Buckingham, commanded his allegiance." Lucy paused, her eyes searching the paintings hanging two, three vertically on the gallery walls. "And the rewards reflected his loyalty. No matter the duke's patronage came of my sister Barbara's marriage to his brother. Family ties bound us all to swim or sink together." A cloud crossed her expression. "This art is not unique to the king. When we lived in the Tower, your father commissioned a portrait of Allen and me to celebrate his newly awarded position as governor."

Luce recalled no such painting at Battersey. "Really? Where is the painting now?"

Her mother shrugged. "I left it at the Tower when we were evicted. I did not want to be reminded of George Villiers's duplicity in raising your father high and ending his life early."

"And yet Father supported the king until his death."

Lucy nodded. "He never questioned the king's commands. I am not surprised Allen continues his legacy, for he worshipped his father." She caught sight of John and turned to walk towards him. "Even if the service of the monarchy resulted in our own destruction."

Luce lingered, the stories overheard as a child vivid. She pictured Lucy as a young girl, beautiful, flirtatious even, dancing at court with her sisters and catching the eye of Theo Howard, Duke of Suffolk. Her mother's first love crushed by a devastating treachery from her sister Barbara. Did that begin Lucy's hatred of the court? Or the crippling debts and horrific lawsuits that resulted from blind allegiance to the Villiers family? Now here Luce stood, surrounded by proof of the king's avarice and his people's resulting deprivation.

God commanded her and John to rebuild England's rightful governance.

Today, another step in their journey.

John led them along the gallery where tapestries draped over tables and hung across stone niches. Luce caught her breath as the enormity of the king's collection settled upon her.

"Parliament intends to sell all?" she asked John. "Where do they even begin?"

"The trustees have been appointed, and inventory starts later this week. They are charged with removing everything."

"From here?" Luce looked around her. "It will take weeks."

"Not just here. From all the palaces. Whitehall. Windsor. Nonsuch. Oatlands. Richmond . . ." He touched a canvas, drawing his finger in the dust. "All will be taken to Somerset House to be sold at market. Those of us who are in Parliament have the opportunity to visit now, to assess which we intend to buy."

Luce could not be sure she heard John correctly. "You will purchase the king's art? For what purpose? Why would you keep a constant reminder of this depraved monarch's oppression of his subjects?" Raising money to pay the army and Parliament's creditors from the sale of the king's goods she could support. But the prospect of John's ownership was a different matter.

"Why, to keep for ourselves to enjoy, of course. Or to sell later, to rebuild our own devastated estates. Nan says opportunity lies to grow rich from these investments, for there is a market both here and on the Continent."

"I am not sure you will want the trouble of this, John."

But he had already moved away from her.

John led them eagerly to the king's privy chamber and paused before an enormous canvas of a satyr creeping up on a sleeping nymph, careless in her nude abandonment, certainly about to be ravished by the creature.

"Antiope and Jupiter." Luce cleared her throat. "Ovid's story is certainly well-depicted." Her cheeks burned at the erotic image.

"The value is in the detailed countryside depiction," answered John. "In fact, Titian called this his landscape painting."

Luce could not help but laugh. "That's not what I'd call it." She took Lucy's arm, ready to leave.

"You are correct, my love. In the El Pardo Palace, where this hung before, they referred by name to the central figures. Venus and Cupid." John peered closer at the painting.

"You seem to know a great deal about this . . . this allegory?"

"I have reserved it to purchase. Nan recommends this as a particularly good investment."

The scandalous painting shimmered before her as if the satyr danced, intent now on ravaging the sleeping nude. "And where will you store this monstrosity? The house in Holborn has no walls to fit."

John took her hands. "My love, you only must look at Nan's collection at Ditchley to appreciate her shrewdness. I have added a cabinet room to the rebuilding of our home at Owthorpe for the purpose of displaying our own collection."

"You have already decided upon this?" She clenched the handles of her pocket purse tightly.

"I had to move quickly, else it would be sent to auction and sold to someone who has no idea of its value. Buying now will serve us in good stead for the future."

The air became close in the gallery, an air of decay now settling in the back of her throat. She thought the privy garden lay ahead and needed to be outside. At the far end of the room, her mother stood before a small portrait obscured in a dark corner. As they joined her, Lucy brushed away a tear.

"John the Baptist. His severed head. How cruel is fate," she whispered. "Would that the king even suspected his own ending be foreshadowed in his collection. It is all so sad. So sad."

God save her. Salome. Revenge. Luce swallowed. "You contradict yourself. You said earlier that the king caused our family's downfall, Mother. You even said how the portrait of you and Allen represented Father's misplaced ambition."

"A portrait?" asked John. "Knowing the company your father kept, it must have been expertly done. We should have it valued. Where is it?"

So now John is an expert in art.

She hated the bitterness in her thoughts and yet could not lose her anger at John's new endeavours.

"He commissioned a portrait of my mother and Allen." Luce shrugged. "She left it in the Tower when Father died."

Lucy turned towards the privy garden. "I'll leave you to your calculations, John, and wait outside. There is nothing more here I care to see."

"This visit troubles her." John watched her leave. "I thought she would rejoice in the financial gain of the sale of the king's goods."

"This visit has brought back sad memories," replied Luce. "And foreshadowed the future, where again she is separated from Allen."

John nodded. "I understand her pain. When my father disowned me for choosing Cromwell over the king, I felt as if a limb were severed from me."

Luce took a final look around. She had no intention of returning to Whitehall again.

"Mother and I will walk to the river steps," she said. "It is time to take the barge to Battersey. Allen and Frances will be there soon. I cannot let him leave without reconciling."

John hesitated. "I have work here. With Walter. We have meetings. I may be late."

"Or you may not come at all," retorted Luce. The stifling heat of the afternoon, the news of the paintings and now John's rejection of Allen again. These were the times she struggled with John's stubbornness. "As you wish. Just remember, Allen was once your dearest friend. And tomorrow he leaves England, probably forever."

Luce and her mother walked swiftly across Battersey's bustling stable yard to greet the travellers. The only news about her brother since the king's execution had come from Nan, reassuring her that Allen had recovered from the brain fever he showed that night. God willing. he would react kindly to her today.

Allen rode at the head of the small party, Frances with Isabella and a guard behind. He dismounted lithely, athletic as always.

"Mother," he kissed her hands, ignoring Luce. "Henry Wilmot is here?"

Lucy shook her head. "You have missed him. Walter received word it was dangerous for him to remain, and so he rides for the coast."

Allen pulled off his gloves, still not meeting Luce's eyes. "So our Puritan cousin feeds intelligence to his Royalist brother-in-law."

Luce was ready for him. "It is the way of the country now, Allen. There are no battle lines to defend, and if we can save further bloodshed, so be it. Of course Walter will tell Nan if Henry is in danger."

"Did your husband inform Walter?" Allen asked, looking at Luce for the first time. "Or did someone else give us that small kindness? Where do your loyalties lie?"

Just as she'd thought. He still wore his anger like armour. He did not attempt to kiss her cheek in greeting.

Luce stepped back. "We can talk inside, in private, Allen. Walter is at Whitehall with John and will return late tonight." Best not to tell Allen of John's rebuff.

Lucy led them to the parlour overlooking the orchard and the Thames. A servant brought fresh cool ale and cakes. As Frances took Isabella to the green-glazed windows and pointed out the boats on the smooth water, Allen stood with Luce and Lucy.

"What danger was Henry warned of?" he asked their mother abruptly. "And does it extend to Nan?"

Lucy answered quietly, "No, Nan is safe, providing she remains at Ditchley. Henry is marked because of his closeness to the royal family. Each time he returns to England, he risks capture and imprisonment. Both Parliament and the army would consider it a triumph if they were to arrest the Stuart's dearest friend."

"And so no new danger?"

Lucy shook her head. "No. But Henry's message is for you to join them in Paris as quickly as you can. The king is on the move." She took his hands. "Allen, I must beg you, for the sake of Frances and Isabella, please reconsider your decision to leave England. Already, I have one son vanished with the prince's exile. You know I have had no word from James these past three years. Do not compound my loss."

Luce's heart contracted. She'd known her mother would ask this of Allen. And she could foretell his devastating response.

"Mother, there is no dissuading me—us." Across the chamber, Frances and Isabella sang as they counted the wherries crowded on the Thames. Suddenly, Luce longed for her own children, ached to hold her own daughter in her arms and be soothed by John's tranquil company.

Allen continued, his words loud in the quiet chamber. "Frances agrees. We are not prepared to live under the yoke of the usurpers in our own country."

As their mother's face whitened, Luce pulled her thoughts back to the present. "Our way is the way of the people, Allen. They have chosen this government, this fair representation. The king betrayed them, and the monarchy refused to compromise. There can be no usurpers when it is the will of the common man."

And here she went again, inflaming her brother's hot temper.

"It is not my will, nor that of a hundred thousand Englishmen," he shot back. "Your husband signed the death warrant. He sat in judgment every day of the mock trial. He could have left; he could have retired to Owthorpe. Our king's blood is on his hands, and by association yours. There will be a price to pay; do not ever let John think otherwise."

"The king deceived Parliament in every way possible. He proved dishonest in his dealings and betrayed his people. His thoughts were only for himself first, never the good of the nation. He left Cromwell no choice." Luce clenched her fists, her stance rigid.

"John had options," Allen retorted. "Like many others of his ilk— General Fairfax, for one—who absented themselves from the court, choosing discretion, refusing to judge the king."

"Fairfax is a wretched turncoat. He betrayed us when he ran from his duty like a frightened maid. John remained loyal to God and his country."

"But not his king!" Allen shouted in anguish. They spoke in circles, unravelling Luce's reconciliation attempt. He continued in a steadier voice. "John chose Cromwell and all he represents in anarchy and mayhem. He was my best friend, and I no longer know who he is. I refuse to live as a hypocrite."

Frances now joined them and handed Isabella to Lucy, who cradled the little girl in her arms.

"We are tired from our journey," Allen's wife said, "and your daughter is ready for slumber. Perhaps her granddame would enjoy telling her a story and singing her to sleep on our last night at home."

Allen nodded. Lucy caressed his cheek with her free hand, a tender gesture Luce knew so well.

"My darlings, always you both must clash before you find harmony," their mother said serenely. "Now sit together and speak the words you really mean, before it is too late. You may not see each other for a while, and you will want no regrets after you part." Lucy turned, clasping Isabella in her arms. As they walked away, the soft strains of "Scarborough Fair" hung behind in the twilight, her mother's familiar voice mingling with Isabella's high notes.

Luce stared at her brother for an age, until her eyes filled with tears and a mist crept across her vision. "She is always the peacemaker. Ever since I can remember, she brought us close every time we fought and reminded us of our first duty to each other."

Allen remained silent. Frances left them to sit again by the window. Luce just wanted to hold her brother close, make him feel her own hurt.

"Please, Allen," she implored. "Please do not leave with words unsaid."

He closed his eyes and rubbed his forehead, a gesture of fatigue as familiar as one of her own. "We have terrible challenges ahead, Luce, events where we know not whom to trust or when. But family . . . family we can always depend on. We've always supported each other in the most difficult of times."

"Even if you choose the Stuart over John and me and our duty here to rebuild England?"

"For God's sake, Luce, do not always seize the last word." Allen turned from her. "My position is absolute. I serve the king. And love my family. Both can share my heart."

Suddenly, exhaustion with this argument overwhelmed her. And her fears stabbed her conscience. She must not be the one whose words made the division unbridgeable. No middle ground existed between them, but there was neutrality. He would never declare false loyalty to please her.

"Allen, I'm sorry," she whispered, not sure if he would hear her. She swallowed and repeated her apology. "Please don't leave in anger."

"Look after Mother." His hoarse voice sounded like their father's. "I wish I could tear myself in two and leave a portion of my heart here with you."

Allen faced her, a sudden ray of the setting sun darting from the window, illuminating his face and erasing the lines from his brow. He was back as a young boy in the Tower, and she facing him across their father's deathbed. The same emptiness and loss inhabited their souls today as it had then.

"Halfhearted has never been your way, Allen," she said. "God be with you and protect you. Go honestly to your king. Though he will never come back to England, know I keep watch here at home, awaiting your return."

7

Frances

In the morning, Allen made excuses to delay their departure. Frances could not determine his reason until she found him standing by the fast-ebbing Thames, staring at the empty jetty.

"John will not come," she said gently. "Not now, not this time."

Allen turned swiftly, his face shuttered, a soldier's blank expression. He strode to the courtyard, and, accompanied by two of Walter's guards, they left the familiar old house with swift good-byes.

As they hugged, Luce pushed a small leather pouch into Frances's hand.

"It's not a great amount," she whispered. "But enough coin to last to Paris. Allen would not take it from me, but I know you will need this."

And then she ran into the house.

When the dwellings gave way to countryside and London's smoky haze faded over her shoulder, Frances rejoiced in the first lark trill. These rolling green hills resembled her beloved Devon, and she could have been riding on her father's estate. A verdant mantle disguised the savagery of the past years of war.

Yet, looking closer at a burned-out farmhouse, a devastated orchard, scars still scorched the countryside. And if the lark's flight over the Weald ascended to heaven, this journey from London to the coast descended into hell. Walter had warned recent clashes had returned the Royalist-occupied defences to the Parliamentarians, but Frances was unprepared for the evidence of the army's ruthless assaults upon the small towns and villages of this peaceful countryside, now plundered by troops and populated by the maimed and homeless. Her heart broke as they pushed forward into Kent.

England suffered. And now Frances was deserting her.

Over the main road, a dust cloud billowed, for troops, prisoners and common citizens alike travelled this route to the Cinque Ports. Thanks be to St. Christopher the safe houses Nan commended were concealed from the main thoroughfares, and the Royalist owners welcomed families such as theirs. Their nights in Bromley and Maidstone passed without incident.

Late afternoon on the third day, they crested the last of the Kent hills. Frances stopped to drink in the beauty of the fertile vale and sparkling water spread before them. Ahead lay their next home, somewhere across the Narrow Sea. Long shadows marked the westerly passage of the sun at their backs, and for a while they were content to dismount and rest their horses. The indigo water glistened with a small swell and as their eyes adjusted to the perspective, Allen caught Frances's arm.

"There, on the horizon," he whispered, his lips close to her ear. "Calais. So near, you see? We will not be far from England. In truth, even in France we'll be as close to Battersey as Luce is in Owthorpe."

Frances shivered, her eyes fixed on the elusive grey blur hinting a distant land.

"And yet a world away. You give me hope one day we will return," she replied.

"I promise you, my darling. It is only a matter of time, and all Englishmen will welcome the king's restoration. We will wear bright clothes, joyfully play our music aloud and ride triumphant in a homecoming procession." He punctuated his words with kisses, making her giggle like a girl. "This blight of the Puritans will eat into people's hearts and souls until all the happiness is starved from them—"

"—and they realise they exchanged one form of servitude for another," she laughed.

"Exactly." Allen clasped her closer and swung Isabella into his elbow's crook. The fresh sea breeze tumbled their daughter's curls as she lifted her petite face and sniffed the air. "Well, it looks as though we have a little seafarer already."

He kissed Isabella's cheek and rubbed noses with her, always the way to make her laugh.

"Come, let's find Sir Edward's safe house." Allen turned from the view. "Nan directed me to follow a path down towards the castle. The side entrance turn is by the White Horse Inn."

They mounted their horses and walked them slowly down a shaded drover's track towards Folkestone. The breeze soughed through the leafy beech trees, carrying a tang of brine mixed with tar and a whiff of wood smoke. As a castle tower appeared, a plume of smoke curled heavenwards. They approached a crossroads where a road clearly led towards the castle, and a small lane wound by several dwellings. The smoke thickened. Allen turned to Frances and their two guards, his expression serious.

"Stay here by this copse and conceal yourselves by riding into the woods a little. Guard, come with me. This is not an ordinary woodman's fire."

Allen set off at a canter, spurring his tired horse forward, Walter's guard at his side. Just after her husband turned by several squat cottages and the sign of the White Horse, a troop of Parliamentarians galloped from the castle, smoke now billowing over their heads. Beyond the inn, large iron gates gaped open. A red glow told of a structure burning, confirmed by timbers cracking and snapping.

Frances hugged Isabella close as the troop pulled up. Half a dozen Roundheads circled, their eyes hard under their helmets. Others rested their horses beneath the trees, laughing and passing flasks and drinking deeply.

"Stand still, my lady," murmured her guard. "Remain still and do not show fear. Sir Walter commanded me to stay with you. I will not leave."

Frances nodded, angry at these men who thought themselves such braggarts, trying to intimidate her. She would hold her ground, play for time if she could. Lifting her chin, she stared back at the enemy soldiers.

Long moments passed as the silent, hard-eyed men continued to ride in circles, playing with her, taunting.

Best break their rhythm.

"Where is your captain?" she called. "And what kind of welcome is this to Folkestone?"

A man detached himself from the troop under the trees and rode towards her. A Roundhead, wearing colours she did not recognize.

"And who might you be?" he asked.

"One who travels on Cromwell's business." Nan's papers had better stand up to scrutiny.

"She is my wife." Allen galloped to her side. "And your name, sir?"

The captain pulled his horse around, the harness jangling. The rest of the troop stood still, watchful. He ignored Allen's question. "Why do you come from the spy's house just now? And why do you travel so light to the Kent coast with a woman and child at your side?"

"I request protection from you," Allen replied roughly. "I ride on Cromwell's behalf, with instructions to inhabit the court in Paris." He pulled their passes from his jacket.

45

"Cromwell, eh?" The soldier took the papers and squinted at them. Frances exchanged a quick look with Allen. Blessed Mary, perhaps he could not read.

"And Colonel John Hutchinson," Allen retorted.

"Friend of yours?" He sneered as he gave up trying to decipher the passes.

"Brother-in-law."

Frances nodded towards the column of smoke. "You and your men are diligent, patrolling for traitors." She wheeled her horse and rode closer to the captain so her leg lightly brushed against his.

Her action diverted the captain from their papers. "Ha. Yes. Those Royalist rebels sheltered Henry Wilmot not two days ago. They won't provide such hospitality to anyone else."

She breathed a sign of admiration and tossed her head. "So you burned them out? How brave of you."

Bastards.

"Cooked them, I'd say," replied the captain. His men laughed. Those who had been riding around Frances joined the others under the trees.

Frances relaxed slightly.

Allen shrugged and looked away from the fire. "Good man. Just as I intend to boil the Frenchmen in their own Bordeaux with our demands." The men laughed and murmured support. Allen held out his hand for the passes. "And if you've finished with these, I'll be sure to write you up in my report to Cromwell. We need more men such as you to keep this country at peace. Your name sir?"

"Patrick Forrester. Captain. Thank you, sir. Most grateful, sir."

Allen ignored him. "Where can a man get a good night's rest here?"

"I'll have you escorted to the White Horse Inn." Forrester wheeled his horse around. "I'll guarantee you the best wine and food in the house."

"Thank you. And leave an additional guard with us. If there are Royalist supporters disturbed by your actions, I would not want my wife and child harmed."

"Yes, sir." The captain dipped his head and summoned two men forward. "Accompany the gentleman and his family to the White Horse. Tell the landlord I expect him to serve them his best, none of that slop he feeds other visitors."

Allen beckoned Frances beside him. As they departed, she could not resist murmuring a congratulation. "Anything hid in plain sight is the hardest to find."

He chuckled and whispered back to her, "A well-executed distraction by my beautiful wife. And when he comes to his senses, he'll realise he knew not my name, nor when my report will be filed to Cromwell. And we'll be long gone."

At least they had a room, while Walter's guards and two Parliamentarian soldiers had been assigned the stable loft, taking turns keeping watch against thieves and rustlers.

"I will be up early to find a fisherman who can take us across." Allen pushed the scraps of unidentifiable flesh around the wooden bowl of greasy broth. Frances did the same, her stomach turning. So much for the landlord's best.

She shifted their sleeping daughter to her other arm and surveyed the filthy taproom. An old man nodded by the cold fireplace, clay pipe clamped between his teeth. Captain Forrester's guards sat a distance from them at their own table, watching intently. She could not shake completely the residue of fear from this afternoon. "Would Dover not be a better choice, with more traffic?"

"The recent battle for Dover's castle and the slaughter of Royalist troops make it completely hostile. Henry Wilmot might sneak in and out with impunity, but he travels alone, disguised. And you heard how close he came to being arrested."

Frances nodded. "I understand. I shall write a cypher to Nan tonight and let her know the news of Henry . . . and the safe house. The note can be carried back by Walter's guard."

Allen beckoned the landlord for more ale. "You did not think you would use your new skills so soon."

Another reminder this journey was not just a move, but a mission.

She nodded. "Forrester may realise he knows little about us and wonder why you were on the lane to the house he just torched. You are right, my love. We should sail as soon as possible with a local fisherman, not a packet boat."

"And he can take us to Boulogne, which will land us nearer to Paris."

He drummed his fingers on the table.

"Allen, we have made the right decision." Frances stilled his hand, clasping it firmly. She spoke urgently, in a quiet tone. "Thousands have gone before us to pledge the king their support and hope for the future of our country."

He listened attentively, as he always did when her voice became this serious.

"We have to summon our courage and enter the unknown," she continued. "And just as the early navigators marked their maps with dragons where mysterious dangers lurked, so shall we encounter our own monsters. But those will be of our imagination, our fears. And when we sail through them and reach the other shore, we'll know that those were simply the dragons of doubt, not to be trusted and certainly not real."

He drank the ale in one draught. And then ordered brandy, and a second, which he drank quickly. Frances sighed. The drink dispelled his fears, but then his sleep was that of the dead, and he would suffer in the morning.

The guards kept watching her. When she beckoned them for help to assist Allen upstairs, one of them nudged her, his elbow rubbing against her breast. She looked up at him sharply, and he leered at her, broken teeth black between his wet red lips.

She left them at the chamber entrance, staring them down until they mumbled and staggered their own way downstairs. Putting her arm around Allen, Frances helped him to the bed and swiftly threw the bolt across the door. She pulled off his boots, drew the covers over him and sat in the single hard chair by the dead fireplace, Isabella wrapped in a blanket on her lap.

She must keep a clear head about her. There would be little sleep tonight.

Frances's simple story of dragons sustained her as she walked along the Folkestone shore early the next morning, Walter's guard following closely. The sea lay with an oily tint to it, flat as could be, with just a small wave lapping on the smooth sand. This was not the rough Atlantic she knew from her childhood in Devon. Her county bred navigators and explorers, dragon fighters and adventurers. And yet a squall drifting on the horizon reminded her of the presence of danger on even the calmest water.

Daybreak melted the fog and burnished the world silver. As she walked by a half dozen one-masted fishing boats tethered to the spit of land, her spirits rose with the sun. Gulls cried as the fishermen readied their boats to catch the morning tide, and a fresh easterly breeze caressed her cheek. She waved Walter's guard to stay out of earshot and approached the boats.

As an intelligencer, proving her resourcefulness must be a priority. And while Allen slept off the French brandy from the night before, she would take care of this next part of their journey.

"You'll be wanting passage, my lady?" A voice broke into her thoughts. Was she that obvious?

She turned and faced a man of about Allen's age and height, shoulder-length blond hair straggling from under a wide-brimmed hat that concealed his expression. His left sleeve was pinned to his chest, flat and empty across the front of a jacket woven of some unidentifiable cloth, beige once and now salt-stained and crusted in white.

"Yes."

The man limped to the boat tied at the end of the small spit, the incoming tide nudging the vessel and rocking it gently in place. His swaying gait mimicked any seafaring fisherman, and yet Frances suspected it came from a wound sustained on a battlefield. Swinging himself on deck, the fisherman deftly sorted his net with one hand, laying it out on the narrow planks and kicking it into place with worn boots.

Holding her guard back five paces, Frances followed him and waited on the shore. The vessel looked seaworthy, solidly made and sitting evenly in the water. Painted a rust colour and thick with a pitch coat below the water line, it appeared well-maintained.

"Tide is best just before sunset," the man replied, "if you're not afeard of the darkening. How many are you?"

"Two and a half."

The man raised an eyebrow.

"One is a child. She is two."

The man shrugged and leaned forward to untether his boat. His legs planted wide, he easily moved with the rocking of the swell. "Same risk. Same price. A crown each. Proper coinage. No useless siege money."

This man assumed a lot and negotiated little. Frances untied the rope and threw it to him. "How can I trust you?"

"Do you have a choice? You're not taking a packet boat for a reason." He caught the rope and coiled it on the deck. "My hut is the third from the end. You can wait there today, for it is safer than the town from those curious about travellers."

As the boat bobbed away from the land, the man lifted his hand in a gesture that almost appeared a salute.

"God save our king across the sea." The words disappeared on the morning breeze. Had she really heard them under the slap and murmur of the waves on the sand?

The boat drifted out on the morning sea. A triangular brown sail raised, and a second smaller one at the stern. Frances stood until it disappeared into the rising sun. Beyond the horizon lay France, the king, her future. After a while, she turned. Time enough for daydreaming later.

Frances could not read Allen's expression as he gazed back towards the cliffs, rearing cream and white from the ocean itself, barricading their precious island from the turbulent sea. The last of the light lingered on the western horizon. He held Isabella tightly in his arms, tucking her inside his coat so just her head peeped out from the dark blue wool. Frances knew Allen needed to embrace his child, protect her from the dragons. As important for him as for her.

"So we forsake England," she mused. Unlike Allen, she left no family behind, for hers had departed this earth long ago, before the war. Yet she knew the emptiness that came with leave-takings. This loss encompassed more than family, for it included her country too. Her courage lay as a hard kernel within her heart, for emotion crushed her soul when the boat left land.

"You choose curious words." Allen stared at the cliffs, his chin resting on Isabella's bright curls. "We sacrifice much for England, but leaving our family to follow the king is surely not renouncing."

"Yet we fight from a foreign land, Allen, not on our own shores. Parliament claims our country while we run away." She was in a strange mood, fey.

"We are not running away, Frances. We are defending our future and the future of England." Finally, he dragged his eyes away from the cliffs, now so diminished they became one with the westerly skies. He tucked Isabella closer into his jacket and smiled. "Are you fearful tonight, my love?"

Her heart swelled as two pairs of bright eyes regarded her, both merry and alight with excitement. Her life, her destiny. Her only family. Isabella struggled and freed her hand, a little pink starfish waving against the brown sail, squealing at the seagulls swooping over the boat.

They laughed at their daughter's delight. If there was to be a crossing over, a voyage to the unknown such as this, then Frances could not have wished for a smoother sailing or a happier child.

God willing, their refuge in France would be as harmonious.

PART TWO

1650
EXILE

8

Nan

The letter arrived tightly sealed and folded many times. Nan flipped over the parchment, noting the worn creases, and confirmed the tiny intricate cutout was undisturbed. This message had travelled far and through many hands, some friendly, some not. She ran her thumb across the fold just above her name.

Yes. She smiled. Frances had learned her new skill well and used it adroitly.

The small tag which projected from the top left corner, no greater than a nail paring, would not be noticed by any but the sharpest eyes. Attention would be on the seal, a perfectly innocent falcon set in red wax. No interceptor would note the tag disappearing when the wax was softened and prized open. Only the recipient would know someone had tampered with the letter and resealed it.

Lady Anne Wilmot, Ditchley Park, Oxfordshire.

A simple address, Frances's dear cousin in England, anxious to receive news of a baby safely delivered or a recipe for a physick.

Innocent enough.

Besides, what woman in a man's world would be receiving cryptography, for surely the fair sex had no mind for the concealment of subtle thinking, politicking or other seditious behaviours? Nan Wilmot may have a reputation for being a shrewd bargainer and a good custodian of her children's inheritance, but these were the confines of her faculties.

And she intended such opinion of her would remain.

Confident of her chamber's privacy, Nan swiftly removed the cushion and lifted the dark oak seat of a large chair by the fireplace. Shifting first the left leg and then the right, she converted the chair into a desk and removed the inset writing box with its ivory-handled pen knife. In a few heartbeats, she slit open Frances's letter. Drawing a candle close, she angled the parchment to catch the golden light.

My dear Nan

We are safely in Paris and greeted with much warmth by Mr. Jonathan Nash, who has taken great pains to introduce us to his friends and make us welcome. I am to visit the Convent of Our Lady this afternoon to continue the charitable works I started in England. I hope you received my note from Dover, and I would be grateful if you could send me Johanna's recipe for the falling sickness, with the ingredients called out. Allen has a friend who suffers from this malady, and we would like to offer him consolation. In haste and in health.

Your affectionate cousin
Frances

Nan placed the parchment on her desk and leaned back, relief in her heart. Allen was safe. Not only safe, but now connected with their cousin Sir Edward Hyde, whose code name Frances had slipped so naturally into her missive. The king's counselor welcomed them into the network, set Frances up with her contacts at the convent and, as agreed, sent a first request. Within the falling sickness recipe and list of ingredients, an update of safe houses would be written in lemon juice between the lines.

The fire flared blue, a hidden bead of resin popped, startling Nan from her thoughts. She took up the parchment again and held it towards the candle. Frances performed well. The convent was the main office for the distribution of news and intelligence in Paris, for who but the spinster daughters of exiled papists and secret Royalists could be trusted with the sacred intelligence of their beloved king?

Satisfied no other news was hidden within the document, yet saddened there was no word of Henry, she held the letter to the flame, teasing the corner to catch before tossing it to the fire. A flare as the note settled, and Frances's writing curled and danced before blackening and turning to ash.

Safe.

A sudden shout from outside the window. Nan tugged the heavy velvet curtain aside. A party of riders clattered to a halt below. Through the rain-streaked window, she could make out a woman enveloped in a hooded tawny cloak. A tall man gracefully swung down from his mount and, reaching up, put both hands around her waist and helped her dismount. She swayed a little and leaned against him, and his arms enfolded her.

God Almighty, she ached for Henry.

Frances and Allen were safely established in Paris. No doubt Henry rode somewhere with the king. And Luce and John had arrived from London without incident. In these times, plenty to be thankful for.

They would be cold and hungry from their travels. Time to welcome them to Ditchley. Time for Nan to enter the Hutchinsons' world.

"Luce looks well." Nan poured John a glass of Madeira and gestured him to sit on the fireside bench. With the servants dismissed and Luce upstairs changing from her damp clothes, Nan valued her private time with him. "She is a strong woman and recovers quickly from childbirth. You are fortunate Lucy is with you to help in her care."

John stretched his long legs out towards the roaring fire. "Her mother is an excellent physician. We are blessed she chooses to live with us. The children are happy to have their granddame with them."

"Aunt Lucy has a great gift as a healer," Nan agreed. She joined John on the bench, where they could speak quietly. "My mother was her dearest friend, and she told me often of visiting Lucy within the Tower."

John sipped his wine and gazed into the fire. "Those were extraordinary times. George Villiers dispensing perquisites at every turn, and everyone scrambling for a piece of the king's benefice." He turned to Nan, the firelight glistening in his hazel eyes. "Little wonder Charles Stuart became so out of touch with his people in that make-believe world of masques and playacting. I saw for myself at court when the royal family could no longer distinguish between man and deity. And so he chose divine rule, unwilling to accept the fate of men."

"And you, John? What did you think of the king ruled through God?"

John ran his finger around the rim of his wineglass. "Allen and I would talk often before the war," he said reflectively. "Your brother Edward too." He looked up at her and smiled. "We three could debate all night the cause of Parliament or the king."

At her brother's name, a lump rose in Nan's throat. Five years since his death, and his memory still pained her.

"Edward was the peacemaker." It was a statement, not a question, for both knew his sweet temperament.

"Edward the peacemaker," affirmed John. They touched glasses, united by a common love.

"And yet you chose ultimately to oppose both Allen and Edward. Why?"

He returned his gaze to the fire, his aquiline profile pale against the dark wood paneling and his long chestnut hair catching a glimmer from the flames.

"I did not know my decision for many weeks, Nan. At first, we all thought it would not come to a choice and there would be no sides. Luce and I would talk about remaining independent, not declaring for either. Allen and I continued our friendship while he fought in Scotland and I built up the garrison in Nottingham."

"What changed your mind?"

Again, he paused. Above their heads, the clicking of heels on floorboards. Luce would join them soon. Nan nodded encouragement for him to continue.

"As the tension grew, our Royalist father bought my brother and me our own sets of armour. Wearing it for the first time, we realised we could not arm for the king. Our home was in Nottingham, the land our family had farmed for so many generations. Our friends, our servants, our farmers—when the king raised his standard at the castle, after demanding our powder and guns, he threatened all of us as one people." John's voice rose. Here was the emotion she probed for. "He took away our very liberties and freedoms. And made no promise to restore them to us except in his position as a father to all of us. A stern and despotic father who would rule us with no counsel but that of God, who spoke directly into his ear." John drained his wine in one gulp. "Well, that was not my God. And at that moment, not my king."

"So you chose against Charles?"

John looked up as Luce entered the room, love lighting his face. He held out his hand. Luce slid onto the bench next to him and curled into his arm.

"I chose for my family, Nan."

All of them in those early years had planned only of how to protect their families as the troops rode through their towns and villages, raiding and pillaging, regardless of who the landlord supported. God knew Ditchley had come under threat so many times. And rigorously had she defended it against the prevailing forces, determined to keep it intact for the inheritance of her boys and the triumphant return of her Royalist husband.

"I understand. We did what we needed to, John."

Luce leaned forward, her face bright from the fire. "And what God told us to follow in our hearts. John and I prayed together for enlightenment. When his true conscience was revealed, God guided us to John's signing of the warrant."

Us?

"And now?" Nan questioned. "Now who owns your heart?"

In the corners of the room, the light pools from the candles ebbed and flowed with John's quiet words.

"I welcome all my neighbours to my home, regardless of their loyalty or belief," John replied. "For now is the season of healing, of rebuilding." He pulled Luce closer, and as she started to speak, he stilled her words. "And just as we have rebuilt our home at Owthorpe, on a fresh pasture, away from the dereliction and devastation of its embattled ruins, so shall our Commonwealth rebuild the friendships among men."

Nan pressed further. "So you are unbiassed, John? One who has put the past behind and looks only to the future?"

"If that is your definition, then yes. For in the future lies hope the past can be reconciled."

John had declared his impartiality.

Soon she could add Owthorpe to the list of safe houses, a neutral Parliamentarian in the heart of Cromwell's territory.

Thus the network extended, stretching back to the Augustinian convent in Paris, where Frances couriered messages from her cousin. And where in the heart of Queen Henrietta Maria's exiled court, Charles the Second schemed with Henry Wilmot in his borrowed, empty rooms, making list after list of who in England could be trusted to support the return of the king.

9

Luce

The paintings he brought down into the country, intending a very neat cabinet for them; and these, with the surveying of his buildings, and improving by inclosure the place he lived in, employed him at home, and, for a little time, hawks abroad; and pleased himself with music, and again fell to the practice of his viol, on which he played excellently well, and entertaining tutors for the diversion and education of his children in all sorts of music, he pleased himself in these innocent recreations. He spared not any cost for the education of both his sons and daughters in languages, sciences, music, dancing, and all other qualities befitting their father's house.

Luce Hutchinson
Winter 1650

Luce paused as she tucked a pair of gloves into her travelling trunk. After a week with Nan, her feelings were torn over returning to Owthorpe, to her children, to their new home. The farther she left London's hubbub behind, the more her isolation grew.

"You are pensive, Luce?" Nan's voice interrupted her thoughts. "Is all well?"

Luce stuffed the gloves deeper beneath her maroon day gown, disturbed by the fine French embroidery and scarlet leather. Too considerate to refuse them from her mother, she deemed herself too godly to wear such finery.

"I'm preoccupied with Allen and the choices he and James made. Allen pledges friendship to our Villiers relations again by joining our cousin Anne in Paris. And you know how duplicitous she can be. How could he even think of trusting Barbara's daughter?"

"Allen and James are their father's sons. They will always think first of service to the throne. And where the king goes, so do the Villiers. I have little taste for them myself, and Anne is one I would keep at arm's length." Nan left the doorway and crossed the chamber to Luce's side, the harsh January light revealing small care lines on her smooth brow. The war exerted its toll on her cousin too. She laid a beautifully manicured hand over Luce's ink-stained fingers, stilling the fidget. "But what concerns you? Something greater gnaws at your heart."

Luce slammed the chest shut. "I dread our return to Owthorpe." The words tumbled from the pressure of being stopped inside for so long. "John sees a life I do not, for I fear his eyes are blinkered and he does not fully recognize the turmoil around us. His dream is to live out his days at the manor, tend to his land, create gardens and beauty and enjoy his books and music as we raise our children."

Nan lifted an eyebrow. "And is that such a bad life? John has made some wise investments and deserves the fruits of his work."

"It is unrealistic and unsustainable. And you encourage him to purchase the king's art, live beyond his means as if he were a courtier, not representing the people."

"Many thousands of Englishmen wish for just such respite after the fatigue of war. John enjoys those pursuits. Surely he has a right to return to the pleasures he loved."

Luce paced to the window. A hoarfrost sparkled across the rolling parkland, coating grass blades and tree limbs in a gauzy veil. A small herd of roe deer stepped delicately from the woodland towards the lake, hoofprints dimpling the white and leaving a trail of green flowers. Such tranquility. And yet beyond the park, beyond the fence, across the water, a king bided his time to return to the hunt.

Tracing the outline of the trees on the pane, Luce tried to explain. "Progress cannot go forward until England is united, and John will be called back to Parliament to bring order through government. Cromwell will never let him leave. His is one of the voices of reason."

The deer tiptoed across the sleeping land, threading between the trees, vanishing as she watched.

"You dreamed of this power, fought for victory, put England's future into play with the king's execution. Does John not want to complete the work he started? Surely he can do both."

The truth in Nan's words cut.

"He has no stomach for politics. There are many days his spirit is not committed, Nan. Days he just wishes to withdraw from government and decisions and break the crucible of change. Hide in Owthorpe and never leave again."

Nan nodded. "These times are not for the faint of heart." She turned from the window as if the view pained her. "You have seen how Allen and Frances could not accept this new England. Their future is dark, and yet they sacrificed the known for the unknown."

"And I fear I am of the same temperament." Luce could finally voice her fears. "I cannot remain quiet, subdued and buried in the life of a country lady. I crave the stimulation of words, debate, the growth of new ideas." She chewed her thumb. "In the heart of Westminster, we were surrounded by great minds, passionate philosophers. I am afraid my restlessness will hurt John, and there is nothing I can do to stop it. For to pretend is to lie, and to lie is to die."

The air absorbed her words, holding her statement between them. Luce feared she'd said too much, even for Nan's forgiving ears.

Her cousin took her into her arms and held her.

"Then write, my darling Luce, write as if your life depended on it. Take your worries and sorrows and fears and write in your notebooks, as you always have done. Write your essays and credos, continue to counsel John with your brilliant thinking, and find comfort in the words you write, the poems you compose, the translations of the philosophers you delight in. There are many who would benefit from reading your work, and so put your heart into your writing. Your words are the intellectual companion you crave."

Over Nan's shoulder, through the window, across the park, the deer reappeared, leaving a chain of tiny prints withering into the ice. The fear blooming in Luce's heart remained, for it was the fear of the known, the suspicion her own restless intellect would bring misfortune. For surely eminence could be both good and bad.

"Thank you, Nan," she replied. "John depends greatly on your business sense. And you are the bridge between Allen and me. I will do my best in Owthorpe. Thank you. For without you, we would be lost."

"Mother! Mother!" Luce's twins raced across the snowy land, the boys' faces laughing beneath their woolen hats, scarlet-cheeked and bright-eyed. Behind, her eldest daughter, Bee, daintily trod a path through the snow, holding Lucy's gloved hand.

Springing down from her horse, Luce held her arms open wide. The children all collided with each other and her, and in the commotion Luce laughed at the sheer pleasure of reunion. John stood perfectly still. A flutter of apprehension trembled through her as he stepped to one side, sweeping a bow and gesturing through tall stone gateposts. He'd been waiting for this moment, seeking her approval. She must not disappoint.

He led her through an avenue of saplings in the snowy, silvery land, his face alight with excitement.

"John," she gasped. "John, this is ours?"

He nodded, his eyes full of love and pride.

In a field of billowing white, the house's honey-coloured bricks glowed in their fresh newness. Three stories high with two wings extending a welcome, the front shimmered with an array of windows, each glazed and reflecting the sparkling landscape. Ornate brick work framed the paned glass, and the curiously designed roof curved and pointed its way to the heavens.

John's gaze followed hers. "The latest in the Dutch style," he announced. "I employed an architect from London familiar with the modern design. There is no such a dwelling from here to London."

A cold wind sliced into Luce's heart, returning fear to her soul.

"And how did we afford this, John? It is a style both extravagant and beyond our means. Your back pay from the army would never have covered this." She hated the way her voice sounded, all pinched and in her throat. John did not seem to notice. He squeezed her hand.

"I have engaged in some commerce with Nan that is proving most profitable, dearest. Come, I'll explain more inside. Settle the children and we shall talk."

Luce pivoted to find her bearings. The last time she was here, Allen and Frances were with them, her mother too, the ruins of their house hidden behind the village, a testament to the devastation of the Royalist armies. The little stone church still stood as it had for hundreds of years, embedded in the landscape as upright and sturdy as one of its yeoman parishioners.

"This was the meadow, wasn't it? The meadow where we saw the skylarks, where we envisioned our future after the war?"

He took her face between his hands and kissed her deeply. "This was our meadow, my darling. And I built a home fit for you and your mother and our children to live in, forever bringing the Hutchinsons home to Owthorpe."

How sweet his touch. A few flakes of snow landed on his auburn hair, delicately laced before dissolving into diamond drops.

"It is a very fine house, John."

"It is home, sweetheart. Let me walk you in."

With the children racing ahead, throwing snowballs and shouting in excitement, they joined Lucy at the front of the house. A flight of steps swept up to the door, a freshly hewn golden oak to complement the brick surround. On either side, tall windows flanked the entry, welcoming Luce home. No dark stronghold this, unlike the last house, cleaved from centuries of protecting the land. This house feasted on the fertile ashes of war, a phoenix rising with all the hope and light the future promised.

Luce laughed to herself. How fanciful her thoughts. Next she would only be writing poetry, not translating Lucretius or keeping the revolution alive with her tracts and essays.

Pushing the door open, John offered his arms, and with Lucy and Luce on each side of him, they entered the hall.

Of course her mother had placed a glazed bowl of snowdrops on the ancient dining table retrieved and restored from the ruins of the old hall. The flowers gleamed in the centre of the lofty chamber, bringing the outdoors inside. The hall was as open and brilliant as the sky, with a huge window at the rear, in front of which a gracious staircase appeared to float on air. All around shone light, scented of the pine forests and woodlands from which the interior was crafted.

Luce thankfully focussed on the small moments. "Snowdrops."

Lucy smiled. "I remember you always greeted the first flowers of the year with joy, my darling. I was so happy to find them in the churchyard this morning, in a sheltered patch under the yew."

John shifted from one foot to another.

"We have yet to bring in much furniture, and there are still carpets and tapestries to hang, and our bedding is—"

"No matter, John. No matter. For this is the most beautiful home I have ever seen. You have brought us together, created our haven and delivered us our future." Luce put her trust in God and Nan. No more worry about money or responsibilities or the demands to come from Cromwell and Westminster's Parliament. No disconsolation with her lot, or fears her brain would shrivel in this country outpost. This moment was theirs to live within, as God intended, full of gratitude and joy.

John took her hand. "Come, let me show you more."

He led her up the floating staircase and threw open double doors. "A ballroom, where we will entertain our neighbours and friends with dancing and concerts and play music in harmony."

Her knees buckled, and the room became a blur.

Almost running in his delight, he opened door after door in giddying succession. "Look, my love. Chambers for the children, for your mother, guests."

She could not find her words. A painful lump sat in her throat.

"And a beautiful room for us to enjoy in private."

A room larger, more gracious, more beautiful than she had ever slept in, with windows to the sky and a fireplace with cushions heaped before.

"And this marvel of concealment." John pressed an engraved rose on a panel. The wood clicked and swung open to reveal a hidden apartment with leaded windows high up in the eaves. Lined with benches, containing a table and stools, with shelves storing blankets and essentials, the space could house their entire family. "A hiding place none will ever find."

"A safe room?" This chamber finally forced words from her. "A safe room, John?

John bowed his head. "Times are still uncertain, Luce. Thanks be to God I could rebuild with the funds from the sale of the art. And spare no expense. When I travel back to London, I know you will be happy and safe in our new home."

She could not bear to hear more. But she must know, know everything. "You return to Parliament, John?"

"Yes." John's voice dropped. The excitement left him. "I cannot be released yet from the Council of State, and Cromwell has commanded me back to Westminster to review the Irish campaign."

"Surely you do not have to rejoin the army? What is happening in Ireland? Do not tell me Cromwell is leading England into war."

The day was ruined. John, this house, this war, this life. None were hers. She did not fit anywhere. Unlike her brother, who knew his mind, followed his destiny. She ignored the traitorous thoughts.

John took her into his arms. "I am simply returning to Westminster. I am no longer active in Cromwell's army, my love. My use is in debate, not battle. Besides, Ireland is just a precautionary campaign to prevent the Stuart establishing a foothold. There is naught to be concerned about."

10

Frances

Never in her life had Frances seen or smelled anything as derelict and putrid as the streets of Paris. She clutched her scarf more tightly to her nose and took small panting breaths through her mouth. Streets! These filthy muddy tracks would not even lead a cow to a byre in Devon, and yet here, the only access to the Palais-Royal swam ankle deep in mud, shite and blood. Picking her way around a heap of steaming offal, slung into the street from a butcher's slapdash knife, she hurried before a pack of stray dogs knocked her over in their eagerness to devour the entrails.

Six months. Six months since she and Allen had tumbled out of a broken-down coach into the mire and muck of this disgusting place, clutching Isabella, shaken from a week's travel from the coast. Bumped, bruised and flea-bitten from the filthy bedding of cheap inns, they'd sought refuge at the court of Queen Henrietta Maria, widow of the king of England, daughter of the royal house of France, aunt to the Sun King himself, Louis XIV.

Court of No Return, more like.

Dear God!

Gagging, she almost vomited in the mud, adding to the disgusting liquid mess around her ankles. How could anything stink worse? Nan certainly knew how to pick a safe convent to exchange their mail. No one ventured into Saint-Germain, the most polluted arrondissement within Paris. Even the cutpurses avoided these poisonous alleys. Turning into Rue Christine— how ironic, named for Queen Henrietta Maria's sister, favourite child of Henry IV—she hurried along the narrow street. Here at least new homes sprang up, and in the spirit of the king's favour they were decently constructed around the bones of the old Augustine abbey.

"Merde!" Frances spat out one of her newly learned French phrases as a fat, barrow-pushing peasant threw a spray of noxious mud over her skirts. Bad enough to venture into this district; to be covered in the toxic filth that would forever stain her gown, and the stink of which would follow her for days, was worse. Her manservant shoved the peasant to one side, which did

little to alleviate her temper; a pile of human ordure tipped from the night's chamber pots barred her passage.

She wished again she'd never ventured forth.

And yet who else would scavenge for firewood, bread, meat?

And who but she to pick up and deliver the network's letters from Nan?

The women of the exiled court foraged for food and delivered secrets while the men dreamed their improbable campaigns to restore the king.

As usual, she must provide the resources while Allen spent his waking hours in men's talk, idling around the palace hallways, creating elaborate plans and yet accomplishing little.

Approaching a small arched doorway, up several worn steps from the street, Frances stayed her servant. He was unhelpful, surly even, but she needed the guard in this chaotic city overflowing with all manner of English flotsam washed in on the tides of war.

"Wait here. *Attendez ici.*"

He nodded and, folding his arms against his bulk, leaned against the wall. He knew the protocol.

The doorway opened into a small courtyard surrounded by the high walls of the abbey and two of the new town houses built in its ruins. Someone had tried to make the space welcoming, and several tubs of lavender and rosemary were placed in the yard, along with a rain barrel and a small bench. Ahead, a heavy wrought-iron gate protected the entrance to the convent, and she pulled and twisted the heavy ring to open it. As she banged on the weathered timber door, the little window within slid open, and a watchful eye peered at her.

Frances whispered, "I come for the blessing of the mother abbess."

"Peace be with you child. Wait here and she will attend you." Another English spinster escaped from Cromwell's Puritan rule.

The window slid shut, and Frances waited with some trepidation for the abbess to come. This was always the moment she dreaded most, for uncertainty always raised a cloud of butterflies in her stomach. Would there be a letter? Would it have been intercepted?

"Madame." A low voice caught her attention. "Madame, for you." A small parchment was thrust from the window, along with a fresh baguette, its aroma tantalizing. "For me, anything?"

"No," whispered Frances. "Not today. But soon, I hope."

"C'est la volonté de Dieu," replied the abbess. "God's will."

Frances bobbed her head and tucked the letter inside her bodice. By the time she turned, the door had slid shut again. She walked briskly across the courtyard to where the servant waited.

"We return to the palace. *Viens avec moi.*"

He bowed his head. "*Oui, madame.*"

His eyes were sympathetic. He was no happier than she, forced to accompany this crazed English lady on her daily quest through the Paris streets. Frances shrugged. Needs must, and if they weren't to starve, she could not rely on the haphazard victuals available within the palace. And if her daily hunt for food took her over the river to Saint-Germain, so be it.

Turning from the spire of Notre Dame, she hurried west and through the crowds on the Pont Neuf. Perhaps a breeze from the Seine would lift the miasma from her throat. Ahead stood the bulk and tower of the Louvre, a fortress against the river front, concealing the Palais-Royal, Queen Henrietta's new refuge.

The broad river rolled past her, a flurry of wind whipping the surface and obscuring the underlying grey murk. But little white clouds scudded across the pale blue sky, and a bloom of hope lifted her heart. Spring. Thanks be to our Lady she maintained her health, for at least on these walks she could escape the miserable conditions at court.

She turned her face to the sky and, rejoicing in the tentative warmth of the first day of spring, took a deep, joyful breath. There. Although the river crawled, fetid with waste, a teasing westerly breeze skipped across the city rooftops, bringing a hint of countryside with it. Frances swallowed the sudden lump in her throat. West, all the way from England.

The servant shrugged in the way only the French could and stomped on, clearing a path through the citizenry with his bulk.

Frances clutched the precious loaf of bread tighter to her chest, put her head down and marched towards the Louvre. At last, she left the mud and filth and reached the relative cleanliness of the palace confines, for at least here were cobblestones and drain channels. Now she encountered hammering and shouting and, heaven be praised, the welcome gritty smell of wet plaster and fresh-cut timber. The scale of the construction never failed to mesmerise her, and she paused for a moment, fascinated as a mass of workers swarmed up the scaffolding and across the face of the palace.

Nodding to the servant to help, Frances picked up a few scraps of wood, stuffing them in the cloth she had brought purposely for such a find.

Pine burned quickly and with a hot, brief blaze, but at least there was a flame, for in their impoverished exile they had no money for firewood and barely enough for food. A few more sticks here, and she would have sufficient for two days of meals and to warm Isabella's possets.

She smiled at the foreman, a big beefy man she saw regularly on her expeditions. He wagged his finger at her and shooed her away, but not before he thrust a handful of tapers into her arms.

"Merci, monsieur!" Frances continued through the grand courtyard, her dignity and confidence forestalling any questions. Besides, the workers were used to the eccentric English ladies who roamed the construction, picking up useful debris. She stopped and retrieved one last piece of wood, oak this time, a treat to burn longer and warmer.

Beggars should not be choosers, and this small gift brightened her morning again. At least she had rooms to return to, for amid this deprivation she was only too aware of the destitution outside the palace walls.

"Ah, our charming vagabond returns. Lady Apsley, I declare you are more skilled at foraging than any of us," Anne Villiers grimaced as Frances unwrapped the wool scarf and shook out the creases of her worn linen sleeves. "I may have disguised myself and the princess as peasants during our escape to France, but you could be mistaken for any common merchant's wife, braced to battle with any shopkeeper who will try to cheat you."

Frances shrugged. "I go to war daily." She spread the contents of her bundle upon the table and gestured for the servant to pile the wood scraps by the cold fireplace in their shared chamber. "Today we have a loaf from the convent, some excellent salted fish and"—here she paused —"the new potatoes of the spring."

Anne looked at her suspiciously. "Potatoes?"

"Allen's mother commends their restorative powers," Frances replied. "She told me of serving some of the first grown in England to your mother and George Villiers when they dined with her in the Tower."

Anne dubiously picked up the small ivory nugget and rolled it between her fingers. "My uncle thought highly of her. He appreciated Aunt Lucy's reports on the prisoners. Especially those who were his enemies." She set the potato down and sighed. "Such different times, when the king's rule was respected—and absolute."

"In truth, our families thrived under the duke's influence. I am sorry Luce still carries the old quarrel with your mother in her heart," Frances replied. "Do you think there is any future reconciliation between Lucy and Barbara?"

Anne flashed a smile of charming brilliance. "The fault does not lie with us. We are the Villiers. We are always looking for allies. And now you can view the world through Villiers eyes and see the advantages of aligning with us." She paused, her sparkling eyes narrowing. "You have the ambition."

"What do you mean?"

"I did not expect Allen to marry you, for when we met first in Exeter, his heart was damaged. Ask Nan. She knew better than any of us." Anne's smile tightened. "He dwelled in a dark world, unreachable by those who had known him the longest. But I can see his attraction to you. You are so . . . capable. And strong. I engaged you to care for the queen's baby. You ended up running the garrison. And pulled him into marriage." Her careless statement hung in the air between them.

Frances surveyed the pitiful empty chamber, a stone floor bare of any covering, the walls rough-hewn. "When we were besieged in Barnstaple by Parliament's army," she replied, "we survived because I persuaded the local merchants to part with supplies. Without securing provisions from Cromwell's supporters, we would have been starved out."

Why did Anne always put her on defence?

Allen's cousin sighed and walked to the narrow window slit. She leaned her cheek against the stone. "How times have changed. And yet you've adjusted, reprised your role. How easily you don the disguise of a merchant's wife. Meanwhile, I am a beggar at the exiled court, and my sweet Princess Minette is one more neglected child of the destitute English queen."

There was no answer to change the facts. In truth, Paris's devastating poverty and cramped conditions shocked Frances. Each day more refugees arrived from England, putting such a strain on resources and tempers that it felt as if the whole palace would go up in flames from the foul mood of the exiled English.

But nothing to be gained from regrets.

"We will find our way again," she replied. "Sir Edward Hyde has your well-being and that of the royal family at heart. He and Allen meet daily to

71

discuss plans for our return to England. This is but a temporary inconvenience."

Anne turned from the narrow opening, the despair on her face quickly replaced by a smile. "I adore Sir Edward, and he has a special regard for me," she replied, the Villiers charm radiant again. "And he is my best ally to remind the king of our loyalty. Yet even in his earnest service of us all, I know not how he will bring this change about. We are surely a people without a home, a king without a country."

No time for further Villiers posturing, Frances turned away and pulled the note from her bodice, folded tightly and addressed to the abbess of the Augustin Convent at Rue Christine. She ran her finger carefully over the red seal with the imprint of the St.John falcon and felt the small tag rough against her thumb in the top left corner.

"What's that?" Anne peered over her shoulder, her eyes fixed on the letter. "More news from Nan?"

Frances regretted her momentary lapse.

"I must find Allen and Sir Edward," she replied, ignoring her question. "Minette and Isabella will return soon from their walk in the gardens. Perhaps you can ask for some fresh milk from my Lady Verney in exchange for half of our bread. Add a little of the cinnamon from Lady Fanshawe, and the girls will enjoy their treat."

She doubted those instructions would be followed. Anne Villiers was not one to nurture a child—unless for political gain. Leaving Allen's cousin sitting disconsolately on the single wooden bench, Frances squared her shoulders and set off to find Sir Edward and her husband. Eager to read Nan's letter, she paused by a narrow stone window, broke the seal and skimmed the brief lines.

I hear that John's new home is quite magnificent, wrote Nan. *And he welcomes family and friend alike. In truth, he is most open to entertaining men of all interests and beliefs, regardless of their history. Pray pass my very best regards on to Mr Nash, and also those of his sister Susan, in the hopes that we will hear of his well-being directly. Kindly remember me to his friend who has the falling sickness. I expect a new curative will be ready soon.*

Frances refolded the letter and stuffed it back in her bodice. A strategic location in the Midlands, much could be coordinated from Owthorpe. And a mention of Susan Hyde. Her work in Wiltshire must be going well. Sir Edward would be pleased to hear Nan's intelligence. As would Allen.

Perhaps now their plans would have a focus, knowing their cousin John Hutchinson declared himself neutral and welcomed visitors—if this was true and not another instance of John's contradictory nature.

11

Nan

Ditchley's herd bred well this year, expanding her livestock holdings. Fine weather cultivated lush grass in the water meadows. England truly flourished this June, and as Nan strolled through the gardens at Ditchley Park, arm in arm with Walter's wife, she calculated the first tranche of income from selling the calves. Very satisfactory.

These were pleasant days when Walter and Johanna visited, for her brother brought much light and laughter to her home, and her youngest son adored his godfather. Johnny was a wayward lad, full of high spirits and a mischievous humour. Walter provided the much-needed male discipline in lieu of her absent husband.

"Will you not come and spend the summer with us at Lydiard?" asked Johanna. "The house is most comfortable now we have brought fresh furnishings to the rooms, and the gardens grow lovelier every week with new blooms."

Nan grimaced. "Much as I love you and Walter, I cannot overcome my childhood boredom with the dullness. At least here we are close to the main highway from Oxford, and I enjoy many visitors. You have to want to go to Lydiard to get there, and frankly—"

"You don't!" Johanna finished for her, laughing. "I know how memories shape us. We moved constantly in my childhood, without a home of our own. My father never spared a thought for his family instead of his political ambitions. Perhaps that is why I love Lydiard so."

"Your marriage with Walter has united our two branches of the family." A little probing here would not go amiss. "Oliver St.John has become a man of great repute in this new Parliament. And now Lord Chief Justice. Your father has successfully navigated his way through these troubles. Perhaps refusing to ratify the king's death warrant was not such a mistake after all."

"I hope he does not live to regret his decision." Johanna reached for the delicate clippers hanging from her waist and cut a handful of lavender. "For your Johnny," she explained, "and his bad dreams. These scattered within his pillow will soothe him."

"Thank you. He is but four, too young to discern between nightmares and truth. How do you know of this curative?"

Johanna handed the lavender to Nan. "Lucy wrote it for me."

"You are in correspondence with her?" She inhaled the pungent scent and immediately returned to her aunt's stillroom within the Tower.

"Yes. We exchange recipes frequently. She maintains a great book of them from her time in the Tower and at Nottingham Castle."

Nan nodded thoughtfully. "So you have a regular messenger service between Lydiard and Owthorpe?"

"And Battersey. Wherever I happen to be. My father requires it of me." Johanna strolled on. "He is careful with his enemies and even more so with his friends. He keeps a close eye on all. Refusing to attend the king's execution and yet serving on the council were all honest judgments. I think that is why Cromwell relies so upon him."

"And your families are related."

Johanna laughed. "Certes, that does not hurt. For if we cannot have faith in family, who can we trust?"

A sudden clattering distracted Nan. A rider galloped into the courtyard, the horse's sides foam-flecked. "John has arrived. He told me he would be staying for a few days after the council retired for summer."

"Then meet him, and I will call Walter from the library." Johanna picked a few more sprigs of lavender. "Let me first find Johnny's nurse and ensure these are ready for him before bed tonight."

John must have ridden straight through from Holborn. His eyes were exhausted, his thick hair plastered darkly to his head. Usually impeccably dressed, his sweat-stained suit was dusty and creased. Nan ran to him and grabbed his arm, for as he dismounted he staggered and swayed.

"You appear ill, Cousin. Have you a fever?"

"I must talk to you, Nan." He glanced at the bustling stables, his countenance intense. "Who else is here?"

"Walter and Johanna. Their children. No one else."

"Then summon your brother, for he too must hear my words."

Nan beckoned a servant to take John's pack and commanded the man to hurry into the house and bring refreshments.

"You should rest first. Your news can wait."

"My soul cannot."

His gravity clouded the bright afternoon. She guided him through the cool hall, straight to the library. As she walked in, supporting John's exhausted frame, Walter started up from his chair. Johanna dropped the lavender sprigs, letting them fall unheeded to the floor.

"Good heavens, John, what ails you?" Walter's shocked face mirrored Nan's own reaction.

John opened his mouth and then sank into a chair. Doubling over his knees, he held his face in his hands. His shoulders began to shake, and sobs burst forth from his throat as if ripped from his very soul.

Johanna knelt, gathering him in her arms. Nan and Walter stood helpless in the face of his anguish.

"John, what is it? Oh God, Luce? Your children?" Nan gasped. "Tell me."

After an eternity, he quietened. "They are well," he choked, his voice still muffled in his hands. "But I cannot say the same for thousands in Ireland."

Nan glanced at Walter. Johanna continued to rub John's shoulders. Slowly, he straightened and wiped an unsteady hand across his face.

"Forgive my weakness, but I have not slept for days, not since the news arrived and I read the reports."

"What news?" Walter and Nan asked in unison.

He swallowed and closed his eyes. "Of Ireland. And the slaughter. The unbelievable slaughter of thousands. Men. Women. Children." He moaned. "Babies. God's innocent babies."

Nan groped for the chair back, faintness assaulting her. "What mean you, John? And how do you know of this?"

He looked directly at her, eyes red-rimmed and mouth trembling.

"Such cruelty, such terrible injustice, oppression, violence, wicked, wicked murderous actions."

"By whom?" Nan dreaded the answer. If orders came from the top, this was no rogue army, but a calculated political slaughter.

"Cromwell."

Walter's voice was a croak, and so he cleared his throat and tried again. "Why?"

"To eradicate the last of Charles's allies. To prevent the Irish joining with him. To eliminate papacy. All of these, some of these, one of these reasons, I know not." John's voice cracked again. "All I know is Ireland's green valleys run red with the blood of innocents, and our country is mad, and the men who run it are mad zealots."

"My father?" whispered Johanna. "Did my father approve of this?"

John shook his head. "No, Johanna. He is as appalled as I am. We have both left the council's chambers, for I cannot face the butcher."

"John. John, listen to me." Nan saw beyond shock to the consequence. "You must still serve. To deny Cromwell support now is to endanger yourself."

"I cannot condone his murderous acts."

"You cannot leave the Council of State. This position is keeping you and your family safe. No one questions your loyalty when you serve Cromwell."

John slumped back in his chair. "In all conscience, I cannot do it, Nan, I cannot. I just want peace. I want this to be over."

She wanted to scream. "You have no choice." Relenting, she continued. "Rest tonight here. Make the excuse business called you back to Owthorpe for a few weeks. But you must return. And Luce will tell you the same." She turned to Johanna. "Please make a posset for John to help him sleep. I fear his demons will be worse than Johnny's tonight."

Johanna nodded. "Yes. I have all I need."

Nan returned to John. "She will take you to rest. No more talking for now. Just sleep."

John allowed himself to be led from the library, and her heart twisted. Such weight upon him. Surely his gentle spirit would collapse under the demands of vile Cromwell.

"What now?" Walter's words broke into her thoughts.

"I know not. There is no undoing of these terrible deeds."

Her brother looked down at his hands, examining them as if the answers were written upon his palms.

"What will the Stuart do now?"

"Advance to Scotland. Lead an army and reclaim his throne. Henry has been preparing for this ever since the Scots recognised the king. All their mission needs is the right time, and reason for the Irish to join."

Walter sat slumped at the library desk. He looked up, and in his eyes glistened the likeness to her beloved Edward. And something deeper, a sorrow that should never be in one so young.

"And so conflict comes upon us again."

Nan nodded. "It never left us, Walter. The war has not ended, not while the king breathes and hope beats in men's hearts."

12

Frances

"Another letter from Nan in cypher. The third this week. Events are moving quickly." Frances opened the clasp on her locket and removed a scrap of paper containing the code. She looked up at Allen. "Quickly, bar the door and be sure no one enters."

Her husband strode to the door and leaned against it, facing her and Sir Edward as they pored over the parchment. "What does she write? What news?"

"Patience, Allen," wheezed Sir Edward. His tremendous girth prevented him from bending over the table. "With the king's journey to Scotland imminent, every piece of intelligence is crucial, and we cannot afford one single mistake."

Frances smoothed the parchment and lay her key next to it, trying not to reveal her weariness to Sir Edward. Her hands were moist. August brought foul smells and relentless heat within their cramped chamber.

She pushed damp hair from her brow and peered at the letter. The lines were spaced widely apart, a clue that perhaps another letter was contained within. Striking a flint, she lit a candle and held it under the parchment. Slowly, brown words emerged from between the lines of ink, revealing secrets invisible just a moment ago.

"The words are challenging. But here is what I understand. *'John devastated over Irish slaughter. Seeks to resign from council. Retires to Owthorpe. Urging delay. Role within more valuable than without.'* Frances looked up. Nan's teaching kept her steady. She must still do her work and do it well. "There is more."

"So now he understands the extent of Cromwell's hideous ambition," Allen's voice was bitter. "How often have we spoken of the rift between John's beliefs and Cromwell's actions?"

Sir Edward abruptly motioned Allen to silence. "What else does our cousin Nan write?"

Frances moved the candle under the parchment. More words appeared. "She suggests Henry visit her and John. He must be convinced to return to the Council of State and assess the attitude of Parliament. The country is appalled at Cromwell's brutality. This is our chance."

Beckoning Allen to rejoin them at the table, Sir Edward picked up the parchment and rapidly read the fading words. "There is no doubt John can bring us much information from within the council. But does he have the duplicity to serve two masters?"

Allen picked up Nan's letter and held it to the light. "She endangers herself with these notes." He contemplated Nan's clear hand. "She is brave in her support of our cause."

"And that's why Henry loves her so," retorted Frances. She had no patience for anyone in this heat, especially her husband and his daydreaming.

Allen dropped the letter, and the thin parchment fluttered to the table. She snatched it up and tore it into tiny shreds to dispose of later with their night waste. She didn't need to act so hastily, but she felt all the better for doing so.

Sir Edward continued as if nothing had happened. "What is John's humour, Allen?"

"Godly. Fair. Civil. His natural leaning favours the victim. He fights for the weak and dispossessed."

"And his political views? Are they malleable?" Sir Edward made a bridge of his fingers. "John Hutchinson held Nottingham Castle for Cromwell throughout the war years. His defence was crucial to the outcome of the war for the Roundheads. If not for his defiance of our siege, we may have won the Midlands. You really think he won't defend his position again?"

Allen hesitated. "Perhaps you should ask of Luce's views. My sister's opinions are those forged in the steel of Calvin in her formative years. Between her and our mother, two formidable minds influence John's thinking."

Sir Edward looked at Frances. "You agree?"

She nodded. "I have always found John a temperate man. He may be stubborn, and sometimes obstinate, but once he has made up his mind, his character serves him well in times of duress."

"And Luce?"

"As Allen says." Frances took her husband's hand, already feeling badly for her shortness of temper. They were all living on a knife edge this summer. "She will always task John to do what she thinks best for the

80

republic. However, I am not sure Henry alone will be able to win John's confidence." She clasped Allen's hand tightly. "Although they are not close of late, John will trust Allen, for their friendship is deep. If it is best for my husband to follow Henry and meet John at Ditchley Park, then he should go too." She tried to ignore the leap of excitement that lit Allen's expression, pushed away her fears for his safety. "Allen and John were once best friends. Perhaps they can be so again. Luce would cherish a reconciliation."

"I will send a messenger to Henry now, instructing him to meet you at Ditchley Park, Allen." Sir Edward took Frances's hand and brushed it with a kiss. "You have done well, Lady Apsley. And thank you for sparing your husband to this mission. I promise Nan will take good care of him."

The court in Allen's absence became a palace of monotony, all activity revolving around the widowed queen and her desperate unhappiness. Frances despised this limbo and avoided the queen's rooms as much as she could. But as the days grew shorter and Allen remained away, she joined the court in the faint hope of some alleviation of her boredom.

Glimpsed across a crowded gallery, surrounded by her maids of honour, Henrietta Maria remained the imperious royal presence Frances remembered from Exeter. But when Paris's silvery northern winter light threw its unforgiving rays upon her, the queen's face was carved with as much sorrow as the saints at her beloved Notre Dame. Deep lines gouged her skin, and although her eyes were still her most beautiful feature, even they were shadowed and sat deep in their sockets. She never laughed or smiled, not even when little Minette came running across the floor to her, and for that Frances's heart saddened. Even in her darkest days of missing Allen, Isabella gave her such joy.

Anne Villiers threw down the book she was struggling to read aloud with a great sigh. Her impatience reflected their mood, for indeed the ladies of the court could do little but read the same words over and over or unpick and re-sew their embroidery, so limited were the amusements within the palace.

Frances kept her eyes lowered on her own book, to not be influenced into irritation. "You are at odds today, Cousin?"

They were at their usual place of an afternoon, on the edge of the queen's circle of women, in their favourite seat by the great window overlooking the palace gardens. The spot may have been drafty, but at least the November chill carried a freshness through the cracked frame. Huddled close to the meagre fire, as the other ladies preferred, only served to heighten the odours wafting from their gowns and bodies. Possessing only one or two sets of clothes made cleanliness impossible. Their solace was that they shared the same predicament.

Anne frowned, her pretty features clouded with frustration. "I have such ennui. This is no court, for we have no king and the queen is a ghost. My cousin George Villiers is gathering support among the Scottish Royalists, and yet we know not if Charles has arrived in Scotland. My son stays on our estates with his men at the ready for the king's arrival with no instructions to mobilise them." As changeable as ever, her expression became sympathetic. She took Frances's hand, caressing her palm. "What do you hear of Allen? He has been gone for many weeks. Has he reached Luce and John yet? Or does he remain with Nan at Ditchley?"

Frances shook her head. "I have heard nothing.

"Such a worry." Anne's eyes glided across the room to the other ladies, smiling and nodding her head as one waved at her. "Did he plan on staying at Ditchley for long?"

"He is to wait for Henry to arrive from The Hague. Allen may also visit our cousin Walter at Lydiard. Sir Edward asked them to gather insights as to the true state of the country's feelings."

"Ah. Feelings. So important, and so often overlooked." She dropped Frances's hand and slid from her gaze, head bent over the book she claimed she was not reading. "And Nan? Does she write?"

"Not since she shared John's terrible predicament."

Anne laid down her book again. "I understand. Wrestling with one's conscience can have such a devastating impact on one's health and state of mind."

Frances tried to understand the hidden meaning in Anne's words, for she had no doubt they were carefully chosen. "Is something troubling you, Anne? This winter is taking its toll on all of us, for we wait for what we know not, in an absence of news from our loved ones." Across the chamber, the queen sat on her chair, head in hand, gazing into the struggling fire. "At least we do not wait in vain for the letter that will never come."

As the queen sat as a statue, so her ladies fluttered and chattered around her, whispering and nodding their heads. An uneasiness grew upon Frances, for many of the glances were directed at her and Anne.

"Frances, there is something I must tell you before you hear it from another." Anne shook her head and moistened her lips before taking Frances's hands. She dropped her voice to a whisper. The unread book thudded on the bare floor. "There are rumours—"

"In this hotbed, there are always rumours." Frances refused to engage in the court's favourite pastime. "Never have I spent worse hours than with these ladies whose constant joy is to ferment the manure of gossip."

Anne's face grew solemn. "These stories refuse to be doused, Frances. I feel it is my place to tell you since it affects our family. And maybe the security of the network."

"Tell me." A sudden fluttering in her stomach, a foreboding.

"It's Allen."

"Yes?"

"And Nan. They were lovers."

Frances gasped. "I don't believe you. This is in poor jest, Anne."

"I am not in jest, Frances. These are old rumours, and yet they refuse to die." Anne traced a finger across her embroidered skirt, pulling on a fraying gold thread.

"Why should you repeat them? What have you to gain by spreading this poison?"

Images flooded her mind, images of Allen and Nan in the garden at Ditchley, across the hall at Battersey, standing silently at the execution block at Whitehall.

Respectably apart. Perfectly together.

Oh God. Had she denied herself the honesty she expected of others?

Through Frances's bewilderment, Anne's voice continued. "It is time to face these stories. I have nothing to gain, but much to lose. If Allen is captured on his return to England this time, he could be tortured into revealing Nan's role."

The fluttering across the hall heightened, whispers now punctuated by stifled giggles.

Frances refused to be embarrassed by an old affair of the heart and an idle woman looking to make mischief. "And so you tell me this because you wish to protect the network? Or do you have another motive?"

Anne Villiers looked at her with widened eyes. "Why would you say that, Frances? I am only thinking of what is best for our king. Perhaps I should tell Sir Edward when I see him next?"

"No need." This rumour must be quenched now. "I know they are fond of each other, perhaps appearing more so than is seemly for cousins. They have been close since childhood and share a special bond. Just as I thought you did with Allen." Frances lifted her chin. She would not let anyone see her pain. Across the room, the whispers had ceased, and all were watching her. "Did you come on behalf of the ladies of the court to spread this muck, served up cold like yesterday's kitchen compost? Have you too joined the queen's gossips, Anne, choosing idle entertainment over family fidelity?"

Anne shrugged her shoulders as she glanced across at the queen's women. "You know I heed neither them nor their petty ways. But I do care about you. I want to save you from hearing this from another's lips who would enjoy seeing you hurt."

I think you enjoy being the messenger, Anne, for this surely lightens your boredom.

"You serve cold news, for whatever this innuendo, Allen left this long ago in his past. Many acted impetuously. In the time of war, we knew not where or when our lives would end."

"This is not about a life that's ended," replied Anne. "More of one that has begun."

"I don't understand . . ."

"Johnny Wilmot. Nan's child. They say Henry is not his father. Allen is."

This time the blow almost doubled Frances over.

Nan's words assailed her.

Allen came to me after Barnstaple, just before I found I was pregnant with Johnny.

And after she had married Allen.

Ditchley worked its magic.

And then the resemblance.

Johnny and Isabella share the St. John eyes.

Such a ringing in her ears and a tightness in her chest she could scarce draw breath. And yet she must speak, must respond.

"Nonsense."

Anne shrugged delicately. "If there is anything I can do, or say to those who spread these rumors, do let me know."

"Nonsense. And you are wicked to repeat this terrible untruth." Frances's voice rose. "It is a disgusting and insulting piece of gossip. I am shocked you would even listen, let alone repeat this poison."

Keep talking. Ignore the pain.

"Ah, my sweet cousin, I can only imagine your hurt and betrayal. It is not my intent to spread gossip." Anne took her hand, and the whispering and fluttering of fans began again. "But you should know what people are saying. And we must protect Allen."

"I care not what these mean-minded, mealymouthed sycophants repeat." Frances raised her voice enough for all to hear and pulled her hand from Anne's. "Perhaps Luce is not so wrong in her condemnation of the Villiers and their love of gossip and sabotage. And if you think this is something I would even begin to give any credence to, you and the court"—she spat the word out in her contempt—"can go to the devil."

A collective hiss of indrawn breath as she flung the words into the ladies, causing even the queen to shift her contemplation from the flames and glance up. Frances rose and slowly, so slowly, walked towards the door at the end of the room in silence, her heels tapping on the stone floor, the silk of her gown rustling. She would not hurry nor leave with her head bowed.

The devil take them.

She turned and approached the queen, the eyes of the wretched gossiping women and Anne Villiers upon her. She made a deep curtsey before Henrietta Maria.

"Frances." The queen held out her hand. "I have not seen you recently by my side. How do you fare?"

"Most well, Your Majesty." Frances took the queen's hand and kissed it. "And may I ask after your health and of your darling Minette?"

The queen nodded, her eyes enormous in their sorrow. "I am here, Frances. I breathe, but I do not live."

The courtiers hushed, trying to catch the words between them.

"I wish I could console you, Your Majesty, as I did in Exeter when you arrived seeking refuge in my town."

A flicker of remembrance crossed the queen's face. "I recall that time, Frances. You brought us delicacies and comfort that no one else could find during the war."

"And you, Your Majesty, you inspired us to bring you the best of all we could find. You were so brave and beautiful and courageous."

A tiny uplifting of the queen's lips. "Those were still times of hope, Frances." She gestured to the threadbare red-and-gold velvet cushion at her feet. "Come, sit by me and tell me more of your memories, for I would hear again of my visit and of my husband and Prince Charles."

Ignoring the glares, Frances sank to the cushion and arranged her skirts around her. She inclined slightly towards the queen and started speaking in a soft tone, encouraging Henrietta Maria to lean forward too, so their heads nearly met. To anyone observing, Frances could have been considered the queen's most bosom companion, her dearest friend.

Exactly her intention.

It was only hours later, after she had put Isabella to bed, that the trembling began. And throughout the sleepless night Frances recalled every moment, every glance, every embrace between Allen and Nan. When morning finally came, she could not say which was true, her remembering or Anne's gossip, for each time she thought of her husband and Nan, she only saw the love between them.

And she had just sent Allen back to Ditchley Park, back into Nan's world.

Isabella woke and climbed onto her lap, wrapping her little arms around her mother's neck, as she did of the mornings. Frances embraced her as she gazed from the window. Outside the palace stirred to another grey November dawn, and people were going about their business as if this were just another day.

"Isabella," whispered Frances, looking deep into her daughter's grey St.John eyes—eyes which she had remarked to Nan were mirrored in Johnny's own face. She kissed her daughter fiercely and rested her chin on Isabella's head. Frances tasted the salt of her tears as they ran unchecked. Isabella fell silent, stilled by her mother's emotion. After a few moments, she twisted on Frances's lap, those beautiful eyes catching the morning light.

"Mama? *Pleures tu?* Why are you crying?" Her little hands caressed Frances's cheeks, patting her face. And the dragons of doubt wormed into Frances's heart, and she knew not what would slay them.

On the Feast of the Three Kings, somewhere in the cavernous empty kitchens of the Palais-Royal a loyal baker had scraped together the ingredients to make *galette des rois*. To the squeals of the excited children of the court, the flat almond cake was broken apart and crumbled in an eager hunt for the paper crown hidden inside.

"I have it! *C'est à moi!*" Minette shrieked as the other children crowded around her. She picked the wisp of paper from the crumbs and waved it above her head. Golden bunches of ringlets bobbed with her excitement, and in the glow of the few candles permitted, her azure silk gown gleamed.

Frances forced a smile to her face. Isabella jumped up and down at Minette's side, clapping her hands in joy. Such a small amusement to keep these children happy, when all around them waited for news of the king and his army of Scots.

Since Anne had delivered the gossip to her, Frances found scant comfort in her days, for always in her mind the accusation burned. She relived every moment spent with Nan in Allen's company, seeing the signs, the hidden messages containing a cypher she did not possess. Her moods swung wildly, her choler one day burning with anger, the next drowning in sorrow. She trusted no one, not even Anne—especially Anne—with the burden of her fears.

As if from a masque's cue, the door flew open, and the queen's guard and Sir Edward Hyde escorted a messenger in the Earl of Morton's livery into the room. Henrietta Maria's hand flew to her breast, as if to hold her heart in place. Anne Villiers stepped forward.

"You arrive from Scotland, from my home," she said. "What news do you bring?"

The messenger knelt and presented a missive to the queen. "Your Majesty, I bring the most welcome news from our allies abroad. Your son was crowned King of Scotland on the first day of January."

Even the children stilled at these words.

The queen tore open the document with trembling fingers and quickly read the contents. "Our time has come," Her voice rang loud and clear and deep. "My son leads an army into England with the Scottish nobles at his side to deliver Cromwell his death blow."

Frances recognised the queen they called "Generalissima," the woman who had commanded her husband's troops, the leader she'd known in

Exeter, who'd left her month-old child behind in the care of Anne Villiers while she fought to save her husband's life.

"My son is with him," responded Anne, triumphantly joining the queen's side. "The Villiers ride to avenge the death of our king and bring back the throne to England, as they have now in Scotland."

With the candlelight illuminating the excited faces of the ladies of the court, and the children now chasing Minette to retrieve the paper crown, dogs tumbling under their feet and a musician playing his fiddle, the scene could have been anywhere, a festive court, an Epiphany celebration.

But the men were absent.

And upon Frances fell the burden of the empty corridors stretching beyond this cozy chamber, the bleak and snow-covered fields of northern France, the wind-whipped black waves of the Narrow Sea. Her mind flew all the way to the desolate Scottish moors and a stone palace stronghold in Scone, where a young king bravely bore a crown weighted with the nation's hopes.

Was Allen with him?

Or was he safely waiting in a familiar manor house outside Oxford?

And so it continues.

The dragons hissed that Allen would not be returning.

And I might never know the truth.

The bulk of Sir Edward Hyde momentarily blocked the meagre heat from the fireplace.

"Lady Apsley." He bowed, his kind face gentle in the dim light. "You welcome the news?"

Frances shrugged. "Our men will be fighting again, Sir Edward." Her breath came shallow, and she squeezed her hands together to prevent the pain from showing.

He nodded, his great head lion-like, gravity seizing his expression. "We will continue to fight to reclaim the throne, Frances, no matter at what cost. And since I do not ride to battle, I must negotiate treaties with our European allies. While the king is fighting for his very existence, we scrap for money and resources to sustain our cause."

"And our means wear thin," replied Frances. "We have no kindling, little food and no prospect of replenishment." She kept silent of her other loss. "Unless we have money soon, the whole court will disintegrate, for hope alone does not feed us."

Sir Edward smiled. "Always the practical one. Nan picked well."

I am not always ruled by my head.

This intelligencer was deceived by the most common cypher of all.

Love.

"And she will now rely on you even more to receive the information she sends," he continued. "You are crucial to the cause, Frances, and we thank you for your sacrifice."

"I am not alone in this, Sir Edward. My husband is somewhere in Britain, ready to give his life for the king again."

"And when we succeed and we are back in England, and the king is restored to his rightful place, you and Allen will be rewarded for your loyalty." He kissed her hand and drew her into his warm embrace, a great affectionate bear hug. "Perhaps this time next year, Frances, we will celebrate in Whitehall, all the pain behind us."

She wished she could share his optimism. She did not know if she would ever return to Whitehall, for no longer was her life with Allen there.

Not while he was in England with Nan.

13

Nan

The pitter-patter of early morning rain kissed her window, and Nan snuggled deeper under the lamb-fleece blankets with a sigh of joy. Beneath closed eyelids, she relived their glorious lovemaking of the past night, conscious of the warmth of him next to her. He moved and laid a muscled arm across her breast, pinning her to the soft feather mattress. Without words, he pulled her to him and she eagerly followed, her lips seeking his in the dim light, his familiar taste rousing her senses. God Almighty, how she had missed this man, how she craved his loving. And now he was here, in her bed, all hers for as long as she could keep him by her side.

"My love," he murmured as he kissed her neck, his lips brushing her tender skin and trailing kisses across her stomach. He paused as he caressed the silvery lines, evidence of the son he loved so much. "My love. Each time I return, it pains me more to leave."

She stopped his words with her own kisses, pulling him to lie on top of her.

"No talk of leaving," she whispered. "Loving, not leaving, is all I will permit today."

He kissed her deeply as the rhythm of their lovemaking took over. And with the soft mist creating a gauzy light, she drove him to love her as he always had, taking her to a pleasure only he had ever given her. Later, the kiss of the rain blended with the sigh of his breathing, and he slept again in her arms.

She awoke to a tapping on the door and an empty place at her side. For a moment, her heart plummeted. And then she remembered Henry stayed for a few more days. He had not left her again, not yet. Nan drew on her shawl and called for her maid to enter. The girl placed a tray of hot chocolate and white sweet rolls on a small table and quickly made up the fire. Nan's room glowed with the leaping flames, and as she curled up in her chair, her hands clasping the warm mug, she stared dreamily into the fire.

Henry and Allen had arrived at Ditchley within days of each other, each travelling on his own, under night's cover. Henry had appeared in his familiar mood of defiant bravado and, as usual, had removed his disguise the minute he arrived on Ditchley land, stuffing his face scarf and battered hat in his saddlebag. Nan laughed. He despised the need to conceal his travels, and his disguise was truly hopeless. She would recognise him anywhere. This man owned her soul.

Allen had less need to be watchful, for his name was not so closely linked with the king's. Still, in these times no harm in precautions, for friend and enemy swung with the wind.

Her cousin appeared dispirited. He should not be kicking around the court of women. He needed to be in the company of men, back in the action of battle.

Precisely where events were leading. The king amassed his army of Scots. Conflict with Parliament's army drew imminent. War fuelled the hearts of men, and revenge raised their standard.

Setting down her empty cup, Nan quickly dressed in her warm woolen house robes and pulled her hair into a hood. Wrapping her shawl closely around her shoulders, she descended to the library, certain she would find Henry and Allen there.

"Good morning." Allen stood by the tall window, his eyes on the parkland. He smiled at Nan and leaned over to receive her kiss on his cheek. "And did you sleep well, Cousin?"

"Yes."

"No." Henry grabbed her waist and pulled her to him. "I had no intention of letting sleep get in the way of love."

Nan blushed, but it was only Allen, and he just laughed.

"You travel here far more often than people ever credit you, Henry," he replied. "And I can see why. Your love for each other glows like a beacon."

Henry shrugged. "When you find your destined woman, you do anything to stay by her side."

"Including wearing terrible disguises," added Nan. "Thank heaven you remove them before you enter the house. I would not want to wake up next to the man in that disgusting hat on any occasion."

Henry laughed, throwing his head back in glee. Truly, this man loved and lived with such intensity. He had no half measures, and she adored him. She found the same in Allen, although tempered by his mother's steadying

91

restraint. Henry had no such caution, his daring legendary. Which was why the king and his men loved him so.

"Does John arrive today?" Allen changed the subject, and their mood sobered. He continued to gaze from the window; a grey mist entwined the bare trees and draped the lush green of the park. Nan crossed to the fireplace and held her hands to the blaze.

"I hope so," she replied. "I sent a message to Owthorpe requesting he visit. I did not give a reason, for I thought it best you explain when you see him."

Allen shook his head. "It will take more than just me to persuade John of our need for support. Your role is vital, Nan."

Nan took Henry's hand, for when she was with him she could not keep from touching him. "Do not be too sure of the difficulty, Allen. When last I saw him, he was greatly disturbed and disillusioned with Cromwell. Talking with John may be easier than you think."

When John arrived later that afternoon, Nan waited for him alone. She could not afford him to immediately turn and leave upon seeing Allen and Henry. Instructing them both to wait in the small antechamber concealed in a library alcove, she sat at her desk to write letters.

As John was shown in, she put down her quill and embraced him. He untied his leather greatcoat and dropped it on a bench, revealing a deep red jacket and black britches. His riding boots were highly polished, and the lace collar of his shirt lay smoothly pressed over his jacket.

Nan kissed his cheek. "John, you are as well-attired as ever. Do you not get accused of being too fine?"

He smiled, and again Nan's heart warmed, for his eyes were always so kind, and his gentle mouth so appealing in his handsome face.

"I will not don brown fustian or Puritan's robes," he assured her. "I am independent, Nan. If men are shallow enough to judge each other by the clothes they wear, I would rather have men not know where to place me than be assigned to a class I do not subscribe to."

Nan led him to one of the high-backed chairs flanking the great carved stone fireplace. She poured him a glass of wine from the Venetian decanter and sat opposite him, her own goblet steady between her hands. After a few minutes of conversation about Luce and their children's progress, she

92

steered the conversation to her purpose, conscious of Henry and Allen listening on the other side of the paneling.

"So you still declare independence, John?" she asked.

"I followed your recommendation, Nan, and continued my work on the Council of State." Swallowing his wine, John placed the glass on the small table by his side. "It cost me dearly in my conscience, for to hear those brag and boast who thought their Ireland campaigns justified caused me to choke down every protest I could think of." His voice was bitter, pain-filled from the slaughter carried out in the name of Cromwell's army.

"And so what next, John?" She hoped his words would be what she anticipated.

"Luce does not agree with me," he started, "and it causes dissention between us, but I have made up my mind."

Go on.

"I have formally resigned my place on the Council of State and intend to retire to Owthorpe. I choose to serve God and his world in a community of harmony and fellowship. I will open my house to any who wish to have discourse about music, books, philosophy."

Is he telling me or rehearsing a speech to Cromwell?

"Luce will be able to continue her translations and studies, and we will teach our children the value of independent thinking and non-judgment of their fellow men. I will transfer the command of Nottingham Castle to another, for I want nothing more to do with war. The time has come to rebuild our country."

"And Lucy? Does she remain with you?"

John laughed. "Do you think it would take any persuasion for your aunt to live in a home of learning, with the prospect of designing plans and taming nature to create gardens of beauty and practicality, safely away from the politics she so despises?"

A safe house indeed, as the king travelled south. "And why does Luce not agree?"

He smiled ruefully and poured another glass of wine for himself, offering to refill Nan's glass. She shook her head.

"You know yourself better than any. Luce is black and white and never seeks the middle ground. Although intrigued with the vision of a peaceful life away from the politics of strife, she avows there are still freedoms to secure, and by leaving Cromwell's council, we will be accused as traitors to

Parliament. She thinks I act hastily and argues I must stay involved with the creation of our Commonwealth."

"And you?"

"I am what my God tells me to be, Nan. And my God speaks of fairness and reconciliation. My conscience tells me that I must no longer bear arms for one side or the other in this war of beliefs. My principles speak of living a life of harmony with those around me, and humility, and rearing wise children. I look to the future, not just the present."

Nan's eyes filled with unexpected tears at John's earnest words, for about him lay such an air of humbleness and yet such strength in his convictions.

"And so what is the solution to this great divide? What can we do to bring England to peace?"

He held his hand out to her. She took it, finding comfort in the warmth and steadiness of his grip. "I know your heart is with your husband, and Allen, and all those who wish to return the king to England." John paused. "Even now the Stuart waits at the border to reclaim his throne. And I would no more ask you to change your heart than cut it out. But perhaps there is another way, one of diplomacy and discussion. My last act on the council was to authorise ambassadors to The Hague, to consolidate our relationship with Holland. Even now Lord Chief Justice St.John travels to meet with the Dutch. My hope is our allies in Europe will sign treaties directly with England, recognising the durability of Parliament, and allow for a peaceful final transfer of power. The Stuart must then accept his place is not on the throne of England."

Nan sighed with relief. Her beloved John did not think the blade the solution to all arguments.

"Thank you, John, for your words are wise indeed." She glanced outside, where the February light dwindled. Time seeped away.

"And what of you, Nan?" he replied. "We have talked much of me since I arrived. Where can I be of assistance to you?"

She pushed back her chair. "Ditchley continues to be the fulcrum to my life. I have invited guests for dinner. I would welcome your wisdom in conversing with them, sharing your vision of our peaceful future. Let me show you to your room, where you may rest. Then we can talk of my situation."

Standing, she led John to the main hall, where a servant met them and escorted John upstairs.

When she returned to the library, Henry and Allen were standing in front of the fireplace, deep in conversation.

"I have a plan," she said. "Listen to me, and listen well. Follow my lead at dinner tonight. Let me speak for us all. And when the time comes, swear by Almighty God you will stand by John."

Nan trusted that John's manners were too refined for him to turn around and walk from her home when he realised who waited for him in the dining chamber. But just in case, she positioned herself between John and the door, so he would have to move her to one side to leave. Instead, after halting for a moment, he proceeded to the table and pulled out a chair. Henry and Allen glanced at each other and did the same, and Nan nodded to the servants to speedily bring the courses to the table. Within minutes, the fragrance of roast meats and fine wines filled the room. After dismissing the servants, Nan held her glass in a toast.

"To our family," she said. "May we always be blessed with a roof over our heads and a table to sit around to break bread together."

Allen and Henry raised their glasses in response, and after a pause, John did the same. Although they were still silent, the men ate and drank steadily, and when Henry stood to bring more meat to the table from the platter on the sideboard, he offered slices to Allen and John. Both accepted.

"You have travelled far to be here tonight," began Nan. She would not let them dine and leave without speaking. "Ditchley, as always, provides sanctuary and a safe haven. John, Allen, I know this is very difficult for you both. And yet here you are, at our table, reunited after all that has passed."

John laid down his knife. "What intent is this, Nan?" he asked. "You brought me under the pretence that you needed my advice, and yet it is apparent you have another motive." He looked down and swirled the wine in his glass for a moment before meeting Allen's eyes directly across the table. "The king's men are here for a reason."

Nan pressed Henry's knee under the table, a warning to be quiet.

Allen picked up his glass and contemplated it too. "How are Luce and my mother, John?"

"Well. You could have written and asked that of me."

"And you? How do you fare in this new order?" Allen put his wine down firmly and folded his arms on the table. Henry moved to speak, and Nan caught his eye and shook her head slightly. This must be worked between the two of them.

"Well," repeated John. "You could have enquired that in a letter too."

"Oh for God's sake, man," Allen blurted, causing John to raise an eyebrow. "Do not play me for an idiot."

"Then what should I play you for, Allen? Last we met, you swore me a traitor and disavowed me as your brother. And now you return to England from exile in Paris with one of the most wanted Royalists in the kingdom, your Stuart was just crowned King of Scotland, and Cromwell has crushed Ireland and is massing troops at England's northern border." John's temper, always quick to rise, flashed. He drained his glass. "You insult my wits, for it is obvious you and Henry are organising an uprising." He turned to Nan. "And you are in the middle."

"Yes, I am." There was no point in dissembling now, for John, always a truthful man, had no tolerance for ambiguity. Besides, challenging him would not diffuse his choler. Nan looked at him directly. "And I hoped you would be too."

"What do you take me for? A traitor?" John drained his glass, and Allen refilled the goblet.

"A man of conscience. A man who wants no more war on his doorstep, no more bloodshed on his land." Nan took his hand, and although he did not respond to her touch, he did not draw away. "A man who rejected the slaughter in Ireland. Who has the power to bring peace to England and return it to prosperity."

"And how do you suggest I proceed? And what part do Henry and Allen play, since you appear to have planned this dinner and conversation so deviously?"

"John, if we can keep neutrality across England, then there are no more factions. You said to me earlier that your only wish was to settle at home, create beauty in your land, raise your children, spend your days with Luce. And if war no longer threatened your doorstep, then this could happen all the more quickly."

John met her gaze straight on. "I am retiring from Whitehall as soon as our Dutch negotiations are completed. Do not look to me to bring any political influence. Cromwell appoints only military advisers, and I have no desire to join his cabal."

"I hear your words. So stand up for your beliefs and help us turn our country into a kingdom of peace, not war."

"Kingdom?"

Nan cursed under her breath, kicking herself for her slip. "Nation. Old words die hard."

John scowled across the table at Allen.

"A—nation—with our Royalist friends ready to reignite war to instate the Stuart on the throne?"

Nan shook her head. "Perhaps there is another way. Diplomacy. Sir Edward Hyde speaks already of a negotiated throne, one where Prince Henry instead of Charles could rule with Parliament. He's young and a staunch Protestant. The people would accept him more easily. The old ways are vanished with the king's death, never to return. There are new solutions, if we can bring men to the table such as we are tonight. Peace is within sight."

John sniffed. "Men are at the table. But the woman is talking. It seems there are more old ways vanished than just the king. How do you suggest we proceed, Nan?"

"Live by example, John." Here came the point of no return. "Make a grand statement within your own constituency. Send the powder and shot stored at Nottingham Castle back to the Tower of London and demolish the castle. Destroy the symbol that had such impact in the war. Bring peace to the land you once fought to keep in Parliament's hands. Then division would end."

Her words lingered in the air and hung over them. Henry and Allen sat motionless, their eyes on John.

He laughed, disbelief in his voice. "That is certainly bold, Nan. You would leave Nottingham defenceless?"

"I would bring Nottingham peace. Yes, keep a small store of powder, as you did before the war, but send the rest to London. I hear the castle is ruined, not fit for habitation. So encourage the townspeople take what they want of the stones and help them rebuild their own derelict homes." She reached over and clasped John's hand. "You will be leading a new world, John, following your conscience and inspiring new ideals with all citizens.

Even Luce would approve of the levelling of all men's needs to a common goal."

John looked at Allen and Henry. "You have been silent while Nan speaks. What part do you play in this new republic?"

Henry spoke first. "I swear by Almighty God, John, if negotiations are unsuccessful and there is war with Cromwell, I will ensure our armies do not approach Nottingham. If there is conflict and we win, I will swear before the king you wanted the best for your entire family, Royalists included. And if there is conflict and we lose, I hope your home at Owthorpe will provide a refuge for those who will flee England's last battle, never to return."

John sat in silence, digesting Henry's words.

"You present a compelling paradigm," he finally said. "And one I will consider. That is all I can say, for I will let my conscience be my guide."

He stood and bowed to both Allen and Henry and kissed Nan's hand, his long chestnut hair brushing her fingers. "I will say good night and good-bye, for I leave now. Thank you for your hospitality, and your trust in me. I do not take your confidence lightly."

"John—" Allen's voice broke. "John, for the love of all we have shared, all we have lost and all we stand to gain in a peaceful land, please make the right decision."

John took a step forward, and for a moment they almost embraced. But it was too soon.

He paused, darkness behind him. "I will leave the decision to God. He will not steer me wrong."

The door clicked, and his footsteps faded and then ceased.

Henry poured Madeira for all of them. Nan wished she was encouraged by her negotiations, but somehow victory tasted bitter tonight. She must write to Frances, for Sir Edward needed to hear his plan was underway. She knew John of old. His conscience would embrace this grand gesture against Cromwell, his action protesting the army's brutality where words alone failed.

Nottingham would not hold for the army. Nor stand against the king.

14

Luce

When Cromwell came back through the country and saw the castle pulled down, he was heartily vexed at it and told Colonel Hutchinson, that if he had been there when it was voted, he should not have suffered it.

Luce Hutchinson
Summer 1651

Luce and the twins climbed Standard Hill as John's militia rolled the final barrels of gunpowder up from the caves beneath the castle mound. Nine years to the month since the king had raised his flag here. Nine years since Allen had remained on one side of Nottingham's castle yard, she on the other, and Lucy's strangled cry carried the anguish of a mother's grief at the chasm that yawned between them.

Another loud bang, and the shouts of her excited boys recalled so many days of the siege, when gunfire and men's cries were the backdrop to her life. Her children knew nothing of war except this aftermath, which in itself was one of the most thrilling days they had ever witnessed. At eleven, their world revolved around the stories of their father's exploits in combat, and they never tired of playing at war.

Thank God. Thank God her children would be spared the horrors of a battlefield, and she a mother's torment.

She witnessed Lucy's pain every day.

Nan wrote Allen travelled in the north with Henry Wilmot and the king's armies. How fortunate Nan had seen him, held him, given him her blessing. The Scots were moving south. Cromwell marched to the west. All around the country, England's warriors rose again.

And in the face of war, John defied Cromwell and the army and sided with his conscience. He destroyed the symbol of war and gave the people the materials to build anew.

She understood. For if she had to pick between her husband and Allen clashing on a battlefield in Nottingham or John's tearing down the stronghold, there was no choice.

Nan's advice divided her. Destroy the symbol of war, remove the conflict. And bring this family disunion to an end. Live now in a peaceful community, their life dedicated to books, music, the country pursuits of a gentleman; perhaps a little hawking, hunting and designing his new gardens.

So. War in her country. Or peace in her home.

Luce had talked to her mother of her own experience, the troubled times of Luce's childhood.

"Your father was a soldier first," Lucy's face had clouded as she spoke of her husband. "Nan's father offered us his home at Purley as a respite from the Tower, from George Villiers's relentless warmongering and all the accompanying strife. But his pride prevented him from retiring, settling to a quiet life. Do not let John repeat my husband's mistakes."

And so Luce had given her support to John's action.

The citizens of Nottingham rejoiced when the final loud explosions rocked the crumbling castle walls. Completely demolished. No longer a beacon of war, just a pile of rubble, ready for carting away to rebuild homes and businesses. Let somewhere else bear the burden of England's dispute. Let Cromwell and the king pass them by.

Pillars of blue-grey smoke plumed motionless in the August heat, evidencing the boundaries of the old castle walls. Dust clouds settled as eager townsfolk dislodged the final stones. A mass of people bustled below her, cheerful cries this time as neighbour helped neighbour pile the precious materials onto shared handcarts, horses with panniers, even bundles slung across strong backs.

Nottingham rose from the ashes. Life flourished.

John's vision of peace was forged from the shadows of war.

"Come," she said to her boys. "Come, let us go to Owthorpe now. Your grandmother awaits, and she will want to hear of your adventures today."

Time to leave this ruined castle, the devastation, in the past and go home.

Scarcely two weeks later, the news trickled in, first from exhausted messengers struggling to reach London, and next in direct commands from Cromwell. *Send arms. Muster troops. Drive fresh horses north to swell Parliament's army on its march through England.*

The Stuart amasses an army of Scots and exiles.

The Stuart reclaims his throne.
The Stuart crosses the border.
The Stuart returns.

"I will not send my honest men to slaughter again." John strode along the bowling green at the east of the house, his eyes on the horizon towards the ancient Fosse Way marking the road north. Luce walked with him, her skirts smooth over the short grass, the lingering dew dampening her hems and scenting the air around them.

"Cromwell requests what of you?" she asked.

"A troop," replied John. "A troop of men, with no oversight from me, just to swell numbers to appease his arrogant commanders. I will not provide them."

Luce caught his hand and stilled his pacing.

"Cromwell's temper is uncertain; we have seen it before," she warned. "Do you not think it best to comply with his request if he is calling out the militia?"

"It is not a request, it is an illegal demand." John took her by the shoulders and kissed her tenderly. "Do not fear, my love, for my command of the militia here in Nottingham is with orders from Parliament to maintain the peace, not march to war."

As they returned towards the house, the clanking of harnesses and weaponry disturbed the tranquil countryside. A storm of hoofbeats cantered on the road from Nottingham.

Pass by. Pass by. Please God, don't turn into our home.

The troop wheeled into their gates and thundered towards the house. In deference to the August heat, they had removed their armour. But there was no mistaking their hostility.

And Cromwell sat high and proud on his charger at the head of his men.

Churning the neat gravel and renting the peaceful morning air with their shouts, the troop circled before the house. Threading their way through the teeming mass of horses, Luce entered their home with John. She would not leave his side. The beautiful proportions of Owthorpe's hall were sullied by Cromwell's anger, his fervour sucking all the air from the room. Lucy stood by the stone fireplace, coolly watching him as he paced.

"On whose authority?" shouted Cromwell. "On whose authority do you dare to bring down the walls of Nottingham Castle?"

His voice fell as John and Luce approached him.

"Colonel Hutchinson." He turned to Luce and bowed. "Mrs. Hutchinson. My heartfelt apologies for disturbing you this fine morning." The abrupt contrast in his manners was unnerving. Luce recalled other occasions where this man's rough temper had shifted to honeyed platitudes on the twist of a word.

"What say you, Hutchinson?" He grabbed John's arm and pulled him to the windows overlooking the vista towards the ancient Roman road. "What say you, when the Stuart's army marches down this vale, destroying all in its path, killing your citizens and raping your women? What say you then, why you could not offer the refuge of Nottingham's castle, the most strategic fortress in all of the Midlands?"

"Parliament," John stated calmly, his natural grace underlining the authority of his speech. "Parliament, not the army, gives me my command. And Parliament approved the destruction of the castle, the re-establishment of a peaceful government and invested me with the power of managing the people's well-being in this county."

"You went around me," spat Cromwell, his voice rising again, his curling Fenland accent strong. Truly, this man's choler raged unpredictable from one moment to next. "You intentionally joined with Parliament, knowing I left the country, fighting to preserve our safety on the Scottish borders, and you did this traitorous destructive act without my knowledge—or approval."

John did not flinch. "This directive needed neither your approval nor your knowledge." Luce curled her fingers into her palms, intentionally inflicting pain from her nails to stop herself from crying out. John showed no fear when defending his conscience. "For your command of the army is not Parliament's authority over the country. And it would be best for all if you remembered your place."

In the hush that followed, the muted clattering of the troop outside was all that could be heard. John did not drop his gaze, and Cromwell spoke first, his voice trembling with restraint.

"You will regret this decision, Hutchinson. You have shown a disloyalty to me beyond a member simply following Parliament's orders. You have intentionally defied me, brought instability to one of the most strategic areas in our nation, and"—here Cromwell took a step closer to John until their faces were just inches apart—"you have taken an irretrievable position many would consider traitorous."

John did not step back, did not blink. Luce could not have been prouder of her husband—nor more fearful for his well-being.

Cromwell burst into laughter.

"Apsley, isn't it? Villiers? And Wilmot? All relatives of yours through your lovely wife's family." He turned and bowed to Luce and her mother, and as he straightened his face once again contorted with rage. "It seems to me, Colonel Hutchinson, the very essence of your loyalty is betrayed by a viper in your own bosom. I would take care of the company you keep, for in the coming months your loyalty to our country and your very future will be sorely tested."

John's anger exploded. "Do not ever question my loyalty nor that of my family." He took a step forward.

Oh God, John, do not put your hand on your sword.

Luce reached for Lucy's fingers.

"Really?" Cromwell did not back down. "Then perhaps you can tell me why your wife's brother tried to assassinate our ambassador to The Hague." He paused, obviously enjoying their shock. "Oh, you did not know of this? Your brother, madam, and your son, madam." He inclined his head with great sarcasm towards Luce and Lucy. "James Apsley plotted with Prince Edward in The Hague and came within minutes of assassinating Sir Oliver St. John. Only the quick intervention of the guard saved our ambassador from death."

Lucy let out a gasp. "James—"

Cromwell cut her off. "They escaped, unfortunately, for I would have run them through without hesitation. And so, Colonel Hutchinson, do not doubt our eyes are upon you and your family. Do not doubt you are being watched. Do not doubt your life hangs in the balance between loyalty and treachery. We ride to Worcester now, but I will return. This is far from over."

As Cromwell strode from their house, Lucy broke into sobs.

"My boy, my boy," she cried. "The first we have heard in years of James's whereabouts, and it is with this terrible news. And against our own family; he attempts to kill Johanna's father. What ruin is he bringing upon us?"

103

Luce's stomach heaved. She could not breathe or find the words to comfort her mother or reassure John.

As the sounds of the troop faded and quiet returned to the beautiful sunlit room, John spoke, "Write to Nan, Luce. Send my good wishes to her and her family. Tell her of Cromwell's visit, of the castle's destruction. And inform her Owthorpe is indeed a safe house."

As September scorched the vale's pastures and John's new plantings withered in the heat, a new kind of visitor arrived at Owthorpe. These callers came by night, stumbling across the meadow, creeping over the bowling green when the golden harvest moon illuminated even a field mouse's darting movement. These men were poorly disguised in tattered jackets, injured, shoeless, devastated. They were the remnants of the army the Stuart had mustered and marched from Scotland and then delivered to a certain death at Worcester.

The final battle, for no man would return to repeat this slaughter.

The king was vanquished.

The republic prevailed.

And, as they had for so many war-torn years within Nottingham Castle, Luce and Lucy tended these men with no distinction to the colour of their coats or the badge on their arms. These were somebody's son, husband, lover. They were Englishmen fleeing from their own friends, cousins, brothers. Luce slipped into the routine again of salves and bandages, stitching sword cuts and administering physics to reduce fevers. The stables became a field hospital of sorts, and when one soldier left, another arrived, carrying the burden of horrific tales of the streets of Worcester running red with the blood of men and horses.

Five nights after the first refugee arrived, Luce and John sat at dinner, the hall quiet, the children in bed and Lucy in her chamber, resting. Her mother's energy had diminished over the years. The war had taken its toll on her too.

"How many more, John?" Luce asked quietly. "And where do they go?"

"I do not know. From the accounts I have heard, this battle was the worst of the entire war. They travel on to France, for there is nothing left for them in England."

Silence crept over them, the sorrows haunting even in this peaceful home. In the lanterns' glow, the furniture gleamed with a rich patina, and the tapestries appeared as windows to the bucolic country scenes they depicted. On the stair walls, the king's art looked down upon them, elegant in its new abode, released from the neglect of the palaces of Whitehall and Richmond, Greenwich, Oatlands and who knew elsewhere. A testament to John's success. And the king's failure.

Some days she walked as a stranger in these surroundings, for the art was lost on her, the finery unappreciated. But the joy in John's eyes as he leafed through a book in his new library or drew his bow across his precious viola reassured her this life was ordained.

And besides, educating their children and pursuing her own joys of writing and translations offered great contentment. She thrust away the murmur of dissatisfaction in her mind. She had no grounds to deny John his happiness.

A servant appeared, Thomas, trusted for many years. He ensured these refugees were bedded down in the hidden bay in the stables, tucked away from the cursory glance of any stranger to Owthorpe. He hurried to John's side, leaning over and whispering, his face close to John's.

Luce stroked the black-edged petals of the wilting late summer rose she had picked and placed in a vase. Her mind drifted to the Lucretius translation, her most difficult work yet. John stood abruptly, white-faced, his chair shattering the peace as it scraped the floor.

"Are you sure?" he demanded of Thomas.

The man nodded, his weathered face worried, darting a quick look at Luce.

"*Quid? Quid est,* John?" Confused for a moment, her mind still in Latin, she caught the edge of the table as the room spun and the pictures danced above the stairs.

"Come. Bring your physicks. Now."

She knew then, as inherent as the blood that coursed in her veins, the marrow in her bones. She knew as only those connected by nature and sinew and tissue and spirit and soul could possibly know.

He had escaped Worcester. And sought refuge with her.

15

Luce

. . . But it was not long before the king chose another way and went to Worcester. Cromwell following swiftly after with his army, and more forces meeting him from several other parts, they fought with the king and his Scots, totally routed and subdued him, and he, with difficulty, after concealment in an oak, and many other shifts, stole away into France.

Luce Hutchinson
Autumn 1651

As Luce's eyes adjusted to the darkness within the stable, she denied her senses, believing the soldier sprawled on the straw just another Royalist seeking refuge. But when John lifted the lantern and the man stirred and groaned, the pain echoed in her very soul, recalling childhood scrapes.

"Allen."

She knelt by him, gently pushing back his matted hair, her fingers feeling for bruises on his head. Fever, certainly, and smears of blood streaked his white face, but no reaction as she tenderly probed his scalp. No injury there. John brought the lantern closer, and she unbuttoned Allen's torn jacket. As she did so, his eyes fluttered and opened, unfocussed for a moment and then locked into hers.

"Sister?"

"Shh. You are safe."

His head rolled to the side, eyes closed again. Luce lifted his blood-soaked shirt and sucked in her breath. She found the source. A sword gash on his right side, under a rough cloth tied tight around his chest.

Edward. A lethal sword cut like Edward's.

She forced herself to look further. The wound had entered him high, no vital organ below, as far as she knew. Ribs cracked from the impact as her fingers pressed and he winced. God be thanked, no piercing of the heart or lungs. If those were damaged, he would not have made it this far.

John knelt beside her. "How does he fare?"

"He will live. But we must get him inside, for already the fever grips him."

"I have instructed Thomas to prepare a bed in the servants' quarters."

She protested, and he lifted a hand to stop her words.

"If the children see Allen in the house, we cannot ask them to remain quiet. He is safest hidden with the servants."

John was right. "Mother?"

"Not to be told, not yet. Not until we understand more and Allen is healed. She is not as strong as she thinks."

Luce nodded. "Then let us move him."

Thomas approached, and together he and John carefully put their arms around Allen and brought him to his feet. She guided them to the stable door, where the moonlit courtyard lay before them. Less than a hundred yards across to the offices, the distance appeared daunting in the brightness of the gibbous moon. As they paused, a barn owl glided across their path, a gleaming ill-omened creature swooping from a perch in the tangled woods by the church.

Luce shuddered, for this bird of darkness heralded an ancient curse, foreshadowing death. Dread froze her step. And then her learning returned to her, and she almost laughed. In Greek myth, the owl forecasted victory for armies. Perhaps this prediction was twofold. Cromwell had won the final war for England. And she would win the battle for Allen's life.

On the second night, the soldiers came. A violent hammering at the door startled them both. Within moments, shouts echoed from outside their window, and John sprang from bed.

"Stay upstairs," he commanded. "Ensure your mother calms the children."

John peered out into the darkness beyond the glass. "I cannot see who it is. But they are not likely to leave without some satisfaction."

He pulled on his shirt, breeches and boots and ran downstairs. Calling to her mother to stay with the children, Luce followed him.

Five Roundhead soldiers stood before John at the open front door, armoured, menacing in their buff leather jackets and thigh-high boots. In the moonlight, their breastplates gleamed. As the leader pushed past John, his spurs rang out on the polished floor.

"Colonel Hutchinson?" he snapped. "We believe you are hiding Cavaliers who have escaped from Worcester."

"No," John said firmly. "I am not. And you are welcome to search my house."

"I don't need your invitation," replied the soldier. He nodded at his men, who immediately spread out. Luce suppressed a cry as they pushed past her and ran into John's cabinet chamber.

"A fancy place for a Puritan." The captain appraised the contents of the room, his eyes travelling from wall to wall, holding a lantern closer to peer at the artwork. "You have an expensive taste in paintings, Colonel."

"They belonged to the Commonwealth and are legally purchased." John's demeanour was calm, but Luce knew he fumed beneath his composure. "Is there anything else you would like to see, Captain?"

The man ignored him and gestured upstairs to two of the soldiers. Lucy stood on the landing, her arms around the twins, her nightgown pale in the darkness.

"You are Pierrepoint's man? Captain Shelby, isn't it?" John questioned. "I recognise you from our days when we defended Nottingham castle. Times have changed that you now challenge my loyalty, when before you would have laid down your life with me."

"I am Cromwell's man," the soldier corrected. "It is not I who has had a change in loyalty, Colonel Hutchinson."

The soldiers clattered downstairs, and the other two returned from searching the ground floor.

"Nothing here, Captain."

The leader glanced at Luce. "Outside, then. Search the stables and the offices."

The fear in Luce's heart bloomed until she thought she would vomit.

"You will find nothing there but my servants and horses," insisted John.

"We'll see," replied Captain Shelby. He turned to leave and, as he did so, intentionally dragged his spurred heel across the wood floor, carving a gleaming white scar. He shrugged. "My apologies, Mrs. Hutchinson. I appear to have left a mark I was once here. Perhaps a reminder I could return."

Luce stood on the steps as the soldiers fanned out through the offices and stables. Shouts arose from the buildings, and the men quickly congregated in the direction of the office. John ran into the courtyard, shaking his fist at the soldiers.

"Do not remove those firearms," he yelled. "Do not dare to leave us defenceless, with no means to protect ourselves."

The men laughed and ignored John. Soon the clatter of metal on cobbles and the scraping of a large wooden crate being dragged across the stones filled the night air.

"Do not take my only defence!" John was livid. "I command you to leave those weapons."

Captain Shelby swiftly drew his sword and pointed it to John's heart. "And I command, in the name of General Cromwell, that you deliver your arms to me."

John froze, his hands helpless at his sides. He had no sword, no weapons. For a minute, they faced off, before John lifted his hands in a gesture of surrender.

Captain Shelby laughed and called to his men.

"Take the bloody lot," he yelled. "Take all the weapons you find, for Mr. John Hutchinson here has no need of a defence. We will happily guard his house for him and protect him, just as we have shown tonight." He turned to John again. "And besides, we don't want Mr. Hutchinson"—Luce shook at his insolence—"tempted to stockpile arms for his fancy relatives, do we?"

The soldiers grabbed armfuls of muskets and, leading a pack pony from the stables, quickly loaded the weapons onto its back. They mounted up and wheeled around in the courtyard, churning the gravel.

Luce ran to John's side, ignoring the stones piercing her bare feet.

"John—"

"Be quiet," he hissed. "Be quiet."

As the troop's clatter faded into the dark, John stood completely still, alert, calm. Thomas emerged from the offices, grinning.

"It worked, sir," he said. "They no more looked for him once they'd got their hands on the guns."

John nodded. "It worked. For tonight." He pulled Luce into his arms, and she felt his heartbeat racing against her breast. "But they will return."

For the next three days, Luce did not leave her brother's side, John making the excuse to Lucy and the children that the Roundheads were searching the countryside for all fleeing Royalists, and one sought refuge with them. He presented a possible infection Luce tended, and she did not want to bring a contagion to them. In reality, she could not bear to leave her brother, for in her heart she knew with every breath he healed, closer approached his departure. And with his leave-taking, the unknown of the future, and the sorrow of a farewell that might be for a lifetime.

"Out of all of us, you were always the one to favour melancholy first, Luce." Allen's whisper interrupted her thoughts. "Are you so saddened by my recovery that a frown blights your face?"

She turned swiftly to deny and relaxed at the amusement bringing a mischievous smile to his face. His cheeks were less hollowed, and the gauntness had faded, colour restored. Now his teasing resumed, she knew him to be well-recovered.

"How do you feel?" She busied herself with straightening the blanket, fussing with the fold to avoid his eyes.

"In my body, well. In my heart, devastated." He pushed himself up, easily moving with just a small wince. "We must talk."

"Do you want me to call for John?"

"Shortly. But there are words we must say to each other first."

Luce folded her hands in her lap, intently studying her reddened fingers. Even the ink stains had faded, nursing replacing writing to fill her days.

"Was it terrible, Allen? What happened at Worcester?"

He lifted his head and took a breath, shallow to avoid more pain.

"We lost the battle before it began. When the king marched from Scotland, he chose to follow the western road. We were full of hope men would join us daily along the way, the Royalists in the north, the fierce Welsh fighters." He paused, his eyes distant as he recalled the ride. "But King Charles did not realise how deep the hatred of the Scots dwelled in the hearts of Englishmen. And asking them to join an army of their enemy was a misjudgment of tactics from which he never recovered."

Luce nodded. "You must have known from your time in the border wars that men would look upon a Scots army upon English soil as invaders, not allies."

"We all knew, Luce. But in our heart of hearts, we hoped our cause would unite all men of Britain against Cromwell's oppression."

110

She could agree there. She would leave the discussion of Cromwell to John. "Men tire of war. They have nothing left to fight for. The promise of a Stuart does not bring change to their world. They care not who rules if their children have bread on the table, and they earn two pennies for an ale. They just want to return to their normal lives, their families, their land, and build a future for themselves again." She needed to tell him the most important news of all. "And the Stuart is dead, Allen. They found a body in Worcester of his description. He is dead. And so is the cause. The conflict is over."

Allen shook his head. "The cause will never die, Luce." He leaned forward and took her hands, his eyes burning. "The king's death is a rumour we put about as soon as we realised the battle would be lost. He escaped, with our cousin Wilmot at his side. He is not dead. I know this for a fact. We live to fight on, to reclaim the throne, to restore England to a kingdom."

She sat in silence, sickened by his words.

"Luce, I will never forget John's help these past few days. He could have rejected me, turned his back on me, stood with his Parliament and turned me away from your home, or over to the army. But instead, his grace and conscience and his love for you saved my life."

She could not see Allen through the tears filling her eyes.

"One day I will repay him for all he has done. He endangered his own life to open his home to me and others, and he continues to risk prosecution by refusing to bend to Cromwell." Allen threw back the blanket and stood up. "Stay hidden here in Owthorpe and make a life for yourselves. Do not worry about me, for I return to Frances and the court in Paris. But John will need your strength, Luce, and your judgment in the coming years. His temper is hasty and his character stubborn. There will come a time when you will have to step in and rescue him from himself, when all are called to account for their actions in this war." Allen folded her into his arms.

Luce welcomed his strength, rejoiced that the wound had healed so well. But what prediction could Allen tell so confidently? "How can you be so sure? What have you heard, what do you know?"

"He murdered the king. And you can be sure his deed will never be forgotten. Be certain that you guide his words, for without your astuteness, he will surely falter." His soft kiss touched her head. "There will be times when you must employ cunning to survive. And know I will always look out for your interest first, sweet sister. At all costs."

Well enough to leave by morning, Luce knew Allen's heart again was torn in two. Just as he wanted to remain with her, the pull to return to Paris, to his child and Frances, overruled. And so it should be. Tragedy dwelled in the choice, not the decision. Even though the fighting had ceased—for without a doubt, Cromwell's victory at Worcester had crushed any remaining hopes of a Royalist army—no national reconciliation existed for Englishmen. Not while men such as Allen and Hyde and the Villiers, all those family names that Cromwell had listed so glibly, still believed without any doubt a Stuart belonged on the throne of England and the old order must be restored.

Allen stuffed John's shirt into his leather pack, along with a second pair of breeches and fresh linens John insisted he take. He looked up and grinned at Luce.

"Not quite a courtier's wardrobe," he joked. "But in the Palace of the Louvre, I will be a man of fashion compared to the poverty of the rest of the lords."

She couldn't raise more than a small smile. Her heart left with him.

Allen sobered. "I must visit our mother this afternoon. I do not want to depart tonight without seeing her. Where is it safe?"

Luce thought quickly. "The new gardens she is creating with John to give employment to our men," she replied. "If you follow the footpath from the stable block east, where the trees hide the building, you will be in the wood. At the first clearing, there are ponds and a bench. Wait there." She crossed to the small window and looked out. "Everyone's at work or at the market. It is a good time. Leave now and I will bring her to you."

Slipping out of the servants' rooms, Luce hurried across the courtyard to the main house. Her mother was bound to be with her grandchildren, as on most days, supervising their writing and reading. Just as she had with her own, all those days in the Tower when the money ran out for tutors. Lucy sat at the table in the hall, books spread out and the children quietly concentrating on their work.

"Mother," she called. "Mother, I would walk with you down to the fishponds. John left me with a direction to give to the labourers this morning before he rode into Nottingham, and I have no idea what he meant."

Lucy stood stiffly and stretched. "Of course, I would welcome the relief. My rheum is worse today with the turn in the weather." She ruffled

Tom's hair. "Now, my boy, you will finish that Latin before the clock strikes three, and we shall celebrate with a sweetmeat."

She picked up her shawl from the back of the chair.

"Show me where John instructed you to meet the labourers. I am sure I can understand what he intended."

Luce laughed. "I would think you could, for you designed most of these gardens."

"My dream, and one shared with John. We are creating the most beautiful property in Nottinghamshire. And keeping the men of Owthorpe working and earning their way again."

From a distance, the figure on the bench was unrecognisable, a hat pulled low, a rough jacket concealing the shape of him. But within a couple of paces, Lucy hesitated and then broke free from Luce's hand. And by the time she reached Allen, she was in tears, laughing, stroking his cheek.

"My son, my darling," she whispered. "Surely this is a miracle. How did you get here, and when?"

Allen shot Luce a glance over her head. "Just last night, Mother, and I am afraid I must leave again tonight. I have just paused for a fresh horse and a hot meal."

Lucy gave a small cry. "So soon? You must leave again so soon?"

"I am needed back in Paris," he replied. "Our cousin Edward Hyde calls on me. And Nan has already sent word I am on my way."

How glibly he lied. Luce realised she did not know this part of his life. And yet his lies were kindness, for if he had told Lucy the truth, her fears would be tenfold.

"And Frances, Isabella? How are they?"

"Most well and living a comfortable life in the grand Palace of the Louvre with our cousin Anne Villiers, Lady Dalkeith."

Lucy nodded her head. "The Villiers. Of course. I remember now. Barbara's daughter. She is the cat that always lands on her feet."

Allen laughed. "Let that old animosity go, for Anne has done much for Frances and has befriended her well. Our daughter plays with Minette, the king's youngest sister, and Frances serves the queen as one of her favourites."

113

"Where?" Lucy's questioned. "Where will your choice take you, my darling?"

Allen guided Lucy to the bench. They sat, Luce standing just a little behind them, all facing the vista east.

"Paris, for now," he replied. "For France is where our lives must be." Through the bronze and gold leaves wafted the evocative scent of the first bonfire of the season. "And when you sit here and gaze upon this view, and look beyond these distant hills and the countryside, and across the Narrow Sea, you will look all the way to Paris, all the way to the Palace of the Louvre." Allen's voice cracked slightly, and he cleared his throat. "And in the Palace of the Louvre, you will see Frances dancing, and Isabella playing with Princess Minette, and me playing cards with Charles Stuart . . ."

Lucy laughed and leaned closer to Allen.

". . . and I'll lift my hand and blow you a kiss, which will fly all the way back home to this bench."

Luce brushed a tear from her cheek, thankful her mother could not see her.

Lucy lifted her face and kissed Allen. "Travel safely, my son. Travel safely to your family. And always remember who waits for you here."

At midnight, her brother stood in the hall, speechless, as he surveyed the portraits and paintings, the sculptures and tapestries. Luce saw the king's riches again through Allen's eyes and was ashamed. His expression grew stern as he walked from one painting to the next. Glancing through an open door, he lifted a lantern from the fireplace and passed into John's cabinet, the room designed to hold his precious collection. They followed him silently. Allen stopped in the middle of the room and lifted the light high. Surrounding them were the gems of the king's art, a grand Titian, a striking Van Dyck.

"We could be at Whitehall or Richmond. And these are all yours now?"

John nodded. "Some. Others I hold for the state, in trust, until we find a buyer on the Continent for them."

Allen shook his head, bemused. "And so the plunders of war feed the victors."

"Has this ever been different?" John raised his own lantern. "Except this time, we do not deface the art, nor spoil the statues, in this house."

114

"Unlike your Puritan friends?"

John's face became shadowed. "The collections are distributed in safe houses throughout England. Or already sold on to the Italian merchants. There is a robust market to buy such works."

Luce touched Allen's sleeve. She must share her justification for John's collection. "We do not keep the proceeds for ourselves. We rebuild our devastated towns and villages, create work for those who survived the war. We must pay the army, put money into the country, redistribute the wealth so long withheld from the ordinary people," she added. "This is one way to do it." Perhaps if she continued to say this aloud, she would believe it happened always that way, and the wealth wasn't being held on to by some.

Allen shrugged. "We will retrieve these, bring them back to the palaces, when we return. Where they are hung is of no consequence now."

Luce let his comment go, and John followed her lead.

"You travel next to Ditchley and then on to the safe houses Nan has arranged for you on your way to Harwich?" she asked. "You will be able to find a fishing boat to take you to The Hague from there, but it will be dangerous riding through East Anglia."

"Nan will be looking out for me," he replied. "And with John's best horse, I have no doubt I will make good time."

This was good-bye, then. Luce could say no more, for Allen must leave now to be safely on his way before sunrise.

In the flickering light, John took a small step towards Allen, and slowly a smile appeared on Allen's face. There were no words, but as John reached out his hand to Allen, Allen clasped it and drew John into an embrace.

Time returned to their early days at Richmond, best friends, and Luce still oblivious of John's growing love for her. The times they all laughed and played and rode to the hunt, drank and danced, sang and read poetry. The three of them, such deep friends, and then joined as family.

"I must go." Allen pulled away abruptly, and Luce caught a glisten of tears. "My thanks to both of you. Keep my love with you. I will return your help one day. Look for notes from Nan, for she will let you know how we fare and call upon you as she needs. And, most of all, watch Cromwell." As he turned to leave the room, he paused. "Remember, you may not have enemies if you are neutral. But equally, you have few to call friend."

16

Frances

As the rustling of autumn leaves blowing across the cobbles of Paris's streets, so came whispers the king lived. And by the time he and Henry Wilmot strode into the queen's rooms at the Palace of the Louvre, the news crashed with the force of a storm over Europe. After surviving the battle for Worcester, fleeing Cromwell, enduring six weeks in hiding and a voyage across the Narrow Sea, the fugitive king returned.

Will Allen be with him?

From Frances's place within the queen's ladies crushed on the dais, the courtiers resembled wheat rippling in a harvest-ready field. As the king and Henry approached, all fell to their knees before him. The rustling of silks, the squeak of velvet and the insistent striking of the king's and Henry's spurs resonated around the stone chamber. A clapping swelled and thundered and broke over them.

Queen Henrietta's eyes fixed on Charles, her hands clasped firmly at her chest. The widow stood as Generalissima first, a mother second, in this critical moment for the throne of England, the future of her son.

Heart hammering, Frances raised herself on tiptoe, peering over Henry as he approached, and then dropped to her heels again.

No Allen.

Is he dead? Does he not want to return? Does he stay with Nan?

How the devil whispered in her ear.

Forcing a smile to her face, she curtseyed to the king and lifted her head for a kiss from Henry.

"My thanks to God and the Virgin Mary for your safety, Your Majesty," she murmured. "Henry, I rejoice you return without harm."

Where's Allen?

Protocol insisted she stay at the queen's side, when every fiber of her ached to shout questions to Henry. And so she behaved as a good lady-in-waiting should. Queen first. Husband later. Waiting.

The young king had grown since last she saw him. She remembered a gangling sixteen-year-old, halfway between child and man, trying out his role as Commander of the Western Armies like a new jacket too long in the sleeve. Now well over six feet, with an athletic body and a grace and presence that drew all eyes to him, he stood virile, confident and adorned with the charm of a man who knew his own power.

Henry also bowed to the queen and came to stand at Frances's side. Road-stained and dusty, he reeked of horses and leather and sweat. A whispering and a stifled giggle behind her penetrated her numbness. She must not show weakness. She forced her words.

"You have been gone long. I have heard recently from Nan. She is well, as are her boys." Frances took a deep breath. "And . . . Johnny, your son, grows strong and handsome."

The whispering intensified.

Henry grinned. His eyes were tired, but the scar puckered his mouth and his crooked smile was as warm as ever. "I am grateful for your news, Frances." He glared at the ladies behind her. They fell silent. "It seems others are interested too."

Frances took his arm and pulled him closer to her, her mouth to his ear.

"This palace is a dung heap of rumours and jealousies," she murmured. "Do not pay attention to these bored women, for they do nothing but construct stories all day."

"The way of the courts the world over." He nodded. "And a reason I can't stand to be in attendance. How's Allen?" Henry surveyed the room.

She swallowed. "I . . . have not heard from him."

Henry turned swiftly. "He has not returned from Worcester? When we were racing from the cathedral tower, I saw him riding out to fight."

Frances shook her head.

"He will not be in harm . . ." Henry tossed these last words over his shoulder as King Charles beckoned and he jumped from the dais to join him. "If he's not right behind us, he'll be with Nan, safe at Ditchley, I'm sure."

Throwing his arm around Henry's shoulder, the king's dark eyes softened with love. "And this man saved my life over and over," he announced. "For if not for him, we would have been seized at the first inn on the first hour of our escape." The courtiers pressed around the king and Henry, eager to hear his tale. "Wilmot is a master of disguise and the most resourceful man in my kingdom. Faith, he even dressed me as a poor serving

117

woman one day and made me practice my curtsey till my knees ached. It is not easy getting down that low when you are well over six feet high. We decided the guise would not work for me."

The court laughed uproariously, and the king nodded, enjoying the attention. The queen seated herself on her velvet chair and settled to listen to her son's stories. As the king recounted his adventures, and the names of all those who helped him spilled excitedly from his lips—Penderel, Father Huddleston, Mistress Jane Lane—Frances stood alone in the crowded room with only her fears for company.

A sudden quiet distracted her. The king solemnly knelt before his mother.

"If not for the secret and courageous network of hidden Catholics, I would have been captured," he said soberly. "I ask your prayers for all those who aided me, who put their lives in such danger, and do so daily to preserve our God-given cause."

One by one the courtiers knelt, and as Frances joined them, her hand making the age-old sign of the cross, she added a fervent prayer for the protection of her husband's soul, wherever it may lie.

Within weeks of the king and Henry arriving at the Louvre, George Villiers sauntered into the palace as though he had simply left for an appointment and returned after a successful rendezvous. The Duke of Buckingham appeared not as a soldier, but as a courtier, and the most favoured in the land at that. Somewhere he had acquired a beautiful red silk suit, a delicately laced white collar and gold-tipped shoes that gleamed as he walked.

He strolled the length of the palace ballroom, a singular figure who walked with such grace, such assuredness, he appeared the prince among men.

Frances found herself next to Anne Villiers.

"Your cousin has a presence," she murmured. "All eyes are on him. Does he always hold the room's attention this way?"

Anne nodded. "George inherited the Villiers magnetism, without a doubt. After his father was assassinated, he was brought up by the late king, became as a brother to the prince. The first Duke of Buckingham was the most beautiful man in Christendom, beloved by the king's father and grandfather."

"I heard more than is natural, by James. Some called him the king's catamite."

Anne shrugged. "'Tis the way of the court. The Villiers have served the royal family well into this third generation, and we know how to make the Stuarts happy. Ask Allen. His father was a favourite of the first duke. He witnessed much at Richmond." Anne opened her eyes wide. "Oh, forgive me. I overlooked that he has yet to return from Ditchley."

No, you didn't.

George Villiers slowed his pace as he approached Charles. The contrast between the duke's fairness and the king's swarthy complexion was arresting.

"George."

"Your Majesty."

"Where have you been?" The king's stern face carried no hint of a welcome. "I gave you no leave to absent yourself from court."

"Sire, I fear I give not a damn." George dropped to his knees in front of the king, his face level with the king's thighs. The court sucked in its breath as one.

"I was occupied with a congenial ma-dam."

The king's lips twitched.

George inched forward until his mouth breathed words just a hair away from the king's body.

"For duty and country caused me to slam—" He leaned forward.

"A poxy whore called Rotter-dam!" Buckingham darted his head, placed a kiss on the king's crotch and jumped up and swept the most beautiful bow Frances had ever seen.

The king roared with laughter. Henry Wilmot grabbed a flask of wine, toasted Villiers and drained it in one gulp, smashing it into the fireplace. People scrambled forward in a confusion of laughter and cheers, surrounding George and blocking him from Frances's view.

"The triumvirate is complete." Anne took Frances and steered her towards the crowd. "Come, I'll introduce you to my devilish cousin George. He'll take your mind off Allen. But be warned. He would have you as soon as look at you."

George Villiers's fairness glowed flawless next to Henry's weathered countenance. Almost as tall as Charles, he draped a familiar arm over the king's shoulder, pulling his head close to his own.

119

"Frances!" Henry called to her and pulled her through half a dozen simpering ladies. "See, another of us returns from battle. I swear Allen will be next. George, meet a kinswoman, and as you can see, a beauty."

Her heart twisted at her husband's name—and Henry's naivety—and she turned away from the rowdiness. The crowd pushed her to stand before the king and Buckingham.

"Lady Apsley." The king held out his hand for her to kiss. "Another of your husband's relatives has arrived safely. May I present George Villiers, the Duke of Buckingham."

"How delightful." Green eyes under fair brows, and beneath his silk suit the body of an athlete. George Villiers looked over her shoulder, his eyes flickering around the crowd. "And Sir Allen is . . ."

She cleared her throat. "Not yet returned from Worcester, my lord."

"Ah. A pity. I thought I was the last to leave." He looked at her bosom and back up to her mouth. "No doubt Allen lags behind me. Visiting his sister and her king-killer husband."

Frances stifled a gasp at the viciousness of his words.

The duke raised the back of his hand to his mouth and coughed discreetly. "Or perhaps he stays at Ditchley. I understand he will always receive a warm welcome from his cousin."

Frances bowed her head to avoid his eyes. Nor could she look at Henry.

"In time, Lady Apsley, we will ensure you do not miss your husband and his disappearance is well compensated. Be sure to call on me for any . . . needs . . . I can service in his absence."

Her cheeks burned. And when she lifted her eyes, she stood alone. George and the king attended the king's mistress and a dozen other ladies. Henry had joined his men in their drinking and carousing.

Never had she felt so isolated, for even in these crowded halls, there were few to call friends.

Edward Hyde pushed his way through the courtiers, an old war horse in a field of flowers, his girth clearing a path to her side.

"I had hoped, in a way, this day would not come," he murmured.

Frances could not be sure she was quite catching his meaning. "You do not rejoice in the duke's survival?"

He paused. "True, I would not lose any more to war," he replied. "But his arrival is a distraction our king does not need." Hyde surveyed the room, his shrewd eyes upon the rapidly deteriorating scene. Henry lay prostrate on a bench while a man poured wine over his unconscious face, and the king and George were dancing with two women on each hand, laughing and stumbling as they misstepped a pavane.

He turned to Frances abruptly. "But I forget your own worries, Frances. Write to Nan," he said. "Tell her of the duke's return and ask for a new list of those she and other houses have sheltered. Perhaps Allen is among them. God knows we need to bring home all the loyal men we can, for there are few left from our once-proud band." His smile was weary, and she glimpsed the enormous weight he bore on his shoulders.

With the return of the king, poverty bit deeply, for there were no funds to sustain him, no allies to maintain him. Anne took Frances to one side as they waited in hope of dinner. No longer did course after course arrive in procession from the kitchens; this king ate ravenously of the wild boar, deer and rabbit hunted by his courtiers in the chases surrounding Paris, snatched from roasting on the fireplaces lining the chambers.

"I am returning to Scotland." Anne dropped a charred rabbit leg on her platter in distaste. "There is naught to do here in the royal household. I would rather be at home, with my son, where my life has purpose."

Anne's news came as no surprise. This court was fragmenting into shards of dissention. Frances wished she could leave too.

"When will you go?" she asked. "You are not the first, nor by far the last, to realise life here in exile is not what we thought it would be."

Anne looked at her sharply. "Are you having doubts, Frances?"

"I do not doubt the cause. I simply disbelieve we have the capacity or the leadership to see us through to a successful ending."

"You don't think Sir Edward Hyde is acting in the king's best interests?"

Frances paused, searching for the right words. A burst of laughter and shouts from the king's end of the room drowned her words. Frowning, she turned to Anne.

"He is most capable, Anne. But there is no money, no leadership, and so many factions and infighting I despair we will ever present one face, ever cohesively be one party for the restoration of the king. And Sir Edward spends more time in the courts of Spain and Holland, begging for money and support, than he ever does here creating a strategy with the king and his sycophants who pose as advisors."

Anne picked up the bone and delicately gnawed at the stringy meat. Grimacing, she put it down again and pushed the platter away from her.

"And that is why I go home," she replied. "There is work to be done there, preparing for the king's return. Much more so than here." She looked out across the hall, dimly lit, for the meagre fires in the hearths struggled to brighten the cavernous chamber. "My cousin George only thinks of pleasure, and I am saddened by what this has become, Frances, truly. When we left England, we had such hopes, such promise we could return quickly. With the shock of the king's execution and now the slaughter at Worcester, I fear all have lost their way."

Including Allen.

Frances followed her gaze, disgusted at the drunks falling over themselves, the young men reeling as they pulled the women from their places and dragged them to dance or to an alcove for deeper pleasures. The king sat at his table, his legs spread wide, a woman on each knee, while Henry stood on the bench next to him, leading an unruly choir of soldiers in a Royalist drinking song.

Such mayhem, such disrespect.

She turned back to Anne. "I understand. You must go if you feel—"

A tremendous roar from the king's table followed by a thumping and clattering as the men banged their tankards on the table, cheering and shouting.

Enough! Frances squeezed her eyes shut. "I cannot stand this either, Anne. I would I could travel with you, bring Isabella, leave this place—"

"Mon Dieu!"

Anne's mouth dropped open as she stared towards the king.

"What? What?" Frances turned, and a rush of blood to her head made her sway.

In front of the king, filthy from the road, ragged and laughing, stood her husband.

Henry leaped from his perch on the bench and pressed a tankard into Allen's hands, and the king grabbed him by the shoulders and pulled him into a rough embrace.

"I don't think you're going anywhere now," said Anne. "Your place is with your husband. And he has returned to the king."

He left her. He came home to me.

Allen raised his tankard, swallowed the entire contents in one gulp and stuck it out for another, his arm flung over Henry's shoulder. Quickly, Henry placed another overflowing mug in his hand, and Allen downed the second.

"He appears delighted to be back in the company of his men," Anne sighed deeply, almost theatrically. "Such is the legacy of war. The brotherhood above all."

Turn Allen, look for me, I beg you.

And then anger at herself for pleading.

Only when Henry leaned drunkenly forward and shouted something in his ear did Allen turn, following the direction of Henry's pointing finger. Only when he left the king and pushed his way through the crowded chamber did she see he was now thinking of her.

"Frances, they are alive," he shouted, straining to make himself heard above the musicians, the raucous shouting, the shrill laughter. He flung his arms wide, his face merry with love. "Frances, I'm home."

With the eyes of the court upon her, she gathered her shabby skirts. Stepping down from the dais, she walked towards Allen, her heart thumping so fast it could have leapt from her chest and run to him, trembling like a deer before a huntsman.

He came home to you.

Why did he take so long?

"Husband," she said as she lifted her face for a kiss, letting his lips brush past her own and land on her cheek. "Praise God you are safe."

"Henry survived. The king lives," he repeated. "Nan told me so, but I dare not believe."

Nan. His first words.

"Yes. Nan's husband brought the king back to us safely. How fares your cousin?"

"My darling, I have dreamed of this moment, prayed to be safely in— Nan? Why, Frances, she is well," replied Allen, his face alight with happiness. "You can learn for yourself. She gave me a letter just for you." He pulled a crumpled parchment from a pouch inside his shirt and handed it to her. "She sends her love to you, and her gratitude."

"Gratitude?"

"You will understand when you read her words. She plans next year for her Lee sons, Frank and Harry, to school here. She sends you gratitude in

123

advance for tending to them as if they were your own." He pulled her close to him and kissed her deeply, his mouth seeking her response.

She turned then, and left him.

"How could you? How could you humiliate me so, foisting your mistress's children on me as if I am some wet nurse, standing ready to defer to whatever bastard you decide to acknowledge?" The months of anger and humiliation smelted a great cannon ball of pain in Frances's chest, a weapon so heated that she wanted to disgorge it at her husband's feet and walk away. Their small chamber boiled with her rage.

Allen reached for her. "Frances, I have no idea what you mean. What in God's name do you say? What manner is this to greet me, my love?"

"Do not touch me," she spat. "Do not think you can smooth this over with your charm."

"What, Frances? What is 'this'? For Christ's sake, woman, tell me what has happened."

"Did you think I would never hear? Did you think Paris far enough away to keep me from your mistress and son that I would never cross their path? Or did Nan plan to get me out of the way here?"

The words flew from her as if a physical blow. Allen took a step back, his face white.

"Nan? What has she done?"

"What have you done, Allen?"

"Enough!" He grabbed her arm, pulled her to him, holding her tightly at both elbows. She struggled, but he would not let her go. "I have been away for months. I have no idea what you are saying."

"You have been away for months, and yet how long were you at Ditchley?" Frances threw the words at him.

Allen blinked. "Ditchley? A few days, enough to change horses, rest before heading for the coast."

Frances leaned forward. "And a few nights between those days?"

"What in God's name are you asking me, Frances?"

There were new lines on his forehead, and for the first time she saw silver glisten in his hair. She knew the same weariness reflected in her own complexion. How much had she given of herself to this man who was not hers?

"Nan. She's your mistress. And Johnny is your child. Anne Villiers told me so. You cannot deny it."

He did not move, did not push her away. He held her tightly, looking deep into her eyes, his moving from one to another, searching, questioning. Before his calm, her own anger drained away, leaving her exhausted and empty.

"You must be mad. How can you even pay heed to such gossip? And from a Villiers too."

"So you don't deny it?"

Allen shook his head, his face still inches from hers.

"Are we in Chancery? Will an innocent plea get me anywhere? You have long made up your mind and chose to believe strangers over your own husband. You have already condemned me, Frances."

"Deny it, then, Allen, deny all of this. Your love of Nan, your son, your deception." Frances spoke low, rapidly. "I've seen how she is with you."

"Nan is my cousin, for God's sake. We've known each other since we were born."

"And loved each other since when? I see how you look at each other, how you are in her company." She couldn't stop now. She must rip this open until the dark, hidden secrets in Allen's heart withered in the day's callous light.

"I have always loved Nan."

"How, Allen? How have you loved her?" Plunging her hands in his heart, pulling out every last lie. "Always as a cousin? Or more?"

Frances's words cracked open an abyss between them.

"You disgust me with your insinuations." His eyes were blank now, cold.

"Truths."

"Not truths, lies. Lies from a jealous woman, a Villiers no less, who has nothing better to do than stir trouble and be entertained by the outcome." Allen searched her eyes again. "Tell me you cannot believe this wickedness."

"Deny it. You still have not denied it, Allen."

"On my father's grave, I deny it. But you choose to believe another over me. I despise your lack of faith."

He dropped her arms and turned away before she could respond.

"I shall find a place to rest with Henry's men," he threw over his shoulder. "Do not expect me back here at night."

"Allen. Please. Your daughter—"

"Tell her what you will. I'll be here when she breaks her fast in the morning."

The chamber door slammed on their argument.

Frances leaned against the unyielding stone wall, her eyes drawn outside to the cramped courtyard, a barren, discarded space, forgotten in the rambling structure of the palace. She could not even see a door, and she had never seen anyone walk across its narrow confines. And yet in a rain puddle, a white dove bathed, splashing in solitary happiness. A sudden burst of laughter from an adjacent room startled the bird into flying away, soaring over the high palace walls. She swallowed the sudden tears that prickled behind her eyes.

And now began a season of revels ushering a frenzy of dancing, drinking and bawdiness the likes of which Frances had never encountered. As if he could not believe his fortune in surviving Worcester, the king and his companions fuelled a lust in the exiled court to drink and swive their way through the days and nights, bewitched by the very demons that stalked their nightmares. Greedily, he led the young men into deeper and darker entertainment until the whole coterie of dissolute, fatherless boys swung through the days and nights unfettered in their craving for life and all the pursuits that validated their survival.

Allen joined the king and Henry in their carousing, for he did not spend his days with Frances. And where he slept at night was his secret.

Furious, Queen Henrietta Maria ordered Charles to desist, to act as a king should, to bear the responsibility of his throne with dignity. Rebellious, her son defied her further until the very halls of the Louvre were defiled, and she fled to pray with her ladies in the sanctity of the chapel, hidden deep in the palace heart. Here, the saints' days measured time, yet devotions fell on deaf idols until the months blurred and the year dissolved into gloom.

And although Frances knelt beside the queen in fervent prayer, the words would not come, and all she could manage was to say her rosary, no more.

17

Nan

Nan reverently caressed the stem of the crystal wine goblet, admiring the deep dark red of her cellar's best burgundy. Ditchley's dining room glowed tonight from the hundred candles she'd ordered to drive the dark from the corners. Lee family silver shone from the table settings, and the hearth glowed with the welcoming warmth of Lee estate oak, stacked high and burning long into the night. Gracing the laden table, a full sirloin of beef, roasted duck and pheasant from the Lee farms—fresh, not salted—slaughtered on her command to entertain her guests.

Walter and Johanna appreciated her warm welcome, seated next to her handsome sons. Nan lifted her glass. Frank nudged his brother, Harry, and her two glorious Lee boys smiled back at her and sipped the wine allowed this evening. Johnny was too young for this occasion, and she had already kissed his sweet cheeks good night hours ago.

"To the health of my Honest John Cary," she toasted the man on her right. "To the dearest friend I could ever ask for, whose care for my late husband, Lee, has extended to that of his children, myself and their inheritance."

Her foreman, a florid man with a worried brow and the unmistakable Cary fairness, ducked his head in shyness.

"It is my honour, my lady," he replied. "Lord Lee was the noblest man in Christendom, and his dying wish commanded me to protect you with my life."

A shadow crossed Nan's eyes at the mention of her first husband. For a moment, she was a young wife, banned from her husband's sickroom by his fear of her catching the smallpox, in tears as the news turned from optimistic to grave to the worst. Married at eighteen, widowed at twenty-five with two young boys and a mother-in-law who despised her. Cary had sat with her in the dark days that followed, sheltering her from the raging of Eleanor Lee, who refused to believe she'd been cut out of her son's will.

"You protected my family from so much, Cary, then and now," she replied. She gestured to her boys, Walter and Johanna, and raised her eyes to the ceiling, above which little Johnny slept sweetly. "And I will always be grateful. You are my friend, and through my mother, my kinsman. I could not wish for a more loyal cousin."

Walter gestured for their glasses to be filled again. "If not for you, Cary, with the wisdom and guidance you showed all those years ago as the executor of the will, there would be nothing remaining of Ditchley, nor its lands and riches."

The man ducked his head again, his colour growing deeper. "My honour and my duty, and one I would do over."

"And now you rescue us again," responded Nan. "For sequestration would have ruined us, and Parliament's fines buried us. Cromwell is remorseless in his personal vengeance for Henry's role in the king's escape."

Walter put his hand over hers. "You have been so strong, Nan, and such a great example to your boys." He smiled at Frank and Harry across the table.

"I fear Ditchley's battles are not over." Cary studied his hands, his innate shyness lending discomfort to his posture, his shoulders hunched. "Parliament looks to our prosperity and covets the revenues that could be diverted to its coffers. And your marriage to Lord Wilmot gives them every reason to persist. His elevation to earl adds even more to your estate. After the Stuart, he is without doubt the most wanted man in England."

Nan took a deep breath. "We have held off the investigations for months. We have preserved our wealth through the worst years of the war. I just need to keep delaying them until a new threat distracts. I would rather die than lose Ditchley. And I have no intention of leaving this earth anytime soon."

"Perhaps that's where I can help." Johanna's sweet voice came from across the table. "I shall write to my father, explain how Ditchley holds these lands for Lee sons, who are loyal to Parliament and the future of our Commonwealth. And my sister-in-law strives to maintain her estate for the good of the men of England who are employed to work it."

"Your father is the most powerful man in England after Cromwell, Johanna. His patronage would help preserve my boys' inheritance. But he cannot be seen to favour me."

Johanna smiled. "But he can support his favourite daughter and her husband. And if we are continually disturbed here at Ditchley by the interruptions from the sequestration committee, he would not be happy."

"If I may suggest . . ." Cary's hesitant voice carried authority in its familiarity.

They turned to him. "Yes, please go on," encouraged Walter.

"Perhaps an administrative approach. Letters go astray, interrogatories unanswered. Clerks appointed and dismissed, leaving their paperwork in disarray . . ."

Nan laughed aloud. "Oh, Cary, your idea is a sound one. And no doubt you have some candidates Johanna's father should recommend to the Oxford sequestration committee, appointments that would be well received and appallingly executed?"

Cary nodded. "I could draw up a list of names."

"Send them to me when you have readied them," replied Johanna. "And I shall see my father acts accordingly. After all, who would refuse an honour from Sir Oliver St.John, Lord Chief Justice of England? I am sure his new appointees will be tripping over themselves to serve on the sequestration committee. Unfortunately, once appointed, they will all be too inept to fill Parliament's purse with Ditchley's wealth."

Nan reached across to Johanna and seized her hand, gratitude and apprehension competing within her. "It is a gamble. But this is the world we live in now. We have no other leverage, for I refuse to pay the fines, and we cannot make the committee disappear."

"Settled," said Walter. He turned to the boys. "You have much for which to thank your mother, for she has only ever acted with your best interests in heart."

Nan's boys nodded and grinned. They were growing so much older, Harry now fourteen, Frank twelve. Another decision to be announced tonight while everyone gathered, and she was with those she trusted most.

"I have some additional news," she said. Her family turned their faces to her. "It is time the boys expanded their education. No longer is the town school sufficient, and if they are to prepare for the entry to university and manage these lands, they need a broader education." She paused. The next words would be hard to say, for once spoken she would be losing her loves to others. "I have decided to send them to De Veau's Academy in Paris"—excited whoops from Harry and Frank interrupted her—"where they will receive the very best education available to England's young gentlemen. Their tutor will ready them for their new school." She turned to her boys.

"Apply yourselves diligently to your studies, and you will become valuable members of the court."

Walter looked surprised. "Sister, are you sure? It is a long journey for your boys, and are you certain it is safe?"

Nan nodded. "The university at Oxford, which has protected this estate over the centuries, has vouched for the safety of the school. There is no war in Paris, Walter. This past year has been peaceful; the great argument sleeps. Even the children of leading Parliamentarians attend. Perhaps this is one way we can bring healing to our nation, through the shared education of our Cavalier and Roundhead children. For they did not choose to fight in these wars, and they should control their own peace."

"Did you talk to Allen before he returned to Paris?" asked Johanna. "Will he and Frances be able to look to their needs, keep them from loneliness?"

Nan's heart softened. "Of course I talked to Allen. We share everything. He has assured me he will care for the boys as if they are his own, and he pledged Frances will welcome them into her heart and home."

She turned to Johanna. There was one more thread to weave.

"Please invite your father and Cromwell to attend a dinner at Battersey next month, Johanna. I can arrange to be there by the middle of March. And include John and Luce. Cromwell's temper has surely softened by now. Best let the Protector be reminded of his bigger debt to John in signing the king's warrant, and his ongoing loyalty. And for him to see how close we all are to the most important judge in the country. For if I am to go into the lion's den to preserve Ditchley and save my sons' inheritance, best I should carry honey with me than a knife."

"Hedging your bets, Sister?" Walter shook his head but could not resist a smile.

Raising her glass again, Nan allowed herself a moment of contemplation. She silently toasted Queen Elizabeth, her mentor in procrastination and delay. All in all, a good evening's work. "Why, Walter, what better way to protect Ditchley than to hedge it?"

The moment she dismounted at Battersey and found the manor in an uproar, Nan's anxiety mirrored that of the Barbary lions at the Tower. Stable lads hurriedly led fully saddled horses from their stalls, hooves striking a volley on the cobbles. A group of armed riders clattered into the yard, wheeling their heavy-breathing mounts, slip-sliding on the wet stones. Everywhere she turned, men were running, some with weapons, others with great armfuls of supplies.

Escorted directly into the great hall and given a glass of ale by a silent servant, she could scream, the tension was so great. How often she had stood with Luce at the Tower, watching the lions patrolling back and forth, their guttural roars reverberating inside her chest. Now she felt their same vexation.

A rustle of silk, and she ceased pacing. Johanna hurried into the hall. She blurted her words as soon as she entered.

"Nan. Nan, I heard from Walter's steward that Cromwell has broken the Parliament. He stormed in and evicted the members. His anger reached a height where he could not be contained. He has shut down Parliament, and today we have no government." She swiftly took Nan's hands, her eyes searching Nan's for reassurance.

There must be more. "What proof, Johanna? And where's Walter?"

This Nan did not expect. A death perhaps, or news of another attempted rising by Henry's hidden collaborators. But this strange twist? She must talk to Walter, hear for herself the seriousness of the situation.

God in Heaven, just when she'd judged Cromwell calmed, his volatility raged again.

"Walter and a troop of our men are even now riding to the Great North Road to locate John and Luce, for they were travelling to their home in Holborn. John is supposed to attend a session in Parliament. We know not what the situation, who is running the country, who is governing, except the Council of State still stands."

"When did this happen? And how did you hear? Is the army in charge now?"

"Martial law?" Johanna paled. "Dear God, we did not evict a king to have generals rule in his stead."

"Your father," urged Nan. "Can you reach him? Can you ask him here?"

Johanna nodded. "He informed us, sending a messenger this afternoon and cautioning us to be on alert. I have no doubt he will respond, if he has not already left for his own estates."

"Insist your father come here first." Nan took control. "Tell him anything that will convey him to Battersey. With the Lord's providence, Walter will find John and Luce and bring them safely here. We must all be together until we know what this means."

"My father can advise us. His first loyalty is to our family, for his disgust for Cromwell is unrelenting."

Nan kissed her sister-in-law and pushed her gently towards the library. "Then send a messenger now, Johanna, before he leaves London. We are entering unmapped land. We must acquire all the information we can."

And she must send the intelligence to Frances to give to Edward Hyde. This could be significant. For out of chaos could rise a new order.

Although she had met Sir Oliver St.John on several occasions, Nan's previous encounters had provided little opportunity to converse with Johanna's father. She thought him an aloof man, unapproachable in many ways, and tonight he appeared to be in the same humour. Walter intercepted John and Luce near Highgate and, diverting around the wild and dangerous heath at Hampstead, brought them to Battersey. After a rapid greeting, Johanna suggested they move to dinner.

"I have plump goose, delivered today from Lydiard, and fresh asparagus. Our steward, Mr. Hardyman, always ensures he sends me the best produce three times a week, for our farms at Lydiard are of a much better quality . . ." Johanna spoke rapidly, as was her way when nervous, her voice trailing when she realised no one paid her attention.

Nan took her arm and gently led her to the end of the table, opposite Walter. She then walked to where Johanna's father had already seated himself. John sat to his left, Luce by her husband. Nan joined the Lord Chief Justice at his right.

"Sir Oliver." His gaze was direct under hooded lids. He appeared stern, but looking more closely, she realized his lines were of exhaustion, and the irregular shadow of his beard revealed he had not been barbered for several days. "Sir Oliver, our thanks for your message this afternoon, for to think of us in this time of national crisis is surely much appreciated by your family."

He nodded and picked up a goose leg from his plate, stuffing it quickly into his mouth.

Not only had he the appearance of not sleeping much, it seemed he had neglected meals too.

"And while we are, of course, most grateful for your message to stay here within the safety of Battersey, we are most curious as to the events of today," she continued. "Do please enjoy Lydiard's bounty, but know we starve of knowledge."

He raised an eyebrow and addressed Walter. "Your sister speaks for you? She has a way with words that could give a man indigestion."

Walter laughed nervously, deferential to his powerful father-in-law. "Nan is always one to speak her mind," he replied. "She may extol the virtues of Lydiard's produce but has called it herself a dreadful, dull place."

"Ah, someone who can speak to both sides of a situation equally and with conviction." He turned to Nan. "A useful skill, madam."

"Or perhaps just a desire for balance," she replied quickly. "One you can understand in your position as Lord Chief Justice, Sir Oliver."

He laughed at that, a brief guffaw before he resumed eating, and the tension around the table subsided.

"And so General Cromwell rejected the proposed bill of government?" John's tone was cautious, quiet. Nan bit back her frustration in his circuitous way but deferred to his experience. After all, he enjoyed a role in writing the language of the new Act. "I had heard that he lobbied hard for the contents to be changed. It appears he did not amend the wording."

"And so he changed the men." Luce pushed her plate to one side and leaned across John to speak directly to Sir Oliver. "He now rules in totality, for dismissing Parliament gives him the status of a monarch, not a republican. How quickly power corrupts principle."

Nan watched Sir Oliver closely. He appeared undisturbed by Luce's outburst, methodically eating the food set before him, gesturing a servant to refill his wineglass. For what seemed like an hour, but was probably only minutes, they sat in silence. With others, Nan would have made conversation, turned the talk lightly to other matters. But with this taciturn man, her instincts told her idle chatter would not distract him from his purpose. And what he left unsaid, unacknowledged, could be the most valuable information of all.

Finally, he put down his knife and stood. "I thank you for your hospitality, Daughter. On days such as today, we are grateful for the comfort of home. And that is my message to all of you." Sir Oliver picked up his gloves from the sideboard and pulled them on slowly. "John, stay here and return to Owthorpe in the morning. Do not go into Westminster. And especially do not take your wife, for a blow with a word strikes deeper than a blow with a sword. Her talent is best kept sheathed for now. Her aim is direct. Which is more so than her brother's, when he attempted to murder me." He bowed to the room and turned. "Nan, return to Ditchley. Take heed of Cary's counsel. The Oxfordshire committee appointments will serve you well. Johanna, return to your beloved gardens at Lydiard, and let Walter play the role of county gentleman. I will retire to the country immediately. Do not expect me back in Westminster, nor at the palace, nor in the halls of justice." He looked around the room, as if summarising a court case, not simply protecting his family. "We are in a time of great deception, and England's citizens fight for power. Even an ape can wear scarlet and be crowned king."

Sir Oliver left the room as abruptly as he had arrived. After the door closed behind him, Walter gave a great sigh and gestured for everyone's glass to be filled.

"Wise advice until we see where Cromwell lands. John, you will head to Owthorpe tomorrow? And keep Luce away. Sir Oliver and his colleagues will not forget easily that James attempted his life in Holland." He looked at Johanna. "I agree with your father. We shall travel to Lydiard and remain there. Nan, you'd be best back at Ditchley. If the Lord Chief Justice of England has no desire to remain where the power of England lies, then neither do we."

John shook his head. "I will venture into Westminster tomorrow to find more of the truth," he replied, "and take my leave of those who are left."

"John," began Nan. "John, perhaps best to leave—"

"In all good time," he replied. "I will retire to Owthorpe. Luce and I both fear Cromwell's sanity and his quest to reign as king. This is not the republic we fought for."

An advent of change? Nan kept her thoughts to herself, but already the composition of her next letter to Frances ran through her mind. For if King Charles had sacrificed his life for an incorruptible throne in heaven, perhaps King Cromwell would succumb to the corruptible throne on earth.

18

Frances

Allen spent time with his men, glimpsed only across the crowded public chambers or when he visited Isabella, his smile reserved for her alone. Frances realised men enjoyed mistresses, and mistresses bore children. But not in her marriage. Allen withdrew to his own world, leaving her at the edge of the abyss.

All through the interminable days and lonely nights, she grew thinner and more on edge as the court swirled in heightened tension. Allen stayed with Henry and the king, George Villiers and his brother Ned. Occasionally she spied him with Edward Hyde, when the chancellor could herd the young men into a council meeting, like an elderly sheepdog fat from lack of exercise.

The women treated her no differently, and Frances found herself on the outer circle of the court. She had no interest in the wantonness and never-ending entertainment the king enjoyed, and yet her faith was not as profound as the queen's, where time was measured by the hours she spent on her knees at prayer.

And so, divided and isolated by her choice, she drifted through the empty days, avoiding Allen and encouraging Isabella to play with the royal children to distract her.

As the spring days lengthened into summer, she befriended Annie Hyde, visiting her father from her own exile at the Dutch court. Beautiful and possessing a charming personality, Sir Edward's attractive daughter caused him fatherly consternation.

"Keep her close to you, Frances," he bid. "For if George Villiers or one of those other rakehells lays so much as a finger on her, I shall be forced to call him out." He looked down at his large girth with a tragic expression. "And I fear I would not get the best of the duel."

Frances swiftly kissed her friend on his portly cheek. She had grown very fond of this serious man, for he always treated her with great respect.

"I shall watch for her as if she were my own," she said. "But she is sixteen, Sir Edward, and you will soon have to make provision for her marriage."

He blew out his cheeks and became even more highly coloured. "Time enough for that. Time enough." As Annie picked up Isabella and twirled her in an embrace, he smiled fondly at the girl. "She will make someone a good wife one day. But not too soon."

Frances smoothed her skirts, carefully pulling a pleat over the worn patch that could no longer be darned. She did not answer, for discussions of marriage only served to sting her own lonely heart.

"Is something amiss?" Sir Edward peered into her eyes, shifting his weight on the narrow bench. It was not much of a seat, but little existed in the way of furniture in these abandoned rooms. "You appear to be sad, my dear. I know these times are difficult, but we are doing all we can. Even now Henry rides to our German allies to secure more loans and men to bolster our position."

She nodded, touched at his kindness. "Thank you, but I am well, Sir Edward," she replied. "Inactivity never did suit me, and it is particularly difficult when there is nothing new in the letters from home."

Sir Edward nodded. "Since Nan last wrote of her dinner with St. John, there is little we can do except hope discord may cause an overthrow. I believe Cromwell has created a struggle for power in evicting Parliament. And soon different factions will clash hard enough to cause his downfall." He took her hand and squeezed it. "I have cautioned the king to not be hasty, to watch and wait. According to Nan and my sister Susan, everyone of influence has returned to their estates for the summer, but as soon as harvest is over, people will start to question their future and look to Westminster for answers."

"Your sister keeps the network alive in Wiltshire, Sir Edward?"

He smiled. "Susan is fervent in our cause and brave as a lion. And still Cromwell's commanders do not fathom that women are capable agents too."

"What would you do next?" Frances appreciated these conversations, the trust he placed in her to share these confidences. "And how can I help?"

"Watch and wait," he repeated. "I am expanding the network in England, spreading our web wider. And here." He looked around to make sure they were still alone. Annie and Isabella were now playing with Isabella's rag dolly; no one else drew close. "Here, I have just authorised the formation of a group of men to actively seek out opportunities in England to cause conflict and rebellion. Anne's brother Ned Villiers serves on it, and there will be a need to recruit more to join him."

Frances nodded. "I want to help wherever I can," she replied. "As will Allen, for I suspect he grows restless here too." Perhaps working together against a common enemy as they did in Devon would be a step towards rebuilding their trust in each other.

Sir Edward drew closer, and she bent her head to listen. "I will talk to Allen, test his appetite for this work. And if the call comes, be prepared to answer it swiftly." His tone was urgent. "You will know when, for the information will come from Ned Villiers through Nan in a letter to the convent, and it will be embossed with the mark of the group."

"Will I recognise it?"

"You will. It is one of the first cyphers Nan taught you. It is a sealed knot."

The west winds from England blew October into Paris, changing the season overnight. And when Frances took Isabella to walk in the palace gardens, the swirl of orange and gold leaves reminded her of the passing of time. Three years since they had begun their exile; none thought they would still be here today. Isabella darted in front of her and picked up a fallen chestnut.

"Look, Mama, *regarde mon trésor!*" The nut gleamed in Isabella's hand, shiny and perfectly formed.

Frances touched it with her finger. It was smooth and unblemished, for it had been well protected within its prickly outer case.

"You must ask Harry to help you thread it," she said, smiling as her girl's eyes danced at his name. "And bring one for him too, so he can play with you."

"Of course. I must look for the biggest and best for him." Isabella dashed to the side of the path and kicked the piles of leaves, searching for more precious chestnuts. Since Nan's boys had arrived in Paris, her five-year-old followed Harry Lee with the adoration of a puppy, for the kind young man went out of his way to play with her. With the instant friendship of the young, they'd bonded, and now Isabella waited for him daily as he and his brother walked over to the Louvre after their lessons were done.

At least there was some sense of family again, for although her heart hardened like a stone against Nan, she could not transfer her anger to Nan's boys. They were polite, helpful young men and brought a welcome change to the monotony of their days.

"And Papa?" Isabella's excited voice broke into her thoughts. "I shall bring a chestnut for Papa too. We shall have a tournament!"

"That would be lovely, *cheri*. Your Papa would enjoy that very much."

If he happened to visit their rooms. Allen rarely joined these walks. She supposed he remained inside the palace, sitting with Sir Edward Hyde, repeating their interminable discussions of how to bring the monarchy back to England.

Did they not realise that nothing was changing?

England did not want a king.

And they would be forever exiled in this foreign land.

She had drifted through the seasons since his return with her heart wrapped in a caul, for after that first terrible argument he had not returned to her bed. Where he slept she knew not, for she did not ask and he did not say. Their conversation remained strictly to that of Isabella's needs or of network business. And anytime she tried to approach him about Anne's gossip, he turned from her and refused to speak to her.

Joined now by letters from Susan Hyde, Nan's listings of safe houses and snatches of news continued to arrive at the convent, and Frances collected and interpreted them for Sir Edward and Henry Wilmot. His recent appointment as Earl of Rochester elevated the significance of Nan and her work even higher in the king's eyes, and Frances must not appear reticent to support her.

But none yet contained the insignia of a sealed knot.

Frances sympathised with the courtyard dove, confined within the walls of her situation, but with her own wing broken, preventing her from flying. She could not tell why this had sunk to such a depression within her, except she was a woman who could only love with all her heart. She'd thought the same of Allen, but she now doubted all she ever believed. He could share his heart quite effortlessly.

And yet, in the darkest hours of the lonely nights, a tiny dragon of doubt kept a ceaseless, insidious whispering. Did she believe gossip instead of integrity? Anne Villiers had long returned to Scotland, and she had never revealed the source of the story.

Was his denial the truth?

Her pride now built a fortress around her heart. And without that strength, what would she have left?

"Lady Apsley! Lady Apsley!"

Frances jumped as the boys rushed across the grass, panting and red-cheeked. Harry and Frank stood before her, their faces flushed, their jackets off. They had raced all the way from De Veau's Academy with the exuberance of youth and were now off again, chasing Isabella around the chestnut trees, pretending she could run faster than either of them.

The complete unfettered joy with which these young creatures relished the present taught a lesson, she thought. *For only in these moments do we truly live, and what has gone before or lies ahead is unreachable and unknown.*

Perhaps Harry and Frank's innocence should be her guide, not the duplicity of their mother.

Today, for happiness must be savoured, they stayed longer than normal. Finally, as the autumn sun dropped in a red ball behind the trees and shadows stretched long in front of them, they readied to return to the Louvre's cramped and noxious quarters. She held up Harry's jacket for him to slip into. He gave a sudden shiver and pulled the fabric close around him.

"The night grows cold," he said. "How strange the weather here, when it can be so hot during the day and cold in a moment."

"It's not cold, Brother." Frank pulled his own jacket off again. "The afternoon is still warm."

Frances looked closely at Harry. Sweat beaded his forehead, yet his lips carried a tinge of blue.

"Time to get you to bed," she said briskly. "You are tired, and rest is what you need."

In her heart, as with anytime a child sickened, she offered a prayer to the Virgin Mary to protect this boy from the night humours.

But the Virgin's attention was elsewhere.

By morning, both Harry and Frank were consumed with an ague.

Within the month, when All Souls Day brought forth the remembrances of the dead, and Frances chose not to leave their bedside to attend the services, she feared their recovery would be a lengthy one.

By Christmas, when they lay wasted and prone, their youth sapped and weakened, their cheerful voices suppressed, Frances wrote to Nan. *Send remedies,* she urged, *send all the physicks Johanna can supply from Lydiard's medicinal gardens, the curatives Lucy writes of in her book.*

And hurry.

Hurry.

Hurry.

19

Luce

. . . While the grand quarrel slept, and both the victors and vanquished were equal slaves under the new usurpers, there was a very kind correspondence between him and all his countrymen. As he was very hospitable, and his conversation no less desirable and pleasant than instructive and advantageous, his house was much resorted to, and as kindly open to those who had in public contests been his enemies, as to his continued friends; for there never lived a man that had less malice and revenge, nor more reconcilableness and kindness and generosity in his nature, than he.

Luce Hutchinson
Winter, 1654

"My boys are settled admirably in Paris, and Cary keeps Cromwell's committee in delightful confusion." Nan sat across from Luce and her mother on a settle in Owthorpe's library. The dark polished wood of the paneling served as a perfect backdrop to Nan's fair skin. "Ditchley is thriving. Of course, I have no knowledge of where Henry is, but no doubt he will appear without notice soon, wearing his dreadful disguise." She laughed, her manner sleek and contented.

Luce sighed. "You manage your life well, Nan. I wish I could say the same for ours. John has been completely distracted with his business matters and ignores his Parliamentary responsibilities. I fear that between his painting collection and Sir Oliver St. John's acquisition of the marble statues, our family has contrived a monopoly in the late king's art." Luce heard her own peevishness but did not care.

Her mother started from her contemplation of the fire. "Do not say that, I beg you. Monopolies ruined our family before. I cannot bear to think of those times occurring again."

"We are not the Villiers, Mother, who build up riches on earth and ignore the rewards in heaven," replied Luce. "Far from it. John is a godly man, and yet he spends little time now on pushing forward with Parliament's reforms."

"You do not think John deserves to be successful in his commerce?" Nan picked up a quill Luce had left lying on the small side table and twirled it between her delicate fingers. "Does it bother you so much you would deny him the method to make money?"

"I think Luce questions John's dedication to the cause, not necessarily his financial success." Her mother always spoke from reason. "His time at his lodgings at Whitehall is spent with art connoisseurs and representatives of buyers from Italy, France, the Netherlands. It is a far cry from compounding Royalist estates to redistribute their monies to back pay those in the army who sacrificed much during the war."

Nan bristled. "Estates such as Ditchley?"

Luce sighed. The same old conflict, and one that constantly troubled her thoughts and her conscience. The country desperately needed money. But to encourage John to plunder Nan's rich estate in the name of Cromwell would be worse than dealing in the king's art.

"There are many ways to raise funds. John must do whatever he desires, for I am sure his wishes are still those of the republic," she added. "But since Parliament was shut down, he has little in the way of responsibility and much time for leisure."

Nan sniffed. She waved her hand airily around the chamber, with its well-stocked bookcases, curiosities and elegantly carved furniture. A beautifully inlaid French clock decorated the wall by the fireplace, and an aromatic fire burned brightly, throwing off a comfortable warmth.

"It seems the republic is doing very well for itself," she remarked. "I counted three violas in the music room, your children are all receiving an education from tutors who once taught the princes at Richmond, and although you dress in sad colours, your gowns are made of velvet, not fustian."

"That's the whole point," Luce burst out. "There are times that I cannot justify John's spending, for he collects paintings and books and plays music and hires dance instructors, all on the back of the king's art. Surely those proceeds are best spent with the people, not for private pleasure."

She caught herself on the verge of tears, the frustration and disappointment lodged in her throat like stale bread. Surely Nan must understand her conflict.

"Luce, a man still has to live, provide for his wife and children." Nan crossed the library to sit by Luce, taking her hands between her own. "If

John seizes the opportunity to do so while still serving his God and country, is he not equitable?"

Luce shrugged. "The money, Nan. There is so much money flowing in from the sale of the art."

"Enough, Luce, enough! John reinvests into Owthorpe, his farms, village, rebuilding the church. He has created work for miles around where just three years ago there was devastation. He employs many and gives charity to countless more." Nan pulled Luce to her feet and pushed her towards the window. "Look up from your books and see what is really happening. In God's truth, John has brought life back to this community and hope for the future."

Nan didn't understand, not really. Her cousin's precious Ditchley Park burst with paintings and tapestries and all the material goods that represented her status and achievements. God forbid Luce would live in that environment for any time; she would go mad. If she did not have her writing to lose herself in, she feared she would run away. Even the responsibility of her children's education was tainted by their dancing and music lessons, which she particularly abhorred. She had no time for these distractions.

"Is there something in particular bothering you Luce? I have not seen you this distraught before. What ails you?"

"The Titian, the painting that John bought which belonged to the Spanish."

"Ah. The Titian." Nan leaned back, a smile playing on her lips. "I thought you might find it offensive. But I insisted John purchase it, for my instinct tells me there is a value attached to the painting which would realise much profit. How much did John pay for it?"

Luce swallowed. "Six hundred pounds."

Nan raised her eyebrows. "A risky purchase for some, perhaps. And yet I think John may have bought well. The market in art is heating now, and between the French and the Spanish ambassadors, a bidding war is on the horizon."

"War has already broken out. And a victor declared." Luce took a deep breath. "The French ambassador has agreed to pay six thousand pounds for the painting."

Nan laughed aloud. "My hunch was correct. I hope John took the offer."

Luce shook her head. "He refused."

"Why?" Nan stood up abruptly. "I must talk to him. He is mad not to take his money. He buys for Cardinal Mazarin. There is plenty more in his purse."

"Don't bother." She felt shameful in some way, for all this talk of money and buying and selling were an anathema to her. "John has already sold it. When the cardinal was so eager to pay six thousand, John raised the price to seven. Even now he is at Somerset House supervising its packing."

Nan hurriedly sat down on the settle again, laughingly fanning herself. "Your husband has an eye for art and a heart for a deal."

Luce shrugged. "It is still blood money, Nan. I cannot stop recalling that day in Whitehall when we could not see the walls for pictures, and every one of them had a price."

"It is as if Buckingham and his decadence lives again," continued Lucy. "We did not dethrone the Stuarts to return to their ways of patronage and perquisites. And now Cromwell governs without Parliament and styles himself Lord Protector; is there a difference between him and the king?"

"Perhaps very little. And if England's future rests with him and he creates a country where we can all live in accord, who is to say it is wrong?" Nan sat back in her chair, seemingly not bothered. Luce wished her cousin was not such a chameleon. "John paid for the art, at a rate acceptable to Cromwell's agents. They were delighted to be shot of the king's possessions and replenish Parliament's coffers. And John reinvests back into the community, creating stability here at home."

"But if Cromwell hears of the price, will he still be as happy?" Luce worried. "You heard of his threat when he visited Owthorpe. He does not trust my family connections or John's friendship with Allen."

A sudden turmoil outside made her jump. Lucy crossed to the window and pulled back the curtain.

"A messenger has arrived. And he appears in a great hurry."

Nan shrugged and leaned forward to Luce, emphasising her words. "There is much to be attended to now, and Cromwell cannot have his eye on every transaction." Nan spoke with a conviction Luce did not feel. "John has proven his loyalty to the cause over and over. He signed the death warrant, God forgive him. And now he is doing the same as others— profiting in the sale of the goods, bringing commerce back after years of war."

144

"Except those others have not already incurred Cromwell's jealousy," replied Luce. "It worries me more that Cromwell is looking for any opportunity to single out John and make an example of him."

"So this is your real fear. You are unusually circuitous, Luce. John is influencing you," replied Nan. "In that case, we shall be sure that John does nothing to attract his attention more. And if my presence here questions his loyalty to Cromwell—" She stopped at a hammering on the front door and loud footsteps echoing on the wooden floor of the hall. Luce's steward burst into the library, followed by a messenger, his cloak dripping rainwater, boots dulled by a horse's sweating flanks.

"For Lady Wilmot." The man pulled a rolled document from his pouch. "I've ridden through from Ditchley Park. A message of extreme urgency."

Nan snatched the message and broke the seal. Rapidly reading the contents, she turned white.

"Is it Johnny? What's wrong?" Luce asked urgently.

She shook her head. "My boys. From Frances. They are desperately ill. She writes for me to come immediately." Nan held the letter with trembling fingers. "This is dated a month ago." Her voice rose. "What took so long?"

The messenger shifted his feet, obviously exhausted. "January storms, my lady. Impossible to cross the Narrow Sea for nigh on two weeks."

Nan flung the document to the fire. "I must leave now. Pray for me. Aunt Lucy, pack me your proven curatives, the possets and tinctures that have saved lives before. And pray, pray I am not too late."

Bundled in soft fox furs against the bitter wind blowing across the flat pastures from the Fosse Way, Luce and her mother walked carefully across the icy gravel paths lining the bowling green. This winter Lucy's steps were more hesitant, the pain of rheumatics slowing her gait and stiffening her back. Today, after Nan's hurried departure left an emptiness in their day, she'd insisted they walk out in the inclement weather. Luce had agreed, tentatively wondering if the weather might be too much for her mother.

"Nonsense," Lucy had responded. "I long for the fresh breezes. And it will do you good to get away from your desk. When you were a little girl, I had to drag you from your studies for fear you would make yourself ill. Don't make me do that again." She'd smiled to take the sting from her words, as she always did when she teased.

145

They had shared so much, the years together, so many challenges and victories. And always they walked in step, their bond forged in both silence and words.

"Remember when we first came to Owthorpe from London?" Lucy turned and gazed past the church to the ruins of the old house. Little remained, for between John's builders and the villagers, most of the stones had been repurposed to serve current buildings. "How fearful we were of the north, and what lengths John went to in his quest to make us feel safe."

Luce nodded. "He withdrew us carefully from the life we had known and did much to prepare us for our new environment." Her eyes watered unexpectedly, for the memory of his devotion brought a tear. "There was nothing he could have done to be more dedicated to our children's well-being."

"And mine." Lucy continued walking, and Luce caught some of her old vigour. "After my disastrous marriage with Leventhorpe, I could not imagine ever feeling secure in a home again. And yet John's care and love for me brought me back to life."

This time Luce paused and welcomed the biting wind whipping at her face. The pain brought clarity to her thinking. "You are recalling this for a reason, aren't you?"

Her mother faced her, blue-grey eyes still sharply intelligent in her lined face.

"I hear discontent in your voice, Luce, and questioning of John's wisdom." She gestured at their home. Everywhere, signs of prosperity and careful planning. From the neatly cut pathways leading to the well-stocked fishponds, to the gardens and recreational walks now sleeping in winter's quiet season, the manor resonated security and safety.

Lucy continued. "In the midst of these terrible times of war and uncertainty, John stayed true to his beliefs, loyal to his people and connected to the land of his forefathers." She looked towards the house. "Tell me what you see, my darling. Tell me what you see, and then tell me what the alternative might have been."

Luce took a deep breath. Her mother knew her well. Well enough that if she spoke aloud, her words would be real.

"I see a well-built manor house, crafted of fine stone, with beautiful windows and in a safe location."

"And what else?"

146

"I see gardens and fields, outlooks and pastures, offices, stables and a prosperous village."

"And what else?" Lucy persisted, chasing Luce to utter the words as only she could.

"A church. A church rebuilt and expanded, where we worship God in our way, with no alter, simply and with no idolatry."

Lucy nodded.

"And how did John manage this, Luce? Do you call this profligate? Do you not think this a wise investment in your children and England's future?"

Chastened, Luce shut her eyes tightly to prevent the tears falling. Shame burned in her heart.

"Sweetheart, it is easy to criticise, to find fault when you are immersed in your own thoughts and enjoy just your own intellect for company." Her mother took her now into her arms, holding her in an embrace as familiar as her own skin. "But you must break your habitual thinking and look at the wider view, Luce. Never lose your fervour, for John is sustained by your passion. But always keep your perspective, for then you will both thrive."

As they walked back arm in arm and heads down into the prevailing wind, Luce was quiet, her mother's words tumbling in her mind. She had been holding on to a righteous resentment to fuel her own sense of importance, her intellectual dominance. She had steered John's actions through her own strategy, pushed him to action, perhaps even in the face of his own uncertainty. She had been herself guilty of the sin of pridefulness. It was time to take stock of her own character.

She laughed at a sudden thought. "Allen would have chastised me in a far more direct manner than you," she said. "Thank you for your kindness."

Lucy joined her laughter. "Don't say thank you. It's a mother's prerogative. And you're right. Allen would have defended John and his love of protecting his land and home over your revolutionary ideas any day."

They entered their home, seeking the company of the children and comfort with a warm posset by the fire. Luce's thoughts flew to Nan, alone on a desperate journey to save her boys, Henry unreachable.

Thank God for John, who made her life possible. A simple yet profound truth she must never forget.

20

Nan

Vanquished below deck, where the heaving of the vessel resembled the contorted bowels of a man with the sweating sickness, Nan prayed without cease.

Hurry, please hurry.

God, if you save my boys, I will dedicate my life to you.

God, if you save my boys, I will dedicate them to you.

God, if you save my boys . . .

Her prayers hammered in her ears, drowning the wind and waves.

Her first crossing of the Narrow Sea. God Almighty, and how often had Henry sailed to join her? His bravery in enduring these fearful passages was unquestionable proof of his love.

Dear God, save me from dying on this voyage, for if you save me . . .

If she stopped praying, God would desert her.

She prevailed.

Landfall at Calais, and France received her, bruised, sick and the prevailing party in her contract with God. Alive, but no warmer or safer on land than on her vessel. And although accompanied by half a dozen of Cary's men, Nan feared the well-worn track plunging into the French countryside. Thieves, highwaymen and other rascals roamed abroad, even in daylight, preying on the stupid English. The route from Calais to Paris proved lucrative for these French robbers, for they knew every exiled Englishman hid coins sewn into garments and jewels concealed in a shoe's hollowed heels.

My boys. My precious boys.

She drove Cary's men hard across this vile, flat French landscape, iced at night and mud-plugged by day. This was no gentle Oxfordshire countryside, tempered by tended cottages and tidy fields. A bleak land. Lazy inhabitants. Squandering the black and arable soil, for nothing grew to encourage useful husbandry of crops or cattle.

Not like Ditchley. Her well-ordered life. Her boys' assured future.

For sanity's sake, she must save them, return them from this alien land to their rightful home.

My boys. My precious boys.

What a ghastly miscalculation, sending them so far away. Most unlike her.

Noxious France. A filthy country.

God, save my boys so I can restore them to Ditchley.

On the sixth day, saddle-sore and weary, she reached Paris's walls. Now a different repulsion clogged her throat with a thick yellow rheum. A river miasma trapping the smoke of a hundred thousand fires and the stink of innumerable inhabitants of this foul city.

Nan pulled her scarf around her mouth and kicked her tired horse.

"Go faster," she commanded the guard. "Tell your French guide a reward awaits if he gets us to the Louvre Palace before nightfall."

Threading their way through dirt-packed alleys and roughly cobbled streets, where their exhausted horses stumbled and skidded on the slippery stones, she confronted filth and ordure at every turn. She had committed her boys to this? What madness. Never again would she let them leave Oxfordshire.

God, I beg you, save my boys.

Thank heaven the hospitality of the palace awaited. There, in Allen's apartments, she would thaw in front of a fire, wash her body, clean her clothes, eat a reasonable supper. Dose her boys with the precious medicines from Lucy's gardens at Owthorpe.

And sleep in the arms of her husband tonight.

Dreadfully fatigued, she concentrated on the space between her horse's pricked ears. Eager to earn his bonus, the guard delivered them to iron gates inset within a long stone building.

"The Palais de Louvre, my lady," he shouted over his shoulder. "Ahead lay the royal apartments."

Negotiating around ragged peasant women collecting wood scraps from a building site, Nan trotted her horse the last few yards across the courtyard and dismounted rapidly. Beckoning for her box, she spied a scruffy page lolling on a flight of steps. Once, his livery may have been an earl's or signified the king himself. Now no recognisable insignia graced his jacket, and from ragged sleeve to broken shoes a filthy grey prevailed.

"Take me to Sir Allen Apsley's lodgings," she commanded. What manner of welcome was this?

"How much?" he responded.

"What do you mean, how much?" she snapped back. "Take me and take me now."

The boy shrugged, his eyes running over the fine Ditchley horses and saddlery. "You can afford it," he said. "We all gets paid something round here."

Nan brushed past him and into the dark hall. Not a sound greeted her, no servants, no dogs lounging by the fireplace and not a stick of furniture in the cavernous stone chamber. 'Struth, surely this was not the palace? These rooms would not house an Oxford cleric.

She stormed through the chamber, the guard's heavy steps tramping behind her. A light flickered at the end of a long corridor, and voices murmured along the empty walls. Summoning the last of her energy, she strode forward through the lit doorway and into a room no larger than Ditchley's hall. A fug of human odour struck her, a stale smell of unwashed bodies unsuccessfully masked by the cheapest pomander scents of lavender and rosemary. She surveyed the throng of people, a meagre fire burning in the smoke-blackened fireplace. An unrecognisable animal carcass turned on a spit, and a knot of dogs and children tussled on the floor.

Where lived the court? Her boys?

In horror, she could not move forward another step.

"Nan? Nan!"

Warmth flooded to her head, causing her to sway. Allen caught her before she fell.

"Dear God, Cousin, we have been fraught with worry for you." His voice the most welcome sound in the world, his arms the most wonderful security. "Frances wrote at Christmas-tide, and now it is February. We thought you ill or in danger yourself."

"My boys, Allen?" She could barely speak. "My boys?"

"They are no worse," Allen folded her more tightly in his arms, "and yet we cannot find a curative."

She started to cry, which startled her, for tears were strangers to her. *They lived.*

As Allen gently wiped her cheeks, gratitude rushed upon her, and she wrapped her arms around his waist, laying her head against his chest.

150

"Nan." Frances appeared at Allen's shoulder. "You have finally arrived."

Nan reached to kiss her and received her cool cheek. "Frances, take me to my boys. Thank you. Thank you for caring for them."

"Any mother would do this for another," replied Frances. "This way." She pushed her way through the crowd, not looking back once to see if Nan followed.

The appalling conditions continued in Frances's chambers. Nan's boys lay on a straw mattress on the floor, covered in a shabby blanket, tallow candles guttering brown smoke in an invisible draft. Frances excused the woman sitting by them, and Nan pushed past her to kneel at her boys' side. Feeling their damp foreheads, gazing upon their thin faces, she looked up at Frances in horror.

"What is this? What conditions do you keep my children in?" Nan stroked their cheeks, and each boy murmured. Harry turned to her and opened his eyes, smiling faintly. "This is monstrous. Have you nothing more than this?"

Frances remained silent, staring at her.

"Speak!" commanded Nan. "What medicine have you given them? What does the court physician say?"

"The last doctor left three months ago, unpaid for a year. And the medicines are those I could brew myself from herbs I could find. Broths, mint, clear spring water. Allen was able to trade for citrus last week, remembering his mother saying the fruit is efficacious for fevers."

Nan was aghast. "That is all? Here? At court?"

"Yes. At court. Not your precious Ditchley," snapped Frances. She pushed a reddened hand through her hair. The candlelight threw lines of weariness across her face. "This is exile, Nan. Like it or not, this is what you sent your children to. And if you think it so bad, take your boys and Allen and go back to Ditchley, and leave me alone."

"What sentiments are these? What brings these dreadful words to your lips?" Nan hissed. "What are you thinking, Frances?"

The door creaked open. Allen brought her trunk to her side. "How do you find them, Nan? They are recovered from their worst, and Frances has

151

spent day and night at their side, never leaving." He looked at her anxiously as he knelt by her.

"She was just telling me of her worries," Nan replied. Surely Frances was hysterical from the strain of nursing. Opening the chest, she removed a smaller box from within. "Frances, please fetch me some small beer, the weakest you have. Lucy insisted the boys should not have water, but a fermented drink only." She pulled the cork from a small brown bottle and sniffed it. "And she gave me coneflower essence. A new medicinal she says brings miraculous curatives to those with fevers."

Allen clasped her hand and kissed it. "Thank God for my mother and her physicks," he said fervently. "And thank God you are here now, Nan. I know the boys will recover."

Nan smoothed Harry's hair and smiled at her boys. "I will take care of you, my darlings," she soothed. "Your mother is here. You will recover."

She barely noticed the chamber door click as Frances left.

"Why does Frances continue to avoid me?" Nan carefully measured the five drops of Lucy's ague tincture into a cup of warm cow's milk.

She handed Allen the brew and opened the window, the first fresh breeze of March bearing the tang of spring grass. He did not meet her eyes, but gently sat Frank up, who gratefully clasped the drink and sipped it.

"Well?"

"It is our own business," replied Allen. The bright spring sun pouring in the window behind him shadowed his face. His words discouraged any further questioning.

Nan shrugged. More lay behind his words. In the weeks since arriving at the palace, nothing surprised her. The squalid conditions, the forced frivolity and the incessant consumption of cheap wine and ale, all these she became accustomed to. But why the obvious aloofness between Allen and Frances—and the arm's length at which she was held by Allen's wife?

"She is so distant." Nan placed her hand on Frank's brow and smiled at him, satisfied no residue of the fever lurked in his fair skin. "And out of sorts." She gestured to the cramped chamber in which she and the boys lived and slept. "These are by no means luxurious conditions, but she is at the court of our king and in a trusted position with Sir Edward. There are not many women in England who have the respect she has earned."

"It has been a long four years," replied Allen. "She pines for England. She has little here except the company of men, for she has no truck with the women of the court." He stood, his tall figure filling the room. Even in this lazy court, he stayed strong and muscular, engaging in daily practice of his sword. Unlike others, such as their cousin George Villiers, he maintained a discipline.

"And she seems to regard me differently than before," pressed Nan. "We were never close friends, and yet now she ignores me unless I speak to her."

"Frances has her torments, mostly of her own creation." A melancholy flickered around his mouth before he pulled on his threadbare jacket and kissed her cheek swiftly. "Come to the palace gardens for a game of bowls. The king commands us all outside to enjoy this first day of spring. Harry has already taken Isabella down, and Frank will rest here quietly."

She thought as much. Trouble between them. And Frances's anxiety would befuddle Allen.

"One moment." She opened her travelling trunk, removing the small crimson leather pouch from that bleak January day five years gone. "I have this for the king. Now I can join the court without fear of carrying contamination, I would like a private audience with him. Can you arrange this, Allen?"

He smiled. "For the wife of his best friend, he will make time. I'm just sorry that Henry is not here too."

Nan nodded. "I miss him terribly. But you tell me his mission in Germany is critical to the king's well-being." She turned to him. "I won't leave Paris before seeing him, though. I cannot bear the thought of staying here and not being with him."

"Without the German funding, we have no hope of mounting any kind of operation. Henry's work is vital." He took her hand. "We will ask Sir Edward when he anticipates Henry's return to Paris. But for now, this moment, let us enjoy a respite from illness and worry. Frank rests comfortably, and spring awaits."

For the first time since the messenger had arrived at Owthorpe, Nan breathed freely. And in this palace garden, where the scent of spring curled and unfurled around her, she could finally think again. When Harry had first responded to Lucy's medicine, and then Frank's fever had broken, her prayers had been answered. These had been some of the darkest times of her life. But today, this moment, she was alive and returning to a world waking from winter and full of thrush song and golden daffodils.

The king enjoyed the air too. Easy to spot, he rose a head taller than those around him. A giant among men, he could be found in the centre of a group of giggling women, each no doubt vying for his roving eye. Seventeen mistresses since arriving in Paris, she'd heard tell. Yes, despite being quarantined with Frank and Harry in those cramped chambers, she kept her knack for extracting information from anyone she encountered. The washerwoman had a keen ear for gossip and shared her news eagerly. But even she only insinuated whispers against Frances, sliding from Nan's questioning about Allen's discontented wife.

"Come, Nan, let me take you to the king." Allen steered her along the gravel path. Weeds grew vigourously between the stones, reinforcing the poverty of this court. With no money to spend on food and clothes, gardeners were not even a consideration.

"There's Frances." Nan stopped. "And look, Isabella with Harry. How lovely to see them together." She pulled away from Allen and walked to Frances.

"How are you, my dear? It is joyful to be able to be out today and to take the air. And how beautiful Isabella looks. She still reminds me so much of Johnny."

Frances turned her head away from Nan's kiss. "I am not surprised. You said they both had the St.John eyes when we first met. Nothing would have changed."

"Nothing has changed. Except a melancholy in you, Frances." Nan gestured to the blue sky, the daffodils in bloom. "Surely today you can forget your worries?"

Frances looked at her coolly. "Not when they travel with me." She took Isabella's hand. "Excuse me. We promised the queen we would pay her a visit." Turning, she did not say good-bye to Allen, and walked quickly away, her back stiff.

"What has happened?" Nan caught the pain behind his eyes. "Can you not confide in me? Is there nothing I can do to help you repair this?"

Allen pulled a lavender bud from a bush and crushed it between his fingers.

154

The pungent scent arose quickly, recalling Aunt Lucy's stillroom, the haven within the Tower that always offered a respite from the fears lingering in the prison walls. He lifted the damaged flower to his nose and sniffed, and she knew immediately he shared her memory.

"For the sake of all between us, Allen, let me help."

He dropped the lavender and bowed his head slightly, not meeting her eyes, his lashes long on his cheeks and his hair falling across his face. "She was given reason to believe a piece of gossip that caused her great grief. Frances does not forgive or forget."

Nan almost laughed. "But that's absurd. She is not a woman to pay credence to court rumours."

"This news came from Anne Villiers, Lady Dalkeith. A woman she trusts from their time together in Exeter."

"And the daughter of Barbara Villiers, who did so much harm to your mother," responded Nan. "What was the gossip?"

Allen took her hand. "That we were lovers—"

"Absurd."

"—and Johnny is my son."

"Oh, dear God in Heaven." Nan snatched her hand from his and stepped away. "How could she believe this?"

"Because a woman she trusted told her. Because I was gone for so long. Because you and I are so close. Because Henry was absent so often from your side. Because Johnny and Isabella share a resemblance." Allen ran his hands through his hair, despair across his face. "Because sometimes the sum of a thousand small truths can outbid the price of one lie."

"What lie?" Nan demanded. "What lie did you tell her?"

"That I have only loved you as a cousin."

"You surely have lost your mind." Nan's anger flashed white hot. "There is no love between us except that of a brother and sister, two cousins who are close."

"But once, after Edgehill—"

"Do not repeat your poisonous words. We vowed never to speak again of this."

Into the stillness between them, shadows fell across the path.

"Nan!" Sir Edward Hyde pulled her into his arms and squeezed her until her breath was gone. "My darling Nan!"

155

"So here is the extraordinary woman who keeps Henry on the straight and narrow path, and whose love causes him to risk his life over and over to join her in England's dangerous land?" The king's deep voice resonated amusement.

She gathered her senses and curtseyed deeply. "Your Majesty."

"Lady Wilmot." He held a beautifully shaped hand out to her. Belgian lace frothed at his wrist, covered by a frayed cuff of fine green velvet. "I see now why Henry must return to you so frequently, albeit in secret." He smiled at her with sensual brown eyes.

Allen's words buzzed in her mind as a hive of angry bees. Now she understood Frances's attitude.

Concentrate on the king.

So attentive, he spoke to her as if she were the only woman in the world. She said nothing, waiting for his next words.

"But I neglect my manners. I understand from my friend Nall—Sir Allen—you have been nursing your sons since you arrived. They are recovered?" How charming his warmth, his kindness, his affectionate nickname for her cousin.

"Yes, Your Majesty. They are almost well again. Now I must attend to Henry, for I yearn to see him." Surely at the talk of her husband, Allen's disturbing words would fade.

"Ah, my loyal Henry. We miss him nightly, for without his company the court is indeed a dull place. And yet he does important work for us in Germany. I cannot recall him yet."

"Then I shall wait here until he returns," Nan replied firmly.

The king laughed. "I admire your spirit, my dear." His face grew sombre. "I heard from Nall you were very brave on the day of my father's death."

"I promised Henry I would stand there for you, Your Majesty. I have waited long to see you and speak of how your father died." Nan pulled the velvet purse from her pocket and handed it to the king. "And within this pouch, I have carried these past years a special relic. His blood on my kerchief."

Charles took it gently and opened the leather thong. He pulled forth the delicate linen, white at first and then stained rust-red. He touched the fabric to his lips, his eyes filling with tears.

"Come, walk with me and Sir Edward, and tell me of the day my father died," he said. "And we shall speak also of the network and the situation in England as you understand it. I hear from Sir Edward that he completely trusts your counsel, and he owes you a great debt."

"A debt of my life," confirmed Sir Edward. "For if Nan had not sheltered Henry and me after Edgehill, we would not be alive today. She is the most intrepid woman I know, and one who can be counted on to resolve any situation. We must discuss her thoughts on the Sealed Knot and its proposed activities in England. I hear from my sister that dissenting factions within Parliament give us great opportunity. I am sure as soon as Nan has seen Henry, she will want to return to Ditchley and the work that is so important to us."

Nan looked back at Allen, standing so vulnerable in the garden, without his wife at his side and Nan about to leave too.

She must sort this terrible misunderstanding with Frances. She must strengthen ties to the king. She must not be alone with Allen. She must wait for Henry. She must plan the future with Sir Edward. So much to arrange. So much to repair.

She would start with the king.

21

Frances

The summons to Sir Edward's apartments arrived the day after the king invited them to the gardens to play bowls. Yesterday had been beautiful, the kind of March afternoon that instilled hope in her heart. At home, the wobbly legged lambs would be exploring the fields and running back and forth in the little packs they formed as soon as they could walk. Primroses would be hidden in the hedgerows, and if she closed her eyes for a moment, she was home.

And then Nan had arrived with Allen at her side.

Frances could not leave the garden quickly enough, ignoring Nan's call. She did not need to see them together. Nor tolerate the whisperings of the gossips. She'd spent the rest of the day alone. And locked the door of her chamber against any visitors that night.

Now Frances walked into Sir Edward's apartments and immediately curtseyed, for the king stood with him.

"Ah, Frances, come here." Sir Edward gestured to the table. "We were just talking about you and the work which lies ahead."

Documents, maps, portfolios overstuffed with letters and a stack of leather-bound journals lay heaped on the table.

"My library and records." Sir Edward smiled ruefully. "For if I do not have my references, I forget what I have written and to whom. I have kept these records since I arrived in Jersey with the late king. One day, when I am retired, I promised myself I would write a history of all we have witnessed, for surely such times will never be seen again."

King Charles laughed. "You will never retire, my friend. For without your guidance, I would be lost."

Sir Edward shook his head. "That's not what Buckingham says."

"Ignore him. He has no mind for strategy, just action and reaction. And women."

"Action. Reaction. Distraction. You could do without his company, Your Majesty, when we have a country to claim."

The king groaned. "I have many mouths to feed here and subjects who plague me daily with their needs. You can manage the business, Edward, while I keep the court amused. Just tell me when and where to appear."

Frances found fascinating the piles of documents and the easy way in which the king deferred to Sir Edward. This, then, was the real distribution of power. Sir Edward effectively ran the exiled community, with the king attending when asked.

A sound behind her, and Sir Edward looked up.

"Ah. Nall and Lady Wilmot. Thank you for coming at such short notice."

Frances whirled around. Allen and Nan stood between her and the door, and she could not leave the room without offending Sir Edward and the king.

Trapped.

"All of you, gather round."

She stood next to Sir Edward, so her husband and his cousin had to face her across the table.

Sir Edward pushed a pile of documents to one side and unrolled a large map of England. Marked across its face were a number of squiggles, all next to rectangles.

"The current location of safe houses," he explained. "I have reviewed these with Lady Wilmot, and to the best of her recollection, the records are correct for the south and Midlands. My sister Susan has gathered confirmations from the west, and we are always in a positive position in the north."

In spite of her distress, Frances leaned over the map with interest. "Are you planning another uprising, Sir Edward?"

He shook his head and glanced at the king, who had drifted to the window, ignoring the conversation. Allen joined him, and the two men stood shoulder to shoulder, laughing at the antics in the gardens below. A sudden squall of rain hit the pane, and clouds raced across the sky, throwing shadows across the map.

Nan stood across from her with watchful eyes. And then turned her gaze to Allen.

Brazen whore.

"I do not believe we should invade or muster an army," Sir Edward replied. "We have neither the men nor the power to do so." He pointed to

159

the maps and then the key cities of London, Oxford, Nottingham, York. "But the safe houses steadily increase in number. And instead, we wait for Cromwell's arguing factions to fracture. We watch for dissention to arise within. We see the effect of what John Hutchinson has set in motion at Nottingham. And to that purpose, we created a new secret group, both here in Paris and in England, which will report as these fissures arise."

"The Sealed Knot," Nan said. "You have heard of this, Frances?"

She refused to answer.

"I told Frances of its formation," confirmed Sir Edward.

Frances caught a glance between Nan and Sir Edward. It was just a flicker, but it conveyed much. "And so where does this affect me?"

Sir Edward smiled. "Not just you, Frances, but Allen too."

Nan leaned over and took Frances's arm, forcing her to look at her. "Sir Edward is expanding the Sealed Knot. Our cousin Ned Villiers leads the operation. And Susan Hyde is a crucial messenger, just like you."

"Yes?" Frances replied. A triumphant smile lit Nan's face. She shook her arm free. "And what is it to you, Nan?"

"Frances, we must speak. We have much to discuss. Allen is of more use in England than here. Sir Edward plans to send you back by year end. I must see Henry before I leave, and then we will all meet at Ditchley."

"NO!" The word tore from her mouth. "Not with you. Not there, not to Ditchley."

She may as well have shot a cannon into the chamber.

Sir Edward reacted first. "Why, Frances? What does this mean?"

The king and Allen detached themselves from the distraction below and joined them at the table. All faced her.

She appealed to Sir Edward. The words buried in her heart burst forth.

"Lady Wilmot is Allen's lover. She bore his child. I will not tolerate being under the same roof as them—"

"Such lies!" Nan's voice cut across her. "Allen told me of these wicked rumours. I have tried to reach you, but you barred your door. Dear God, Frances, why do you insist on believing this idle gossip?"

"And you deny it? Or is it because Allen warned you? You, whose husband is never present and yet miraculously sired a child upon you?"

"Frances!" Allen's voice thundered across the room. "Do not bring others into our dispute."

"You leave me no choice." Frances could not stop now. "You arranged this, you and your mistress. And what will happen when we return to England? Will I be conveniently sent to Lydiard while you remain at Ditchley on the king's business and Henry is exiled here?"

"Lady Apsley," the king's mellow voice commanded her attention. "Lady Apsley, those are serious allegations. What basis? I have nothing but the greatest respect for Henry and Lady Wilmot."

She cared no more. She had nothing.

"Anne Villiers, Lady Dalkeith." She turned to Hyde. "Your lover, I have heard."

"Oh dear God, Frances," Allen groaned. "You go too far."

She whipped around to Nan. "And you? You have no defence? You say nothing to clear this gossip. And now, once again, you manipulated Allen and me to your desires."

Outside a dove cooed, over and over and over.

Frances stood alone at the table. The king, Sir Edward, Allen and Nan opposed her. If one of them didn't speak, she would surely fall to the ground and never rise.

"Lady Apsley." The king again. "Anne Villiers told you what exactly?"

"John Wilmot is Allen's son, not Henry's. My husband and Nan are lovers." She turned to Allen. "How could you do this to me? And how could you continue to break my heart?"

Sir Edward, silent until now, walked around the table to her, his expression agitated.

"Lady Dalkeith told you this?"

"Yes."

"On whose authority?"

"She did not say. But the whole court knows it."

He took a deep, shuddering breath. "And so she does more damage than even I thought."

The king looked at him. "She is your good friend, Sir Edward. What say you?"

"She was."

"Oh?"

"Before she left for Scotland, we had a falling out. I discovered things about her I did not know. Facts which belied her character, led me to believe she was duplicitous."

161

The king laughed humourlessly. "Not a first for a Villiers."

Nan stepped forward. "And so you confirm she is lying, Sir Edward? For in truth, there is no basis to this rumour. Johnny is Henry's child, and nothing lies between Allen and me except the love of two cousins."

"Henry did not live in England when you conceived Johnny." Frances clutched the facts with all her strength. "Allen was there, with you. Henry travelled with the king in exile."

"On what authority do you say this?" repeated Sir Edward. He moved swiftly for a man with such bulk and started pulling the leather-bound journals towards him. "Who challenges Henry was not in England?" He looked directly at Nan. "When did you conceive? And no modesty, Nan, for a marriage depends on your honesty."

She looked directly at Frances. "August 1646. Johnny was born in April 1647."

Just after their wedding in Owthorpe.

Just after she had pledged Allen her life, her love.

Sir Edward opened a volume and ran his finger down a line of entries. He impatiently flicked the pages back and forth.

"June, July . . . August. Here we are. August 15. Letter to Lady Wilmot. Relieved to hear Sir Henry has arrived safely. August 22. Letters to Lord and Lady Wilmot at Ditchley Park. Topic: stay until you hear from me about returning to France. September 18. Letter to Lord Wilmot. Do not travel to France yet. September 30. Remain with Lady Wilmot, do not leave." He looked up. "Henry was at Ditchley throughout August and September, on my secret business, Frances. He may have been condemned to exile and had to flee England, but he hid at Ditchley until the last possible moment."

Frances swayed on her feet, a sickness rising in her throat, shock and humiliation combining to take her legs from under her. She could not cry, could not talk, could not look at Allen or Nan. For she could not bear their pity.

These months of doubt, suspicion corroding her heart.

All avoidable if she had just confided in Sir Edward. Casually asked for Henry's whereabouts. Looked for evidence to combat Anne Villiers's poison.

Pride undid her. Strength became her weakness. And her precious independence an assassin's knife.

An arm around her, a strong arm, steady. "Come, Lady Apsley. Come sit with me." The king drew her to the window and steadied her on the sill. She refused to look at Nan or Allen.

"If there is something I have learned in these difficult times," he continued, "it is the poison which enters a man's soul through the simplest of gossip. You have fallen victim to foul play by words. And Anne Villiers plunged the blade into your heart." He held her hand between his with great tenderness. "This viper's nest of rumours and gossip is not for you. I recall your bravery and honesty when you cared for me in Barnstaple. You have no duplicity and cannot believe others would harm you through jealousy or envy. You befriended someone at court who betrayed your trust for their own amusement. And I, of all men, know the cost of disloyalty." The door clicked. She looked up. Only Allen remained.

"Talk now to your husband, Frances." The king stood. "Talk for as long as it takes to dispel the doubts and step forth from the shadows into the light of truth. I hope to see you both in the morning, reconciled. For there is no replacement for the love of a good man and woman. One day I hope for the same myself, when I can abandon the allure of these unprincipled Villiers. Their fire burns bright, and we seek them like moths to a flame. One day I desire to enjoy all you have in Allen. A devoted, honest and faithful partner. Do not let idle tongues destroy true love, the most precious gift of all."

He left her then, his words burning in her heart.

Alone in her prison of misery.

"Do not ever speak to me again, Husband," she said, still not lifting her eyes. "For I did not trust your word. I do not deserve you. I have damaged you and your family."

Allen came to her, close but not touching. "When you entered my life, my world was dark, and I could see nothing in the void. Twice over you saved me, for without your love I would not survive, without your support I could not endure."

She listened, fiercely concentrating on her hands, choking back her tears.

"And today, I tell you that I cannot live this way any longer."

This was good-bye.

"The dragons of doubt," she whispered. "They have defeated me."

Allen took her hand, and at first she could not move. He insisted, and she followed him to the fireplace, where cushions lay on the floor and a small blaze cheered the fading afternoon.

"Sit with me," he said. "For I have much to tell you."

He pulled her down next to him, and as the afternoon closed around them, he told her of Worcester, and the slaughter, and the refuge he sought with Luce and John. She leaned against him, leaned back against his strong body, his arms closing around her, his chin resting on her head. They had sat this way often in the garrison in Barnstaple, planning their survival, how they would escape the siege.

And then he took her back farther, to his war years, to the opening battle.

"Edgehill was the first action I saw," he said, telling her of times never shared before. "Edward and I witnessed hundreds slaughtered that day. And when we took refuge with Nan at Ditchley, she sat all night with us, in silence, knowing we would never be the same again."

"I wish I had known Edward." Frances stared into the fire. "You and Luce and Nan loved him dearly."

Allen did not answer immediately, and she knew the tears ran down his face. The fire flared, a drop of resin awakening a spark.

"The past is behind us. Edward is in his grave. We chose to fight on. As did you." Allen smoothed her hair, kissed the top of her head. "All the time you were dealing with the horrors of living here, fending for our family, begging for food and kindling, I was trying to take us home again. Working with the king and Sir Edward on plan after plan that would restore us to England."

"I did the best I could for us," she cried. "And then you were gone. I fell into despair."

"We both were trying the best we could," he replied. "We just were trying in different ways, where we thought we might succeed."

"When you returned from Worcester. When you chose your men over me. When you did not come to me for so long. And still have not?"

He shifted and yet did not loosen his hold on her. "These months have been lost forever, Frances. There are things in battle I have seen I can never speak of. We drink to banish those demons. When you closed your heart to me, my brotherhood was all I had left."

"And Nan?" She needed to hear his final truth.

"Nan." Allen paused, his arms now even more tightly around her. "Nan has been with me my whole life. She understands me as only blood can, instinctively and without words."

Although her heart beat faster, she did not pull away.

"And yet I could never be with Nan as I am with you, Frances. You are my life, my soul, my love through eternity. You are my comfort in the dark, for you chase away my shadows with your starlight."

And what next? Is that enough?

"Come back to me, Frances. Come back to my life, my love."

She bowed her head again. With the gentlest of touches, he turned her in his arms, lifted her chin and brought his face close to hers. Tentatively at first, he kissed her lips. And then cradled her face and kissed her deeply.

As she responded to his familiar touch, and the taste of him and the tang of his salt tears, she kissed him back, with her heart and soul and all she had to give.

"I love you, Allen," she whispered.

As they discovered each other again, he murmured words against her skin. "Bring us back to ourselves, my darling. God willing, we may be blessed with another child. And if she is a girl, we will call her Frances. To remind us of what we almost lost, here in France, and what we found again."

PART THREE

1655
HOMEWARD

22

Nan

Nan dashed through the midnight air on her swiftest horse, the hoofbeats a steady thrumming in her ears as she raced across the western hills of Oxfordshire and into Wiltshire. A hunter's moon lit the path ahead, where flints and shale glistened in the creamy light. Cary's men cantered with her, their black flapping cloaks blotting the landscape.

From Ditchley to Lydiard, two full days following a lady's pace, and in November's miserly daylight, she pushed the boundaries into the evening hours. Tonight, they rested just a couple of hours at Faringdon, the Talbot Inn providing water for the horses and stew for her men. Too nervous to eat, Nan contented herself with a glass of sack. Enough to warm her brain but not befuddle her thoughts. And send her on her way again at a stride even Allen would be hard put to maintain.

"*Meet me at Lydiard,*" Susan Hyde's letter had commanded. "*Meet me in the church early Sunday before the parishioners arrive so we may pray in private for the souls of Mr. Fitch and Mr. Edwards. I would hear of your travels and how your sons fare in Paris. Come by return, though, for I would have you listen to this curate. You will find his sermon most inspiring.*"

The wax had been stamped with the device of a sealed knot.

Sir Edward had warned her of this before she left Paris. A sudden message from his sister. A demand to attend St. Mary's church at Lydiard. And the names of Ned Villiers and Charles Stuart written in code entwined within the simple note. Obey Susan, he'd insisted. Especially if she places a time limit within her honeyed words.

A sudden clattering as the horses sent up a brace of pheasant. They flapped into the air, causing her mount to stumble and recover, yet she barely broke pace. A quick glance over her shoulder confirmed light in the east, red streaks spearing into the darkness. She had perhaps three more hours to reach the church before it filled for Sunday service. The guard ahead turned back to her and raised his gauntleted fist, one finger pointing to the sky. One hour, he signaled. *One hour and I will have you at Lydiard.*

At Cricklade, they crossed the Thames and swung south towards Swindon, then veered west and into the hollow way leading to St. Mary's church. Dawn had chased her these last miles, and by the time they pulled into the stable courtyard between Lydiard House and the church, sleepy lads were stumbling down from their lofts and lurchers bayed from their kennels.

Horses were already tethered to the church gate, and Nan dismounted rapidly, her legs buckling slightly as she touched the cobblestones. Pulling off her gloves and smoothing her hair under her hood, she strode towards the south door of the church, the private family entrance leading from the house.

The house.

She'd ignored this memory so far in her rapid flight from Ditchley. Nan glanced up at the blank windows, the flat plaster absorbing the morning light and sucking the life from the rising sun.

A stone's throw from the church tower and the deep cold tombs of the dead in her family, reproaching her absence from the weight of the centuries.

For only once had she returned.

And now the resting place of her father, mother and beloved brother. Her childhood home, the dullest, loneliest place she had ever lived.

Perhaps she had come home for a reason. For she had yet to make her peace with them.

The war had never encroached upon Lydiard.

And now she brought it into its heart. She and Susan Hyde.

The woman sat in the St.John family pew, a dark oak enclosure to the right of the nave. Nan walked towards her along the ancient stone floor, an old pilgrim's route where colourful wall paintings told of St. Christopher and Becket, martyred to the people. The great painted royal court of arms hung on the north wall, an admonition and a reminder of Lydiard's loyalties. A surprise Walter had not hid the carving in the attics, for it would not last long if Cromwell's men came to call.

At her footsteps, the figure turned and beckoned. Nan joined her in the pew on the hard oak bench, grimacing slightly from the saddle bruises she'd collected in her flight from Ditchley. The woman silently looked towards the north wall. Nan followed her gaze and gasped aloud at the man in full military uniform standing by the window, his back to the grey dawn light.

174

"Edward!"

And then leaned back against the pew as she realised he was carved of stone.

"A remarkable likeness, don't you think?" Susan Hyde reached out and took Nan's hand. "I did not realise you have not returned since he died."

Nan shook her head, overwhelmed from the ride and the emotion of Edward's appearance.

"Your father placed Edward's statue there not long after his burial," Susan went on. "He visited every day until he died himself."

Nan's eyes flew to the canopied marble effigies of her father and his two wives, her mother on one side, his second on the other, united in eternal rest. And although she could not see from where she sat, she knew of the small girl kneeling at his feet, a carving of herself when she was but seven years old. A lesson that one day she would join the ranks of the dead.

Enough.

"Your letter was insistent, Susan." She turned to the woman, who slipped down her hood and untied her cloak. "We have communicated all these years by written word. What has caused this urgent request to see me now, and under what secret circumstance?"

Susan's fair skin flushed, and her large blue eyes shone in the early morning light.

"Information I cannot trust to paper. And too complex to write in one letter. An uprising," she said. "Beginning here, in Wiltshire. And spreading across the country with Royalists ready to stand up and fight, to overthrow Cromwell, to ready the country for the return of the king."

Nan shrugged. "We've heard rumours of this since I returned from Paris in August. In three months, naught has come. Why now?"

"This time the Sealed Knot has organised with men across all of England," Susan said fervently. "Your husband must cross from Paris and lead the northern contingent. From the south and west, our men rally and fight. In Nottingham, York, Oxford, hundreds of men prepare to be awakened to the call of freedom and the return of the king."

"Are you sure?" Nan searched Susan's eyes for the truth. There was no mistaking her fervour, the intensity of her words.

Susan looked around the empty church and leaned closer to Nan.

"I am sure. I have been party to the planning for months," she said. "There is much to be done before now and February, when it is to take place. But most importantly, you must get word to Henry to be prepared to lead the north to victory."

"What sign should I give him that this is a real cause?"

Susan nodded. "Tell your husband that on my life I can guarantee I have heard the plans, witnessed the secret meetings. My brother has authorised me to liaise with you and those others who are consequential to the mission's success."

"And who leads this uprising?"

"Penruddock. Sir Thomas Penruddock, of here in Wiltshire."

A creak as the door opened and the first footsteps of the parishioners shuffling in for the Sunday service. Susan reached for her prayer book and settled back in the pew, her eyes fixed on the altar.

Nan's mind filled with the news, her heart thumping in excitement.

"The time has come," she mouthed. Edward's statue gazed impassively upon her. "We will prevail."

"I need to know exactly what you expect of me." After the sermon, Nan took Susan's arm and they strolled across Lydiard's parkland, two cousins partaking of exercise on the brisk November morning.

Susan did not turn but kept her eyes fixed on the woodlands. She spoke rapidly. "What you do best, Nan. Organisation. Communication. There are so many diverse groups coming together. We cannot afford to have any break in the chain."

"Leaders on the ground? Safe houses?" Nan's mind immediately flew to the practicalities. "Messengers to carry advance news or changes in plan?"

"Exactly." Susan turned to her, paused in their stroll. "My brother will move the king to The Hague in preparation for sailing once the uprising is complete. He needs to be assured there is a clear path to London."

"Who else knows within the family?"

"You are the first," replied Susan. "Except for Ned Villiers, of course. He's here in England now, working from inside the Sealed Knot."

"Who else needs to be informed?" Nan thought for a moment. "John and Luce are strategically positioned in Nottingham. They could certainly be a safe house."

Susan nodded. "We have a large group of two, three hundred men at Rutherford Abbey, just a few miles from Owthorpe. It would be good to know there is sanctuary close by."

Nan nodded. She would reach out to John, ensure his views had not changed.

"Where is Allen?" Susan's question interrupted her thoughts.

"Safe in Norfolk," replied Nan. "He spent the summer with me at Ditchley, but Cary warned me the sequestration committee had heard of his return, and I cannot risk them suspecting me of hiding Royalist sympathisers. I sent him to Feltwell, where his father had a manor. It has not been inhabited by our family for many years, so none will suspect him there. He will be well-concealed."

Susan pulled her cloak around her more tightly. The watery sun provided no warmth. "Have him on alert for the second wave. When Henry has raised the northern armies, he will need roads cleared down to London. Allen should join him in the Midlands to ensure open passage."

"This is really happening?" No wonder Sir Edward had instructed her to respond immediately if she heard from his sister. "How long has this been in the planning?"

"No matter. Suffice to say that this time we will be successful. Cromwell has no idea of our plans." Susan broke into a smile. "This is too wide a network, too large a campaign for him to have any idea of the extent of our organisation. By the spring, King Charles will be crowned in Westminster, and England's monarchy will be restored."

A movement caught Nan's eye as they turned and walked back towards the house. Walter and Johanna were waiting for them by the bowling green, their dogs scampering on the grass as their children played chase on the smooth lawns. A more peaceful, harmonious scene she could not imagine. Curiously, the prospect of Lydiard was no longer dull. It was safe, secure, a place that had resisted centuries of change. And Walter was the perfect custodian of its future.

"Not a word to Walter," hissed Susan. "He may be your brother, but he is not on our side."

A fear gripped Nan's heart, a tremble of anticipation that Susan's fervour was misled. Did men really want to upset England's peace? The old argument slept deep. Would she be the one to awaken men and lead them to war?

She shook her head, put her fears aside. Henry and the king counted on her level thinking to bring order to their plans. Susan's fervour might drive men forward. But Nan's caution would secure the plan.

23

Frances

"My father called this 'The Ship of the Fens.'" Allen paused as they crested a small incline. The fog blanketed across the land as far as Frances could see, silver waves mingling with grey rivers. And from nowhere, a cathedral tower sailing from the mist, floating above the land. "I was eight years old when we came to inspect Feltwell Manor before the tenants moved in."

"It is beautiful," she gasped. "And mysterious. How can it be real? Surely this is an illusion?"

Allen turned to her, shifting Isabella a little closer to him on his saddle. "The cathedral has stood for hundreds of years," he replied. "And in the recent wars, a timely surrender by the Royalists saved it from Cromwell's ruination."

"Are we travelling to see it?"

"No. Ely is Cromwell's town. We may be hiding in plain sight when we get to Feltwell, but to ride the street by his home would not be wise." Allen's face became serious. "How are you feeling? Will you be able to travel all day today? I think we are about twenty miles from our new home."

Frances smoothed her hand over her pregnant belly and smiled. "I feel wonderful," she said. "My time is yet two months away. Women feel their strongest in these weeks."

He nodded. "Tell me when you tire, my love. Let's push on to the manor so we arrive before dark." He turned his mount and, followed by the pack pony and in the rear, a guard provided by Nan, they made their way across the drovers' track. "Keep straight on the path," Allen called over his shoulder. "There are marshes on both sides, and a horse and rider can be lost in a blink of an eye if you veer sideways. We turn at the crossroads about ten miles hence."

As Allen led their horses into the fens, Frances's own emotions heightened. In truth, she had not been to this part of the country before, and she looked around her with interest at the activity across the marshes. Everywhere were the shapes of men digging and mules pulling carts piled high with soil. Fresh-cut ditches running in straight lines divided the land like a giant chequerboard. The track widened, and she urged her horse forward to ride side by side with Allen.

"What an endeavour," she marvelled. "For to drain these marshes is an enormous undertaking."

"Thousands and thousands of acres," confirmed Allen. "Cromwell knows the richness of the soil that lies beneath the water. His vision to create arable land from swamp is ambitious; but once completed, Anglia will feed all of England, and the famine years will never return."

"Is our land fit for farming too?" She knew not the conditions at Feltwell, and this landscape intrigued her, reminding her of the bustling manor farms of her Devon childhood. The endless Fenland skies arched overhead, and Frances caught her breath at the space and unique light shimmering from the pale blue heavens.

Allen caught her interest. "Yes, I believe so" he replied. "My father was always proud of the property, and although we never lived here, he invested in the farms surrounding the manor house. I am sure the land is good for crops, and I also have an idea to establish a falconry, for the terrain is perfect for training and breeding."

After years in cramped filthy Paris, imprisoned by stone and stagnant river, Anglia's winter wind gusting across the fens sharpened her senses and promised a tantalising freedom. Overhead in the wide skies, a peregrine hovered over the ditches, seeking the mice and rabbits dislodged by the digging.

"It seems you already have residents."

Allen gazed up. "And more to come. The king promised me the office of Master of the Hawks upon his return. I must have a mews ready for him."

"How will we afford this, Allen?" She did not want to pour cold water on his enthusiasm, but they had no money.

He grinned. "John is entering the venture with me. He wishes to invest, and what better place than with his brother-in-law? The wealth of the country is no longer just with the Villiers and their kind."

Frances tried to reconcile Allen's words. "So you will be in business with John, share our lives with him and spy on him too?"

And what happens when the Sealed Knot calls upon us, Allen?

"Not necessarily John," Allen replied. "But certainly the encounters he tells us of, and others around him who hold power in the Midlands. Nan informed me Penruddock's men are assembling near Owthorpe. I would find out what John knows, what the climate is in Nottingham for the king's return."

Frances took her eyes from the activity on the horizon. "Penruddock? Who is he? What do you mean? Is there an uprising planned?" She and Allen were alone. And this countryside so flat anyone approaching could be seen a long way off. "I thought Sir Edward's plan was to watch and wait, to wait for Cromwell's fall through his own misgovernance. Is there an uprising?

Allen glanced over his shoulder and back at her. "We hear from Susan Hyde that Penruddock is organising men across all of England. Hyde has finally agreed with the Action Party to move now, and not wait for Cromwell's factions to implode. Henry is leading a contingent from Paris. The Sealed Knot is sending out orders to all the safe houses to be prepared and to rise with him. On March 8, all across England, from the western counties to the northern moors, men will stand up for the king and overturn Cromwell for good."

Frances's heart pounded. Allen's words were said with brevity, and carelessly. "Are you involved, Allen? Will you leave me and our new baby to go and fight again?"

"This time, no," he replied. "I am part of the second wave, the men following Henry to London to open the roads and prepare the country for the king to reclaim the throne. This time I stay here with you and the children, and we will wait. Wait in our new home for the news that Henry has been successful and the king sails home."

And so it came. Hope lit a small ember in Frances's heart. Her baby would be born into peace, into a united England.

They fell into quiet, and by late afternoon Frances sighted a small copse of trees indicating habitation, and perhaps a mile beyond, the tower of church.

"I believe we have arrived." Allen glanced at Frances. He paused by an ivy-covered red-brick archway on the side of the track. "Here is our home. Here is Feltwell."

Through the archway, along a path tangled by briars and erupting in mole hills, squatted a grey building, its uneven tile roof sprouting moss. Splintered shutters hung awkwardly from broken hinges, and as they dismounted and stood at the edge of the path, a flock of crows rose from the skeletal bare trees, cawing hoarsely. They startled Isabella, who began to cry from exhaustion.

Allen took his sword and hacked at the brambles, slashing a way through to the front door. Frances followed him, holding Isabella by her hand and soothing her as they walked. The guard remained with the horses, wordlessly looking around him.

The house was a hovel. Allen looked back at Frances, his face white.

"I had no idea. The tenants must have left years ago."

She could have cried. "Did Nan not know when she advised us to hide here?"

Allen shook his head. "Nan knew only that the lease expired and the manor was vacant."

Close up, the evidence of neglect overwhelmed her. Frances laid her hand on the front door and pushed. The rotten wood gave way under her pressure and fell through into the house.

"We cannot stay here." Allen turned, his shoulders slumped. "I have brought us into a ruin. I know not where else we can go. We cannot return to Ditchley, and there is no safety at Owthorpe for us."

The despair in his voice broke her heart. Frances threaded her hand inside the hole in the door and felt for the latch. She tugged at the iron till it gave way, and with a heave of her shoulder she managed to shove the door open. A foul odour of mice assailed her, and choking back her breath, she walked into her home.

"We must stay here the night," she called over her shoulder. "For it grows dark, and we have nowhere else to go. Pick up Isabella and bring her in from the cold wind."

The room was empty save for a bench and table, sturdy enough if the woodworm had not invaded. The wattle-and-daub walls were cracked from the cold, and old rushes lay scattered on the floor, hosting God knew what vermin. Frances kicked them to one side, ignoring the scuttling sound as she did so, and crossed to the windows, relieved to see intact panes of glass in the frames. She pulled one open and pushed the shutter back. A fresh breeze carrying the scent of water filled the room. A green-gold light from the setting sun softened the damaged walls.

"This is not a ruin, Allen," she said. "But simply neglected, forgotten, lost to the war." She opened her arms wide and pulled her husband and daughter into her embrace. "Like all of us, it needs hope and love. Together, we'll make it home."

A silence fell between them. Outside, a fox yapped and was still.

"And yet . . ." Allen looked down at Frances, his expression serious.

"And yet Henry and Hyde plan war," finished Frances. "And men rise in the king's name, and you are commanded to spy on the king's behalf, and Nan will play both sides—"

He pulled her close to him again, his heart beating steadily beneath his linen shirt.

"That is for tomorrow," he replied. "Tonight, we are secure in this moment, our daughter is safe, and our child will be born into peace. For once, let us not worry what the future holds."

The plight of the manor house was clear by morning light, and within an hour of waking, Frances had sent Allen into Feltwell village to find out where they could obtain provisions, workmen to repair the immediate needs and a woman to help her clean. She also dispatched Nan's guard back to Ditchley with instructions to return immediately with a cart full of essential furnishings. By the time Allen returned, Frances had lugged the filthy rushes outside to a heap by an old midden pile, opened all the windows and doors and sent Isabella to picking the last of the autumn apples from the overgrown orchard. Content that the house was solid in its construction, and a victim of neglect rather than abandonment, Frances rested on the wall surrounding the well, cherishing the peace that flowed over her. Home.

Allen joined her, reaching for her hand and turning his face to the wintery sun. "The village is well-kept, and the people are friendly," he said. "My father was respected, and his reputation still stands."

"Is it wise to put about that we are here?" Frances asked. "We do not want to draw attention to ourselves."

"These fen villages are isolated and keep their secrets well," he replied. "I have no concerns we will bring danger to our doorstep. In a few days, the interest in our return will dwindle, and we can build our lives in safety and obscurity."

Across the overgrown garden, Isabella skipped through the orchard, her apron full of apples.

"It is a good home for our children." Frances smiled to see their daughter so carefree.

Allen nodded. "Nan arranged for us to call on Lord and Lady Heveningham next week. If you remember, they are relatives on our grandmother's side and maintain a good household not far from here. Lady Heveningham will be able to help you when your time comes." He caressed her stomach and pulled her close, and she relaxed into the warmth of his arms.

In the following days, Allen walked the entire manor and assessed the repairs needed. He worked hard himself, throwing off his coat and joining the labourers in restoring the manor house to a livable state while Frances swept and cleaned the inside, rejoicing in the strength she felt in being active in the last few weeks of her pregnancy. As soon as Nan's wagons returned with beds and furniture, so she filled the rooms and made the manor home. She saw few people and yet rejoiced in the holy silence of the fens and the endless heavens arching over their land. As the year turned, so Frances reflected that the simplicity of their life was the real healing between her and Allen.

She knew this time was borrowed, and soon they would be called to court, to serve the king when he returned. For return he would. But this respite would heal their wounds and restore the health of their marriage. And bring new life to their world.

Her pains came late upon a Sunday night in January, and with the advent of dawn, Lady Heveningham's midwife was summoned. She was of the old ways and kept Frances's chamber darkened, the shutters firmly closed. As the waves of pain arched her back and nature took over her body, Frances did not mind the darkness. And as she was helped to the birthing stool by the hearth, and the room reduced to the fire's flames and the pressure of the baby's head, she travelled with her child on its journey into the world. Her body knew what to do, and she rode each wave of pain with increasing urgency until she and her baby reached their destination. A final body-splitting pain and an overwhelming relief as the midwife reached and pulled the child from her. A sharp smack, a wail and an exclamation.

"A beautiful boy, Lady Apsley. A strong, hearty boy."

She lay back against the hard wood rails of the chair, and as the midwife swaddled the baby and placed him in her arms, the joy this child represented warmed her entire being.

My beautiful boy.

Our son.

Named for her family, to complete the circle.
Peter.

24

Luce

Colonel Hutchinson hath upon all occasions been ready to assist and protect the king's friends in any of their troubles and to employ all his interests to serve them.

Luce Hutchinson

Spring 1655

"We must be on alert." Dressed in his thick waterproofed outdoor jacket, John's usually polished boots were mud-spattered from his ride. The lanolin on the coarse wool reeked, but at least it kept him dry. "Remember when we used to sit in the castle at Nottingham? You would be writing in your notebooks, and I reading the dispatches, trying to predict when the Royalists would next strike."

"Those days are long gone." Luce wondered at his restlessness, for anxiety did not normally govern her husband. "What disturbs your peace, John?" Putting her pen down, she crossed the room to kiss him and still his anxious pacing.

He absently returned her caress and peered through the window. She followed his gaze and shivered. A hard rain beat down across the fields, spray dancing from the muddy furrows. The bare ash trees holding their clusters of crow's nests swayed like storm-tossed ship's masts in the March gales.

Weather not fit for man nor beast. She pitied anyone out today.

"What cause do you have for concern?" she repeated, for in recent weeks his rides had taken him wider afield than Owthorpe's boundaries. Although he made little of his discovery of Penruddock's group of Royalists and their cache of arms, she knew he had told Nan of the incident.

John turned back to her. "A messenger came from Nan late last night while you were sleeping."

Luce searched his face for a clue to his feelings, but his expression was blank. "And so? She has more advice for your art dealings? Or perhaps a recommendation for a new piece of commerce? Nan is never still in her pursuit of a business opportunity—"

"The messenger was riding on through to Allen," he interrupted. "She advises in cypher of a movement and warns to stay within our homes."

"A movement? Or an uprising?" A familiar powerful emotion coursed through her blood, the reaction when they were under siege in Nottingham's castle.

John's eyes searched through the blinding rain as if any moment he expected an armed troop to thunder across his peaceful fields. "An uprising."

"And Allen's role?" Dear God, not another war, not more battles in this beleaguered land, not more danger for her brother.

"The messenger carried him the same instructions. To wait until she sent more news."

Luce nodded. "He'll obey Nan. Not many others, but he will note Nan's words."

"I must go out again." John reached for his hat, which he had thrown on a chair, dripping wet. "I cannot stay inside the house and wait for news to come to me."

"Do not ride far, John. Do not think to leave our property." Defending the peaceful manor of Owthorpe was very different than guarding fortified Nottingham Castle.

He turned as he opened the door. "I will just ride as far as the inn on the Fosse Way. If there is movement, troops will use the direct thoroughfare to move quickly. The landlord will tell me if he has seen increased numbers of strangers."

"And I will gather the children and mother and be prepared to bar the doors and windows." Luce knew her mother would share the practical tasks of readying for defence. And activity would keep them occupied until more news arrived. She paused her step. "John, why did Nan write to us to warn us before the uprising began?"

John pulled on his gloves and strode across the hall. She hurried at his side to catch his words. "Because Henry is heading the insurrection. Even now he rides to Yorkshire, to Marston Moor, to lead men south and take London. Penruddock's men span out across the country, not just here. Our family is indisputably in the centre of this, Luce, and I know not what the outcome will be, nor who wins or loses."

The following days were as if preparing for the siege of Nottingham Castle all over again. Only this time Owthorpe Manor had no moat, no thick walls or secret escape tunnels. And their only defence was faithful servants and the men of the small village. No fighting force, no troops, no stores of gunpowder and arms. Just hunting guns, pitchforks and scythes.

John made the rounds to his strongest labourers and loyal villagers, ensuring all were close in case of need.

Worse, they could give no indication they knew of the happenings in the outside world, for to reveal their knowledge would be to disclose their secret message from Nan and compromise their family.

After a week of living on nerves alone, Luce and her mother could not stand another day inside. And when a late afternoon break came in the March storms sweeping across the valley, they pulled on their boots, wrapped up in their cloaks and headed out into the muddy bare garden. Luce's first thought was to walk towards the Fosse Way, to see for herself if anyone was on the road. Lost in her thoughts, she trudged along, her head down.

"Spring comes late this year," remarked Lucy as they made their way around the bowling green, where pools spread across the waterlogged soil. A flock of migrating geese had taken up residency and waded in the shallow water, pecking at invisible grubs. "Planting will be delayed if this rain continues."

"I feel the whole world is waiting." Luce swallowed the anxiety lodged in her chest since she'd heard of Nan's warning. "John rides out daily to the Fosse Way and beyond and spends hours looking for troop movements. There is such a silence, for not even Cromwell's men are riding past in their usual patrols."

"We can do nothing here," replied Lucy. "It is a woman's lot. And yet, when the time comes, we have the opportunity to influence events perhaps more than men."

"What do you mean?"

Lucy smiled. "Look how you supported John in his most difficult times, when decisions were elusive and fear froze action."

"You speak as if John had no power over his own thinking."

Her mother tucked her arm in Luce's, and they walked, heads down into the wind.

"John logics well and reaches his own conclusions." Her mother's voice was caught by the breeze. "But we know that sometimes his obstinacy gets in the way of clarity."

"Did you encounter the same with father?"

Lucy did not slow her pace. Although a rheum caused her mother pain, she still walked strongly. "His stubbornness was of a different kind," she replied. "His devotion to the king and Buckingham blinded him to their faults. And even in the last years of our life in the Tower, when he was so ill, he refused to speak of them with anything but a loyal heart."

"That's where Allen learned his beliefs," Luce mused. "And Nan."

"Nan and Allen were always in concert." Her mother stumbled, and Luce quickly steadied her. "They may not have spent much time together, but when they did, they were inseparable."

"Let's turn back now, Mother." Luce worried at how quickly her mother tired. She never tripped, usually so sure-footed in her beloved outdoors.

"A few steps more. The scent of spring on the wind makes me feel young again."

"You are always young," protested Luce. "Just yesterday I caught you sitting on the floor with your granddaughter, playing with her dolly as if you were five years old too. That is your special gift."

Lucy laughed and stopped. The wind had whipped colour into her cheeks, and although her face was lined, the wrinkles were smile lines around her eyes and mouth, and no frown marred her forehead. And still her blue eyes sparkled, although a rim of grey outlined her irises.

"Five minutes more, and then we'll turn—what's that?" She abruptly pointed to the distant bank of the Fosse Way. A lone figure in a long cloak stumbled down the steep slope, leading a limping horse. As they watched, the man reached the bottom of the incline and stopped, looking directly at them and the house at their backs. He pulled his hat down and lurched towards them.

"A traveller. And one who has come far, it appears," Lucy said. "He is alone. He cannot do us much harm, and his horse is in no fit state to gallop off."

"Should we raise the alarm?" Luce recalled John's warnings. "We cannot be sure he is not leading a whole troop behind him."

As they watched, the man wavered and appeared to lose his balance. The horse stopped, uncertain of its direction.

"He is no troop leader," Lucy replied firmly. "I fear he is wounded or ill. We shall do what we've always done at Owthorpe, and at Nottingham. Treat him as an injured man first, and a friend or enemy second."

Her mother was right. In all the years they'd defended the castle for Parliament, they never distinguished between nursing the king's men and their own. And today was no different.

"Let us help him these last few yards, then," replied Luce. "For at the rate he is travelling, he will collapse before he reaches the house."

They hurried forward as the man continued to meander towards them. His back was curved, as if only by studying the ground in front of him could he put one foot in front of the other. Only when they stopped in front of him did he lift his head.

"Henry," gasped Luce. "Oh God, Henry, what has happened to you?"

By the time John returned, Henry was slumped in the fireplace chair, wrapped in a thick fur mantle, clasping a large brandy, his feet bandaged and propped on a footstool. His trembling had reduced to the occasional shiver. He withdrew into himself, staring at the fire's blue heart.

Luce put her finger to her lips the moment John opened the door as Lucy looked up from dressing a cut on Henry's forehead.

"Henry?" whispered John, his eyes round with shock. "What is he doing here?"

"He has not said," replied Luce. They stood in the half darkness, for the March night had closed in again, and once more a gale whistled around the house. Henry started at a sudden clatter of hail on the window and subsided back into the chair again.

"When did he arrive? And where are his men?" John eased off his coat and hat and dropped them in Luce's arms.

"Late this afternoon. He came alone." She placed John's outer garments on a bench and drew her mouth close to John's ear. "Talk to him, if you can," she whispered. "We have to know what happened. And if we are in danger. I can get no word from him."

John nodded and sat in the chair across the fireplace. Henry barely acknowledged him. Luce followed, keeping in the shadows so she could hear but not distract him. Lucy dabbed the last of her salve on his head wound and joined her.

"Henry, my friend." John leaned forward and put his hand on Henry's. "I am so grateful God guided you to our home."

Henry moved his eyes from the fire to stare at John, as if he was just registering him for the first time.

"And certainly it is with God's grace that you sit here now, safe and warm, your wounds treated and secure with your family."

A tap at the door, and Luce swiftly went to retrieve the hot stew brought by a maid. She set it in front of Henry, and as soon as he smelled it, he leaned forward and hungrily spooned the broth into his mouth.

"It appears you have been on the road for a while," John observed. Henry ignored him and continued to wolf down the savoury stew. "Eat, my brother, eat and fill your belly. And then tell us what this means."

After scraping the bowl and tearing a hunk of bread from the loaf, Henry finally looked at John. And with a final gulp of his brandy, he began to talk.

"I arrived here in February," he said. "And at first all seemed on plan. True, we'd had a false start when the Wiltshire faction began early—"

"Penruddock?" John interrupted.

Henry nodded. "But we were told Fairfax was throwing his support behind our plans, and so I left London for Yorkshire. Before, the north has always held for the king."

John leaned forward. "And this time?"

Henry fell into silence. The wind rushed around the house, rattling the window catch and blowing smoke down the chimney.

"This time no more than two hundred men came to Marston Moor. The gates of York remained shut against us. I tried to rally them—" Henry's voice broke. "I tried to convince them more men would join us. Even from Nottingham, John, even from Rufford Abbey."

"The men I discovered and disbanded," John said under his breath.

"I sent Wagstaffe to the West Country to meet up with Penruddock. I disguised myself and came south to rally Royalists in the Midlands." He sank into quietness again. This time John did not prompt him.

Henry lay back in his chair and threw his head back to the ceiling. The shadows from the fire cut great grooves in his features, and his face appeared cadaverous, his eyes hollowed, his cheekbones razor sharp. Luce drew in her breath at the premonition of a death mask.

"They are all gone," he said. "Captured, tried and executed."

No one moved. Not a sound. Even the wind dropped; the rain paused.

"It's over." Henry took a deep, shuddering breath. "Cromwell will crush this insurrection with his entire army. We have no chance now. The cause is lost."

Luce never thought to hear those words from Henry, always so optimistic, so jovial, a man's man, full of laughter and jokes, a soldier and a leader.

She quietly knelt by his side so as not to disturb his poor bandaged feet.

"Where do you go now, Henry?" She hardly dared ask the question.

He started, as if seeing her for the first time. "I return to Paris, Luce, as quickly as possible. For I cannot stay here. Cromwell will triple his effort to arrest and execute me now."

Henry struggled to his feet.

John put a restraining hand on him. "You will rest and recover your strength first," he said firmly. "You cannot leave in this state, man, and no one will look for you here." He ignored Luce's shake of her head. Cromwell would look exactly to Owthorpe. Had he not threatened them with a list of their Royalist relatives?

"Rest here," John repeated. "And tomorrow, I will escort you with a fresh horse as far as the Nottinghamshire border."

Luce's eyes filled with tears at John's kindness, and yet she trembled at his words. Her mother walked over to stand by Henry and placed her hands on his shoulders.

"Is there anything we can tell Nan, Henry?" she asked gently.

He nodded and turned to Luce.

"Write her a letter for me, Luce, for I am hopeless with words," he said. "Use your beautiful poetry and your love for her. Tell her that her soldier adores her and will return one day. For the time being, he cannot risk bringing the hunt to Ditchley. She should kiss Johnny and tell him his father is proud of his boy."

Luce nodded. "Of course, Henry. Of course I will tell her."

He smiled, his scarred and weathered face softening in the dying firelight. "And tell her she must do whatever is within her power to show her loyalty to Parliament and protect her sons and Ditchley. Anything within her power. For her very survival depends on it."

25

Nan

Nan opened her fist and turned over the bride's lace in her palm. She examined the delicate fabric briefly and then closed her fingers over it again.

Do whatever you must do, Nan.

"Your father would be proud of you," she observed to Harry, lounging opposite her, his long limbs taking up most of the leg room in the carriage. What tricks time played. At twenty-two, her son neared the age of her first husband when he died. Today, Harry so resembled his father that her heart climbed into her throat with emotion. Time blurred between past and present, and she was the link between life and death.

Her boy leaned forward to glance from the window and sank back in his seat. "You promised this journey to Wiltshire would not be all business. Can I hunt tomorrow? This morning was perfect, had you not insisted I take a bath."

"No. You will have other duties, and ones I have little say in." She reached out and straightened his drop-lace collar, smoothing it over the blue silk jacket. "You know how important this is to me."

"What about me? Have you considered my life?" He pushed her hands away. "And please stop fiddling with my clothes. I am not a child."

The carriage lurched to a stop.

Nan took a deep breath. If she could just run, leave this all behind, ignore her duty, be as free as a girl again at Battersey and follow the river to her fate.

Do whatever you must do, Nan.

She nodded to her son. Harry unfolded his legs and reluctantly departed the coach. The door swung back on its hinge, clicking shut. A final moment to compose herself.

She edged back in her seat, where she could view those lining the path to the church door. In the darkness of the carriage, they could not see her.

John and Luce. Lucy, Walter, Johanna.

Johanna's father, Lord Oliver St.John.

Allen and Frances absent.

All summoned to witness this next clause in her contract with God.

And by the church entrance, eagerly waiting, the influential Danvers family, recently bereaved of the old lord. Thank God his untimely death a month before had done nothing to delay her arrangements.

Stalwart Parliamentarians all. God Almighty, the old lord had signed the king's death warrant with John. *Take that as a show of loyalty, Cromwell.* At least she'd convinced them of the need to read the old prayer book along with the newly ordered oath in the forthcoming service.

Combined, the Lee and Danvers holdings would straddle Wiltshire and Oxfordshire.

And their joint family power would halt the progress of Cromwell's thugs.

"Mother." The carriage door opened, and Harry held his hand out to help her alight.

"Walter says it is time we went inside."

She nodded.

Henry, you instructed me to do whatever I must to save myself and my family. To protect Ditchley, the children.

Nan drew in her breath and held it for a count of five, filling her lungs with fresh country air, and squared her shoulders. As she alighted, Luce caught her eye and pulled a small face of sympathy. Nan turned her head quickly, lest the sudden rush of emotion break through her reserve.

And at Harry's side she walked into the Danvers' family church.

And she gave away her son, her boy, her beloved eldest whose life she'd saved in Paris.

She gave him in marriage to this little chit, Ann Danvers, daughter of one of the most influential Parliamentarian families in the country.

There, my husband. It is but three months since I received your letter. Did I work swiftly enough to protect us all from the failed uprising? No one can question our loyalty to the Commonwealth with this marriage.

Or would Cromwell see through the scheme and continue his harassment?

The minister stood, dark-gowned, sombre like a crow in the sunlit church.

She handed her son over to God and Parliament and preserved the future of Ditchley.

Soothed by the hedges full of wild roses and the dusty scent of cow parsley lingering in the air, Nan furled the leather blinds on her coach when she reached the gates of Ditchley Park. She had left the wedding party as hastily as she could, pleading a need to return to her own estates to take care of urgent business. In truth, she could not tolerate the nest of Puritans one minute more. Nor Harry's reproachful look as he'd pledged fealty to his new bride.

She sighed with relief. Her view was of Lee land as far as she could see. From the fat cows cropping fresh spring grass to the recently shorn sheep, naked of their valuable fleeces, this year's yield promised most lucrative.

And free from Cromwell's grasp.

She'd secured Harry's future. Now to look to her own. The carriage trundled across the rolling parklands, through the deep woods marking the boundary of the gardens, and pulled into the deserted courtyard.

Frowning, she walked briskly to the house. Away for a week, and her people had disappeared. There was no excuse for laziness. She must summon them immediately, address the importance of maintaining discipline.

And yet something was amiss. When she demanded of her houseman the reason her staff were absent, he nodded wordlessly to the library.

The officer stood with books scattered on the floor around him, haphazard, spines broken and pages carelessly creased. His spare frame leaned towards the shelves as, with bony fingers, he prised another volume from her collection, leafed through it and dropped it to the ground with an exclamation.

"Sir!" In three steps, Nan reached his side. "Good God Almighty, who are you and what is your intent?"

He ignored her and continued rifling through her precious books, his thin nose pinched and red, his eyes squinting.

"Enough!" She snatched the book from his hand and stood between him and the bookcase. "Enough! Your name, sir?"

"Lady Wilmot, I presume?" He stepped delicately away from her and walked to where Henry's collection of French brandy stood on a silver tray. "The devil's brew, I see. Fitting, with a husband such as yours." With a flick of his wrist he tipped over a crystal decanter and observed as the contents gurgled to the floor.

He turned back to her. "My name, madam, is William Packer. Major General William Packer."

"Should I know you?" Nan stood the decanter upright and faced him.

Moving back to the shelves, he intentionally trod on a volume of Master Shakespeare's plays, rotating his boot to grind it into the floorboard. "There will come a time in this county I shall ban theatre completely. You will have no need of these or any other seditious literature I find on your shelves."

"And until that time comes, I am free to enjoy reading whatever I wish in the privacy of my home," she shot back. "And you, Major General Packer, have no authority to tell me otherwise. I shall inform General Cromwell of your rudeness."

"Oh I am sure he will be most happy to hear from you," replied Packer. "For he tells me since he can get no satisfaction from the sequestration committees, it is my personal mission to ensure you comply with all of Parliament's requests."

"I comply already," replied Nan. "And if you require further proof, simply ask my family, the Danvers, of my obedience."

"Ah, the Danvers," replied Packer. "Do permit me to offer my congratulations to you on your son's marriage. I am sure you thought such an arrangement would ensure your immunity."

"Immunity?" she asked guilelessly. "Surely, Major General, you know how pliable immunity is when the alternatives are so enticing?"

Packer looked at her sharply. "Let me make this very clear, Lady Wilmot. Your husband recently led yet another insurgence against the legal rule of this country. We believe your family helped him escape to France."

Nan bit the inside of her cheek.

"You are now under close observation. You may have befuddled the sequestration committees with your administrative mazes and helpless correspondence. You may have even thought securing a marriage with the Danvers would protect your son's considerable inheritance." He stepped forward. She refused to cringe. Refused to drop her eyes, although her heart was racing and her palms sweating. "But I am here now, and there will be no more confusion. Ditchley Park is under my jurisdiction, and within six months I promise it will be completely in my control."

How dare this intruder threaten her? She took a step forward, determined not to cower before him. "You will never have evidence to prove I am other than an honest woman who lives by the law of this land and wishes for nothing but a peaceful existence."

Major General Packer drew even closer, the sharp scent of fanaticism on his skin. "May your peace be eternal, Lady Wilmot," he whispered. "As I wish the same of your husband. I fancy he may find his rest earlier than you. Long and everlasting, which you and all your Royalist allies deserve."

Without even a cursory bow, he strode from the room.

When she was sure he had gone, she let herself sink to the floor, her legs trembling, her arms wrapped about her. She tasted the salt of her tears as she caressed her books and stacked them gently to a pile by her side. There she sat until the light faded and her nervous servant tapped on the door, ready to make up the fire.

Cromwell's wrath smote rapidly. Throughout the summer, rumours swirled of a crackdown on liberties, and by September Nan realized the worst had arrived upon them. Sitting with Honest Cary as he outlined the instructions, her horror grew at Cromwell's edict.

"He has introduced a new system of government." Cary pulled a parchment and quickly sketched a map of England. "The country is divided into twelve regions, each with a major general appointed to govern." He drew careful lines around Oxfordshire, Wiltshire, Norfolk, Nottinghamshire, Surrey, all the locations of her family's estates. "And all the governors will report directly to Cromwell."

Nan traced her finger on the boundaries. What were lines on a map when she had fences on land? Just men's fancies, for she held the power of her own boundaries. "And so? Why should this pretender king and his counterfeit nobles be of bother to me? They can play with their paper lines. I have England's dirt under my feet and barricades secure against encroachment."

Cary lifted worried eyes to hers.

"Lady Wilmot, this is not just a map," he said earnestly. "These governors are all military men—major generals. They are authorised to enforce any rule to suppress Royalists. And they raise their own militia to carry out their orders." He paused. "Major General William Packer is in charge of Oxfordshire."

She refused to let even Cary see her fear. "And so we will behave as model citizens." Nan's words were braver than her thoughts.

Oh God. Allen.

"What about the others?" she continued. "We are protected here at Ditchley, and Harry's marriage assures us the appearance of Parliamentary loyalty. What about those who live outside the protection of Parliament's allies?"

Cary met her glance directly. "Life will be extremely difficult for your cousin Allen. He will be compelled to post a bond to guarantee no sedition and imprisoned if that bond is forfeit."

Nan shuddered. Did anyone yet suspect Allen's involvement in the Sealed Knot?

Sedition.

"Known Royalists will be forced to pay a tax to fund the militia." Cary pulled the map towards him again. "And he will require permission to leave home and travel. Any movement will be fully monitored."

Nan was aghast. "This is full military rule," she said. "Has Cromwell gone mad? He cannot enforce this on good Englishmen."

Cary's face creased with sorrow. "There is more. He is shutting down all play houses, and horse racing and bear-baiting are abolished. All the old English pastimes are eradicated."

"So this upstart clod now intends to rule the morals of England as well as its finances?" Furious, Nan jumped to her feet and swept her hand across the table, scattering the map, tipping over the inkwell and dashing quills to the floor. "Over my dead body will I bend to his command." A red rage fuelled her words.

"My lady, this is dangerous talk." Cary picked up the paper with trembling hands. "I do not know how much I can protect you in these times."

Compassion washed over her as she observed his balding pate, his shoulders weighted with worry. This man had been so faithful to her for so many years. She must take care not to punish him as the messenger of Cromwell's dictates.

She knelt to gather the rest of the papers and stood the dripping inkwell upright.

"Honest Cary, I would never jeopardise your role in the sequestration committee. I know you come to deliver the news, not to enforce it. And I thank you, my friend, with all my heart." She put her hand on his arm. "Now return home to your wife and your hearth, and take comfort in the knowledge that you are my dearest, most loyal friend. And you serve Cromwell to the best of your own ability. I would not have you tied up in these matters. This is for Allen and John and me to sort."

Cary bowed and left Nan alone in the chamber.

She paused for a moment and then made her way to Elizabeth's portrait.

One foot on Ditchley, and the map of England spread beneath her, the old counties, the ancient boundaries of the kingdom, coloured and painted in glowing jewel-like tones. A stark contrast to Cary's black ink on yellow parchment.

The queen's face gazed upon her.

"He will never take England from us," Nan avowed. "I would rather die than give this devil his false boundaries."

26

Frances

Henry's failed uprising and fear of reprisals confined them to their home, and although they were isolated in Norfolk's fen lands, Frances and Allen waited with trepidation to be persecuted under a charge of rebellion. But throughout the endless bleak winter, no troop appeared, and although they were half out of their minds with boredom, they were safe. Nan had chosen their hiding place well. Finally, when spring arrived and Frances could no longer stand the confinement of their land, she and Allen ventured forth to a public gathering to celebrate May Day.

Gaily coloured silk ribbons rippled in the soft breeze, lifting from a fresh-cut pine maypole. Feltwell's village green thronged with parishioners, and as Frances strolled arm in arm with Allen through the May Day fair, her spirits lifted. Isabella caught the festive mood, and crowned in May blossoms, she dodged through the crowds. Even Peter, clutching Frances's hand and staggering in his first pair of shoes, shouted with joy at the juggler.

As they stood before the maypole, a gathering of Puritans across the green cast a cloud upon the afternoon. After locating Isabella happily dancing with other girls of the village, Frances took Allen's arm and led him towards the dour group of men.

"Why are you approaching them?" Allen hissed under his breath. "There is no good reason for you to engage with Hezekiah Haynes."

Frances smiled. "He comes from Essex, not far from my cousins. I thought perhaps I could reach out to him, find a common ground. We must look for ways to survive the rule of the major generals, and he directly carries out their commands."

Allen looked at her suspiciously. "You mean you want to find out more about him to send to Nan and Susan Hyde. I don't have to acknowledge him, nor tolerate the major generals. I will leave you to pay your compliments. I cannot abide his Puritan leanings." Allen detached his arm and, taking Peter, returned to the maypole. Frances shrugged, pulled her shawl across her chest and walked across the flattened ground to where the man stood.

"Major Haynes." She stood before him. "My good wishes to you on this beautiful day."

He bowed slightly, his long dark hair brushing the lace collar of his black suit. In truth, he dressed plainly but expensively. There was money behind him. "Madam . . . ?"

Frances dipped a curtsey. "Apsley. My maiden name is Petre. My family hails from Essex too. Ingatestone, not far from your home, Major Haynes." She smoothed her skirts demurely, kept her eyes lowered. "Do you travel home often? I am sure you must be most busy with your position."

"Petre." His voice was hostile. "Recent recusants."

"I come from the Devon branch," she said quickly. "We share a common grandsire."

"That is fortunate. I have no tolerance for Catholics, even those claiming to have renounced their idolatry." His black eyes bore into her, and she regretted her move. A shadow cast upon the day.

"Old history in these times, sir," she said.

"And yet memories are long." He gestured to the soldiers standing around him. "Go now. Follow my orders."

He brushed past Frances, pausing only to grab her elbow. She took a step back, surprised at his intimacy. "I intend to eradicate all such memories," he said. "Do attend and learn, Mistress Apsley. You may find this a useful lesson."

Before she could say more, the soldiers pushed through the villagers and approached the maypole. She followed, her heart pounding as Allen quickly gathered Isabella to his side and picked up Peter. Moments later, the closest two soldiers swung their axes, hacking deep blows into the pine, shocking the villagers into silence.

As the maypole teetered and crashed to the ground, ribbons knotted and soiled, Haynes raised his fist to heaven.

"And so endeth your wickedness," he shouted. "Go home. Pray to God. And be thankful I have saved you from certain hell and damnation."

"Nan will still not leave Ditchley." Frances warmed the letter over the candle, moving it slowly across the flame as the hidden words emerged between the lines. "With Henry's role in Penruddock's uprising, she fears they will finally sequester the estate and evict her." She looked up at Allen, sorting a bag of jesses, bells, hoods and leather straps at the kitchen table. "She also says Cromwell can go to the devil."

Allen chuckled and continued working. In the eighteen months since they had moved to Feltwell, he had established the mews with John's investment and did not appear concerned at the restricted life he now led.

"My cousin is a fighter, for sure," he replied. "Henry warned her of the consequences of Penruddock's venture. None of us can leave our homes, for every movement is watched now."

"She plays a dangerous game. Henry pushed Cromwell into establishing martial law. And forced the Sealed Knot to go deep underground." Frances turned the letter sideways to read the hidden lines between the ink. "Your cousin Ned Villiers is freed from the Tower, desperate for intelligence. Even Susan Hyde is unable to get news through from the Wiltshire network."

Frances lay down the letter and reached for Allen's hand. "Do you think this purgatory will ever end?"

Her hand stilled his work, and he looked up. "Purgatory? Strong Catholic sentiments, sweetheart. You should take care not to use that term outside of these walls."

"I would not be that foolish, Allen." Yet the old faith whispered in her heart, and she leaned upon the comforting prayers before she drifted to sleep at night. "But this limbo is truly exhausting."

"And so what does Nan expect next?" He rubbed hard on the leather, not looking up. She was used to his skittering away from such talk of faith, for had not his own been lost in the bloody battlegrounds of the wars?

Frances held the letter to the candle again, searching for any other cypher or hidden instructions. "She does not say. I have never seen her speak so vaguely. I will write we are still well hidden here in Feltwell. News passes us by, for we are just farmers now. Court intrigue is in our distant past."

Allen pulled her towards him. His rough linen shirt and breeches were those of a countryman, and he smelled deliciously of leather and the outdoors. Frances told herself that she should enjoy Norfolk's solitude. But she could not shake the constant anxiety from the restrictions imposed upon them. She was as one of Allen's falcons, hooded and jessed, when she longed to soar free in the wide Norfolk skies.

Ned Villiers appeared in October, when St. Stephen's little summer illuminated the fens and transformed the murky ditches into ribbons of gold. Frances was already abroad, for she loved the early morning promise and the empty land's illusion of freedom. As the sun rose in a great bronze orb, she turned to head back to the house and halted at the sight of the man hidden in the shadows of the brick gatepost. A traveller heralded change.

He stepped forward into the dawn. Behind him, a horse cropped the dew-drenched grass.

"Lady Apsley."

She nodded, cautious, holding her dogs to heel.

"Allen's cousin Ned Villiers." He reminded her of Henry Wilmot, restless and cautious. "Barbara St.John's son."

"And Anne Villiers's sister." Bitterness infused her words. "I know of you. You ride far out of your way to see us. We are not in any position to share news of value. Why would you visit us, when Allen tells me of the contempt between his mother and yours?"

And me and your sister.

She rested her hands on the dogs' heads. One word from her and they would attack.

He bowed his head politely. "That is old history. My brother William and I made our peace with Allen a long time ago." Ned gestured to the house. "Nan warned you would be suspicious. I am simply bringing you news, piecing together information."

Across the empty landscape, nothing stirred. Yet soon workers would fill the fields and spies would be about again.

"Come inside. Strangers in these parts raise suspicion."

He moved swiftly then, catching the reins of his horse and leading the creature quickly into the stable yard. Ned's movements were efficient, and although he had the voice of a gentleman, his care of his horse proved his solitary life. After walking the creature into an empty stall and removing the saddle and bridle, he pulled an armful of hay and dropped it into the manger, filling the trough with freshly pumped water.

"You treat your animal well," Frances remarked.

"He has carried me far," replied Ned. "And we share a long road ahead."

"Come," she said. "Come inside. Allen will be glad to see you."

She led the way into her home, and the founder of the Sealed Knot followed her. The network lived.

"I cannot say this any other way." Ned embraced Allen roughly and threw himself into the chair by the empty fireplace. "Susan Hyde is dead."

"She was ill? I had not heard." Allen sat at the table to face him, his expression concerned.

"Tortured. And died from fear."

Ned's words shattered the morning. Frances doubled over, her reaction visceral.

"God Almighty, what happened?" Allen leaned forward, his hands clasped. "Does Nan know? Is she safe?"

Ned rubbed his eyes and nodded. "Nan is safe. But must not move from the protection of Ditchley." He took a deep breath and turned to Frances. "You may not want to hear this."

Frances shook her head. "I must hear. Sir Edward is a dear friend."

Allen rose abruptly, returning with a black leather pitcher of ale and three tankards. He set them down on the table and poured the ale until it foamed. Ned drank thirstily.

"It happened at her home in Grittenham—"

"My God. Just miles from Lydiard. Is Walter involved? Did he order her apprehension?" Allen asked fiercely.

"No. Neither he nor Johanna are implicated. Cromwell's men broke into her chamber. They searched the house, her room, her person, and found papers. They deprived her of sleep and food and kept her isolated." He paused, rubbed his eyes. "And then forced themselves upon her until she lost her mind."

Vomit scorched Frances's throat. "Oh, Mary Mother of God," she whispered. "This poor woman. This poor, poor woman."

"What next?" demanded Allen.

Ned filled his tankard again. "They took her to Lambeth. That dark house where so many others have been tortured. She died a week later, without ever speaking."

They sat in silence, then, for what seemed like hours.

Eventually, Frances propped open the kitchen door. A breeze from across the fens drifted into the warm room, and her dogs stretched out upon the cool stone floors, their paws occasionally twitching as they chased rabbits in their dreams. Upstairs the children awoke and were singing a nonsense rhyme that involved counting and laughter. This could be any day in any farmhouse kitchen across the land.

Susan Hyde is dead.

"Susan was essential to the cause," Allen said slowly. "I wondered why Nan wrote she wasn't receiving letters from her anymore. We are dismembered with this news. The network is compromised." He strode to the door, where he leaned against the frame and gazed out over the fens, his back taut. After a few minutes, he turned back to them. "What can I do, Ned? Where can I go? Put me to use. For Susan must not have died in vain."

They went through the motions of the day, Allen and Ned in the parlour, Frances with the children. And by the time evening fell, the shock had settled and action had taken the place of captivity. She put Isabella and Peter to bed early, promising adventures the next day in return for obedient sleep. As darkness crept over the land and filled the kitchen with its security, Frances lit lanterns and the men returned to eat.

Allen pushed back his bowl. "Tell us more of the last years, Ned. I would have Frances hear too. We have been isolated here at Feltwell and know little of what has been happening."

Ned smiled. "Being imprisoned in the Tower hardly kept me in the centre of things. But you'd be surprised at who is secretly loyal to the king while posing as Cromwell's guard."

"Start from Penruddock's uprising," Allen pressed. "For why did this fail?"

"King Charles ordered Henry Wilmot to England to settle the conflict between members of the Sealed Knot and the Action Party and unify the resistance efforts. Alas, neither talked to each other, nor to the other factions that exist now. The whole network is a misalliance of men. And although Henry escaped, I was not so fortunate." Ned flexed his back, a gesture of weariness that spoke much. "A year in the Tower for me. And not in your mother's hospitable house." He smiled at Allen.

"You remember our home there?" Allen's face brightened. "Those were lighter times, when your father had the rooms in the Royal Mint. Luce and I enjoyed when you and William visited from Battersey."

"Except when my mother accompanied us." Ned's face was rueful.

Frances recalled the old family stories told by Luce. "Was the quarrel so bad? Allen's mother never speaks of her sister Barbara. And circumstances since the war have prevented us to speak of this again."

Ned grimaced. "On two counts," he replied. "Not only did they fall out, I married the daughter of Theo Howard. Stories of his love for both sisters and their grave jealousy still scar our family."

Frances was anxious to hear of the outside world. But she would be patient. "And the two sisters, your mothers, still do not speak?"

"No, never. Even though their feud died with Theo a lifetime ago," Allen remarked. "My mother avoids London and is happiest in John and Luce's garden, planting her medicinals and playing with her grandchildren."

Ned took a tankard and raised it to toast Allen and Frances.

"You are fortunate. Mine still pursues preferment and spends her time filling her granddaughter's head with stories of the old king's court and the entertainments and masques she enjoyed."

"Aunt Barbara spends time with William's daughter?" Allen drank from his own tankard and stared out of the window as if seeing something from long ago. "I remember her christening, at Whitehall, with Prince Charles standing for her. None of us quite knew how to behave around a baby. And she grabbed his hand and wouldn't release it."

Ned snorted into his ale. "Not much has changed," he said, his voice muffled as he drank another draught. "Barbary's sixteen now, and every man within five miles of Westminster is pursuing my niece's hand. It's already rumoured that the Earl of Chesterfield is enamoured of her."

Allen raised an eyebrow. "As ambitious as always, you Villiers," he teased. "She sets her sights high."

"Which brings me to your brother-in-law, Hutchinson." Before Frances's eyes, Ned turned from a casually gossiping cousin to an agent seeking information.

Allen sat up in surprise. "John? He is not ambitious."

"And yet he spirited Henry Wilmot safely on his way out of England after the uprising. He surely knew his action would find favour with the exiled king."

"He's a fair man, and Luce is Nan's dearest friend and beloved cousin. He acted from loyalty, not ambition," Allen replied. "Why do you ask?"

Ned glanced at Frances.

"You can trust my wife, Ned. She has Hyde's confidence and Nan's training. All of the intelligence coming from Nan to Hyde in Paris was transmitted through Frances."

"My apologies." He flashed a quick smile at Frances, sparkling with the Villiers charm. "I am not used to trustworthy women."

She nodded.

Not surprising, given your sister and mother.

"Go on, Ned. What business would you have with John and Luce?"

"We are hearing rebellion by the people against the rule of the major generals. Dissention in Parliament. Sooner or later Cromwell will realize he cannot maintain martial law, nor impose such dire moral restrictions on the good people of England."

"And what would John have to do with this?"

"Nan reveals Johanna's father, Oliver St.John, is generating support for a new way of governing. He has always been a moderate, has looked for diplomatic solutions."

Allen refilled their tankards and pushed up his sleeves. He pulled a set of falcon jesses towards him and fiddled with the buckles. "Go on."

"We hear Sir Oliver proposes a new constitution. One to return power to Parliament."

"And where do John and Luce fit in this?"

Ned shifted in his seat. "Nan cannot openly leave Ditchley, and even Johanna and Walter are reluctant to visit for fear Henry's legacy will taint them. They stay at Lydiard, as Sir Oliver advised. But John and Luce can travel and entertain Parliament's men. They can discover more."

"And what is so interesting about revising the constitution?" Allen pulled another set of jesses towards him and smoothed the leather.

"Lord St.John's petition has a clause that will turn the major generals out of power." Ned's voice tightened. "He recommends the re-establishment of a second house in Parliament. And recognises a single head of state with defined powers based on precedent is the best constitution for England. And the single head of state would still be named king."

Frances clasped Allen's hand to still his restless energy.

"And so he returns," she said. "Legally, with no bloodshed, welcomed by all England."

Allen pushed the jesses away, the bells tinkling loud in the quiet kitchen. "And why would Cromwell accept this? He would rather tear the guts out of England than turn power back to the Stuart. I think you are deluded, Ned."

"That's what we need to find out from John." Ned leaned forward. "He'll tell you what Cromwell is thinking, not me."

"And what do you suggest I do? Invite them both for dinner?" Allen's wry tone made Frances laugh. Their conversation was so tense she could not help herself.

Ned smiled in return. "No. But John is commanded to return to Whitehall. In the coming months, he can check Parliament's pulse, discover Cromwell's intent. And gauge how loyal his puppets really are."

27

Luce

Colonel Hutchinson being at that time at London, by chance came to know all the plot. Certain of the conspirators coming into a place where he was and became perfectly acquainted with the whole design; and weighing it, and judging that Lambert would be the worse tyrant of the two, he determined to prevent it, without being the author of any man's punishment.

Luce Hutchinson
Winter 1657

The command came, direct from Lord Protector Cromwell himself.

"Return to Whitehall, John, for I would seek your counsel. I am surrounded by men who do not honour our vision, nor obey God's word."

Within a week of leaving Owthorpe and opening their town house in Holborn, John arrived home fraught. As Luce sat with him at dinner, she coaxed his worry from him.

"This council is a serpent's nest of conflict." He threw down his linen and pushed his chair back. "Today I overheard men talking of a scheme to assassinate Cromwell."

"What?" Luce gasped. "Where were you? How did you overhear?"

John shook his head. "I was in an alcove, waiting to enter the Painted Chamber. I did not realise I was concealed from those who were walking by."

"What did you hear?"

"A stupid, simple plan." John drained his wine. "If it wasn't so stupid, I would think nothing more."

"Tell me."

"A shove, a push, an open window. And in a blink, Cromwell would be in the river below."

"Let them do it." Luce clapped her hand over her mouth.

John ran his fingers through his hair. "I cannot, Luce. And your words do not help my conscience."

"And yet you have not reported them? Do you know who spoke?"

He nodded.

"I cannot condone an assassination." He paused. "And besides, they plot to replace Cromwell with John Lambert. He challenges the very core of our Commonwealth. He would undo all that we have accomplished. If there is a man I despise more than Cromwell, it is he."

In the quiet of the chamber, the ambitions of Nan and Allen haunted her.

"You hold a powerful piece of information," she said quietly. "One to change the course of history. For the second time in your life, you possess extraordinary power, John."

He lifted haunted eyes to her. "You think I haven't thought of that?" Standing, he walked to the window and gazed out upon the dark street. "If I say nothing, Cromwell's rule could be over, and Lambert will seize power, driving us into the greatest rift of all. If I say something, I will prolong our family's suffering."

She came behind him then, sliding her arms around his waist, resting her cheek against his back. "You must act with your conscience, John. And think of how life will be each way. Perhaps the devil you know is better than the devil you don't."

In the chill February night, Whitehall's Banqueting House stood swathed in fog drifting dank from the river. From the landing pier, the white stone beckoned, and as she and John walked up the incline, Luce drew her black velvet cloak closer against the damp. Translucent haloes wavered around the torches flaring orange, weak beacons in the darkness. The street teemed with Parliament's men and their wives, and the clatter and swish of boots and skirts on the cobbles struck loud and sank mist-muffled. She gripped John's arm to avoid slipping, for her old court shoes were thin-soled and the bumps and cracks of the pavement slick.

A state dinner. How peculiar to be returning to the scene of so many courtly masques of her youth. She glanced sideways at John to see if he too felt the echoes of the past urging them forward. Under his shadowed hat brim, he bore a firm expression. After discussing the situation with Walter, he appeared willing to attend Cromwell's banquet, steered by Allen's letter encouraging a firsthand account of the event. The closer they drew to

Whitehall, the quieter he became. Yet to refuse to attend as Nottingham's representative would be a grievous mistake. Cromwell himself commanded his presence officially. John's absence could not be excused.

They passed the site of the execution, no trace remaining of the day. And now Cromwell claimed the palaces for his own, refurnished them with the king's treasures, raised his farming cronies to courtiers and married his baseborn daughters to the highest lords in the land.

Nothing changed. Was all for naught?

Luce turned as John said something, dragging her mind away from the ever-circling questions.

"Do not frown, so, Luce," he insisted. "We are here at the Lord Protector's invite. His intent is to show the foreign ambassadors he has the support of his countrymen and demonstrate the true wealth and stability of his Protectorate." John beckoned to a servant and helped Luce off with her cloak. "Play along," he whispered. "If not for your sake, for mine and your family's."

She wondered at his words, for anxiety's edge sharpened his tone, but the chance to question him passed. The crush of arriving guests swept them through the doors and up the staircase, launching them into the hall on a tide of perfume and excited whispering.

The grand room appeared the same since last she walked through on the morning of the king's execution. Then, she'd stood with the other wives in the upper gallery, looking down upon their husbands as one by one they entered, wiping the ink from their fingers and the deed from their consciences. The king had made his procession, the crowd had wept and fallen silent, and the commissioners had completed their business.

This evening, illuminated by a thousand candles, King James remained on his painted ascension to heaven across Rubens's ceiling, and the colourful finery of the women recalled the most extravagant of Henrietta Maria's masques.

Nothing changed.

"John, this is all wrong." She drew him to the side, away from the flow of people and the cacophony of Cromwell's own musicians. "What aspirations does Cromwell have? What is he thinking?"

John looked around at the gathered members of Parliament, shoulder to shoulder with titled nobles, and she followed his gaze. There were his old colleagues from the commission, and many new faces, people she did not recognise. None came to pay their respects to John and directly snubbed them by averted glances and whispering behind fans.

She longed to be home. "What is he thinking?" she repeated. "And why are we truly attending tonight?"

"The military bill was struck down," he replied. "The rule of the major generals is over. Never again will martial law prevail over our citizens."

A great surge of relief swept over her. "Cromwell permitted those tyrants to rule without law or justice. Surely this is a step towards normality."

From the dais at the end of the hall came a swelling of applause and cheers as Cromwell entered, his plain wife dressed in scarlet velvet and his daughters tricked out in lace and silk. The finery did not conceal their country manners and posturing. And this sycophant crowd encouraged their aping of the old courtly ways.

John continued talking, his eyes searching the crowded room, following the procession of Cromwell. "The end of the major generals is significant. His grand experiment proved to Cromwell our citizens will not be governed by a militia. And now he has set his sights on uniting the country a different way."

"But why this banquet now? Why all the trappings of monarchy?"

John bowed as Cromwell walked by, and Luce dropped a curtsey. Not the deep court obeisance she had learned at Richmond Palace. But a dip, the smallest possible acknowledgment.

"I told Colonel Fleetwood of the assassination plot. He passed the information along to Cromwell."

"And so this is to celebrate his escape?" The hall filled with those who claimed loyalty once to the king, nobles who had not fleed to the Continent, but married into Parliament's families, bringing titles and land to the basest of men.

"Yes, and more. He is the target of many assassination plots. Sir Oliver St.John and the Parliament are concerned for the ongoing security of the country."

Another group approached. John bowed again, this time to the Venetian ambassador. The court had reformed as if never fractured.

"England needs to resume its rightful place as a world leader. And so Parliament has offered Cromwell the crown of England. We believe tonight he will announce his acceptance." John's face was white, his jaw clenched.

"Oh no, no. Why? That was exactly what he fought against," Luce whispered vehemently. The crowd of people pressed closer, and God only knew who listened.

"He fought against the divine right of kings. Not the election of a monarch." John smiled grimly. "If anything happens to him, a monarchy will provide a transfer of power immediately to his sons, securing economic stability." He pulled her back farther into the shadows under the overhanging gallery. "And with King Oliver on the throne here in England, there is no kingdom for the Stuart to claim. He is eternally banished."

"His sons? A succession? Never were there a more debauched pair of Cavaliers than Henry and Richard Cromwell. One a rake, the other a country clodpoll." Luce's words flew from her mouth without guard or thought.

John looked over her shoulder, and his eyes hardened. "Turn," he commanded swiftly.

Luce's response froze on her lips as she twisted to face Cromwell and his wife.

"Colonel Hutchinson," he greeted them. "And Mrs. Hutchinson." Cromwell's red face and thick neck bulged over his tight white linen collar. Yellow britches ballooned over lace stockings, and square-cut leather shoes made his feet enormous. "How kind of you to travel all the way from Owthorpe."

John bowed his head, and Luce trembled inwardly at the tension in her husband. "And how is country life, John?" Cromwell continued. "Does your hide allow you the obscurity you desired?"

"Yes, sir."

"And your brother, Mrs. Hutchinson. How are Sir Allen and Dame Frances enjoying their farm in Norfolk?"

Luce swallowed, her throat dry. "Well enough, sir," she replied. "They are content in their life and raising their children."

Cromwell nodded. "Well enough, well enough." He repeated her words back at her. His eyes narrowed, and he leaned forward. Luce resisted the instinct to flinch. "But not your cousin Wilmot, I think. She has no satisfaction with a quiet life in the country. She continues to plague my officers and even wrote to me directly with some cock-and-bull story of revisionism to the Lee family that neither I nor my council can make head or tale of."

Luce stifled a smile, for she knew Nan's strategy well. "She cares deeply for her home and her boys' inheritance, my lord. I think she does what any mother would do to protect her young."

"More like any she-wolf to protect her pups," he retorted. "The Earl of Rochester may be the one wearing the armour, but she is the warrior in that marriage." Cromwell laughed loudly at his own joke, his abrupt shift in mood as unsettling as always. He glowered, running a stubby finger around his tight collar.

"I have much to thank you for, John," he continued. "Fleetwood told me of your discovery of the latest plot. We look kindly upon you for your protection of our well-being."

We? Our? He even speaks a king's language now.

Cromwell shifted from foot to foot, clearly uncomfortable. "They say I make an announcement tonight," he muttered. Sweat stood out on his forehead under his thinning hair. "But such an important decree must have the weight of Parliament behind it. And, more than anything, the blessing of God Almighty. I do not seek to rebuild Jericho, and this is what they expect me to do. Your conscience, John, is one that I look to for guidance in keeping to the Lord's ways." Cromwell's face cleared, and he threw back his head and laughed. "Tonight is for entertainment, for music and feasting." Truly, this man's temperament shifted as the wind. "And when you return to your manor, John, ensure the people know I want what is best for them. The major generals overstepped their command."

Luce bit back a remark, for had he not been the one who established the military rule, put the major generals in power and confined her brother to his home under the threat of financial ruin? Her contempt for Cromwell's artful words threatened to choke her. John squeezed her hand.

"I am happy to return to Owthorpe," replied John. "For in England's heartland lies men's dreams."

"And why do you not come back to serve me here at Whitehall, John? Your honesty is missed among these deceitful men."

John paused for one heartbeat.

Do not declare your thoughts too plainly, John. Do not let your honesty be your downfall.

He cleared his throat. "Since you broke Parliament, tyranny rules the land. And I fear we return to the old ways of bondage and suppression of men's rights, regardless of their party. I cannot before God belong to a

Parliament that strips men's freedoms and parallels life under the old king. There must be fair representation of the people's will, not just the Protector's orders."

Cromwell's face froze. The musicians broke into a Spanish galliard, and at his side, his plump wife adjusted her scarlet gown and tapped her foot impatiently. Luce searched her mind to come up with the right words to defuse John's unguarded reproach.

"My lord, what my husband means is—"

"My enemy Lambert put these grievances in place. I have dismissed him, along with the major generals." The Lord Protector nodded his head slowly, sagely, disavowing responsibility, his eyes now wide and innocent. He held out his arm to his wife.

Truly, this man is like a child, one minute a tantrum, the next all smiles.

"England needs truthful men back in council, John. I shall be calling on you in the coming months as I restore a sober and honest Parliament. Your absence is over. I desire guidance from godly men such as you. Return when I command. Do not refuse." He abruptly embraced John, kissed Luce's hand and then disappeared.

As they digested his words and deed, others around tried to catch Luce's eye and wink while others openly nodded and smiled at her. John Hutchinson was back in favour.

The musicians struck up a processional, and servants in yellow livery carried plate after plate of roasted meats head-high on golden dishes. Luce could tell no difference between now and the days of the Stuart court, when the king and queen presided over their subjects and the royal mood determined failure or favour.

Three days later, Cromwell announced to Parliament his refusal of the crown, stating God's personal message to him to rebuild Jericho would be the antithesis of the spirit of the rebellion. His words echoed those of the banquet, almost as if he had been rehearsing the points of speech with John to test the veracity of his words.

No matter. So a king by any other name was his compromise, and one still allowing the succession of his son, Luce could only voice her frustration with John. Her anger did not make for peace; for weeks, her husband was torn between loyalty to his constituents and his desire to turn his back on

Cromwell and leave Parliament forever. And when he chose to resign, chose the anonymity of Owthorpe once more, it felt like her own personal exile.

Throughout the summer, she fluctuated from scribbling furiously in her notebooks to striding across Owthorpe's pastures, returning dusty and exhausted only to write again.

Finally, her mother suggested a visit to Allen and Frances, and an invitation to Nan to accompany them.

"With the end of the restrictions, it is safer to travel." Lucy sat at the writing desk, reading a letter and simultaneously drawing pen and paper towards her. "We have yet to meet their new baby. We shall travel to Feltwell and enjoy a change of scene." Her head bowed, now more grey than brown, she quickly wrote a note, her penmanship no less for the arthritis gnarling her fingers.

"You leave me little choice," responded Luce.

"You leave *me* little choice," retorted her mother. "You have been out of sorts all summer. And if you want peace at home and in your marriage, absence will make you fonder of both."

With grudging acceptance, Luce packed up her notebooks and writing chest and permitted her mother to sort gowns and house gifts.

Within a week, accompanied by two servants, they were bound for Feltwell, and as the land flattened and the sky broadened, the magnitude of the landscape soothed her. The uniformity of the scenery created a hypnotic state, and between the swaying of her horse's gait and the unending fields of crops stamped in squares across the land, Luce's agitation subsided.

"You always know what is best for me," she called ahead to her mother, riding her own chestnut mare. Lucy kept a good pace, and on horseback she appeared as upright and graceful as Luce ever remembered her.

"That's what a mother is for," Lucy laughed. "Remember how many times we escaped Leventhorpe Francke and took the horses out to ride or the cart to market? The fresh air is always an antidote to your bookish ways, Luce."

Luce smiled wryly at her. "Your husband was a cruel man who kept us under his yoke. John is not a bit like that."

"No," agreed Lucy. "No, he is not. But habits die hard, and when I see you working without pause at your writing, and your eyes are blue-shadowed and your brow furrowed, I know the same anxiety has its mantle over you as it did in those days. And then it's time to break your habits."

A lump came to Luce's throat at her mother's wisdom, and she quickly changed the subject to avoid any further introspection. "I wonder how Frances is enjoying her life in the country. She must find it very tame after Paris."

Lucy turned back and urged her horse forward faster. "If I know Frances, she has been keeping busy with her children and Allen. I have no concerns she yearns for change."

Presently, a copse of trees indicated a settlement, and as they drew closer, a whitewashed farmhouse emerged with a row of outbuildings and stables. Surrounding it were neat fields and a healthy orchard. And leaning against the gatepost, his shirtsleeves rolled up to reveal brown forearms, stood Allen.

Luce's heart soared at the sight of her brother.

The following day Nan arrived, and the women gathered in Frances's parlour, dressed in their loose country gowns. Frances produced the most delicious foods, and between the elderflower cordial, blackberry tarts and the first crisp apples, her simple country style provided an antidote to their anxieties.

"My new granddaughter is beautiful." Lucy rocked the little girl in her arms. "And such a sweet name. Franny."

Frances smiled. "Allen pledged to me once that if we were to have another girl, we would call her Frances. To remind us of our time in Paris, the hardships and joy we encountered in exile."

"Now we are all of the country rather than city," observed Lucy. "My youth at Lydiard was the happiest. Although the Tower formed your early years, Luce, time at Owthorpe has convinced you of the healing airs of the gardens and rivers."

"I thought Lydiard the most boring place on earth," Nan laughed. "I could not wait to escape to Battersey with the excitement of London on my doorstep. But now, try to take me away from Ditchley Park and I would surely die. I never want to return to Whitehall and all its pretence again."

Luce smiled. "I found it shocking to see Cromwell aping the monarchy in the Banqueting House," she replied. "He has installed himself in the king's rooms as if crowned, his musicians rivalled those of Charles and Henrietta's, and I have heard that he has even more art in his collection than the king ever did."

Frances shook her head. "What next, Luce? Do you think he will be crowned?"

"No, I don't." She paused, measuring her words. Here, within the privacy of Frances's home, in the secure bosom of her family, she could speak the truth. "John thinks he will continue to rule as Protector, but he has secured a succession for his son Richard, should anything happen to him."

"And of the Stuarts?" Nan leaned forward. "Does Cromwell believe the real king will give up his pursuit of restoration and remain in exile in Paris?"

Outside Allen strolled towards the mews. Luce wished she could capture this carefree moment for him as a gift.

"Does the king really have a choice?" she asked. "He is without funds, without an army, and most of the nobles who remained in England have resumed their lives. They are either managing their country estates or married into the daughters of the Commonwealth."

Nan stood, restless as always. "Henry treats secretly with the Spanish. Last year he rode to Germany and France to raise funds for the king. Now he raises a regiment in Bruges. The royal families of Europe will never cease supporting Charles Stuart. For to disclaim him is to foster their own decline."

Luce agreed. "And how long will the royal families of Europe stay in power? For truly, if commerce is flowing again, and we are not at war, does it really matter who is at the head? Perhaps this is a sea-change across Europe, not just England. For once men taste the freedom of a republic, can they ever return to servility under a crown?"

Frances walked to the window to watch John and Allen. "Our husbands are finding their own peace," she said. "I don't think England has the stomach for more war, more slaughter of its sons. Perhaps Henry should consider coming home too."

"Never!" Nan's voice rocked the peaceful parlour. "He will never desert the king. And just as he saved the king's life after Worcester, if anyone can bring Charles Stuart home to his rightful throne, Henry can."

Luce put her finger to her lips. "You must take care, Nan. Cromwell's eye is still upon you. He made a point of singling you out in conversation when we were at Whitehall. Do not get caught uttering these statements where you do not trust your audience."

Nan tossed her head and gathered up her shawl. "I fear neither Cromwell nor his lackeys. Honest Cary and I run rings around them and will do so for as long as it takes to preserve Ditchley for my son and heir, and for Henry to come home."

The women fell silent for a moment, each in her own thoughts.

Lucy joined Frances at the window and put her arm around her waist. "My son is well," she murmured.

Frances leaned against her mother-in-law.

"Very well," she replied. "Allen is at peace here, Lady Francke. He loves his hawks, his land, and the children thrive on our wholesome food and fresh air."

"And his mind is not troubled?" Lucy's voice dropped lower, and Luce could not quite catch her next words.

Frances shook her head. "He has put aside his love of strong drink," she replied.

Lucy turned to Luce and Nan. "Come, let's enjoy this beautiful afternoon and ask Allen to show us his mews. Perhaps he can even fly a falcon for us before the light goes."

"You go on." Frances kissed Lucy's cheek. "I will join you after I've seen to the children."

The women left the farmhouse and crossed the clean-swept courtyard to a long plaster building set at a right angle to the house. A tidy reed thatch sank low over the walls, and small square windows with bars but no glass were evenly spaced along the front. From inside came the rustling of wings and Allen's voice. Lucy opened the door, and Luce recalled her mother's stories of Lydiard, where hawks were part of her privileged upbringing.

As she stepped inside, her eyes adjusting to the dim light, Luce cried in delight at the row of perches, each with a tethered, hooded falcon perched upon the wood. The creatures were exquisite, no more than a foot high and speckled in a glorious blend of grey and white. As the nearest bird to her spread its wings, brilliant white plumage and grey stripes appeared.

"Allen, they are beautiful," she whispered.

He turned to her, his eyes alight in the dusky interior. "Aren't they just?"

"John said you were breeding the best possible bloodlines," she replied. "But I had no idea they were this gorgeous."

Allen laughed, his voice causing the bird to flap its wings again before settling down on the perch.

"Only the very best," Allen replied. "Only the very best for the king's Master of Hawks."

Luce looked at him sharply. Had she heard him right?

"The king's?"

Allen nodded proudly. "He promised me the position before I left Paris. And when he returns to England, Frances and I will move to Richmond Palace and take up residence by the royal mews." He reached a gauntleted arm out to the bird, who quickly hopped onto the leather glove. "Now, my beauty, let's take you outside and set you loose. Show my sister what it's like to fly free."

Allen walked outside with the falcon on his fist, out towards the wide open Norfolk countryside of his home.

"You see, there is always in men a longing to be free, to take charge of their own destiny." Nan stood beside Luce, watching with her. "I think John does too, in his own way. Your husband has courage, defying Cromwell, refusing to attend Parliament and acknowledge him acting as king. Perhaps he regrets his decision to sign the warrant. Or your persuasion for him to do so. You tell me to be concerned for Henry. And I think you should be aware of John's vulnerability."

Her cousin turned and walked after Allen. They crossed the courtyard arm in arm, resembling courtiers at the royal hawking parties she'd witnessed as a young girl.

Luce, with heavy heart, slowly joined them.

28

Nan

Ditchley's hunting had always provided much sport to the men in her family, and Nan loved when Harry took the hounds out to hunt in the deer park. Her son had grown to be a skilled horseman, and a model for Frank and Johnny, teaching them the fine art of bravely taking a blind fence and landing safely across a ditch. Three beautiful boys and a safe haven in which to raise them. As she watched from the library windows, they galloped across the park in a race against the creeping February dusk, determined to squeeze the last out of their day. Beautiful boys.

She had been wise to marry Harry to Ann Danvers. Since the wedding, they had assumed the active role of Baron and Baroness of Ditchley, a handsome young couple making the rounds of the local gentry, visiting friends near and far and yet entertaining modestly and soberly at Ditchley Park.

And two beautiful granddaughters. Nan's heart swelled as she considered the blessing of Harry's girls, born into a house of boys and doted on by herself and her sons. An unexpected benefit of a marriage arranged for political reasons and now proven a love match.

Still, she must maintain caution, not revel too much in her success. They were always mindful of Cromwell's eyes on them, and it would not do to raise his antagonism higher against his greatest enemy's wife

She rang a bell within the library, and when the servant appeared, she ordered the fire to be piled high with fresh logs and for wine, ale and food to be brought as soon as the boys came inside.

And it wasn't long before their laughter and shouting, the tramp of boots and the slamming of doors heralded their arrival. She sat on the sofa, positioned herself to appear the stern but loving mama they knew her to be, while inside her heart rejoiced at the rough-and-tumble young things they were. She refrained from showing how much she adored them, for she had to be mother and father to them all, and discipline was essential to their well-being.

"Mother!" Johnny was always the first to her side. "Mother, it was my hound Penelope who downed the deer. I trained her, and she repaid me with the kill today!" In his glorious excitement, he sounded just like Henry. And when he came close to the fire, the crimson gore from the deer's belly streaking across his face confirmed his news. He'd been bloodied in his first kill. Nan pushed away the sinister comparison to a battle wound and attended instead to his happiness.

She smoothed the hair from his flushed forehead and wondered at his beauty, as she did each time she realised he'd grown again. "And we shall celebrate right now." She looked up gratefully at Harry and Frank, who obviously had let their young half brother lead the hunt today. Her Lee boys winked and smiled behind Johnny's back, and her heart swelled at the affection between all of them.

"I can have wine?" asked Johnny. "I am now almost ten. Just another two months."

"Double digits, all but a few weeks," confirmed Harry. "I had my first drink by then, and I think you should too."

Two servants appeared bearing a tray of savoury hot pastries and a large flagon of wine.

The boys crowded round excitedly, immediately wolfing down the food.

Harry, as the head of the house, poured the wine and handed out glasses. As Nan accepted hers, two more riders galloped past the window. The last of the hunt were home.

"To Johnny!" Harry raised his glass high.

Johnny grinned at his family. Surely he would break hearts with that melting smile and beautiful eyes. And more than a touch of Henry's charm. Nan shook her head to chase away those thoughts. Plenty of time for Johnny to grow up, but not yet

"To Johnny!" they all repeated and drained their glasses, Johnny included. How convivial, with the roaring fire, the laughter of her boys, the warm room and the day drawing to a close outside. The room was peaceful, with just the generous firelight and the boys lolled on cushions before the flames, still talking about the hunt, the stories now growing in magnitude, the fences higher, the deer cannier. Nan allowed herself to dream of how life would be when Henry and the king came home.

The door flew open. Surely she had not summoned Henry simply by visioning him? Her heart fluttered, and she jumped to her feet. Two men entered, their faces indistinguishable. Both wore long cloaks and hats, and as they strode forward, chased by a servant who quickly took their garb, she recognised them.

"Allen? Ned! Why—it's been far too long." She walked swiftly to greet them. "What brings you to Ditchley?"

"Come and sit down, Nan." Allen's face was serious. She searched his eyes, registered the frown on his forehead. Sorrow abided there, and pain.

Nan's heart started beating hard.

The boys jumped up and surrounded them. "Uncle Allen! Uncle Ned! You should hear what we did this afternoon."

"Not this minute," Allen replied.

"Tell me . . ."she whispered, her hand to her throat, the other reaching for Johnny. He came to her side, and her Lee boys stood with Ned.

"Ned has just returned from Bruges," Allen continued. "I want you to prepare yourself, Nan."

"Henry." She knew the minute she said his name his light had extinguished.

Allen's eyes held the truth she could not bear to hear. "He's gone, Nan."

A trembling started within her core, spread through her body. So many times she had rehearsed this moment in her life, dreaded these words, planned for this news. But she had not prepared for his death.

This cannot be true. Not now. Not now.

"Mother?" Johnny's voice broke through her grief. "Uncle Allen?"

Allen kneeled to be eye to eye, gathered him in his arms. The comparison between the young boy and the seasoned soldier was stark.

"Johnny, my boy, your father has died. In Flanders, doing what he loved the most, soldiering for the king."

A great sob racked from Nan's body. Surely this was someone else who cried? "My love. My own true love."

Johnny took her hand. She must be strong. She clasped his firmly.

"Was he injured in battle?" her son's young, clear voice asked. "Did my father die a hero?"

Allen gently wiped the smear of deer's blood from Johnny's cheek.

"Yes, he died a hero, for during his life he saved the king from death many times." Allen paused. Nan swallowed. "But in January, while forming

224

his next brigade to support the king's restoration, he caught a fever." Allen held Johnny by his shoulders, looking directly into his eyes, forcing him to trust his words. "He died peacefully in a hospital, surrounded by his men, who loved him so much."

He met Nan's gaze over Johnny's bright head. She knew the ghastly conditions of the impoverished king's army. But for the sake of her son, she confirmed Allen's words.

"He would not have suffered, my darling," she said quietly.

"Did he not write to us?" Johnny's voice trembled.

Nan gathered him closer. "Henry never was one for writing," she replied. "But you know he died with your name on his lips, for he loved you so dearly, my son."

Ned Villiers stepped forward. "He did send you a message, Nan," he added. "I heard it directly from the colonel who was with him when he died."

She squeezed her eyes closed, gathering herself against another sword-thrust into her heart.

"His words, Ned?"

"That one day his body would be returned to Ditchley. But until then, his heart flew free to be with you and Johnny and would rest forever within yours."

Nan fought back the tears threatening to stream down her face, the scream of denial that lodged in her throat. She must be strong; she must be strong for Johnny.

"Then I will embrace his heart," Johnny spoke before she could. "And I will care for my mother and protect the king, just as my father did. And when I am old enough, I will ride to the king's side and bring him back to England. I will finish what my father began, I swear."

His Lee brothers came and stood by him, and Harry placed another full glass of wine in Johnny's hand. Nan did not demur, and as she stood by herself in front of the fire, Allen came to her side, and she joined them in raising her glass in the toast proposed by Harry.

"To Henry Wilmot, the finest man who ever fought for the king," her son said. "And to John Wilmot, Second Earl of Rochester, who now assumes his rightful place among England's lords. May he continue in his father's footsteps and raise a Stuart on the throne again." He drained his glass, and they all did the same.

Not once did Johnny cry, and as he stood tall with his brothers, she saw Henry in him, and the light of her husband's legacy within his eyes. At that moment, she had lost her boy and gained a man.

Allen put his arm around Johnny and drew him to a bench by the side of the fireplace. He leaned over and picked up the flagon of wine and poured her son another glass. As she stepped forward to stop him, Allen looked up at her. His eyes were unreadable grey pools in the dim light.

"Tonight is a night for men," he said, his voice rough. "We will sit together, your boys, Ned and me, and we will talk of the wars and Henry and the Stuart."

She stood still, her hands clasped in front of her to prevent her from reaching and snatching Johnny back to childhood.

"And we shall get very, very drunk," Allen continued. "As all soldiers do when lamenting their losses." He gestured to Harry and Frank to join him and motioned Ned to give them more wine. "Be with the women of your household, Nan, and mourn your husband. Tomorrow, we shall plan the future. Tonight, we honour the past."

"There is no future!" The words tore from Nan's throat unbidden. "And you will not take Henry's child into the abyss with you." She ran at Allen and hit him, pounding her fists on his chest, sobbing her pain.

"Nan . . . Nan." Allen's voice came from a thousand miles away. The red haze in front of her eyes narrowed until the fire merged and all blurred from the hot tears. He grabbed her wrists, folding her in his arms.

Still, she struggled. "You and Henry think wine and song and jokes will cure all evils. What jokes will you tell tonight, Allen? What ballad will you sing to my dead husband?"

"Shh." Allen wrapped his arms around her. "Shh."

He rocked her then, and when she could no longer make a fist and her throat was raw and her tears were exhausted, a gentle hand caressed her cheek.

"Mother?" Johnny's voice. "Mother, we will always remember my father, and I will be proud to follow his legacy." He stroked her tears away and, taking her from Allen, put his own arms around her. Her other boys joined them, and as they embraced they wept softly for the man who had loved her like no other.

Finally, she left them, fumbling her way from the room, the weight of her loss now doubled with Johnny's passage into the world of men. She choked back a cry. Only one woman could comfort her now. For only one woman she knew had survived losing the love of her life.

She walked through the dark house to the portrait.

Elizabeth.

Painted as she turned from dark clouds to golden sunshine.

Nan stood before her, hands clenched within her skirts, fists squeezed tightly, arms rigid. "Tell me how you continued to live when your love died. Show me the path forward."

Elizabeth gazed back at her steadily.

Balance the light and the dark. In the shadows lies survival.

Her own Privy Council, Nan called them. For just as Elizabeth relied upon Cecil, Walsingham, Hatton, she must take guidance from men. And now that her earl had left her too, she existed as a woman alone.

With three boys and their inheritances to protect.

She had commanded Allen to stay and had hidden Ned in the secret room behind the library. A Villiers was too close to the king for her Parliament men. She'd sent messengers across the land to her brother Walter, to John Hutchinson, even to Sir Oliver St.John deep in his retirement. They all came.

For was she now not the Dowager Countess of Rochester, and her son the second earl? And although granted by the prince in exile, the moment he returned home the title would be ratified in English courts.

Of that she had no doubt.

And if Cromwell's predatory ways were a threat when Henry was alive, he would swoop in and take everything if he thought she was a woman undefended.

"Where am I vulnerable?" Nan asked, looking at the men of her family assembled around the huge oak table, polished to a high shine. Perhaps Elizabeth had once held a council meeting in this room. The thought gave her courage. "And what intelligence are we missing?"

She had no time to tread delicately today. Even now, as news spread of Henry's death, she must act to prevent Cromwell's aggression.

"Johnny's inheritance, for one," Walter spoke first. "You've done well to secure Ditchley for your Lee boys—"

"Marrying to Danvers was an excellent strategy," interrupted Sir Oliver. "You have little to fear, for the family continues to stay in favour with Cromwell."

"So it's really Johnny's well-being, his future," Walter continued. He looked squarely at John. "Do you think Cromwell continues to pursue Wilmot land?"

"I don't know," he replied. "I am not in Parliament, and I have no plans to attend. I am like Sir Oliver. Retreated to the country."

"And the likelihood of the king's return?" She turned to Sir Oliver and Allen. "What if the king can muster the army Henry was building—or sail under peaceful terms? What if the king returns? You've been in Paris, The Hague. I've seen for myself his persistence, his belief in his own destiny."

"If Hyde had been able to control the dissidents, the king would have prevailed, I believe." Sir Oliver sat back in his chair. They all looked to him, for he was surely the most senior and experienced in these affairs. "You know as ambassador I once tried to negotiate a peaceful settlement. But with no resources, no money and a fragmented support here, Hyde has no rallying point, either in exile or here at home. Everyone has scattered to the wind, died, or sunk to the depths of depravity in an exiled court without a purpose."

He looked at Nan, his rugged features softening. "Best keep Johnny close to home for now," he said. "Educate him here locally. Employ a good tutor; place him in school at Burford. Put his name down for Oxford. Live a normal life, and a quiet one." He shifted in his seat and looked at Allen. "And teach the young earl the ways of court—the old ways."

Nan nodded at the hidden message in his words, at the hint that perhaps all was not lost.

"There's something else." Walter leaned forward, his arms folded on the table. "Cromwell is furious that you did not follow through on your promise at Whitehall, Cousin. You hide in the country, John, and you are absent from his plans."

"My decision, and I intend to stand by it," replied John. "The men of Nottingham ask me to be their new governor, and I have much to attend to at home."

"The Protector has commanded Thurloe to investigate you." Walter's words lay before them, and for a moment none spoke, and then they all began at once.

Nan rapped on the table. "What means this, Walter? Why should Cromwell instruct his spymaster to investigate John?"

"Worcester. Rumours continue to grow that the king's invasion was aided by allies in the Midlands who lent horses and gave sanctuary. A witness has come forward and named John as one of them."

John sat very still, then shrugged. "I have no doubt many men come forward when Thurloe offers bribes or torture to furnish a story. All I know is that the men of Nottingham are loyal to me and that I will overcome any questioning of my conduct."

Sir Oliver stood, and as he did so, the rest of them followed. "Take care, John, for your obstinacy also turns like a worm in Cromwell's heart."

Gathering up his gloves, Sir Oliver bowed to Nan. "I cannot stay longer, my dear. I do not think you have much to worry about at this moment. Continue your low profile and keep Johnny close to home." He turned to John. "But you, you must be cautious. For the words that you just uttered confirmed my opinion. Cromwell now fears betrayal from within his own party. Those who are popular inevitably make him unpopular. He wanted you by him so your goodness and honesty would transfer to his own cruel visage. By staying in Nottingham and holding yourself to these standards, you have triggered a loathing that amplifies his insecurity. If you choose to remain close to home, then be on guard. Be careful, Cousin. Be very careful."

Wrapped in her warmest woolen cloak against the raw February afternoon, Nan let herself out of the side door. Across the stable yard, only Allen's and Ned's horses remained. She would talk with them later, ask them to watch out for John, pass on to Luce Sir Oliver's warning in case he refrained from telling their plain-spoken cousin of Cromwell's threats.

The yard was deserted, the boys inside.

No longer would she walk out in the morning, sweetly sore from a night's loving, and greet Henry's horse in its stall, reassuring herself that indeed her husband was in her bed, his caresses not a dream. Past the rose garden where so long ago, in that June gloaming, he had talked Allen and Frances into supporting the king's cause. Now the roses were pruned to mere stumps, their blooms buried beneath the soil, the promise of a summer still months away.

She let her cloak fly open, welcoming the razor-sharp north wind that sliced into her body and threatened to blow her from the footpath. At least she felt something, for all other emotions were buried beneath the shroud of winter's cold news. Head down into the wind, she marched to the church at Spelsbury, where she could be alone with her God and her thoughts.

Through Ditchley land, now secure for Harry. Next she must talk to Carey about Adderbury, the Wilmot estates, and ensure those would be protected for John.

Tomorrow.

For today, as she walked through the dozen houses of Spelsbury village and approached the lych-gate of the church, today belonged to Henry. A sudden squall made her pause under the roof of the gate, a fitting stop. Henry's death was not marked by coffin or clergyman. No one attended his funeral. Her heart was his crypt, and she vowed in front of the church that she would never marry again, never love another as she loved him.

A carpet of white and yellow narcissus lined the path, and a few fresh-carved headstones marked the vivid green grass. She stood under the shelter of the gate, and as the flowers bent under the weight of the wind and rain, she resolved to be as them, to bow under the prevailing forces, but never resist them enough to break.

If only she had a lock of Henry's hair to make a mourning ring.

Or a letter, to keep by her bedside and mark as "his last."

She had nothing.

Except his heart in hers.

And his son to raise to his father's legacy, to serve his country and king.

"I'll care for our beautiful boy," she whispered into the wind. "I'll watch out for him and give him to the king to continue your legacy, Henry."

The gale dropped for a moment, and the rain pattered loudly on the lych-gate roof before a yellow shaft of sunlight lit a distant hilltop.

She faced east, where somewhere he lay, alone in a foreign land.

She let the wind whip the tears from her eyes and blow them down her cheeks.

She crossed her arms over her heart, stepped from under the sheltering roof and lifted her head to the sky and the wind and the rain.

"Good-bye, my love, good-bye."

29

Luce

Cromwell would have been king but for fear of quitting his generalship. His court was full of sin and vanity, and the more abominable, because they had not yet quite cast away the name of God, but profaned it by taking it in vain upon them.

Luce Hutchinson
Autumn 1658

Luce abruptly sat up before she realised she was awake. The wind pummeled her bedchamber windows with such power she feared the glass would shatter. Never had she heard such a roaring and moaning as the storm shrieked like a banshee across their pastures and slammed into the house.

Lightning scorched the horizon, and moments later a thunderclap rattled the very foundation of their home.

She reached for John, finding only an empty place in their bed. Knowing him, he already walked around the house, securing windows, checking doors, peering outside to survey damage. Luce grabbed her shawl and hurried to the children's rooms. She found them huddled in Lucy's chamber, all tucked into one bed, Lucy in the middle teaching them to count between lightning and thunder to judge the storm's distance. Luce smiled, her own childhood memories of her mother's reassuring presence rushing back to her.

Lightning flashed across the landing and hall, illuminating the art and bringing life to the portraits. As she walked by the large picture windows, John caught her hand and hurried her downstairs.

"Don't pause there," he said, guiding her towards the western aspect. "I do not know the glass strength, or if indeed anything can withstand this wind." He wrapped his arms around her and stood behind her at the small paned window by the doors. "We can watch safely from here. There is nothing more I can do to secure us." The storm raced across the sky, by turns flashing fire and pouring rain. As the grey dawn light crept over the land, a final huge gust of wind shook every window in their house. With an agonising creak, the oak tree by the bowling green fell, its roots laced in black dirt.

And afterwards, silence.

"The storm has blown itself out," murmured John. "God knows what omen this was, but men will talk of this tempest for years to come. I have never witnessed the like."

Luce was reluctant to leave John's arms, but thumps and laughter from above indicated the children were about, and they would be hungry after their vigil. She turned and kissed him, delighting in his lips on hers, the very strength of him.

"Perhaps later we can catch up on our sleep," she said. "Or at least go to bed."

Three days later, the sun shone brightly, drying up puddles and brightening spirits. John put the children to work picking up all the sticks and debris from the lawns and rallied the villagers with chopping the fallen oak and hauling firewood to their own homes. Now only bruised earth remained and a sense of emptiness, like a missing tooth, a gap in the view where there once was a barrier.

"Once again, John, I have beaten you." Allen strode across the bowling green, his head thrown back in laughter at John's rueful expression. "A score of twenty-five, and the game is won."

"Only because you had me on your side," said Luce. She caught Allen's hand and held it aloft in triumph. It was so good to have her brother and Frances with them again.

"We let you win," announced Frances. "For better to have you both celebrating in success than arguing in a loss. I would not want to trouble your mother to referee once again."

She ducked away as Allen pretended to spank her and threw herself down on the bench next to Lucy, fanning herself.

"How quickly the climate changes," she said. "For between the sun and Allen's wins, the heat is relentless."

Luce laughed. "We'll be kind to you now. Rest and enjoy my mother's company while you can, before Allen challenges us to another game. I swear he did not come to stay to collect more falcons from John, but to beat us in bowls, day after day."

Frances groaned, and Lucy handed her a glass of minted elderflower. Her hand shook, spilling a little on Frances's gown. With a cry of apology, she tried to dab it off.

"No matter, Lady Francke." Frances set the glass on the bench. "The children have made more mess on this gown than you can think. A little cordial will probably be as good a cleaning agent as any!"

Lucy nodded, still dabbing at the gown. "I am sorry, Frances. I simply slept awkwardly on my arm last night, and it has left me with a spasm."

Before Luce could ask more, the children arrived, Isabella and Franny with the twins, and Peter staggering under the weight of a fat puppy. The moment passed.

"Come, Luce." John held out his hand. "Walk down to the fishponds with me, for I would see how the latest project progresses. I have challenged the men to finish by St. Stephen's Day, and I think they are well on schedule."

She took his hand, and as always, loved the sense of belonging when they touched. They strolled across the pasture, under the shade of the young chestnuts John had planted the first year they moved in. September heralded a subtle change in the season, and no longer were they immersed in the deep green of summer. A hint of orange hovered around the curling edges of the leaves, and in a sudden quivering breeze, the colours twinkled like chaffinches.

This land, so dearly loved by John and her mother, was cultivated now to an exquisite bower of gardens and ponds, streams, lakes and woodlands. As they reached the gate to the fishponds, a lark rose from the field of cut hay, the creature's hymn piercing through the somnolent afternoon.

"Remember when we first returned, John?" Luce turned to the man she adored. "Remember you told me of the home you would build, the life we would enjoy here with our family."

She gazed across the undulating land, from the ridge of the Fosse Way to the silver gleam of John's lake, with their beautiful home nestled in the dip and the church tower solidly beside.

John held her face between his hands and kissed her long, his love on his lips, in an embrace so familiar.

"And I promised you happiness, Luce. I hope you can look at your life and agree it is so, even with our share of sadness."

Luce's eyes returned to the Fosse Way, remembering Henry, and across to the church where two of her stillborn children slept in earth's blanket. "God has comforted us when we have been sorrowed," she replied. Her thoughts went back to the night Henry had sought sanctuary with them. "I feel for Nan's loss. We may not have agreed with his politics, but Henry was a loyal servant of the king, and Nan believed in his cause with all her heart."

"As you do mine, my love," he replied. "And thanks to you, our independence has brought us the friendship of many, and Allen and Frances back into our life. God willing, we have avoided Cromwell's ire all summer. And his attention is on greater things than my refusal to attend his Parliament. I love this land, Lucy. I cannot imagine being away from it ever again. And so here we are."

"Here we are," she repeated. "And here we shall endure."

John kissed her again and then broke away, his attention caught by something over her shoulder. Luce turned as four riders crested the Fosse Way, reined in for a moment and then advanced towards their house. Soldiers, their half armour shining, horses stretched out in a full gallop.

"Get the children. Hurry. Take them indoors with your mother." John was already running towards the house. He called back over his shoulder. "I am not expecting anyone, and riders who travel this fast do not bear good news."

Picking up her skirts, Luce ran to the house. Allen and Frances were playing bowls with the children while Isabella and Lucy sat quietly on the bench, threading daisy chains from the last of the summer flowers. They had not seen the riders, did not realise the danger.

"Frances," she called. "Frances, take my mother and the children inside. Now."

Frances looked up, startled at the command. "What has happened?"

Luce gestured to the children and helped Lucy to her feet. "Soldiers are coming. We know not why. Isabella, stay with your grandmother. Do not let her return outside."

Frances scooped up Peter and Franny and gestured to the older children. "Come. Quickly. Come with me." She hurried the children towards the house while Allen and John ran to the stable yard. For a moment, Luce hesitated and then followed her husband, her heart hammering, thoughts racing.

Cromwell had finally come for John. Their idyllic summer was over. He was recalled to Whitehall to serve in Parliament, to prove that Cromwell had fair and just men in his cabinet. Dear God, perhaps not even that. Cromwell's envy had poisoned his temper. John had challenged his integrity one time too many. Now her husband would be sent to Nottingham's prison, all because he stood by his own truth and refused to follow Cromwell's brutal ways.

John, John, your stubbornness was always your Achilles' heel

She ran up to Allen and John. They stood, the three of them, as they had in the old days.

"Allen, if they take me now," muttered John, "go to Sir Oliver or Walter. Do not attempt to intervene yourself. And do not drag Nan into this."

"I will ride immediately," replied Allen.

The riders approached, dust kicking up in a cloud and the ground trembling from the pounding hooves. Allen put his arm around Luce. John stepped forward.

The leader dismounted, pulling off his gloves and reaching into his pouch.

"Colonel John Hutchinson?"

"Yes. What would you have, disturbing my peace this way?"

Oh, be careful, John, be careful.

"I come from Sir Oliver St.John." The messenger handed John a letter. "On Tuesday, the night of September 3, the Lord Protector, Oliver Cromwell, died."

"Cromwell is dead?" John repeated.

"Yes."

The other men dismounted, began walking their exhausted horses. The heavy air was disturbed only by the puffing of the creatures.

John hurriedly broke open the letter and read the contents before handing it to Allen and reading again over his shoulder.

"So he died in the palace and secured the succession." Allen's voice was bitter.

Luce took the letter from him. "The storm that raged that night brought more than devastation to the land. You were right, John. It was an omen that heralded death."

John nodded. "His son Richard Cromwell is now the Lord Protector of England."

"The clodpoll," muttered Luce. "Who has no desire to govern a country and no backbone to command men."

Allen's eyes narrowed. "God be praised that you are finally safe from Oliver Cromwell's jealousy," he said. "But God only knows what his son will do in his place. Or the army. There will be a struggle for power between the generals and Parliament again." He turned to Luce. "And God only knows where this leaves the king. For Richard is no Oliver, and the army will not follow him as it did his father. Lambert, Monck, Fairfax—they will all fight like crows over carrion for control of England."

Luce's heart contracted. "I hear in your voice the old excitement, Allen. Surely after all this time, and the measures Cromwell put in place, you cannot suggest the Stuart thinks to rule?"

Allen looked swiftly at John and then back at her. "He never stopped believing, Luce. And with this news, Hyde will have a reason to gather all the fragments and create one whole army again. Especially if yours is in disarray."

Those last words, bringing all the old wounds to the surface again. And she'd thought them safe now.

Sign, John. Sign the warrant. And with your deed, our new Commonwealth will live forever.

Allen kissed her cheek, as he had done so many times before. "We must leave. I need to talk to Nan, find Ned. We will ride to Ditchley immediately."

"Why, Allen? Cromwell has secured the succession on his son precisely for this reason," Luce replied. "What could change?"

Allen did not answer as he strode ahead. Frances opened the door.

"What news?" she asked urgently. "What must we do?"

Allen reached out to hold her. "Cromwell. Cromwell is dead." He glanced past her into the hall.

Luce followed his gaze to the children and Lucy. How frail her mother looked, not much more than a child herself. She pushed the thought aside and turned to Frances. "His son Richard has succeeded. We know not—"

"Grandmother!" Isabella cried out. Luce spun around.

Lucy slumped on the bench, daisies spilled around her on the dark floor. Her eyes fluttered, and she moaned.

Luce ran to her and held her in her arms. "Mother? Mother, what is wrong?"

She opened her eyes. "I . . . I felt dizzy, Luce. Help me sit up, please."

Allen leaned over his mother. "You fainted, Mother. Here, let me carry you to your bed, where you can rest." He scooped her up into his arms as if she were a child and carried her up the stairs, Luce at his side holding her mother's limp hand.

"You shall feel much better when you have rested," she said, pushing aside the fears that threatened to take over her voice. She did not want to worry the children or Allen. But this was not the first time her mother had fainted, and this time the muscle pulling down the corner of her mouth did not release its hold on her still face.

30

Frances

Frances and Allen rode directly to Ditchley Park, the children bundled in John's coach, heads nodding in motion with the swaying and bumping. Frances preferred horseback. She needed the fresh air and challenged Allen to ride fast and hard over the tracks, as eager as he to enjoy the wild wind on her cheeks. Within two days, they were pulling into the stable yard at Ditchley, for although the roads should have been busy, a strange quiet hung over the country. Nan brought them immediately into the library.

"I've heard from Ned," she said without hesitation. "He wants you to join him in Westminster as soon as you can."

"Events are moving quickly now." Allen drummed the table with his fingers. Frances gently put her hand over his. "The Villiers home is in the centre of Westminster, and with Ned's invitation there is no better place to keep watch."

Nan gazed at him thoughtfully. "It is unfortunate Aunt Barbara is there too. I have no dispute with her, but I recall the old family rift and know why Luce is so angry."

"I remember them too," Allen retorted. "And I also recall Barbara was the only one of my mother's sisters who intervened with Chancery Court on our behalf. She alone engaged the king to make good on Father's debts when everyone else shunned us and debtors' prison was a breath away."

These family arguments, stretching back decades. Frances agreed with Allen and hoped that Luce would understand their need to stay with the Villiers. They would rather be in London, in the centre of the turmoil, than waiting in the distant fens for a messenger to appear on the cold horizon.

"What will you do in Whitehall?" Nan's eyes were alight, the most animated Frances had seen her since Henry's death.

"Discover where the real power lies," replied Allen. "Luce may think life will continue as normal, but I disagree. Richard Cromwell is not his father; he is weak and easily led. I don't believe he has the strength to govern. And if he loses control of the Parliament, the army will claw back military rule." He paced with excitement. "This is our chance to unite the country and return the king."

"You'll need clothes." Nan's statement startled Frances. She hadn't even considered her wardrobe for so many years. What a strange conversation, and yet another indication perhaps normality was returning and a visit to the dressmaker would be part of her routine again. "You can borrow my court gowns. They may no longer be fashionable, but they are well made. We are of a similar size."

"Thank you, Nan. You are very generous." Frances smiled at the woman she'd once jealously despised. Now she valued their friendship, nurtured by a shared love of Allen. Much as she had rebuilt with Luce until Cromwell's death uprooted their lives.

"Don't worry about Luce," Nan responded brusquely, reading her thoughts. "She knows Allen has to look to his survival, and she and John cannot thwart his future with the king."

"Do you think they realise how quickly events may change?" Frances thought for a moment. "It seems they are denying the existence of the king."

"We have lived with this desire every day for the past ten years," Nan said. "To contemplate the king's return to England is second nature to us."

Allen walked over to Henry's brandy collection and poured himself a glass. "And with every day, we get closer to this dream becoming a reality. John and Luce choose to absent themselves from court, from Parliament, from the centre of power, and retire to the country. And in doing so, they abdicate control of their own circumstance."

"Hiding in the country continues to be their best option, given their past and John's role in the king's death," remarked Nan. "I, for one, will not return to London again unless it is to my advantage. But you, Allen, you have much to gain. Both of you do. So make haste to Aunt Barbara and ensure your relationship with the Villiers family is as strong as it can ever be. And then tell me exactly what they have in mind, so I can get my own messages through to Hyde—and caution Luce."

"This could be the start of the king's restoration to England and the throne," Allen's voice grew excited, louder.

"Make your part count, Allen." Nan leaned forward and took his hand. "For Henry's sake, and Johnny's. Do all you can to make this count."

Within the week, their children happily settled at Ditchley Park, Frances and Allen were riding for Westminster, accompanied by a trunk full of Nan's best court gowns.

As they rode through St. George's Fields, the first colours of autumn limned the chestnut leaves copper. Frances had spent little time in London, for her visits had been limited to Battersey. Now, riding between the hedges and with the first glimpses of buildings and chimneys heralding the city proper, a leap of excitement shuddered through her. True, there had been little change outwardly to their lives, for as far as they could tell, the transfer of power from Oliver to Richard Cromwell had been successful.

And yet something shifted within them.

They were as they had been when first joined together, that unforgettable journey from Devon to Owthorpe, with nothing but the packs on their horses and survival in their hearts. The first time they made love, in the stable loft at Exford, she knew that this man would always be with her. And last night, as they lay in an inn at High Wycombe, the same passion had ignited their lovemaking.

Allen caught her glance and smiled his lazy smile, the one that reached the depths of his grey eyes. And she responded, the memory of his beard on her skin colouring her cheeks and making her blush like a young girl. He laughed then, to see the effect he had on her, and she laughed back before urging on her horse and riding ahead of him into the London street.

Two flint-lined gateways guarded the entrance to Dean's Yard, and through the iron bars lay a peaceful square, verdant with manicured grass and canopied chestnut trees. Above the refined stonework soared smooth brick walls, interspersed with windows indicating elegant residences within. Frances looked questioningly at Allen. She had not expected this fine a house, for truly Ned had always seemed down on his luck, with threadbare clothes and worn boots.

"Aunt Barbara managed the family wealth through decades of political upheaval." Allen showed the guard their papers, and they were waved into the yard with no questions. He folded the passes and stuffed them back in his jacket. "There may still be debts encumbered on the estate, but she held on to the house and their position and arranged for Ned to marry the Earl of Suffolk's daughter."

The square was a haven from the clamour of the surrounding streets, a charming patch of countryside within the city.

"She sounds formidable." Frances straightened her shoulders and tweaked the collar of Nan's navy velvet travelling cloak. They stopped in front of one of the first buildings, a fine architecture of golden stone blocks and ornate carvings.

"Nothing you can't match." Allen grinned. He dismounted and held out his hand. "Come, let's see what the Villiers network has to say about Richard Cromwell's longevity."

A groom took their horses, and another servant appeared and escorted them through the black-painted door of the fashionable town house. A heavy fragrance of musk and something sweet, gardenias perhaps, greeted Frances as she stepped into the parlour. She halted at the sight of a figure by the windows, gazing out to the square.

Allen stepped forward and knelt. "Aunt Barbara."

The figure did not move.

"May I present my wife, Lady Frances Apsley."

Frances curtseyed to the woman's back and stood again. If Barbara Villiers was attempting to intimidate her, she would not succeed.

Inclining her head slightly, but still not turning, the woman held out her hand.

Allen stepped forward again and kissed it.

"And so circumstances bring us together again, Allen." The woman's voice was husky, a rich timbre unimpaired by age. "Your mother will not like that you run to be with the Villiers again."

She turned then, the light behind her, an advantage Frances recognised. Aunt Barbara's dress was of the old style, made over to now carry a drop-lace collar rather than a stiffly starched ruff. A rich green silk, exquisitely embroidered with gold-threaded falcons, the fine workmanship of a court seamstress. And rich enough to distract from the aging countenance above.

"You are pretty, my dear," she continued, her eyes appraising Frances from head to toe. "And, Allen, you favour your father more each time I see you."

"It has been a while, Aunt Barbara."

"Long enough."

Frances looked curiously at Allen's aunt, catching the resemblance to Lucy in her features and yet absent in her tone. This woman carried none of the warmth of her sister and all of the arrogance of a lost royal court. A bitterness pulled down her mouth, and pridefulness infused her movements. Frances could understand why Luce could not tolerate mention of Barbara. All her senses were on alert, for this woman was not one to trust.

"And Ned?" Allen prompted.

"With my granddaughter Barbary," she replied. "We have had occasion to discuss her marriage prospects with her mother, and Ned is best suited to their temperament in these delicate matters. He will join us for dinner."

She walked to the fireplace and rang a small hand bell. Immediately, a servant appeared and bowed.

"Show my nephew and his wife to their chamber," Barbara commanded. "We will dine at seven."

Dismissed, Frances curtseyed again to Allen's aunt, but did not bow her head. For a moment, she and Barbara locked eyes, and then, with a small nod of approval, Barbara turned again to her contemplation of the square.

In the privacy of their chamber, Frances lay back on the bed as Allen pulled off her riding boots.

"Your aunt is quite daunting," she observed. "I can see why Luce cannot stand her. Between her pride and her manners, she represents all the old ways Luce and John rebelled against."

"It goes much deeper than that. Luce remembers the difficult times in the Tower and the stories our mother told her of their jealous history. She blames Barbara for the ill that befell our father and his debts, for if it was not for her influence, the Villiers patronage would not have led him to his great ambition . . . and failure."

"What stories, Allen? Your mother is very private about her past, and Luce did not speak of much either." Frances rolled over and sat up, intrigued by this history.

"My mother was in love with Theophilus Howard, the Earl of Suffolk. He paid her great attention when she first went to court as a young girl. She was considered the most beautiful of all the St.John sisters. Barbara hated her for it."

This was a side of Lucy that Frances did not suspect.

"Go on. How did Barbara hurt her?"

Allen sat down next to her. "Women's stories, my love. But apparently Barbara and his sister tricked him into marrying another. And when he discovered Barbara's deception, he went out of his mind with grief." He stretched out and pulled her to him. "Distrust can do terrible things."

Frances pushed him away. "And then what?"

"It's old gossip. Barbara then took him as her lover, for her jealousy of my mother and all she loved was extreme."

"That's terrible. No sister should turn against her own like that."

Allen shrugged. "It happens. Lucy swore never to speak to her again. And Barbara never confirmed or denied her relationship. But in her lifetime, she was able to secure much in the way of perquisites and privileges from both the Villiers and the Howards."

Frances recalled Allen's earlier words. "Ned." She nodded. "Ned is married to a Howard."

"Theo's daughter, and an heiress in her own right." Allen reached for her again. "And so it continues. Now Barbara has successfully managed the marriages and lives of her own children, she looks to her grandchildren to see what advantages she can influence there. She is not stupid."

Frances let herself be pulled into her husband's arms as he started to unlace her gown.

"Far from it. She has proven herself a survivor. And in these unknown waters, her experience will serve the family well."

Ned arrived just as the torches were being lit in the square, turning the small close into an enchanting fairy village of golden flames and shadowy trees. Frances watched the lamplighters from the parlour window, excluded from the conversation Barbara conducted with Allen. She realised his aunt was significantly more interested in the company of men than women, and rather than sit on the edge of their conversation, Frances chose to remove herself completely and stand in Barbara's place by the window. A subtle challenge, but one Barbara would understand.

You can have my husband's attention. But I am now distracting yours.

A carriage pulled up. Ned sprang out and turned to assist a woman who was alighting. In the gathering darkness, Frances caught sight of long curling hair which flamed auburn by the torchlight. A door slammed, and Frances turned as moments later they entered the room, laughing. The girl stepped from behind Ned, and Frances recognised a rare and beguiling beauty. She was a little above average height, and as Ned removed her cloak, her bare shoulders gleamed ivory in the candlelight. Her face took Frances's breath away, for her almond eyes beckoned a sensuality that belied her years, and her red mouth, with its slightly parted lips, looked as if bruised already by a thousand kisses.

"Grandmother!" The young woman ran to Barbara and transformed to a child as she held her face up for a kiss.

"My naughty girl," scolded Barbara. "What have you been up to, Barbary, that your mother is in fits and your uncle Ned here had to spend all day calming her nerves?"

"It is not my fault the earl declared himself in love with me." Barbary shook back her hair, revealing again a curious mixture of seductress and girl-child. "I did not encourage him—" She broke off as she saw Allen and Frances. She held out her hand but waited for them to come to her.

Such assurance in one so young.

"I believe you were friends with my father," she said to Allen. "Uncle Ned says you fought together." Her voice was of a similar timbre to Barbara's, husky and throaty, as if woken from a restless sleep.

Allen bowed, kissing her hand. Frances simply stood. Age required Barbary curtsey to her. After a moment's pause, the younger girl did so.

"I fought at his side at Edgehill and stood next to him when you were christened at Whitehall," replied Allen. "He was a fine man, and he would be proud to see his daughter today."

"My William." Barbara rang the bell by the fireplace. "He was the noblest of all my sons, a true hero and friend of the king."

Frances glanced at Ned to see if he begrudged this favouritism. His face remained expressionless, but she read resentment in the set of his shoulders.

"Let us eat," continued Barbara. "And this evening we shall toast King Charles at our table, in our home, not hidden in secret in the cellar as in previous times. Change is advancing upon us. Tonight, we shall discuss how we all will benefit."

"A toast to the king," repeated Barbary. "Uncle Allen, will you take me in to dinner?"

She walked in front of Frances and held out her arm. Allen shot a quick look to Frances and then escorted her from the room.

Frances lifted her head, determined not to be the least put out by Barbary's rudeness. As she did so, she caught Aunt Barbara's eye upon her. The old woman smirked and followed her granddaughter to dinner.

31

Luce

Lambert, with a heart full of spite, malice and revenge, retreated to his palace at Wimbledon, and sat there watching an opportunity to destroy the Parliament.

Luce Hutchinson
Winter 1659

General Lambert's rebel officers descended with nightfall, thundering into Owthorpe's court, circling and wheeling and digging great furrows into the gravel. The full snow-moon cast a bleak and cold light over the land, turning the men into faceless figures, their cloaks blending with their horses. Six heavily armed soldiers—once friends, now enemies.

Bidding the group of local men who dined with them to stay seated, Luce joined John at the window.

"We've prepared for this," he said calmly. "You know what to do."

Luce nodded. A stillness bloomed within her, every sense heightened. How quickly she returned to fighting, her body and mind swiftly recalling those years at siege within Nottingham's castle. This was no different. She would defend her home, her children, her life. Royalist invaders or Lambert's rebel army, the night made no choice between sides now. They threatened her home, and she would protect it with every last breath.

"I am not afraid." She kissed John's lips. "Let us face them now. And prevail."

John pulled her to him, kissing her deeply in return. "Go. They could not have picked a better time to understand what it is to challenge us, my love."

He turned to their dinner guests. "Hold here. I will call for you if I need you."

Now shouts and a hammering on the great outside door. John put a hand on his sword and ran swiftly into the hall. Luce darted towards the stairs. Already, her servants gathered in a stalwart group by the service area, and she pushed them all quickly into the kitchen.

Her children stood with her mother in the gallery, awakened by the commotion. "All of you, move into the hidden chamber now," she commanded as she ran up the stairs. They scampered, their white night robes gleaming in the moonlight, Bee taking her grandmother's hand and helping her walk as swiftly as she could. Renewed pounding echoed within the hall. Any minute John would be forced to open the front door to prevent it from being broken.

"Hide. Do not move, no matter who says it is safe." Luce followed them into her chamber. "You know the code word your father and I will use. Bolt the door and do not leave."

Luce took a final look at her children, their faces brave. The maids stood with them, resolute. She had picked her servants well. All she could trust.

She locked the heavy wooden door to the safe room, where it immediately became one with the paneling. The children slammed bolts from the inside. One. Two. Three. Four. Five. All in place. Then, as she passed through three more rooms to the ballroom, she locked each of those behind her, thanking God for John's insights. A house designed in war would defend in war too. His secret compartments protected them tonight.

And God's providence. Back in the great hall, the guests of the evening stood in the shadows, neighbours, local men, loyal friends, ready to fight. Lifting a hand to warn them to stand still, she entered the lobby, carefully shutting the door behind her.

God's providence. Tonight, of all nights, a meeting of John's constituents. His hospitality welcoming them, his door open to all.

Except Lambert's militia.

John and their minister stood together, an older man, his white hair thin upon his pate. Such a small detail to notice now. John slid open the bolts. A soldier appeared on the doorstep, an army man. She recognized him from the castle days. A local. Lambert had recruited those closest to John to bring him down.

She stepped forward.

"What means this?" she demanded, using every ounce of her strength to steady her tone, manage her anger. "How dare you disturb us with no reason, no warning?"

First, a woman's touch. First, try to diffuse conflict.

Over his shoulder, a block of men all facing their house, silent. Pistols glinted in the moonlight, weapons held by their sides, ready to use against them.

Her anger rose.

"We come for money owed to the army." The soldier pulled his own gun. John moved to her side, his hand close to his sword. "Colonel Lambert has assessed by order of Parliament you are to give us your money. All of it. Let us in, or we will let ourselves in."

"You have no right," John's voice was steady, low. "I do not recognise Lambert's authority. And I will not fund his treasonous army."

"You have no choice, Royalist." The man took another step forward, now across her threshold. He had violated their house. Enough.

"Get out." Anger gave her voice. "Or regret your action. And take your foul rebels with you."

John drew his sword and pointed it directly at the man's heart. "Do not advance another step, you dog." He thrust his sword a foot closer to the soldier. "You are no friend of the people, and you are an enemy of mine now."

The minister held John's sword arm. "John, not in front of Luce," he cried. "No bloodshed, not in your home."

The soldier locked eyes with John and held his hand up to his men. A shuffling as they formed a line. He gave a signal. As a group, they lifted their pistols and cocked them, the clicks echoing around the courtyard.

John broke himself free from the minister's hand and, holding his sword high, brandished it towards the armed men.

"Now, Luce, now!" he shouted.

The soldiers marched towards John, guns aimed. John stepped to one side, and they crowded into the lobby. At the same moment, Luce threw open the door to the great hall, revealing the fifty men assembled within.

God's providence. For tonight, the loyal men from Owthorpe, from Kinolton, from Hickling attended John to discuss a county matter.

God's providence, Lambert's rebels chose this night to challenge John's authority.

And when they ran into John's hall, pistols cocked and ready to steal his wealth, they came upon a wall of local men, loyal men, men who had followed John through all the years of the war.

God's providence. Luce laughed aloud. Never had she seen such shock on men's faces as she did on Lambert's soldiers that moment.

Now who had authority?

They stood white-faced, guns dropped to their sides. John's followers stepped forward from the shadows, surrounding them.

Captured in the moonlight, overwhelmed by the surprise defence, imprisoned by their own fear, Lambert's men placed their guns on the floor.

John sheathed his sword and put his hand out to the soldier. "May I offer you some wine, gentlemen? For although your insolence nearly cost you your lives tonight, you will find us all quite hospitable here in Owthorpe. Especially when united against a far greater enemy than each other."

The soldier frowned, humiliation refusing to let him meet John's gaze. "We are only carrying out orders, Colonel Hutchinson," he replied, his voice low. "General Lambert commands us to acquire as much money and powder as possible to prepare for the fight ahead."

"Lambert is fighting the wrong enemy. Richard Cromwell may not be able to hold power for much longer, but this time is not for insurrection, but preparing for a greater danger," John replied. "Think well, my friend, on the consequences of these orders. Turning against your own will only result in providing free passage for the Stuart to return unhindered."

The soldier placed his hand on his own sword. "Never while I wear this," he swore.

John shook his head. "You are mighty conflicted my friend. Now return to your homes, and leave me at peace in mine."

The soldier bowed to John and his men, beckoned his own to follow him. They marched from the house, and within minutes the clattering of hooves faded.

Luce drew a deep, shuddering breath. "They are gone."

"For now." John gestured to the local men to fill their tankards. "But this won't be the last."

Later, as she lay in his arms with her head on his chest, Luce reflected on the evening. John's even breathing soothed her and calmed the anger that still boiled.

"You knew they'd come?" she asked him. "What is happening, John?"

He paused before answering in his measured way. "It was only a matter of time. As we feared, Richard Cromwell is unable to control either Parliament or the army. I believe he will be ousted within the year. There is now a struggle for supreme command of both. And neither faction includes Cromwell's heir."

"And where does that leave us?"

"No different than before," John's voice was reassuring. "We are independent and so have no argument with any side."

Luce traced a finger over his chest, so calm and strong. "Even with the king's army?"

In the silence that followed, a barn owl hooted outside the window, followed by a sharp scream from a hunted rabbit.

John turned on his side to look at her, the waning moon still strong enough to light his handsome features. "Would you consider Allen an enemy?"

"Of course not."

"And yet he sides with the king."

"And always has."

John smoothed her hair in a gesture she knew so well. She turned her head in response to his caress.

"You are saying this is different?"

"Our enemy is within now, Luce. And I fear our republic is at stake."

She broke away from his touch, abruptly sitting upright. "You cannot mean this. If Cromwell does not last, Fairfax or Monck will take his place. Even Lambert was once offered the Protectorate."

John sat up too and took her hands in his. "And is that what the people want, my love?" A series of army generals ruling over them, winning election by whomever can quell the population and rule by fear?"

Luce fell silent at his words. She may have contradicted him in previous discussions, but she'd witnessed the faces of the men facing each other in her hall. Each was prepared to kill the other, for no reason either could later justify.

"And so what does this mean, John?" she repeated.

John gathered her closer, enfolding her in his arms. "Perhaps it means the Stuart will return," he said. "And perhaps he will work with Parliament and bring peace to this land. For men will not tolerate a return to war. And especially a war within a war, faction against faction under military rule."

She searched his eyes.

"And for us?"

"We will stay quietly in the country and let the world pass us by. God will look after us, and I trust in his safekeeping." John leaned forward and kissed her and slid the gown from her shoulders. Tenderly, sweetly, he made love to her, taking her to their familiar place, the very heart of their life together.

Only when she was drifting to sleep, satiated and drowsy, and the dark night closed around her, did she start awake from a shiver of fear.

If the king returned, what vengeance would he impose on those who had signed?

John quietly slumbered. He trusted in his God, in his own conscience. But was that enough?

Luce lay on her back, staring at the ceiling, eyes wide open, as she imagined the worst possible outcome of the king's return. She resolved to fight for John's life as if her own depended upon it.

And the small, still voice inside whispered to her of the memory of the night when she'd also lain sleepless, the cold January night when she'd rejoiced in John's signature. The night he'd written his name with the courage of her conviction.

Dear God. In signing the king's death warrant, had John sanctioned his own?

32

Nan

Nan approached the princess in the Long Gallery with a slow, measured pace. Perfectly poised beneath the portrait of Queen Elizabeth, the child watched Nan closely, her little chin lifted just slightly arrogantly, her head held imperiously. As Nan approached and swept a magnificent court curtsey, she stayed in her position of obeisance until the princess's voice rang out.

"Arise, Lady Rochester, and tell me how you fare."

Nan rose slowly, keeping her head bowed as she kissed the little girl's hand. "Most well, Your Highness, thank you."

"Did you travel far to come to court, Lady Rochester?" The little girl was most self-assured, for she could be no more than three years of age.

"Many miles across the land," replied Nan. "But I had a magic horse with wings that flew by night across the stars and whisked me here in the blink of an eye."

The little girl nodded her head wisely. "And the magic horse, Lady Rochester, where is he now?"

"He is eating breakfast, Your Highness. Just as you should be." Nan lunged forward and picked up her beautiful granddaughter, whirling her around to helpless giggles. "For if your mother knew you played at princesses instead of your sewing, we would both be in big trouble."

"I won't tell if you won't, Grandmother." Eleanor's voice was serious, her blond curls bobbing as she shook her head. "My mother doesn't approve of kings and queens and princesses."

"Then we keep this our secret," assured Nan. There was no harm in teaching her granddaughter of the importance of the royal family, for certainly she would be marrying a duke or an earl herself and attending court. "And one day, when the king comes home, you will go to court and meet him, and you will know exactly how to behave."

Eleanor giggled. "Just as you do?"

Nan laughed. "You had probably best not look to me for guidance, for I fear perhaps I go too far in expressing my opinions." She turned as footsteps hurried along the gallery. "Ah, Cary, I was just being chided for my forwardness in courtly behaviour—"

"Madam, I request you come with me urgently." Cary's fair face was flushed, his skin covered in a sheen of sweat. He had hurried from somewhere.

"What now?" Nan put down Eleanor and took her little hand. It felt so delicious, and again she revisited the pleasure of her granddaughter's company. "There cannot be anything so urgent that it disturbs my princess's breakfast."

Cary's expression did not lift, and deep worry furrowed his brow. A sudden dread came upon Nan.

"What, Cary? Speak, man."

"It is Lord Harry, my lady. I have just left his chamber. I fear he sickens. I fear the signs my lady, for it is just as his father was."

Oh God, no, no, no.

Nan turned swiftly to her granddaughter. "To your room, sweeting, and stay there until I send for you." Her sudden fierceness caused Eleanor's little face to crumple in tears. Nan kissed her and gently pushed her away. "Run to your room now."

Honest Cary twisted his kerchief between his large hands. "I have sent for the doctor, my lady. But I fear this disease strikes quickly. Harry calls for you, with the little strength he can muster."

A single candle guttered on the mantel, for to light more caused Harry to groan in pain, the brightness searing his wounded eyes.

Nan gently dabbed his face with a damp linen, careful to avoid the open pox where the pus ran. Beneath the terrible disfigurement, her boy existed somewhere between life and death, and this last day of March she called a scribe to Harry's bedside.

Her mind was clear, washed by the thousand tears she wept in private.

Time to pen a document no mother should have to write.

Time to write Harry's last will. *Dear God, please give him strength for his testament.* For she could dispose of his worldly goods, but eternal redemption lay beyond her command.

The room narrowed to just her, the scribe and her beautiful boy.

"Harry," she whispered. He turned his blind eyes to her. "Harry, the time has come to make your will. I am going to help you, for there is much to sort for your wife and your daughters, your Ditchley inheritance, your bequests to your brothers."

God give me strength as I write my son's dying declaration.

Nodding to the scribe and taking Harry's swollen hand in hers—for surely the pox spores would not dare invade her now—she logically dictated the disposition of the worldly goods of Henry Lee, Third Baronet of Ditchley. For two hours, she spoke without cease, listing sums of money for his wife, his daughters, his friends. Bequeathing property, manors, revenues among family and friends. Appointing Walter as executor.

"I trust only him," Harry's damaged voice broke into her monologue at his uncle's name. She poured a drop of Johanna's smallpox tincture from the small flask into Harry's cracked lips.

"Walter will safeguard all on your behalf," she reassured her boy. "He and Honest Cary will guarantee the welfare of your family, my darling."

Harry nodded his head slowly.

Nan continued, for God Almighty, if she allowed her heart to rule her head, she could make a mistake in this disposition, and Parliament would swoop in and deny probate and take everything.

The scribe's pen scratched her words into the parchment, hasty in his drafting hand. At her command, he read her dictation aloud, preparing for his final copy.

"Harry, you must agree, so we have evidence and witness you are in sound mind, albeit weak body." She touched his poor face gently, and again he rolled his head towards her.

"My chestnut mare. My grey gelding." He licked his lips, his tongue swollen. "Ensure they are well treated."

The memory of the day she'd heard the news of Henry, her boys joyful from the hunt, flooded into her mind. She nodded, for if she spoke now she would break down.

"And my wife, my girls. Tell them I love them."

"I will, Harry. They love you dearly and wish only for your eternal peace."

She gestured the scribe gone.

And in the quiet of the night, she sat with her eldest son until the candle died and the light was no more.

Nan pulled her gaze from the library fireplace, where such a short time ago three boys had lolled and laughed and teased each other about their hunting prowess. Now the grate was empty, the fireplace swept clean of ash. And only two boys remained to carry on.

Soon the first fire of autumn would be lit. The seasons continued, refusing to heed her grief.

Strong. She must remain strong.

"Thank you for visiting me, Allen." Nan adjusted the black skirts of her mourning gown and crossed her hands in her lap. Somehow folding her hands and holding them reduced the sense of loss. For the knowledge she would never feel her child's hand in hers again was too painful to contemplate. "Richard Cromwell has, to all intents, resigned his position. No one is taking orders from him, and England is rapidly falling into anarchy. I will tell you simply you must make plans to go to the king in Holland."

"I didn't come to Ditchley to be ordered away again. I'm concerned about you, Nan." Allen put his arm around her, and for a moment she leaned into him before straightening again. "This terrible sadness of Harry's death has affected you more than you care to admit. You were barely through mourning Henry. I don't think you should be alone here."

Nan shook her head. "Ditchley is home. There is nowhere else I should be. Harry's daughters need me. His wife is ill with grief." She struggled to stop her face from contorting, swallowed hot, fierce tears. "I tried everything, as did Johanna."

Why could she not save her own child?

How could she fail him?

How could you leave me, Harry?

"You could have done no more, Nan." Allen took both her hands in his, and his strong grasp reminded her of Henry. "The smallpox rarely lets go once it bites. Harry was a prey you could not rescue."

So much loss.

"I know it is God's will. I will watch after his family. And I have Edward and Johnny . . . John . . . to care for, and my darling granddaughters." Nan pulled her hands from Allen's to convince herself they were not Henry's. "My life is here. But you must go. Go to Holland, as the king and Hyde make decisions. He will value you more if you are at his side."

"We are hearing the same," confirmed Allen. "Ned has suggested Barbary Villiers go with her new husband, Palmer, for favours are distributed generously to those who go to support the king. He writes from Holland that Englishmen are arriving daily as the tide ebbs here for Richard Cromwell."

"Ned predicts well. But do not take Isabella with you."

"Frances has it in mind. She thinks she is of an age where being at court will be an important experience for her."

Nan snorted. "Sounds to me our Aunt Barbara has been filling Frances with ambition. She did well marrying off her own grandchild to Roger Palmer after Barbary's scandalous affair with the Earl of Chesterfield. Watch she does not have eyes on your daughter for an advantageous marriage next. Do not let the Villiers use your children as marriage bait."

Allen laughed. "You are one to talk, Nan." And then he bit his tongue, guilt on his face. He looked as he did when they were ten and she'd caught him in a lie.

She patted his hand. "I will not deny Harry's was not a love match, not at the beginning," she replied. "But he and Ann grew devoted to each other, and my son died well-loved. That much I have to be grateful for."

Clearly uncomfortable with the direction of the conversation, Allen stood and poured himself a glass of wine. He gestured with the bottle to Nan, but she shook her head. She would save the malmsey for later, for when the comfortless night descended upon the silent house and sleep eluded her.

"What else do you hear from Ned?" Nan steered the conversation back to the business at hand. There were decisions to be made, and Allen needed her advice to make them.

"The Sealed Knot and the Action Party are working together now. The different factions are finally united in one objective. The king seeks to treat any way he can with Monck's army and the impending new Parliament." Allen's face was bright with hope. "Charles offers religious freedom, concedes much in his future role in ruling the country, freely forgives those who rose against him."

"Except for the regicides."

The new word coined just for the signers tasted bitter in her mouth, for not only did it remind her of the day she'd stood at the scaffold at Whitehall, it described the taint in her own family.

Allen's mouth tightened as he looked into her eyes. "Except for the regicides."

They both sat in silence then, with only the fashionable wall clock's mechanism for company. And with each tick, change crept closer. Nan took a deep breath.

"John is in danger. Mortal danger."

"Yes." Allen threw back his wine and poured another glass. This time she took one too.

"Does Ned say more?"

"No. There is no negotiation with the king on this point. He seeks revenge against all those who killed his father."

"Dear God. Do you think Luce realizes the peril they are in?" Nan stood too and walked to Allen's side. "Or John? His stubbornness clouds his mind to the point of obtuseness."

Allen shrugged. His nonchalance did not fool Nan. "We have not discussed the matter."

Nan sighed. This brother and sister, who fought like dogs over a bone and loved just as fiercely. Her clear thinking was the only hope to steer them to safety, for she loved them both deeply.

"Then do not write to her except to bid good-bye," Nan said. "Do not bring this worry to their doorstep yet. Keep your own counsel and leave before you say more than you ought."

A calm coldness crept across her, pushing aside the grief, filling her with resolve. She must put her sorrow behind her and save her energy for the family living. And if this meant she needed to call on Walter and Sir Oliver, as well as all those who were flocking now to General Monck's army, she would do so. All her instincts forecasted the king's return. Monck foresaw where old loyalties must be replaced by new. She would tread his path. And it would serve her entire family well to declare an allegiance to the king and forget their differences. England was joining as one again, and they must too.

She needed Allen in Holland, with Frances collecting information. For who knew where loyalties lay again as the rats deserted the sinking ship of the wrecked Commonwealth. Nan kissed Allen's cheek, this man who meant so much to her and Luce.

"Make plans to go to Holland, Allen. Renew your friendship with the king. Secure your position at court. And have Frances gather intelligence as soon as you arrive. I must think carefully on John's defence."

33

Luce

My mother, while she was with child of me, dreamed that she was walking in the garden with my father and that a star came down into her hand, with other circumstances, which, though I have often heard, I minded not enough to remember perfectly; only my father told her, her dream signified she should have a daughter of some extraordinary eminency.

Luce Hutchinson
Autumn 1659

Luce moved the last of the roses closer to her mother's bed, standing them on the sturdy table now piled with notebooks, an inkwell and several freshly cut pens. She cleared a space where the deep crimson flowers could be seen, and the fragrance drift towards the bed, caught by a gentle breeze from the open window.

Lucy's eyelids fluttered open, and she smiled, her mouth still slightly twisted, but it was her familiar smile, loving and sweet.

"How beautiful, my darling," she whispered. She reached out a thin hand and brushed the blooms. "Such joy. But they will not last long. Is it October now?"

"Yes, the first today. Did you sleep, Mother?" Luce sat on the bed, careful not to disturb her mother's slight form. "May I bring you a cordial? Johanna has sent more recipes for your fatigue."

"That darling girl. She sends me a curative a day, and yet I think there is little for the weariness of age upon me."

Luce took her mother's hand. "Don't talk so. You simply had a bad turn, and your choler is unbalanced. A tonic from Johanna will bring you out of bed and back to your garden."

"I would like to walk outside again," Lucy's voice grew determined, and she struggled a little to sit. "John is eager to start the pruning, but it is too early with this late summer."

"Then if you eat, and drink what Johanna prescribes, you will gain your strength within a few days." Luce arranged the pillows to support her mother. Three weeks since her mother's collapse, and although each day came with a small improvement, she did not want Lucy's melancholy to affect her recovery.

"I'm not hungry." Lucy turned and faced the wall. "I dreamed of Allen last night, and I feel him close to me today."

"Allen will come soon, Mother. He plans to visit by the end of the week. He writes he has news for us."

"Your father, not your brother." As Luce reached for her hand, a tear appeared on her mother's cheek. "He was my love, Luce. There was never another. Barbara never realised the truth."

"I know." Luce smoothed her mother's hand. "He loved you dearly and was the best father to us."

Lucy turned her face back to Luce. "He was strict and disciplined. But a generous man and well-respected. Our life at the Tower held moments of great joy, do you remember?"

"I remember his ordering Allen's tutors to teach me, to spur my brothers to compete with me and overcome their own laziness." Luce shook her head and laughed. "Remember how furious they were when I outstripped them? Father held up my work as the best."

"And so it was, my sweetheart. You are gifted beyond all measure. Your writing, your brilliant mind. Do not ever think to give that up, for your words will bring light to the truth and serve you in times of need."

Luce frowned at her mother's riddles. "What do you mean?"

Lucy fell silent, appearing to gather her thoughts. "Uncertain times. Richard Cromwell is not his father." She stopped, the effort taking a toll. "And the king waits and watches for his chance."

"The country is united, and there is no returning to the king's divine rule." Luce refused to question her faith. "Parliament will sustain the continuity of the republic."

"Yes, it will." Her mother's voice was soft, and her eyes closed. "But will they work with Richard, or another?"

Luce started to speak but was stilled by her mother's next words.

"The king will promise anything to return to England's throne. Including being managed by Parliament. And when restored, he will avenge his father's death." Lucy's voice drifted, and Luce leaned forward to hear her more clearly. "Have a care for John, Luce. Intervene, lest his stubbornness cause his downfall. The king will never forget who signed his father's death warrant. And you share responsibility with John." Lucy sighed. "I think I'd like to see Allen now."

Allen must have ridden through the nights, hardly pausing to break, for he arrived at Owthorpe within three days of Luce sending for him, white with exhaustion and anxiety. Luce embraced him before he hurried towards their mother's chamber.

"She is not in pain," she said. "But her thoughts travel, and she sometimes mistakes me for her sister Eleanor, or speaks to Barbara. Do not be distressed, for her mind is not troubled."

"What mean you?" Allen's eyes darkened to grey pools. "She is not in her right mind? How could this happen so quickly? What is wrong?"

"Allen, you must prepare yourself. She is frail. There are some days she is with us, others where she journeys to be with those she has loved." She eased his riding coat off his shoulders, and he let her, like a child. "Now we must soothe her mind, sit with her, help her go where she will. You will see: she is not in pain. Today is a good day."

At Allen's footfall, Lucy turned her head. She lay in her bed, propped by pillows, the morning sun streaming into the room and throwing a patch of sunlight on her covers. A calico cat slept curled up in the sunshine. A single rose remained in the vase.

"Allen?" she called. "Are you here?"

Luce led him forward. "He is here, Mother. Your son is here."

Allen knelt on the floor by the bedside and kissed his mother's hand. Lucy smiled and stroked his head. Luce quietly left the room, closing the door behind her. Time for them to be alone, to remember their own way

Later, she returned with John and found Allen sitting next to Lucy, she with her cheeks rosy and her eyes following his hands as he told some story. As Luce approached, her mother turned to her.

"I feel the best I have in weeks," she said. "Allen tells me of the court in Paris and of the falcons he keeps at Feltwell, awaiting the king's return. I caution him to not be in debt, for we know the king is not always prompt in payment."

Luce looked swiftly at Allen. He answered, "Wise words indeed, Mother. I promise I will not over commit us or go into debt."

Lucy nodded. "Good." She looked at Luce. "I have a desire to see the garden, my plantings."

"You are not strong enough to walk today, Mother," Luce said gently. "Perhaps later."

Her mother's face fell. "I miss my garden, Eleanor. Our special corner, in the sunshine, away from the White Tower's shadow. I can walk, I am sure. Allen has made me feel so much better."

Luce shook her head. "You are not steady—"

"We can take you to the garden," John interrupted. "Allen and I can take you." He dragged the chair by the window to her bedside. "Here. Luce will bundle you up in blankets to keep you warm, and Allen and I will carry you upon Titania's throne."

"Titania," Lucy mused. "Once someone called me Titania . . ." She shook her head. "No matter, I cannot recall now." She smiled. "Then, John, please take me to the bower. I would sit on the bench where I last saw Allen and look towards the court, and Paris, and think of him playing cards with Ned Villiers."

Allen's face clouded, and Luce swiftly pulled shawls and a blanket from the chest. "Mother, we shall go now before the sun falls behind the trees. Come, wear these, and we shall escort Titania to her bower."

John and Allen lifted Lucy from the bed and into the armchair. Carefully, they stood on either side and raised the chair, their strength making easy work of her lightness.

Luce followed them into the garden.

The sun threw dappled shadows across the green, and from the chair, Lucy lifted her face to the warmth. The men carried their precious burden, evenly in step, matched in height.

They set Lucy down by the bench, and Allen sat next to her while John handed Luce to her mother's side. They rested together, as they had in their childhood, each in their shared and singular thoughts. The afternoon quieted around them, a tranquility only disturbed by a chance leaf loosening and fluttering to the ground from the sheltering oaks. Peace stole over them, and a hush. Luce could not say exactly the moment life changed. All she knew was when the lark song pierced the silence, Lucy had left them.

For the last time, Lucy travelled through the ivy-wrapped gate from the house to the church. Never again would she walk with flowers in her hands and spring at her heels, eager to place the blossoms on the simple table John had installed in place of the old popish altar. Luce swallowed her tears and walked behind her mother's coffin, secured by John's steady arm. The small procession wended through the gate and into the church, where the villagers waited, their faces solemn. They had loved the lady. Her mother's maid lifted her sorrowful face as they walked in. Faithful Susan. Luce would ensure that she was given a new position within the household.

Luce followed Walter and Johanna into the pew while Allen and Frances sat with Nan across from them. Ned Villiers surprisingly attended, silent by the rough stone wall, his face in shadow. John stood next to the minister, his hair falling forward as he opened his Bible. A clear light shone through the ancient stone church, bright now that John had removed the stained-glass windows and replaced them with translucent panes of glass. Nothing was left of the old, dark chapel. Luce's mother was happy to be laid to rest in such a modest building. The one time Luce had spoken to her about being returned to Lydiard, Lucy had vehemently shaken her head.

"Not with my brother's popish monuments and garish displays," she'd said.

"Not even to be with Edward and Anne, Mother?" Luce had asked gently. "You loved them dearly in life, and I thought you might wish to join them."

"I will see them in heaven," Lucy had replied. "Owthorpe is my life, and one day you will join me here. I will be waiting for you."

Luce's eyes burned as John read the words from the twenty-third psalm, her mother's favourite.

"Good-bye," she whispered. "Go to the arms of your beloved husband, for my father stands for you at the gates of heaven. Godspeed."

After the simple ceremony, the family sat in silence while the villagers filed out. All were invited to the hall for refreshments, and Luce wanted a few moments before they must attend to their people, listen to the condolences, act as if it were not painful to speak of her mother's life.

She stayed behind, aware John and Walter and Johanna had left. And thought herself alone until she opened her eyes from silent prayers.

Allen remained, his head in his hands. And Ned Villiers still in the shadows, sitting stoically at Allen's side. Luce walked across to her brother.

"She is laid to rest in a place she loves," she said. "And she is with our father in heaven."

Allen looked up, his eyes red-rimmed. "She should be back at Lydiard, with the family, not here alone with John's."

Luce gathered her thoughts before she spoke, remembering her mother's caution to pause before speaking.

"I can only tell you it was her wish, Allen," she replied. "She regarded Owthorpe as her home. And one day John and I will be interred here too. Her earthly remains will have our company; already her soul resides in heaven."

In the pause, Ned Villiers cleared his throat. "I came from London as soon as I heard the news from Allen. My mother sends her condolences." His voice was overly loud in the empty building.

"Your mother? Aunt Barbara? They have not spoken in ten or more years. Why should she care, when she did my mother so much harm?" So much for discretion in her words.

"Those times are long gone, Luce." Allen stood, and her cousin followed suit. "Ned and I have no care for the old, long-held grudge. Our aunt simply sends her sympathy to us at the loss of our mother, her sister."

"Barbara never did or said anything simply or without a motive," Luce retorted. "Thank your mother for me, Ned. I do not wish to hear from her again."

She turned to leave and paused as Allen and Ned stood still.

"What?"

"Frances and I return to Westminster tomorrow," replied Allen, "and then sail with Barbary Villiers to Holland. Aunt Barbara is paying for our passage as we work to understand what may be next for the country and the king."

Luce looked up to the ancient beamed roof and back at Allen. "You might have waited," she said angrily. "You might have waited until after today to tell me you are now in league with our mother's greatest enemy." How could he betray their mother's memory so quickly? How could he take Frances into the bosom of the woman who had done everything within her power to destroy their mother? "What is this talk of the king again, when Richard Cromwell succeeded as Protector and Parliament is content?"

"I do not need your permission to decide my future, Sister. And today of all days, honour our mother, not your failed rebellion." Her brother turned his back and strode from the church.

Ned Villiers pulled a small leather pouch from inside his jacket. "There's something my mother wanted you to have."

"I don't want anything your mother wishes to give me," Luce snapped.

"She told me it was meaningful to Aunt Lucy." He held the pouch out to her.

She ignored his hand. "You have no idea what was important to her."

He smiled, with all the guile of the Villiers charm. "I think I do. This belongs to my wife. And she and my mother wish you to have it, to remember Lucy's youth, as Barbara does."

In spite of herself, she looked down as he drew a miniature portrait from the pouch. A handsome young man smiled up at her, framed by a twisted lock of auburn hair, bright in the gloom. She met Ned's eyes again.

"Theo?"

He nodded. "Theophilus Howard, the Earl of Suffolk. My deceased father-in-law. And someone once very close to your mother . . . and mine."

She dashed the portrait to the stone floor and pushed past Ned, running for the sanctuary of home.

For the rest of the day and night, until they left the next morning, she avoided her brother and cousin and only kissed Frances good-bye.

Later, sleep eluded her. The tree branches tapping on the window caught the hunter's moon, throwing a pathway of light across her chamber. Luce pulled on a robe and stepped outside.

She pushed open the unlocked church door. The air smelled different, tainted by the disturbed vault, the stone only rolled back in place today after her mother's internment. Luce felt her way across the rough wall and sat on the wooden bench. Thoughts did not come, but emptiness did not worry her. This discourse was deeper than words, mere letters in a pattern, lines on a page. This love and loss flowed through her body and heart and soul. In the sacred silence, she understood the wisdom of her mother's last wish. Luce would never have joined her at Lydiard. And so Lucy waited for her here at Owthorpe.

A moonbeam fell across her lap and onto the stone floor. A sudden glint. Luce bent down before she knew it. The miniature lay face up, concealed under the bench before her.

She picked up Theo and held the portrait, turning it this way and that so the auburn hair glistened in the moonlight.

"You do not belong here," she whispered to her mother's first love. "And one day I will return you to your world. For you are not part of mine."

PART FOUR

1660
RESTORATION

35

Frances

The crossing of the Narrow Sea to the Continent proved as different from the last as could possibly be. No furtive hiring of a fishing boat, no hurried disguised departure. This fine March morning Frances stood on the ship's prow, a fresh breeze tugging at her hair, the water sparkling and shimmering as if a mantle of sapphires. She looked forward to the emerging shore of Holland, not back at the fading cliffs of England, eager for the future, not clinging to the past.

Allen's strong arms enfolded her, and she leaned into his embrace.

"Happy, my love?" he whispered against her ear, his words soft under the creaking of the ship's ropes. Across the deck, a fiddler played, and the Earl of Oxford led passengers in a joyful Royalist victory song. This day she would never forget.

"Without reserve, Allen," she replied. "Unimaginable only a year ago. And now we travel to court to bring the king home."

She turned to her husband, her love. "And yet a bittersweet moment, for others do not travel with us."

His eyes reflected the indigo waters, and this time there were no shadows, no pain. "Edward and his brothers, Henry, each of our loved ones will remain in our hearts, my darling. Their sacrifice made this possible. We'll not forget them, and we will always honour their memory."

"Always they are with us," she repeated. "And now we resolve to protect Luce and John. No more death, Allen, no more dying for this cause."

"We sail to The Hague that I might pledge my loyalty to the king, join with his army to return him to England. Upon my honour, I am a soldier first and will always serve the cause. I live to defend the king."

"And your family?

"I will die to protect. But those times are no more."

In the spring sunshine on the open sea, with a clear horizon around them, she knew the liberty of survival. She knew the indomitable spirit of her faith and her belief in her husband. Together they sailed into a bright new world. And the dragons finally disappeared.

Upon approaching land, the sea being very shallow, the ship moored several hundred yards from the shore. A stiff offshore wind picked up, making the landing challenging. Truly, the Dutch were most accommodating, and a host of small boats of varying sizes rowed out to transport the English to the town. There was no jetty, no wharf as such, and as they beached with a shudder, waves splashed into the vessel and soaked them. Allen jumped over the side, the water just below his boots, and with laughter carried Frances and set her on her feet as he reached dry land. Nothing could dampen their mood, nor that of those around them.

There was no mistaking the warm welcome when they reached the neat and well-maintained town. The streets were crowded with all kinds of carriages, carts and horses for hire. The enterprising Dutch put to use every possible transportation for the foolish English and charged appropriately for the use of their farm nags, hay carts and even wheel barrows. The whole town was reminiscent of a harvest festival, for the procession of farm carts drawn by Dutch peasants contained merry lords and ladies, joyous merchants and clerks—anyone and everyone reaping a successful crop by joining with the king to celebrate his homecoming.

The spring sunshine warmed them as Frances and Allen trundled to The Hague in the back of a hay cart, their fine clothes stuck with straw darts, noisy children and barking dogs running alongside them.

The palace overflowed with people, where English was the only language Frances could hear, and the mix of freshly made court gowns and threadbare velvets of twenty years past created a riot of colour. Allen helped her down from the cart, and she paused while he brushed the straw from her skirts and straightened his own sleeves and hat. He held out his arm to her, patted his bag to make sure he still carried Nan's money.

"Ready to greet our king, my love?"

She took his arm and laughed in delight. "Ready, Allen. We have Nan's gift of money, Walter's letter and ourselves to present to King Charles."

Ordering two of the boys to follow with their trunk, they entered the palace.

The crush within was even greater than outside. No Louvre was this, with long galleries and open halls, where the exiled court had gathered in miserable groups huddled around meagre fires in empty rooms. This palace hummed with activity, and as Allen pushed his way through the mass of people, Frances held tightly to his arm to avoid being separated from him.

Allen grabbed a clerk carrying an armful of papers. "Where are Sir Edward Hyde's apartments?" he asked.

"Lord Clarendon?" The clerk nodded to a passage. "He's in his office until evening." He looked disdainfully at Allen and Frances. "You'll have to get in line for your petition. And don't expect it to happen in a hurry."

"Thank you." Allen guided Frances around a group of merchants, each garbed in velvet so fresh it still carried the scent of the dye upon it. He smiled at her. "We'll see if we can request a favour here."

Pushing through the crowd and encountering a line of people winding along the narrow corridor, they walked to the head, ignoring protests from those waiting. Allen greeted the guards at the door.

"Sir Allen Apsley and Lady Frances Apsley to see their cousin Sir Edward Hyde," he announced.

The guards looked at them dubiously.

"Oh, let us in, for God's sake," Allen ordered. "We've travelled far, and Sir Edward is expecting us. We come on the king's business."

"So does everyone else, sir," replied the guard. "We've orders not admit anyone who has not presented their name and is on the list."

Allen pulled Nan's letter from his pocket, carefully ensuring her money remained hidden. "Give Sir Edward my compliments, along with this letter," he said. "Now."

The guard nodded tersely, stood for a moment undecidedly and then chose to obey him and went into the chamber. Moments later, Hyde's enormous bulk filled the frame. Over his shoulder, Ned Villiers stood beaming.

"My dear Allen and Frances, welcome, welcome," Sir Edward roared. "For sure, you are a sight to see. Come, come free me from my business and tell me of Nan and yourselves. Let me put commerce aside for an hour and enjoy the news from home." He beckoned them in and ordered the guard to refuse entry to anyone else.

"My deepest condolences to you, Sir Edward, on the loss of your sister." Frances sat with her old friend by the window while Allen and Ned stretched out on elegant armchairs in front of the fire, deep in conversation.

He frowned at his hands and shook his head. "I thought by never mentioning her name, by keeping her from the letters, she would be safe."

"You did the best you could."

"Not enough." Sir Edward's voice broke. "Thurloe must have been following Susan for months. But she was so brave, Frances, so brave. She gave nothing away. She protected the network with her silence. And paid for it with her death."

He lifted pain-filled eyes to her. Frances leaned over and touched his arm. "Susan died to safeguard the king. As would any of us in the network, Sir Edward. Her sacrifice will not be forgotten. I am so very sorry."

They sat in silence while shouts and laughter echoed into the chamber from the courtyard outside.

"And now we return our king safely to England." Sir Edward cleared his throat. "So, Allen, what say you?"

Allen looked up from his talk with Ned. "To the return of the king?" He walked to the window to join them. "I say I have waited eleven years for this time to come. I am here to pledge my service and my sword to restore him to the throne of England."

Sir Edward nodded. "Your sword will not be necessary, Allen, for we return in peace. Monck has guaranteed our safety. But your service will be most welcome."

"I am here to pledge loyalty. I hope I will have the opportunity to tell the king so myself."

"You will. He is eager to meet all those who trouble to come here to join him."

Allen drew the pouch containing Nan's money from his doublet. "And hopefully those who cannot travel but send a welcome in their place." He handed Sir Edward her gift. "For the king. From Frank Lee."

Sir Edward opened the pouch and smiled. "Nan knows the expedient way to find favour in the new court," he replied. "Thank her for me. Her kind gesture will be most appreciated." He groaned as he adjusted his leg on a footstool, his swollen calf bumpy with veins under the cream silk stocking. If possible, Sir Edward's girth had increased even more, and it was obvious to Frances that his gout pained him greatly. "And what do you have in mind for yourself, Cousin?"

"The king once remarked that when he was restored to the throne, he would need a keeper for his hawks," replied Allen. "And to that end I have been stocking a mews at my home in Norfolk for the past three years. I can guarantee some of the best falcons in England will be ready for the king's return."

Sir Edward nodded. "A thoughtful venture. And one to please the king very much."

"They are beautiful creatures, for sure," interjected Ned. "When I was last back, Allen showed me the progress he has made in breeding. He has always had an eye for a peregrine, and now I'd say not even Cromwell's mews could outshine his."

"That is a bold statement." Sir Edward unwedged himself with difficulty from the chair. "Cromwell prided himself on his horses and his hawks."

"Allen's are better," Frances said firmly. "For he has not just the eye, but the heart as well. A hawk is like a woman, she needs to feel worshipped, as well as respected."

The men laughed at her, and Sir Edward held out his hand to Allen. "'Pon my word, Allen, we shall see that you are made master of the king's hawks. How soon could you take up residence at court?"

Allen glanced at Frances. She nodded, smiling.

"As soon as we return, Sir Edward," he replied. "The country life has served its purpose."

"Our daughter Isabella approaches the age of twelve," continued Frances. "Your consideration for a position at court, once the king marries, would be most appreciated."

Sir Edward appeared amused. "And you, my dear? While we are arranging positions, where would you like to serve?"

"Wherever I can be of most use to the royal family," Frances replied. "My favourite memories are of the time I spent with the queen and Lady Morton in Exeter, when the queen's daughter was born. If I can be of assistance in the royal nursery when the time comes, I would consider it an honour."

"Hmmph." Sir Edward gathered up a stack of papers on his desk and shoved them ito Ned's arms. "That may be sooner than you think. The king

275

is already considering Catherine of Braganza as a possible wife. She brings a tidy dowry." He turned to Ned. "Make sure these are all recorded, Ned, and include Allen's appointment."

As Ned nodded and Allen began his thanks, Sir Edward held up a finger. "Do you owe on the hawks, Allen? I do not want the king to inherit a liability from you."

Allen shook his head. "No, Sir Edward. The hawks can be purchased outright. I have no debt on them, nor creditors who would place warrants."

"How did you manage that? A good falcon is not cheap."

"My brother-in-law, John Hutchinson, underwrote the acquisition," Allen said.

Before her eyes, Sir Edward's expression hardened.

"You are in business with the king-killer?" he asked coldly.

Frances stepped in before Allen could defend John. Here was the temperature of the king, evidenced immediately in his most trusted advisor.

"Times have changed in England. John is respected in his county, and of course he is married to Allen's beloved sister Luce."

Hyde's face grew more solemn. "In a few days, the king will declare the terms for truce, for amnesty upon his return. He is willing to forgive those who fought against his father. But not those who murdered him."

In the silence, Frances became aware of shouts and merriment echoing in through the open window. A shooting star larger than any she had ever seen lit up the night sky, exploding into a shower of sparks across the roof.

"What sign is this?" she gasped, surprised at the casual reaction by Ned and Sir Edward.

"These are called fireworks," replied Ned. "The king has ordered them to be let off every night of the week he stays here in The Hague. They announce the start of the evening's celebrations." He stuffed the papers under his arm and took Frances's and Allen's elbows. "And you must join us. You can refresh yourselves in my chambers, for I have an extra room to spare in this overcrowded hive. Sir Edward, will you come too?"

The older man shook his head, his expression clouded. "Not at present. I have work to finish that will last long past the fireworks. But enjoy yourselves." He looked up at Frances under his heavy brows and smiled. "Go, Frances. I have no doubt that Nan prepared you for your stay here and packed suitable gowns. Go and enjoy yourself." His glance moved to Allen. "But don't do anything stupid and get yourself mixed up with that regicide brother-in-law of yours. Not now, when we are so close to restoring our lives to their rightful place."

Frances curtseyed, her opinion of Sir Edward now cautious. No longer were they old friends and fellow conspirators. Attitudes had changed with the anticipated return of the king. Statehood had fallen upon him, and those easy days of shared intrigue had vanished.

Ned walked them quickly to his apartments, and by his expression Frances knew not to say anything until they were safely inside.

"Is the court opinion that grave?" she asked. "We thought perhaps the king's declaration had been manipulated by Parliament for its own jealous use." Frances glanced at Allen, his back to them. She dreaded his old anger was going to rise again.

"I'm afraid so," replied Ned. "The king is prepared to tolerate much, to give way to the people's desires, to return under new terms. But he is not prepared to pardon those who executed his father. And can you blame him?"

Allen turned. Frances was anticipating his blankness, the emptiness that came over him at times of great anxiety. Instead, his gaze was clear and his words calm.

"Then we will find a way around this, Ned," he said firmly. "And we will. Between us and Nan, we will not let John die. Frances, you must write to Nan now, for she waits for news at Whitehall, ready to guide John's path."

"I'll send her a message this evening." Frances's heart beat faster. She had not expected to take up her intelligencer role again immediately upon landing.

"Hyde and the king may not be the direct route to securing John's freedom. But don't underestimate the rest of our family," observed Ned. "Now let us join the court."

36

Luce

Colonel Hutchinson told them that for his acting in those days, if he had erred, it was the inexperience of his age, and the defect of his judgment, and not the malice of his heart, which had ever prompted him to pursue the general advantage of his country more than his own; and if the sacrifice of him might conduce to the public peace and settlement, he should freely submit his life and fortunes to their dispose.

Luce Hutchinson
Spring 1660

Candles gleamed in the windows of their Holborn home as Luce and John rode into the familiar street, worry-weary and exhausted. The Great North Road from Owthorpe teemed with southbound travellers, all intent on reaching London and seeing for themselves the changes occurring each day. Relief flooded over Luce, for she'd worried their servants had not been able to make headway in time to prepare the house. Ever since receiving General Monck's command to return to Parliament, John had been quiet, reflective of the time spent in Owthorpe away from the centre of power. His detachment bordered on indifference. Even after all their years of marriage, Luce could not understand this quality in her husband.

"Here we are." John swung down from his horse and patted its neck before handing the reins to the stable boy. "A safe journey, one without incident. I am hungry."

She swallowed a retort. They were in London, not out for a day's ride to Nottingham market. Did he still not realise the implications of tomorrow's Parliament?

Not like her. Luce could not sleep for the worries that plagued her nights, could not eat for the words that stuck in her throat. Did John not think of the king's revenge, his role in the proceedings against the king's father?

They crossed the muddy stable yard to the door. The shouts and rumbling of the city wrapped around them, neighbours arguing, dogs barking, children crying, a group of drunk apprentices shouting a Royalist song as they staggered forth from the inn at the corner. There was no peace on this street.

Each time they'd stopped along the road from Owthorpe, the rumours had grown wilder, the truth stronger

The king was on the move.

The king would arrive in London by Friday.

The king was already living in Whitehall Palace and had reopened the theatres and bull pits.

The unknown fed gossip at every tavern, every landlord the latest authority on the day's news.

When John once again sat with Parliament on the morrow, he would hear for himself of the Stuart's return. And yet still her husband refused to talk of his own future.

"We shall see, God will steer my destiny," he kept repeating. "I have nothing to fear, for God has safely guided me to this point and will continue to look to my well-being."

They crossed the threshold into the old familiar Holborn home. Luce turned to John.

"We step from our old life to our new," she said. "The opening of Parliament decides our future."

"It is in God's hands," he replied calmly.

Dressed immaculately in his best red velvet suit and fresh lace collar, John's fair handsomeness twisted her heart as she fastened the tiny buttons on the jacket front. His thick hair curled on his shoulder with hardly a thread of grey, and his neatly clipped mustache framed the sweet mouth she knew so well. Luce's fingers trembled slightly, and she bowed her head closer to the task. Her man. Her love. Her destiny.

"And so you are ready, John?" she asked, looking up at him into his soft brown eyes.

"Yes," he replied. "I do not choose to be a part of General Monck's cunning new government, but I am obliged to attend on behalf of my people."

"You will be strong? You will bear this news?" Luce tried to still the fluttering of anxiety in her heart.

He nodded, his face sombre. "Today is a turning point in our country's future. I must hear for myself the Stuart's declaration. Finally, Monck's secret dealings with the royal court will be disclosed for all men to judge."

"As will the king's terms for returning to England." Luce choked back a sob and turned away then. Holding herself tightly, she could not bear for John to see her cry. His arms came around her, drawing her close to his strength.

"Hush, my love," he whispered against her hair, brushing kisses across her head the way he always did to soothe her anxiety. "Hush."

She twisted free of his arms. "I cannot bear it, John." Her anguish broke through, calm fleeing as he strapped on his sword and pulled on his hat. "It's gone, it's all gone. What we fought for, what our brethren died for." Sobs choked the rest of her words, and she waved her hands in despair.

He paused, his own shoulders slumping briefly before he straightened and adjusted his sword. "I must go. Pray for me, Luce. Pray our Parliament keeps strong." He kissed her. "Work on your writing, and worry not. I will return before curfew."

Alone with her thoughts, the ghosts of the past crowding around her desk, Luce could neither write nor read, for each time she dipped her quill in ink, the words of the past eleven years crushed her. And what use now, all those letters and proclamations, pleas and pardons? Hopeless were her fervent treatises for equality, for men's rights for representation, for the abolition of the divine right of kings.

Worthless. Lost to the winds of change like dust motes in sunshine.

Finally, giving up on being able to write at all, Luce pulled a chair to the window and gazed out at the Londoners going about their business. The sticky buds on the chestnut trees promised spring. Her mother's favourite season. Luce let the tears fall and, alone in her room, surrendered to the fear and guilt she concealed from John.

By the time darkness crept along their street, stiffness and cold had set in from sitting by the window. The lamplighters walked with their flares held high, and wavering orange flames now lit the buildings, flickering from the iron brackets. John approached on his mare, for Luce recognised her high-stepping gait, and disappeared under the window. The smell of roasting meat curled into the chamber. No more time to mourn. This one day of grief for her lost dreams, and now to hear what Parliament and the king had ordained.

And find a way forward.

Standing and wiping her eyes, smoothing her hair and brushing her skirts, Luce nodded quietly to her mother's ghost in the shadows.

"Be with me, in my heart," she whispered. "Bestow upon me the strength you gave my father when the Tower walls confined you and the prison isolated you."

And, as so often with the spirits of the departed, a welcoming warmth swept over her.

Her mother would walk with her on this journey. She was not completely alone in her mission to save John from the king's vengeance.

"Forty days we have to declare ourselves and receive clemency." John sat at the table, his face weary, the strain of the day hollowed in the shadows under his eyes.

"Like our Lord in the wilderness," replied Luce, flippant in her relief. "So just as he wandered in the darkness, now you walk to the light."

John bowed his head, his hands clasped around the glass of Rhenish. He did not respond to her joke.

A quiver struck her heart. "John?"

"Forty days to declare our loyalty and obedience."

"God is wise, John. He knows what lies in your heart, your conscience. Your loyalty and obedience is with your people. And you represent them to the king." Luce drove her point forward. "For declaring loyalty to the king in the absence of conflict is no more than declaring loyalty to your people."

"You play with words, Luce." John remained sunk in his chair.

"There are only words now," she flashed back at him. "The time for swords is over."

"And so you ask of me to erase the past with a single declaration."

"I ask you to speak of the present and look to our future." Surely he could see where this led. A declaration, a pardon, home. "And you can say that; you can pledge your loyalty."

John did not meet her eyes. "Yes," he whispered, almost to himself. "Yes, I can say that."

Luce took a deep breath. "Then you must swear your oath now, John. Be the first to declare, be the leader among men, and lay claim to the king's pardon."

John drank his wine in one gulp. "Parliament returns on May 3. I shall be the first to step forward and declare myself a subject of the king."

"Your decision is God's will," she said firmly. His declaration would erase the stain of the signature. And wipe clean her own conscience. "Swear your obedience, and then we retire permanently to Owthorpe, never to return to London again."

And now every man who had previously opposed the king stood and made his declaration, following John's leadership and appearing before Parliament and each other. In truth, Luce could hardly keep up with events, for each day a flood of men appeared, hats twisted in hands, begging forgiveness for their moment of rebellion. Each night John sat at the table and told her of their words, of Ingoldsby's tears, of claims of Cromwell's holding their fists to make them sign the death sentence, and of his own impromptu words when called upon a second time.

"I told them it was my youth and my inexperience that drove me to sign," he said. "Not malice, not hatred for the king."

"And did Parliament believe you, John? It seems peculiar to me that the king leaves clemency in the hands of the very men who turned against him." Luce pulled her notebook towards her to write John's observations. "How can they act impartially when they are judging themselves among equals?"

John shook his head. "The king is canny," he replied. "For he leaves it to others to pass judgment. He has just provided the means, not the end."

Luce looked up. "What else did you say? Surely you included some oratory to speak of the king's mercy and his bounty, the words we thought would sway opinion of you."

"Not really, for they called on me with no warning." Her husband reached for her hand, stilled her writing for a moment. "I admitted I had made a shipwreck of everything except my conscience."

Luce waited for more. "The words we discussed, did they not come to you?" In the silence, a carriage clattered on the cobblestones on the street outside and a shout from the driver echoed across the room. "What else did you say?"

He shrugged. "Just that I had spent my money on maintaining Nottingham's security, and if there were any additional ways to prove my loyalty, I would place my fortune and my time at their disposal."

"Did they ask you to explain your condemnation of the king's father?" Luce grew more concerned with every statement John made, for surely his speech declared sacrifice, not defence.

"They did not ask me, but in clear conscience, I told them my act was that of an Englishman, a Christian and a gentleman."

Luce groaned aloud. Was John serious in his recounting? She kneeled in front of him so she could look deep into his eyes.

"Do you think that was enough, John? Do you think they are persuaded you are no threat to them or the king?"

John nodded. "I believe so, my love. They would recognise the clear and simple truth I spoke. For at the end of the day, the House has suspended me and forbidden me from serving. My time is over. I have no more obligations. We can go home."

Still, he did not look directly at her, and still something did not seem right. Just as she was about to question him more, footsteps clicked along the corridor outside. Nan entered, dressed in fine court clothes and bringing with her the scent of pomanders and brandy.

Luce jumped up. "You are looking very fine, Nan. What is the occasion?"

"I just came from Whitehall, from the nobles assembling there."

"You still attend?" Luce asked. "I thought you spent most of your time at Ditchley now."

"It is my choice." Nan's face grew serious. "And while Allen and Frances are at The Hague with the king, best I be close to the messengers."

"With the king?" Luce repeated. "Why is Allen there? And why do you seek royal company so actively?" Truly, events moved swiftly, and she struggled to find steady ground.

"For favours, of course," replied Nan. "They must be of the party to escort him back to England. And I sent them with salutations from Walter— and a gift of five hundred pounds from Frank."

"Five hundred pounds?" John whistled. "That will buy a few offices."

She nodded. "We must always plan for the future." Her face grew serious, and she drew John and Luce closer to the table.

"John, tell me how your time has been at Parliament these past days."

John turned away and poured wine. "Well enough," he said over his shoulder. "How are things at Ditchley? Have you had a good lambing season?"

Nan refused to be redirected. "And you have said the pledge?"

John nodded and handed Nan a glass.

Nan sipped slowly, concern wrinkling her forehead.

"And the Act?

What Act? John has not mentioned an Act.

Her husband sat still, cradling his wine.

"John, what about the Act of Oblivion? Are you named?" Nan reached for Luce's hand and held it tightly.

Luce turned to John. "What does this mean, Husband? What are you named in?"

John put his glass down and clasped his hands in front of him. "I hoped to spare you from this, my darling, until I had more clarity." His voice was gentle, reasonable. "Within the pledge of loyalty, the king also specified an Act of Oblivion. For those who signed the death warrant."

Her stomach rolled, and the room shuddered before her.

Nan spoke, breaking through the mist, "You are on the list."

"Yes."

"And you have pled before Parliament, asked for repentance?"

"Yes."

"Have you been suspended?" Nan's voice was urgent.

John nodded his head.

"But not released?"

John took his glass and drank deeply. "No. So I should surrender, then?"

"Not yet." Nan turned to Luce. "I must excuse myself. Would you kindly direct me to the privy?" She imperceptibly motioned towards the door.

Luce recognised her cue. "Yes. Come with me."

The moment they were in the dim corridor outside the library, Nan closed the door firmly and leaned against it.

"John is in extreme danger. I have received word from Frances, quoting Sir Edward Hyde. If John does not surrender, he will be imprisoned. If he does surrender, he will be tried as a regicide, a king-killer. The king will show no mercy. This I have on good authority."

"Never. Never will I let him sacrifice himself for his conscience," Luce hissed back, fear feeding anger. "What now?"

"Get John into hiding immediately," Nan replied. "Conceal him at Feltwell, where he is out of sight, where no one would think to search in a Royalist household."

"And then?"

"Return to Holborn. Wait for the king to cross over and you hear from me. For with Charles, we have power. With Parliament's vengeance, we have nothing."

"Power? We have no power with the king." Luce was frantic. Events were moving too swiftly. She needed time to think, to plan.

"You may not," Nan replied, "but as the widow of the king's best friend, I do. Look to your family for once, not to your absent political allies." Her cousin held an elegant hand in front of her, ticked off her long fingers. "Edward Hyde, who has remained loyal to our family since his first marriage. My niece Barbary Villiers, the daughter of the king's loyal colonel William St.John, who died in his service. Barbary is also cousin to his favourite, the Duke of Buckingham. And remember Ned Villiers is her uncle. She could intercede with the king."

Family ties indeed ran deep. Luce clasped Nan's hands within her own and brought them to her lips in prayer. "Then rally our family, Nan. Plead for John's life. And I will send him into hiding and await your return."

37

Frances

Frances giggled as Allen cursed while trying to adjust the sleeves on her claret-red silk gown, struggling with the fine cords. The slippery lace from her collar kept getting in the way of his knots.

"Truly, I am more skillful at taking these off than putting them on," he teased her. No maids were to be found anywhere, so great was the demand by the court; they were on their own to dress and prepare for the evening's festivities, the grand masquerade ball before they left for England. Finally, after a few more tugs they were ready, and for a moment they stood and admired each other in their finery.

"We have come a long way from Barnstaple's siege," Frances laughed. "And our first night together in a hayloft."

Allen drew her close. "And through it all, you have been my rock, my love, my beautiful girl," he responded. "Promise me you won't fall for some court fop and leave me?"

She pretended to think. "Only if he has better prospects than you." She kissed him. "Never. I would not change this moment, our hardships and our victories for anything, Allen. For to be standing here is to know we have survived. And that is the most joyful of all."

Allen bowed to her, took her hand and kissed it. "Then, Lady Apsley, the king awaits. Let us take our rightful place at the court of King Charles the Second."

Following the sound of the musicians, they walked through the palace and arrived in the banqueting hall. Here the cacophony of a thousand voices mingled with the orchestra. This was the court Frances had imagined in her darkest moments: extravagant clothes, the scent of exotic perfumes and the laughter of the most beautiful people on this earth.

The opulently furnished room boasted glorious wall hangings and an ornately carved ceiling gleaming with jewelled colours. A huge chandelier blazed over the dancing area, and around the walls unique sconces in the shape of outthrust arms bore two-foot-high candles. Never had Frances seen such affluence, such a richness of colour and scent and music all blending together.

"I surely have returned to Whitehall," Allen exclaimed. "And we could be arriving for a masque with King Charles and his queen. After all these years . . ."

"This must remind you of the time before the war, with William and your Aunt Barbara," Frances replied, stroking his arm. The orchestra, sitting on a raised dais, struck up a pavane, and the floor cleared to reveal the king, darkly handsome in a suit of black velvet with tawny trimmings.

"Oh," Frances gasped. "How marvellous." He looked nothing like the impoverished king-without-a-home she remembered from Paris. Or the gangly youth missing his father that she'd nurtured in Devon. "And that must be his brother James, the Duke of York."

Allen glanced across. "Yes. His fairness is such a contrast to the king's dark complexion."

"Goodness, is that Anne Hyde next to him?" Frances stood on tiptoe to get a better look at the woman at the prince's side. "She's grown since last I saw her."

"More like she's grown very close to the Duke of York, I'd say," Allen replied knowingly. "Nothing like a dashing soldier to turn a girl's head. Ned said Prince James had been recalled from Spain. He is an excellent strategist and a leader any soldier would think worthy of serving under."

"You should ask him," said a voice at their shoulder, and they both turned to greet Ned. Frances was impressed with his ornately embroidered jacket, so stiff with metallic thread the fabric beneath was barely visible. "You could hold a position with Prince James in his cavalry, Allen. He would welcome an experienced soldier such as you. An alliance with him would serve you well."

"You think acquiring a position is that easy?" Allen questioned.

"It is right now," replied Ned. "We'll approach him later this evening, when the wine has flowed and Anne Hyde's company has made the duke even more gracious. Royal favours are being distributed like Maundy silver. Especially to those of us who cared enough to travel to support the king and his brother here in Holland, to aid them before they arrive back home. Nan judged the right timing, for sure." He caught Frances looking at his clothes and shrugged. "We still own the patent for gold and silver thread. My mother puts our resources to excellent use."

They laughed and turned back as the king finished the dance with his sister Mary. A new tune struck up, this time more sensuous, a rhythm slithering into Frances's blood, creating an excitement she had never felt from music before.

"Oh. Here we go," Ned whispered.

"What?" Frances asked. "What's going on?"

"Watch," he replied succinctly. "I thought this might happen."

As the sensual chords pervaded the chamber, a woman emerged from the group gathered beneath the musician's dais. She was tall, taller than Frances, and dressed in an exquisite gown of turquoise and silver, which shimmered with every languid stride. A waterfall of auburn hair cascaded over her bare shoulders and down her back, rippling as she moved purposefully towards the king, now standing alone on the floor. Masked, she walked knowing the eyes of the room were upon her, slowly, until the beat of the music and the swish of her dress were in perfect harmony.

"God's nails," exclaimed Allen. "Who is that?"

"The king's latest mistress," replied Ned.

And as she gracefully sank into the lowest of curtseys, her dress spreading around her, her hair flowing over the floor, Frances gasped.

"It's Barbary."

The king leaned forward and slowly untied her mask with as much sensuality as if he undressed her completely in front of the assembled court.

Ned nodded. "Yes. She has not left the king's side within an hour of her arrival. And when we depart for home at the end of the week, she will be on the *Royal Charles* with him."

"Did she not just marry Roger Palmer a year ago?" The king had taken Barbary away from the floor and now sat with her on a bench, just the two of them, winding her hair around his wrists as if binding them with rope.

Following Frances's gaze, Ned laughed. "That is of no consequence. The Stuarts have a desire for Villiers love again. It is as if we never left."

"Speaking of which." Allen nodded across the room. "That is a sight I never thought to see."

Frances followed his gesture. Standing across the ballroom, Sir Thomas Fairfax, their opponent at the siege of Barnstaple, the general who had ended their war, stood next to George Villiers, Duke of Buckingham. Between them stood a fair-headed woman, her hands clasped in front of her.

"She is not happy." The words flew from France's mouth before she had time to think.

"Who would be, married to George Villiers," murmured Allen. "He is the biggest rake in Europe. He only wed her for political gain. And her property."

"And so Mary Fairfax became the Duchess of Buckingham?" Frances wondered aloud. "Dear God, that must have sat well with Fairfax's Parliamentarian supporters."

Ned leaned over. "By then Cromwell was struggling with approval for his ideas for succession, and Fairfax sided with Monck," he whispered. "The tide was turning. My cousin simply hitched his sail to the prevailing wind."

"George would sell his mother if he thought he could pocket the profit." Allen's face darkened. "His father ruined mine, if you haven't forgotten, Ned."

"He is without scruples," agreed his cousin. "As is the rest of my family. I think I must be a cuckoo's egg, for I don't sing their song."

Allen's face broke into a smile. "We have always been truthful with each other, Ned. Don't think I've forgotten all you did for my mother in our troublesome times."

Frances nudged Allen. "The king comes."

Amid applause, the king, followed closely by Barbary and her husband, made his way through the crowded ballroom. As the king walked in front of them, Barbary spotted Allen and tugged at the king's sleeve. Frances gasped at the intimate gesture and quickly recovered as the king turned to his mistress.

Barbary drew him towards Allen and Frances.

"My cousin Sir Allen Apsley, Your Majesty."

The king threw back his head and laughed. "Nall! And Frances." He kissed her soundly on the lips. "What a wonderful pleasure to welcome you here. Sir Edward mentioned he entertained you."

Allen bowed deeply, and Frances curtseyed, Nan's beautiful ball gown spreading around her. Barbary caught her eye, puzzled at the king appearing so affectionate.

Allen dropped to one knee. "Your Majesty, I pledge you my loyalty, my service, my sword. I would not be anywhere else in the world but in your presence at this time. I will follow you wherever you command, as my father followed yours to his death."

With tears in his eyes, the king raised Frances's husband and gathered him in an embrace. "Remember Barnstaple? Remember our walks, your advice to a young boy who had just lost his father to exile?"

Allen nodded, and Frances swallowed the lump in her throat.

"That young man has never forgotten your kindness, Allen, nor your tenderness, Frances." The king took a deep breath. "We have waited for this time and lost many dear to us along the way. Henry. Barbary's father. Your cousins. All men who have died in our name and without whose sacrifices we would not be here today."

"They will never be forgotten, Your Majesty. Their names will endure. I shall see to that. As will Nan and their children." Allen glanced at Barbary. She smiled proudly.

"Nan! How is she? And where is she?"

Allen grinned at the king. "She is well and is raising Henry's son, John, to become your loyal subject. They wait to welcome you home."

"Nan and John Wilmot. Home. There were days I thought I would never live to see home again." The king glanced at Ned. "Do you return to England with us?"

Ned nodded. "Allen and Frances are guests upon my ship, Your Majesty."

"A good arrangement." The king embraced Allen again. "Ride with me into London. Our procession will be magnificent."

Allen bowed again.

The king paused, and his next words came quietly. "I know in what high regard your cousin William Villiers was to you, Allen, as he was to me. How curious that I should now be reacquainted with his daughter." He turned and smiled at Barbary. "The love of a Villiers is never far from the Stuarts."

For their remaining few days in The Hague, Allen and Frances made the rounds of acquaintances from Paris. The Duke of Buckingham's faction grew strong, George Villiers now replacing Henry as the king's confidante. His father-in-law, General Fairfax, one of the archenemies of the king's father, now joined him in a curious alliance.

"Fairfax absented himself from the original commission," Allen told Frances. They were waiting at the quay to embark on the flotilla of boats accompanying the *Royal Charles* and amused themselves by people-watching as they stood. "And so although a fervent Parliament man, Fairfax was not a signatory to the death warrant. As far as King Charles and Buckingham are concerned, that is enough to excuse him from prosecution."

"Luce calls him a coward. He actively pursued the king to his death more fervently than John ever did and yet refused to put his name on paper." Frances scowled. "Surely the commanders should be responsible, not those who serve under them."

"Someone has to be made an example of," replied Allen. "Cleaner and quicker to pursue those who signed than those who fought." He glanced back up the wharf. "Look, I think the royal party is coming. Let's move closer to the ship."

Frances took his arm, and they made their way to the edge of the quay. A line of Dutch guards stretched as far as she could see, holding back a throng of Hollanders that numbered in the tens of thousands. Not since the execution had she witnessed such a mass of people. This time there were cheers and shouts and music playing. A very different atmosphere. She shivered despite the warm sunshine.

Catching her thoughts, Allen held her close. "No looking back, Frances. Those times are behind us."

She smiled at him. "No looking back," she confirmed. "Here is the king . . . and Barbary. We should board."

They followed the king to the tender and stood on the shore as he boarded and headed for the *Royal Charles*. Shortly afterwards, they climbed into their own boat bound for Ned's ship. Frances gave a prayer of thanks for the position they found themselves in and the extraordinary opportunities ahead. She and Allen returned to England. And the court of King Charles.

38

Nan

Nan's hired coach pulled to a shuddering halt, and she disembarked just north of Scotland Yard. Pausing outside Wilmot House, she let the pedestrians and horses on King's Road rush past her as she gazed up at the four-storey brick building. The sturdy Elizabethan structure endured, and although Henry had not lived here since before the war, the house of his birth was hers, as custodian for their son.

Thank heaven for God's providence. Nan's tenant, Lady Harvey, now being unable to afford the lease, had informed she was leaving the house, having subleased it to Mr. Willoughby. Until June 7, the empty house was solely Nan's.

Furious as she was that her rents were interrupted, Nan could not think of a better refuge for Luce than right under the nose of Parliament. While John was hidden away in Norfolk, Nan was going to have to use every contact, every possible favour she could think of to extricate him from his pending sentence. Positioning herself in the centre of power was the only way to effectively control events. Ditchley was too far away, and thanks to Walter's stubbornness, Battersey still considered a Parliamentarian house.

Walter. Another of her challenges. Really, he appeared incapable of recognising the forthcoming changes and was most tardy in kissing the king's hand. She sighed. Another matter to attend to. A generous gift to the king in her brother's name should smooth over any suspicions that his loyalty to the king carried any hesitation.

Her thoughts returned to John. At her request, Luce would arrive later this afternoon. Together they would find a solution, even though Luce may not yet realise the role she had to play.

Her eye was caught by Thomas Alcock, her husband's trusted servant, scurrying along King Street. Fortuitous, for when Nan had written to him at his house next to the Wilmot mansion, telling of her intent to visit, she had no assurance he even still lived in the vicinity. The war had displaced so many. When Thomas saw her, he hurried more, and within a minute he was in front of her, breathless with anxiety and excitement, his fair skin flushed in the late May heat.

"I have the keys," he puffed. "Lady Harvey left them with me for the new tenant."

"Thank you, Thomas." Nan held out her hand for them. "And thank you for your confidentiality in this matter. I shall only be here a few days. And my cousin may be joining me."

Thomas gulped. "The house is empty, my lady, and all Lady Harvey's servants were dismissed. You'll find little comfort here."

Nan touched his arm to reassure this kind man. "After our privation of the past eleven years, this is a palace. For there is no price to pay for peace of mind, no luxury equal to quiet enjoyment."

She pulled some coins from her purse. "Now if you could kindly fetch some ale and wine, pies, perhaps some cheese and bread, sustenance is all I need. And if you could see my travelling case into the house, I shall be most thankful."

He bobbed a bow and picked up her trunk. Turning back to Henry's home, she took the heavy iron key and slid it into the lock. And walked into the safe haven she and Luce would inhabit while waiting for the king's return.

Luce arrived later that afternoon, and when Nan opened the heavy front door, she embraced her cousin and quickly drew her inside, shutting it against the rain that now danced on the road.

"You answer your own door?" Luce drew off her gloves and looked around.

Nan took her bonnet and cloak and laid them on the bench in the otherwise empty hall. There was little furniture, for she had wisely removed all the costly pieces to Ditchley before leasing the house.

"We are alone here." Nan steered Luce to the front parlour, where she'd made up a fire and laid out Thomas's bread and cheese on the table. "No one saw you come from Holborn?"

"Other than my coachman, no," replied Luce. "And as you instructed, I sent him home, to wait for a message from me." She drifted over to the corner shelf, her eye caught by several small books. Trust Luce to find her written friends first in an empty house. "Why all the secrecy, Nan?"

Suddenly, she turned. "Is there news? Is there news from Allen and Frances?"

Nan led her to the bench in front of the fire. Rain pattered on the windows, and a sudden squall rattled the glass and made the fire hiss. She retrieved Luce's cloak and wrapped it around her. "Spring has disappeared on us again," she said. "And it's June next week."

"I didn't rush here in secrecy to discuss the weather, Cousin." Anxiety sharpened Luce's voice. "Tell me, please. What has happened? Is John in deeper danger?"

"I have heard from Allen." Nan ignored Luce's abruptness, for she knew fear tainted her words. "Sir Edward does not think well of John. There is no clemency from his influence."

Luce swayed and grasped the bench's wooden arm. "What does that mean?" she whispered.

Nan sat next to her and clasped Luce's other hand, forcing her cousin to meet her gaze. "This means we fight on a different front, Luce."

"Than the king?"

Nan shook her head. "No, the king's favour is what we seek. But the method of reaching him is not through our cousin Hyde."

Luce looked searchingly at Nan. "Who, then?"

"Allen has a suggestion," replied Nan. "But I have to see for myself if his idea is viable."

Luce shook her head. "You must not endanger yourself by saving John's life," she said. "I will ask Allen myself and follow his advice."

"I don't think so." Nan gathered both of Luce's hands into hers. "Your time will come, for I am sure we will need your assistance in persuading John to cooperate."

"Cooperate?" Luce's voice rose again. "Cooperate in what?"

Nan sighed. "Prepare yourself, Luce, for this will not sit well with you. Allen says the king returns with a mistress at his side. He has witnessed firsthand her influence on the king. At her request, he is restoring forfeited lands to other families who have expressed contrition for their part in the war."

"And? Does Allen think we may be able to reach the king through her?"

Nodding slowly, Nan stood.

Luce gazed at her steadily. "I can overlook moral depravity if it saves John's life."

294

"The king's new mistress is our cousin Barbary Villiers. And according to Allen, she has more power in her little finger than Sir Edward wielded in his whole history with the king."

Luce gasped. "Barbary. Ned's niece? There is no justice in this world if yet another Villiers ruins our lives."

Nan poured two glasses of wine and handed one to Luce. "Drink this. You'll need courage. And instead of rejecting them, let us toast to family ties. You may despise our Villiers relatives and the injustices they wreaked on your mother. But I intend to find a way to exact a favour from them that will avenge old hate and bring your husband home to you again."

Luce drank deeply, her hand trembling. "And so you return to court?"

"The king rides in state from the Tower to Westminster tomorrow." Nan poured more wine. She must be firm with Luce. "And in the evening he dines at Whitehall. Allen and I will seek out Barbary and beg her intervention. We have no time left for diplomacy."

They drank together then. And Nan silently prayed for the success of her plan to rescue John from the scaffold

The church bells woke Nan, crashing and clashing and shattering the early morning stillness in their jubilant pealing. She threw aside the blanket and jumped from the one bed she and Luce had discovered in an upstairs chamber. Luce was already sitting by the window, gazing out across King Street and the handsome houses across the way. Her profile was sombre, and as Nan walked to her side, she put her arm around her cousin's slight shoulders.

"Be strong." Nan held her tightly to steady the trembling in Luce's body.

"It is over," whispered Luce. "Until just now, until the bells rang, I could imagine this a dream and that our republic still stood. But the king has returned. Today, he enters London. It is over."

"Yes, he returns," Nan replied softly. She knew the same sorrow dwelled in her brother Walter's heart and preoccupied John's thoughts far away in Norfolk. "But he does not evict Parliament, Luce. He works alongside England's representatives. Your fight was not in vain. We will never return to the old king's way of divine rule with no thought for the people of this land."

Another peal of bells, this time from St. Martin's across the fields by Charing Cross. Below in the streets, people were gathering, setting up stools and opening hampers of food, determined to be at the front of the crowd as the king rode by. And as the hours passed, and Luce remained a silent sentry to the demise of her rebellion, Nan brought water and bread, which stayed untouched at her side.

Finally, by midafternoon the sporadic cheering swelled into a sustained roar and the bells clashed even more wildly, now all at once, a cacophony sweeping over the buildings and bouncing from the walls. Luce opened the catch and leaned from the window, and Nan squashed herself next to her so they could both look towards Charing Cross.

And here came the tramp of foot soldiers, the king's guards, pikemen marching to peace, not war. Next the Cavaliers, their horses caparisoned in richly decorated fabrics, replacing their usual worn, battle-scarred leather. The nobles rode next, then the king's brother and the Duke of Buckingham. All paraded in this victory procession, and suddenly, without warning, tears choked Nan's throat and sprang from her eyes. The king, on a white stallion draped in cloth of gold, a young god riding at the head of his army. And next to him, a horse with no rider, led with stirrups turned. Was this for Henry? Was this the horse that Henry should have ridden at the king's restoration? She did not know for sure, but she could think it in her heart, that the king would remember his faithful friend, the man who saved his life, who helped him escape from England. Who did not return with him.

Now the procession passed below their window, making the last turn before the Banqueting House and Westminster Hall. Luce sat motionless, and as the king rode beneath them, she silently leaned forward. They both watched him disappear from sight as he approached the place of his father's execution, each lost in their own memories of that day.

"There's Allen . . . and Ned." Nan nudged Luce, who returned her gaze to the street. The men did not look up, for they were not to know of Nan's hiding place.

"So you go to the palace today?" Luce's voice was a monotone, crushed. Never had Nan heard such defeat in her cousin.

"I will. The king speaks first at Westminster. And then, when the ceremonies are over, I will return to Whitehall, to Barbary's lodgings, and put forth our case for John."

Nan's solemn words seemed to break through Luce's mood. She pulled herself back from the window and closed the catch, shutting out the rejoicing. Nan recognised the resolve of Lucy in her expression, the steel in her words.

"Thank you, Nan," Luce replied. "And God bless you. Go with Allen. Meet with Barbary Villiers. Plead for John's freedom. I will wait here for instructions from you. And pray for my husband's life."

London's families had long returned to the safety of their homes by the time Nan slipped from the back of Wilmot House. Threading her way past the night-fragrant gardens of Scotland Yard, she pulled her hood farther over her head. She should have had an escort, for the crowd about now was of a different mood. These were the apprentices and soldiers, the careless men and wild boys, and with the fountains flowing wine since the morning, not many remained sober.

Nan sucked her breath in surprise as a shadow detached from the rough wall.

"My lady." The man raised his lantern, and she exhaled with relief.

"Thomas. How long have you waited here?"

He lowered the lantern again. "I have been watching out for you, Lady Wilmot," he said. "I thought perhaps you might have an errand at the palace."

Her husband's servant had seen much in his day. Why would she be surprised? "So you accompany me?"

"Of course. Whom do you seek to see?"

She could trust him. Henry told her he had staked his life on Thomas more than once, arriving secretly in London in some halfhearted disguise and allowing himself to be properly costumed and concealed from the Roundheads.

"Barbary Villiers. Lady Castlemaine." Nan grimaced. The king had already granted Roger Palmer an earldom. Rewards for services given. And those of his wife.

"I know her new lodgings. Come, I will guide you."

Thomas lifted the lantern and led Nan through the crooked streets and alleys and a series of courtyards. The May evening was gentle, yesterday's showers had washed the streets and released a perfume of jasmine in the air.

The drunks stayed in the gutters by the taverns, and together Nan and Thomas entered the heart of the king's palace, where she would meet Allen at the Castlemaine apartments.

"Here, my lady." Thomas stopped before a door set in a long row of town houses. The palace had certainly been cleaned since she was last in Whitehall. Was the renovation Cromwell's? She thought as much, for he had lived here as a king himself. Several women in splendid court costume were entering the house, and, nodding a thanks to Thomas, she slipped in behind them.

Following the courtiers, she handed her cloak to an attendant and carefully shook out her skirts. The black silk cast a suitably respectful tone, for she wanted to bring attention to the king's debt to Henry. If her husband hadn't smuggled him out of England after their crushing defeat at Worcester, Charles would be dead. She adjusted the heavy pearl necklace so it lay smoothly around her neck and touched her hair to make sure it was neatly in place. Dressing without a maid was not the easiest, but Luce was handy, and together they'd managed.

"Nan!"

She turned at her name and walked straight into Allen's arms. He held her tightly, and for a moment she relaxed, his familiarity reassuring her that she was not on this mission alone. Once more they joined forces, only this time it was not against Luce, as in their childhood arguments. Tonight, Luce's future depended upon them.

"I saw you in the procession." Nan stood back a little to look at her cousin and admired his beautifully cut jacket and britches. A froth of lace tumbled at his neck, and, most glorious of all, he was wearing one of the new French wigs that the king had made fashionable. Dark and curling past his shoulders, the carefully styled hair enhanced his handsome eyes, and she had to look hard to find the boy she'd known, the exhausted soldier she'd tended after Edgehill.

"And painful it was too," he muttered. "I have never taken six hours to travel from the Tower to Westminster."

"You've never ridden with a king before," she teased. "Well, at least with one in peace." She tugged at his wig. "It suits you."

Allen smiled and smoothed the hair. "'Struth, this is hot. I'm not sure I can keep this on all night." He looked around the crowded reception rooms, where powder and wigs were the order of dress. "It's a new world to get used to Nan, for sure. And one that Frances is eager to embrace. Money flowed to the court the moment the king made his declaration. How quickly we all transformed."

Nan laughed to witness his discomfort. "You've been with your hawks too long, Allen. You'll need to recover your court ways now." She looked around. "Is Frances here?"

He shook his head. "No. She was requested by Sir Edward to chaperone his daughter Anne. Seems he thinks she's been seeing a bit too much of the Duke of York." He looked down at her, and a smile played around his generous mouth. "Well? You look set for battle. Are you ready to meet the king's new mistress and her cuckold husband?"

Nan straightened her shoulders. "She had best remember her place." The young chit was not going to get the upper hand in this meeting.

"Apparently, she is receiving guests in her drawing room. Let's see how far she has come since last you saw her." Allen held his arm out to Nan, and together they climbed the wide staircase and threaded their way into the formal rooms.

The display of wealth in Barbary's apartment was overwhelming, and Nan suspected that every suitable piece of furniture that could be moved into these rooms had been done so on a day's notice. Paintings crowded the walls, tables and chairs were at every turn, and cabinets full of crystal and curiosities filled the corners of the rooms. The candle arms carried blazing tapers, and the smell of expensive wax mingled with that of ambergris and musk and fragrant spiced wines.

By the large fireplace, flanked by Villiers relatives, a tall woman with cascading auburn hair stood aloof. There was no mistaking the Villiers charisma, and as she glanced across the room, Barbary's striking almond-shaped eyes flickered up and down as she appraised Nan's dress. A man standing sullenly behind her, Nan guessed, was her husband, Roger Palmer. Conveniently close to deter gossip, but very obviously at a loss as to what to do with his wife.

Nan walked up to Barbary until they were face-to-face. She knew Allen was at her side, but she did not break her gaze from the woman's eyes.

"Cousin," she acknowledged and held her hand out. As the senior ranking woman, Nan expected Barbary to curtsey to her. After a minute's pause, she did so, with exquisite grace and a great deal of exposed bosom.

"Lady Wilmot. And Allen. I am glad you could join us this evening." Barbary leaned forward and affectionately kissed Nan's cheek, girlishly, and suddenly Nan understood her allure. No wonder the king was captivated. This woman-child was magnificent. And very aware of her power.

Tread carefully.

"We are honoured to be here. It is not often I venture abroad. But on such an occasion, I felt I must represent my husband and all that he did to bring the king to this moment." Nan watched Barbary carefully for a reaction and saw knowledge dawn on her beautiful face.

She turned to Allen. "Cousin, you sent a message that you had urgent business with me. Can it not wait? The king will be here momentarily, and I—"

"We will not take long," interrupted Allen, drawing Barbary to one side. Nan walked with them, and together they stood in front of their cousin, blocking her from the rest of the room.

Resting a hand on Allen's sleeve, Barbary drew him closer. "You are most eager to ask for a favour, it seems, Allen. Surely you can join me tomorrow at bowls. We can talk then as much as you wish."

Nan refused to let Barbary distract Allen. She took her niece's hand, ignoring her widened eyes at her presumption in touching the king's mistress. "We should talk now. It is an important family matter, and one that you can assist in."

She lifted an eyebrow and turned her attention from Allen. "Family? Which family is this, Cousin?"

"Yours," Nan replied firmly. She was not going to let her divide them. "Your cousin Luce, Allen's sister."

"The little Roundhead?" Barbary's voice echoed the sneer in her face. "She thinks to ask a favour of the king for her regicide husband?"

Nan stepped closer. "No. I do." Eye to eye, the two women measured each other. For now, Nan had the upper hand. A thought crossed her mind that this woman would soon be her equal in negotiating.

"Why?" A disturbance at the other end of the hall and the sound of clapping in the entry hall. The king had arrived. And Barbary was already trying to look over her shoulder to see him.

"John Hutchinson saved my husband's life. He has worked tirelessly for the king's cause for the past seven years, opening his home as a refuge

300

to wounded Royalist soldiers, storing guns and powder for the safety of the county." Nan would not let Barbary be distracted.

"John tended me after Worcester, risked his own life to hide me," Allen continued. "Luce nursed me back to health. As long ago as then, he was independent and concerned about what was best for his countrymen."

The king approached the outer receiving rooms. Time to exact more, to remind Barbary of her beginnings. Nan stepped closer, her words for Barbary alone. "Once, your grandmother betrayed Luce's mother and caused her terrible unhappiness. You will know the story. And this is your chance to repair the harm she did. And perhaps earn my respect." She could see the last words piqued Barbary's interest. Nan had just a few moments left. "Act on this for Luce, and I will see that your own star continues to shine at court. You need Hyde's approval. I can't guarantee he will like you, but I can make your ascent one he will not block."

Barbary tossed her hair back and adjusted her gown, revealing more creamy skin and curving bosom. She glanced over Nan's shoulder, and a languid glow burned in her eyes. She replied to Nan between almost closed lips so none but Nan could read her words. "And so I ask the king to spare his life? I will not do this alone. If I whisper in the king's ear, you both will speak in public."

The clapping increased. The king was entering Barbary's drawing room. Her husband walked towards them to hand his wife to the king.

A bargain, then. Nan spoke clearly and urgently. "Allen and I will formally declare our support for John. And you will remind the king of his love for Henry. Put the word about that the king looks favourably upon John for his service. And tell your uncle the Duke of Buckingham you would consider it a great favour if Parliament heard from him directly of the king's kind disposition."

"My kind disposition?" the king's voice echoed her words from behind, and Nan turned and swept the king a curtsey. "Lady Wilmot, you always know how to flatter me, just as your husband knew how to make me laugh." He raised her from her curtsey and kissed her cheeks. "'Struth, it is good to see you here at Whitehall, and you too, Nall."

"Your Majesty." Nan smiled at the king, for in her heart this was truly a most wonderful sight. "My husband gave his life for this moment"—here the king's eyes filled with tears—"and I pledge loyalty and honour from the Wilmot family and to serve you to the end of our days."

301

Kissing her hand, the king nodded. "Most appreciated, Lady Wilmot. And for Henry's sake, I shall welcome his son at court. How old is the boy now?"

"John is twelve, Your Majesty, and up to Oxford this year."

"Send him to us when he is ready," replied the king. "We shall take good care of him."

Barbary stepped forward, with her husband just behind her. "As you take care of me, sir?" she asked with a hint of laughter in her husky voice.

"As I take care of all the Villiers, as my father did before me, and his father before him, Barbary." The king bowed to Roger Palmer and held his arm out to his mistress. "Now tell me how else I may take care of you."

Barbary gave Nan a final glance, nodding her head slightly before turning to the king and whispering something that caused him to lower his head to hers and burst into laughter.

Time to return to the empty house, where Luce awaited alone, and tell Henry's ghost his king was restored to Whitehall. "Come, Allen. We are done here. I must go home to Luce, and we have to put the next part of our plan into motion. I fear that might be our most difficult task yet."

"Will Luce do as you ask?" Allen put his arm around Nan, and once again she leaned into his reassuring frame. "She would not for me, I know."

"She will. She has no choice. All we can do is set the stage. Now she must use her words to plead for John's life. It will be the most important letter she will ever write."

39

Luce

She devised a way to try the house, and writ a letter in his name to the Speaker, to urge what might be in his favour. This letter she conceived would try the temper of the house; if they granted this, she had her end, for he was still free; if they denied it, she might be satisfied in keeping him from surrendering himself. Having contrived and written this letter, whereupon she writ her husband's name and ventured to send it in.

Luce Hutchinson
Summer 1660

"No." Luce turned to Nan in horror. "John will never write a letter contradicting his signature on the warrant." How did her cousin even begin to think her husband would deny his conscience and lie before Parliament and God?

Nan tossed her gloves onto the bench and reached up to pull the pins from her hair, letting it fall around her shoulders in disarray. The formality gone, she became again Luce's beloved childhood friend Nan, accomplice against her brothers, her childhood defender.

But tell John to lie? This duplicity was too much to ask.

"No, he won't write it." Nan crossed the room swiftly and gripped Luce's hands. "But you will."

"What?" Luce recoiled, trying to pull her hands from Nan's. "He will never sign such a statement."

Nan would not release her. "But you will," she repeated.

Luce struggled and broke free. "What do you mean? What are you asking me? Is this your idea of a plan to save John? To falsify words and forge his signature?"

"And our family and friends will certify the truth to it." Nan grabbed Luce's shoulders and pushed her to the window. "Look. Look at a new London."

The street below pulsed with people, and the torches stayed lit despite the curfew. Tonight, London celebrated a king on the throne again. The city did not sleep. Luce thought she never would again either. What trap was

303

Nan devising for her? To lie to God? Or lie to her husband. Be damned on earth, or for all eternity. This was a Faustian bargain she could not make.

Her heart aching, Luce searched for guidance in the cold, distant stars. And found none. "I cannot deceive John this way. He would never forgive me."

"And if you don't, John will be paraded along King Street to Tyburn, where he will be hanged until barely alive and then pulled down from the scaffold and thrown to the ground to suffer the unspeakable anguish of witnessing his own entrails drawn and his body quartered."

Bile rose in Luce's throat at Nan's ferocious words. The image of her love's beautiful body lying broken and bleeding on a filthy street blocked out the world. All she could see was his chestnut hair matted and soaked in a puddle of blood. Her mind pulled memories of the king's death and substituted John's beloved face. The result was unbearable.

She was John's executioner.

Turning back to Nan with a sob, she searched her cousin's resolute face for a shadow of hope. "I will not see him desecrated and slaughtered as a traitor."

"Then write the letter, Luce. You have told me yourself how often you wrote for him, signed his name on his behalf. You have his hand. You can forge his name. Write John's apology with eloquence and passion, write with his words and your emotion." Nan sat at the window and leaned her head against the glass. "Write well because your husband's life depends on the truth of these convictions. Only then can I muster others to certify his intent."

Luce had no choice.

In the clarity of making her decision, calmness flooded Luce's body. Already, she sorted words, phrases, statements to prove his innocent intent. "Who else is joining us in this? Where's Allen? What does he do now?"

"Allen travels to Feltwell directly to bring John back to London and keep him hidden. He may be called before the Lords, but we cannot let him appear before we've persuaded the Commons. Of course Allen will certify. Along with Ned and your cousin Broderick. Others of the court who visited Owthorpe and were saved by John's fearless hospitality." Nan looked at Luce. "And as the widow of the king's favourite soldier, Henry Wilmot, the man who saved his life after Worcester, I will lead the signatures."

Luce digested Nan's words. "So you keep John in darkness while we play counterfeiters. You stand to lose much, Nan, by signing your name to a document pleading for the life of a regicide."

Nan clasped Luce's hands again. "It is a risk I am willing to take," she said. "I have survived the war by flying in the face of fear. We have but a few days before Parliament brings the final regicides to justice. We must act now before the proceedings open formally. And if I am right, Barbary Villiers will persuade the king to urge our case before the others."

"Do you have parchment here? Ink? A pen?" Every word she had ever written in her life had led to this moment. Best begin now while horror stalked in the shadowy corners of her mind and passion fired her thoughts.

"I will ask Thomas to bring writing tools in the morning." Nan gathered her into her arms, and once again Luce was a girl, secure in the embrace of her beloved cousin. "Sleep now, my darling, for you will need your strength these coming days."

Gratefully, Luce allowed herself to be put to bed.

True to her word, Nan found parchment, ink and a dozen sharpened swan's quills. And by the time Luce arrived in the drawing room, her cousin had dragged a table to the window and moved the bench alongside. The morning sunshine streamed through the dusty panes, casting a golden light over the oak, illuminating the parchment. Normally, Luce would have been delighted to spend hours writing, lost in the beauty of creating poetry. Today, she approached the table as a prisoner to the dock.

"It is to your liking?" Nan asked anxiously. "I told Thomas to bring us the very best quality instruments he could find."

Luce nodded slowly. "These are excellent. I am not sure if I can match with my words. I have been awake most of the night searching for them, and when I catch one, it slips through my fingers like quicksilver."

Nan pulled out the bench, and Luce sat down, staring at the paper.

If she picked up the pen, she would betray her husband.

If she didn't, she would kill him.

She had no choice.

 SIR—Finding myself by His Majesty's late proclamation proceeded against as a fugitive, after I had so early claimed the benefit of that pardon the king's Majesty was graciously pleased to extend to all offenders, I fear what I spoke in so hasty a surprise as that I was in when I had last the honour to declare myself in the House, was not a sufficient expression of that deep and sorrowful sense which so heavily presses my soul, for the unfortunate guilt that lies upon it; and, therefore, I beg leave, though my penitent sorrow be above utterance, to say something that may further declare it, and obtain your belief that I would not fly from that mercy which I have once made my sanctuary. They who yet remember the seeming sanctity and subtle arts of those men, who seduced not only me, but thousands more, in those unhappy days, cannot, if they have any Christian compassion, but join with me in bewailing my wretched misfortune, to have fallen into their pernicious snares, when neither my own malice, avarice or ambition, but an ill-guided judgment led me. As soon as ever my eyes were opened to suspect my deceivers, no person with a more perfect abhorrency detested both the heinous fact and the authors of it, and I was as willing to hazard my life and estate to redeem my crime as I had been unfortunate, through a deplorable mistake, to forfeit them by it. For this cause, even before Cromwell broke up the remaining part of the House, when his ambition began to unveil itself, jealous of those sins I did not sooner discern, I stopped and left off acting with them . . .

And, as Luce finished the letter, she did not pause before signing John's name, for as she wrote, she became him, and his words became hers and his again.

This was the final truth, for if she failed in this, all was gone.

I cannot but beg the honourable House would not exclude me from the refuge of the king's most gracious pardon, and pluck me from the horns of that sacred altar to become his sacrifice; and, if I thus escape being made a burnt-offering, I shall make all my life, all my children and all my enjoyments, a perpetual dedication to His Majesty's service, bewailing much more my incapacity of rendering it, so as I might else have done, than any other wretchedness my most deplorable crime hath brought upon me, in whom life will but lengthen an insupportable affliction that to the grave will accompany your most obedient and most humble servant.

John Hutchinson

Luce waved the letter gently to dry the ink and placed it in a pool of sunshine. The June sun had moved across her desk unnoticed while she wrote, and now finished, she realised she was both hungry and thirsty. Nan stood by the empty fireplace watching her, a flask of ale on the table, along with bread and cheese.

"I am done." Luce reached across and pulled a piece of bread from the loaf. "Do you want to read it?"

Nan crossed to her side and sat next to her on the bench. She put her arm around Luce, resting her cheek on her shoulder, and read the letter slowly, once and then again.

"It is a marvellous composition, dearest Luce."

"But are these words enough?" Luce was drained, all the emotion turning her blood to water.

Nan placed the letter down carefully. "Along with our other work, I believe they are."

Luce lifted the ale mug with both hands to steady as she drank thirstily. "And now what happens? When can John return? I must confess my sin to him; I cannot carry this unbearable burden long."

"Soon," replied Nan. "But not yet. Roger Palmer and Ned Villiers go before the House of Commons on Saturday. They will not only plead for this letter to be entered into the records ahead of the Proclamation, they will put word about that the king would be most delighted if John were exempt."

"Should John not be there? It was a condition of his parole that he appear in person as soon as the court sat."

"For now, no." Nan picked up the letter again and tested the ink. It was dry. "For if John appears again before them, I fear he may not speak with the eloquence and humility that you have captured in this letter."

"And so you defy the order?" Luce struggled to follow the cat-and-mouse games of her cousin.

"We appear before it is formally announced." Nan stood up. "I have just heard confirmation from Ned that the house is well disposed to hearing John's plea tomorrow. The letter must go to Whitehall this afternoon and be placed into the hands of the Speaker. Let me find Thomas and ask him to deliver it in person."

Luce stood too. "No." And then, without hesitation, took the letter from Nan.

"If I am to deceive my husband and the Speaker, I will deliver this myself. Then no one else can be blamed if the crime is discovered. Give me your pass so if I am stopped, I can use the Wilmot name."

A curious lightness of spirit came over Luce as she descended the steps from Wilmot House and entered the busy thoroughfare of King Street. The afternoon was full of sunshine, and from across the way a gentle breeze carried the scent of fresh-cut grass from St. James's Park. With a sudden trill, a blackbird flew to the stone wall that separated the house from the dusty street, and a ginger tomcat stretched his plump body under the shade of a bush. Luce leaned down and stroked him for the pure joy of a touch of normality in this illusory day.

Pussycat, pussycat, where have you been?
I've been up to London to visit the queen.
Pussycat, pussycat, what did you there?
I frightened a little mouse under her chair.

The rhyme came unbidden, her mother's words ringing as clear as a bell. "And now you have a king to visit, pussycat," she whispered. "Now you have a king."

Encouraged by her mother's memory, Luce turned to her left and walked into the glare of the afternoon sun towards Westminster and the Banqueting House. She determinedly looked straight ahead, where the abbey spires of the minster soared into the impossibly blue sky, ignoring the place of the king's damnation to hell.

Now she was back in familiar land as she drew near to Westminster Hall. How long ago, when she appeared before the Chancery Court, forced into giving evidence against her father and his debts. No brick or stone or wooden beam changed. The fabric of power resisted England's fracture. How fierce she was then, how angry against the king, ready to take on a court, a city, a country. Now she fought to defend one man's life, not to start a revolution.

She passed unquestioned through the guarded gate and walked right up to the weathered wooden door to the hall.

"Your pass, my lady?" Sentinels blocked her way.

Luce summoned every scrap of arrogance she could muster. "I am here on the king's business."

One of the guards moved his pike to one side. The other seemed doubtful.

"What business might that be, my lady?"

308

So far they had not asked for her pass. Now she had no choice. "I am the widow of Henry Wilmot, Lord Rochester. I have an important letter to deliver to the Speaker."

The guards immediately stood to one side and bowed their heads. "Lord Wilmot is sorely missed. We served under him," said one of them. "Please, pass through."

Luce stepped into the shade of the cavernous hall and immediately looked up. Yes, there were the flying angels that had brought her so much comfort during the darkest days of her father's hearing. She walked the length of the hall, where booksellers still sold their wares, and clerks bustled with piles of parchments tucked under their arms. She had to see one more thing before she delivered the letter. Drawing close to the chancery screen, she reached up and gently stroked the forehead of the carved white deer that embellished the arch.

"Give me courage, in the memory of my father and my mother," she whispered. "You bestowed me strength before in this hall of justice. Now please grant clemency to my husband and allow us to go home again."

She stepped through into the Chancery Court, knees trembling as the weight of the moment bore down on her. She quailed inwardly before the justices, the lawyers, the clerks, the stacks of papers and pleadings, dusty and fresh, all debating the outcome of men's lives in the torrent of suits heralding the return of the king.

And then pulled herself together. Hers was not the responsibility of the nation. Hers was the fate of one man. The man without whom she would die.

"Sir Harbottle Grimston," she whispered to an usher. "The Speaker of the Commons. I have an important delivery for him."

"I'll take it to his office," the man replied. "Give the message to me."

"I must deliver this personally."

The usher hesitated. She did not drop her gaze.

He shrugged and gestured towards a screen. "He's there."

Luce withdrew the parchment from her purse. The whole world narrowed to the document in her hand. Three steps, and she rounded the wooden partition. Two steps, and she stood before the Speaker. Before she could change her mind, she pressed her letter into his hand and marched from the chamber, leaving behind her counterfeit words and heartfelt plea.

It was done.

On the fourth day, Luce received word from Allen that he and John were back in Holborn. Allen did not know how much longer he would be able to restrain John from walking right into Westminster and turning himself into the Commons.

"I must go to him, Nan." Luce buttoned her cloak and turned to her cousin. "John is strong-willed and will not be dissuaded from appearing. I must forestall him, confess and beg his forgiveness.

"Go now," replied Nan. "I'll wait here. Ned believes a ruling will come from Parliament today or tomorrow. Remain at the house in Holborn, and I will send news as soon as I have it. Whatever happens, do not let John leave to represent himself."

From Scotland Yard to their home in Holborn was less than an hour, but to Luce it was one of the longest miles she had ever walked. The fine weather held, and Londoners were out in force. The streets were crowded with merchants' wives, apprentices, clerks hurrying to the inns of court, and all kinds of tradesmen shouting their wares. The mood of the city had changed so drastically she could not believe she was in the same town, for it seemed overnight the black-clothed preachers had been replaced by bright-coated dandies. Overnight, new shops had sprung up in empty premises, and the closer she walked to Covent Garden, the more commerce and bustle she confronted.

The city disoriented her with its jubilance, and she swept her memory back to the times of the old king, when she was young and visiting her family in their luxurious new Cheapside homes. The old splendour was back a hundredfold, and with each step closer to John and the truth of her deed, her heart rebelled at every outward sign of the celebration of the king's return and the circumstance that forced her lie.

Standing in front of her own door, she took a deep breath and banged on the solid oak. Allen pulled her inside.

"Luce."

Her brother looked tired, his eyes red from lack of sleep.

"Where's John?"

"In the library. He does not know of the letter. If I had told him sooner, he would have gone straight to the Speaker of the House and denied it." Allen rubbed his face, the stubble shadowing on his chin. "You know how to handle him. He will not take this news well."

Luce drew breath. "Let me see him on my own. Thank you for bringing him back, Allen." After all their arguments, they still stood side by side. "And thank you for all you are doing to save his life. I know this is not easy."

Allen took her hand and kissed the palm. "I do it for you as much as him, Sister. And for the sake of our mother and father in heaven."

So he felt close to them too now, in these fearful times.

She nodded and walked through to the library. There were still many books on the shelves, and John was standing with his back to her, reading the titles as if looking for something.

"John," she said.

He turned swiftly, and a delighted smile lit his face, the smile she had loved for so many years, the smile that had won her heart when first she saw him by the lantern light at Richmond Park.

"My love," he cried, holding out his arms to her. "My darling! Allen brought me back here to meet with the Commons, for we signers are all to appear to plead again. I did not expect to see you here. I thought you were with Walter and Johanna at Battersey."

"No," she replied. "I have been in town. There was business I needed to attend to."

He dropped his arms at her tone. "What business? With whom?"

She couldn't reply. She who always had the words at her fingertips lost them on her lips.

He knew her too well. "What business, Luce?" His tone grew suspicious. "What have you done?"

Still, her mouth refused to obey her.

"You must tell me what you have done," he repeated. Now worry crept into his tone. "Are you well, Luce? Is there something wrong with you?"

"Nothing which cannot be forgiven," she replied.

"I don't understand."

His dear face, his handsome countenance. She touched a chestnut curl that rested on his lace collar, traced the outline of his lips. Whole, beautiful, unharmed. He stayed still under her hand, his eyes searching hers.

"The Commons were ready to receive your new apology—"

"Ah, that is why Allen brought me back. We must go now—wait, you say *were?*" The significance of her word stopped him.

"It was delivered four days ago."

He struggled with her statement.

"How? How could my apology have been delivered four days ago? I have yet to write it. I must redress this mistake."

She had to explain quickly, tell him of her betrayal before he left. Already, he turned.

"I wrote it. And I signed it. And I delivered it myself to the Speaker of the House."

John froze.

A bitter cold crept across her body, and she started to tremble. "We only had one day, John."

"We?"

Say more, shout, be angry. Say more, John.

"Nan. Allen. Ned. And Barbary Villiers."

John laughed harshly. "A full conspiracy of Royalists."

Now her anger flashed. "Who united to save your life, Husband."

"And what fine words did you devise to satisfy the Commons? Or are they even satisfied?"

Luce dug in her purse. "I made a copy. You can see my words. I do not betray your conscience, John. Only do I say that Cromwell betrayed you and deceived you and many others. And how you were a friend to all men."

John refused to turn. Still, he would not look at her, nor take the paper she held out to his back.

"And you forged my signature?"

Luce dropped her hand again. "John, ever since we were under siege at Nottingham I have been your secretary. I have your hand, your signature, and I have written many dispatches on your behalf, when you were too exhausted to write."

Finally, he turned. "I dictated those to you."

"And my heart dictated this to me." She threw the letter to the ground. "I understand if you will never forget this, John. But forgive me, for I did it for love of you, to save your life, to bring you home."

"And you think me incapable of defending myself?"

Luce shook her head. "It is not that, John. If we had not expedited this letter to the Speaker, if Ned had not spoken for you, if Barbary had not convinced the king that he should treat you with compassion, you would be before the Commons today and sentenced to death."

"How do you know that still won't happen? And you've publicly made me crawl like a worm on my belly in front of this Parliament, begging and pleading for my life, lying before God in the words and deeds of this . . . this counterfeit."

This was worse, so much worse than she'd imagined. She could handle his anger, his outbursts. He was a man of passion, and she could meet his passion and fight fire. But this cold contempt gave her no weapon to parry, no lunge to strike home her point.

A sudden banging, words rapidly exchanged and footsteps striding to the library. They both turned, and Allen ran in, a message in his hand.

"It is done. The order has come from Parliament."

Luce hugged her arms around herself, for if her letter was mistrusted or not believed, all this had been for nothing and she had sent John to his death, and he would die hating her.

Allen unfolded the parchment.

> *"On June 9, the House went on to vote that Colonel John Hutchinson,*
> *(1.) Be discharged from being a member of this House;*
> *(2.) Be incapable of bearing any office or place of public trust in this kingdom;*
> *(3.) In respect of his signal repentance, shall not be within that clause of exception in the Act of general pardon and oblivion, as to any fine, or forfeiture of any part of his estate not purchased of or belonging to the public."*

Allen's voice choked on the last. "We did it. We got the Commons to discharge you. You are halfway to freedom. Now we go to the Lords with our certificate and ask them to exclude you from execution. The Indemnity Bill is going before them. We now have the authority from the Commons to remove your name from the list."

John slumped in a chair, his head in his hands, his shoulders shaking. A broken sob wrenched from his throat. Luce exchanged a quick glance with Allen, and they both crossed swiftly to him, kneeling on either side.

"Hush, my love," whispered Luce. "Weep for your wounded pride. Weep for the men who will not be pardoned. But do not weep for yourself. We are almost there. You are almost free."

40

Nan

As Elizabeth assembled her council of men, so Nan secretly convened at Henry's house those who could influence the Lords. And with no less cunning, she laid out the request to them. Just as Elizabeth had used her councillors to mask her own brilliant mind, Nan would control this appeal, for did she not know the way to persuade men? Her survival of the war years was proof in itself. Just as Elizabeth's survival against Mary was a testament to her own ingenuity.

The table stood in front of the fireplace. Diverse chairs from the kitchen to the bedchamber surrounded it, and the bench held the arses of two Villiers and a Biron. Best of all, Anthony Ashley Cooper, the king's ascendant councillor, sat at Nan's right hand. Barbary had done well in identifying a group of men who would carry weight. Now Nan must secure their signatures.

"John Hutchinson saved my husband's life after Pennruddock's disastrous rebellion," she stated, looking around the room. By candlelight, at eleven of the clock, the men's faces were shadowed and half-recognisable. As she'd planned. Tonight's meeting must not be stamped in memory. "And for more than seven years, he stored guns and stockpiled powder accessible to the king's cause. As he helped us, now he deserves our aid."

The men nodded. Lord Viscount Grandison, Barbary's uncle, leaned forward, his handsome countenance now illuminated by the candles. "I will support this measure for you, Nan, and for the family that first brought me my title."

"You honour the memory of my uncle, Grandison?" She wondered at his loyalty. He was a king's man through and through. Barbary had done well to bring him to the table.

Grandison nodded. "Barbary reminded me of her father's debt. My brother lived in gratitude to Oliver St.John. If not for his bequest and the support of the St.John family, we would not have the wealth we enjoy now. You have asked little from us in return over the years."

Nan turned to Ned. "And you sign too?"

"Yes, of course." Ned looked around the table. "You all have a reason to be thankful for John Hutchinson and his family. The time is crucial. The Commons have approved his omission from the regicide death list. Now we convince the Lords not to reverse that ruling and to ratify his petition for forgiveness."

Nan pulled the parchment towards her.

"Allen and I have drafted this. We believe it accurately states John's position." She turned to Ashley Cooper. "Sir Anthony, as one of the twelve lords who brought back our king from Holland, and who now serves in Parliament, your name should be prominent. Would you sign after me?"

Sir Anthony bowed his head. "It would be my pleasure, Lady Wilmot. This is a politically opportune pleading for the king to demonstrate mercy, and who better than your cousin John to receive it."

Nan kept her face impassive, masking relief. He did not mention his own obligation to the Villiers family, and she did not want to leverage that debt unless necessary. Up until this last moment, she could not be sure all would capitulate. But she'd picked her first choice wisely. Sir Anthony sat as one of the most powerful men in Parliament. The others would follow his lead.

And frankly, with her signature and Sir Anthony's, the Lords would not need to read further. Sir Anthony had the power now. And if his star waned, John Wilmot, the young Earl of Rochester, would wield great influence with the king when he came of age in just a few short years. She would save her son's sway for later too.

Nan brought a candle closer to the document. "Let me read this aloud," she said. "And then place your signatures beneath mine. We will put it before the Lords immediately.

"These are to certify that about seven years ago, and from time to time ever since, Colonel Hutchinson hath declared his desire of the king's Majesty's return to his kingdoms, and his own resolutions to assist in bringing His Majesty back: and in order thereunto hath kept a correspondency with some of us, when designs have been on foot for that purpose; and hath upon all occasions been ready to assist and protect the king's friends in any of their troubles, and to employ all his interests to serve them. He gave the Earl of Rochester notice and opportunity to escape when Cromwell's ministers had discovered him the last time he was employed in His Majesty's service here in

315

England. He received into his house, and secured there, arms prepared for the king's service, well knowing to what intent they were provided, and resolving to join with us when there had been occasion to use them. For these, and other things, Cromwell some time before his death had a very jealous eye over him, and had intentions to secure him, which some of us understanding gave him notice of; that usurper being the more exasperated against him, because he could never, by all his allurements, win him to the least compliance with or action under his authority. Nor were his resolutions of serving the king only in Cromwell's time, but when the army invited the remainder of the House of Commons to return to Westminster, whither he was summoned, he declared to some of us before he went up, that he only went among them to endeavour to settle the kingdom by the king's return, and to improve all opportunities to bend things that way; and accordingly so acted there, openly opposing the engagement, to be true and constant to the Commonwealth, and endeavouring to bring the army under a civil authority, opposing also in the House the commitment of these gentlemen who brought up the addresses for a free Parliament, as also the destroying and pulling down of the city gates. All or some of these particular actings and declarations of his, tending to His Majesty's service, every one of us who have here subscribed are able to attest."

One by one they signed and left, disappearing into the night as if they had never been.

> ANNE ROCHESTER
> AN: ASHLEY COOPER
> ROBERT BIRON
> ALLEN APSLEY
> EDWARD VILLIERS
> RICHARD BIRON
> G. GRANDISON
> A. BRODRICK.
> JACK MARKHAM
> A. BABINGTON

And when they were gone, she locked and bolted the door against the outside and stood alone in the shadowed house of her husband. She felt his arms around her, his beard on her cheek, heard his distant laughter. Henry approved.

My work is done, Henry. My dearest Luce and John are safe. And now I can leave, leave London and the court and these political games.

Ditchley called to her heart. The future belonged now to her sons, their inheritance. She would look for another property, a second manor close by. Where she could be near but give them room to grow. One day Johnny would attend court. Serving the king was his destiny. But before then, she still owned his heart. Still kept her favourite son close.

Home. Almost there.

John arrived on her doorstep the following day, and as she welcomed him in, he glanced at her travelling trunk standing in the hallway.

"Your part is done? And now you disappear back to your other life, Nan." His face drawn, his eyes hollowed, John had aged ten years since last she'd seen him. "By God, you are a chameleon. Will we ever know your true colours?"

"My colours are my family's." She bit back her anger at his churlishness. "As they always have been." She guided him to the parlour, where he stood, ignoring her gesture to the bench. "And that includes you, John."

"I don't need your charity."

"But you did need my loyalty."

He paced, his grace hobbled by anxiety.

"John." She tried another approach. "John, your anger with Luce is misplaced. She is but the object; your disappointment is with the failure of the Commonwealth, the corrosion of your dream. Don't take your defeat out on her."

John turned on her, his face tight with anger. "And you? You who led her to deceive and lie on my behalf, who tricked the highest court in the land with counterfeit? Your conscience is clear, Nan? For I think you have a role in this God would find hard to forgive. You risk damnation for your deceit."

"And you are already damned for your murder." *Fight fire with fire.* "I know not your eternal fate, John. But at least I can affect your mortal life."

He sat, then, slouched on the bench. The July sun fell on his hair, bringing gold to the chestnut tones, highlighting the worry lines on his face.

"They demanded I give them a list. Of all whom I saw sign the death warrant. Even at this last moment, still they asked more of me, to betray my

317

fellow men, point out who signed with glee and laughter, flicked pens full of ink at each other, pushed each other like eager school boys in a rush to kill the king."

Nan held her breath. Did he even now balk at the last fence? Did he refuse to cooperate?

"What did you tell them, John?"

He looked down at his hands, methodically rubbing the fingers of his right hand as if to wipe clean the ink stains.

"The truth. Each signed separately, alone. I witnessed no man signing. And only God witnessed me."

"And did that satisfy them? Did they exclude you from the Act of Oblivion?"

He lifted his head, eyes full of tears. "Yes."

"And yet still you weep. Are you determined to be a martyr to your conscience? Or a survivor for your loved ones?"

The tears fell then, and she crossed to him, held him in her arms, this poor conflicted soul. "You are too good for this earth, John. But you have been spared, and your family needs you more than your country now. Go home. Leave now. You need never return. This is no longer your world nor your responsibility."

As he wept, she heard him whisper his thanks. Whether to God or to her, she knew not.

Sir Edward Hyde, eager to execute and move on, was furious. He called upon Nan as she rested at Battersey with Walter and Johanna, the Wilmot house now leased to its new tenants, all evidence of summer's drama erased. Later, she intended him to escort her to the Villiers at Whitehall, where she could say her good-byes, retire officially to Ditchley.

Now, however, he rebuked her in private.

"Your cousin Hutchinson is unreliable, is not a good witness, Nan. He could have easily identified the signatories and not been financially penalized. His conscience appears at the most convenient times," he railed at her. "And you endanger yourself and your sons by publicly endorsing him. After all your years of caution, you made a foolish move."

She faced him down. "He saved Henry's life. And so I save his."

"And that whore Barbary Villiers enjoyed making a fool of me too, no doubt." Sir Edward sat on the bench, his huge girth rolling over the sides of the narrow wood, his gout-swollen feet spread wide. He thumped his cane again on the oak floor for emphasis. "She has a witch's power with the king. And she enjoys parading it in front of me. I believe you knew how to harness it to your benefit."

Nan nodded slowly. "She is high in favour, for sure. And with her rise the fortunes of the family again."

"You forget all that I have done for you and your cousins?" Sir Edward now sounded peevish, and more. His voice was weary, care-worn. "Do not desert me at this time, Nan."

She crossed to him and laid a hand on his shoulder. "Never, Sir Edward. These days flow like a fast-moving tide. There are hidden currents that drive the fleet forward, and gales that blow some off course. But we are all in the wake of the king, and we all sail to the same destination. Peace, prosperity and a settled government and monarchy."

He glanced up at her, the wisdom in his domed forehead at odds with the doubt in his eyes. "You're right, Nan. It has been a long voyage to reach this moment. I cannot afford a shipwreck on the shoals at the last league."

"The king loves you," Nan reassured her old friend. "He will need your wisdom in the coming years. And he trusts you beyond all others."

At her words, Sir Edward's broad face cracked into an anguished scowl. Without warning, he broke into sobbing, great heaving wails that shook his whole body. She pulled her hand back in shock.

"Edward, Edward, what ails you?" Nan recovered herself, for here clearly was a man in great pain.

He continued to sob as if a dam had broken, and the torrent of grief poured down his cheeks unstopped. His eyes pled to her, his words trapped by the ferocious bondage of tears.

She slapped him, hard, to prevent the hysteria. And waited.

Sir Edward reeled back, his eyes wide. And then he spoke.

"I would rather commit her to the Tower than disgrace our family, the monarchy, this way."

Nan tried to gather her thoughts. Clearly, he was in shock and yet made no sense.

"Barbary? She is the king's mistress, but it is really no disgrace. She is married, and the king conducts his affairs with dignity."

Shaking his head, Sir Edward sprawled on the bench in such a careless manner Nan feared he would fall. She sat beside him and took his great hand.

He looked at her then, looked directly into her eyes. Never had she seen such shame and anger mixed in her old friend's face.

"My daughter. Anne." He could barely get his words out, emotion rasping his voice.

"Anne? To the Tower? What mean you, Edward?"

"She is pregnant. With the Duke of York's child."

Nan took a breath. A pregnant daughter out of wedlock. A shock, but not insurmountable. She rubbed his hand. He must be exhausted, and this last news the feather on the horse's back. "I understand your concern, Edward. But she is not the first to have her head turned by the king's brother. And I suspect not the last. An arrangement can be made, and quickly, to marry her to a suitable young man who will be only too grateful for the patronage of His Royal Highness—"

Sir Edward gripped Nan's hand until she winced with pain.

"I cannot do this."

"Yes, you can. And I can help find a willing suitor."

"She is married already." His words were muttered now, a monotone that Nan could hardly catch. "She married the Duke of York in a secret ceremony when in Holland. And now the king insists his brother publicly acknowledge her as his wife and make it official."

Unbelievable. And yet believable. A royal prince marrying a pregnant commoner. And sullying the royal bloodline, making a travesty of the monarchy. And just when the spirit of England welcomed the royal family back into power.

She stared at Sir Edward. "This cannot be," she whispered.

Tears fell down his face unchecked. "The king insists his brother stand by his child. And his vows. In two days, they will marry officially in front of the king at my house."

"You will be reviled for this." Nan's thoughts went immediately to the politics. "The people will say you did this intentionally."

He nodded. "Villiers hates me. Now she and her family have cause." Sir Edward tried to take a breath and gave a sharp cry, his hand on his chest. "I am undone, and our family will be disgraced."

"Calm yourself," Nan soothed him. "Calm, and we must think. The king will attend the wedding, you say?"

"Yes." His face was ash-white.

"Then all is not lost, for he knows of your own integrity." Gently placing his hand back on his lap, she crossed to the fireplace and rang the bell. "I am insisting you rest. Johanna will take care of you. I shall go to Barbary tonight on my own. Bring her thinking round to mine. Best you stay here, in your present state."

Sir Edward did not try to stop her. What an unexpected twist this day had taken. One family crisis averted, another appeared. As a servant arrived and she gave instructions for Sir Edward to be taken to a guest chamber to rest, she already planned how to turn Sir Edward's shame to their advantage. And this time Nan considered Frances ready to be the beneficiary of their good fortune.

41

Frances

Fitting to their new positions, Frances and Allen hired a hackney coach, for surely as king's favourites at court, they should be seen availing themselves of the latest fashion for travel. The vehicle wound through the streets from their rooms in Westminster to Whitehall. As she stared from the window at the early evening London bustle, Frances could not but think of how fast their fortunes had climbed. Already, the poverty of Paris and the isolation of Feltwell fell away from her.

Across the dim interior, Allen sprawled, relaxed in his usual way, careless of disrupting his wig. Frances considered his fashion. Truth be told, he cut a fine figure in his new embroidered jacket, and Ned Villiers's tailor ensured that gold and silver thread embellished the garment from collar to cuff.

Fit for court. And their future.

Her thoughts turned to the evening before them. How different Luce's life would be if only John had followed Fairfax and excused himself from signing the warrant. A year ago John sat in Parliament, commanded the trust of all. Now he was nothing, stripped of all offices, fined into financial oblivion and banished to the country.

And yet Luce appeared to regret nothing. Before her arrival from Holborn to join them in this outward display of deference and indebtedness that Barbary demanded, Allen had charged Frances with chaperoning his sister's outspoken tongue.

"Luce will have difficulty in stopping with a mere gesture," he'd warned her. "She is never one to let an opportunity to speak her mind pass her by. And this occasion with Barbary is exactly one she would enjoy."

"Perhaps she should stay away?" Frances had asked. "We can thank Barbary on her behalf."

Allen shook his head. "That won't be enough . . . for either of them."

She fell back into contemplating the evening ahead, lulled into a daydream by the rolling of the coach.

"We're here," Allen broke her musings. "And I believe Nan is right ahead of us. For God's sake, be sure to look out for Luce and stay by her side. Barbary may demand a public display of gratitude from Luce, but we can't afford her to insult the Villiers." He helped Frances down from the Hackney and waited with her for Nan, who was just alighting from her carriage. When she saw Frances, she smiled broadly and held out her arm.

"Ready to visit the lioness in her den?" she asked cheerfully.

Frances laughed. "Where is Sir Edward? I thought he was escorting you?"

Nan's face grew solemn. "He is indisposed. I will tell you more later." As they entered the house, she whispered, "And if the king comes tonight, take your lead from me. Do not question my suggestions or doubt my motives."

Before Frances could respond, they were greeted by Barbary's servants and shown to her drawing room.

The sophisticated woman seated at the window was hardly recognisable as the free-spirited girl who had winked at Allen and Frances on the wharf in Holland. Now her hair was elaborately dressed and curled, with great ropes of pearls intertwined within the masses of auburn locks. A huge ruby nestled above Barbary's pale forehead, dazzling as it reflected rays of light from a hundred candles. The sheerest gauze draped over her shoulders gave the illusion of modesty, but as Frances drew closer, she could see the low-cut pink silk gown grazed Barbary's nipples. Only the translucent trim covered her unblemished skin.

Frances curtseyed, and Allen bowed. They walked forward to receive Barbary's cousinly kiss, but even that had changed. Formality reigned in the gestures and greetings, and an invisible barrier separated family from courtier.

Frances caught sight of Aunt Barbara, concealed within a shadowed alcove. From what Frances could make out in the gloom, her dress was most fashionable, glistening with gold thread and a familiar motif of falcons embroidered along the front panel. She did not move, and Frances's attention was soon drawn to new arrivals. When she did look back to the alcove again, Barbara had disappeared.

"We will talk when Luce arrives," Barbary dismissed them as others came forward to make their bows to her. "Please enjoy our hospitality." She gestured to the room and turned to speak to those next in line.

Musicians began to play, and laughter and animated conversation filled the rooms. There were no more sightings of old Lady Villiers, and Frances was grateful for her retirement. She cast a pall upon the atmosphere, and in truth she probably only appeared to unnerve Luce.

Nan beckoned to her. Allen joined Ned, sitting at a table of piquet with Barbary. It was fortunate that Allen's new position of Master of the King's Hawks came with a healthy stipend, for it was not cheap to live the life of a courtier

"Is something worrying you, Frances?" Nan's eyes were sharp.

"No. Nothing that won't wait." This was not the place to air her concerns of maintaining their lifestyle. All were taking pleasure in the restoration of recreation, fun and the gratification of their starved senses. No one wanted to hear of poverty or privation.

"I heard the king arrives soon," Nan murmured as they watched the gamblers. "And probably the Duke of York too."

"I hope not before Luce; for them to meet would be most unfavourable." Frances glanced at Nan. "If they do, you will have to ask Allen to stay with the king while we escort Luce."

Nan glanced at the door. "I agree. It is one thing for him to have been persuaded to order clemency to John. And quite another to meet the wife of his father's murderer face-to-face. Barbary plays with fire. As she always has."

"So the Duke of York comes too, you think?" Frances continued. "King Charles has been nothing but kindness to me. I do not know much of Prince James."

"Allen has been confirmed as a captain in his household too?" Nan asked. "I know Ned planned to arrange this."

"Yes." He was commissioned earlier in the summer, to both of their relief. Additional revenue would be much welcomed.

"So he spends his time in service with both the king and the duke?"

"He does. He enjoys the Duke of York's company, for he respects him as a soldier."

Nan watched as Allen threw down a winning hand to the groans and cheers of Ned Villiers and his party. "Allen has entered court life again with ease."

"It is where he is happiest."

"And you?"

Frances paused, seeking the words to explain her ambition. "I have served the king and his mother for many years, often at great hardship. Committing to the king has been a difficult journey, Nan, with no money, no prospects and only a dream to keep us alive." Nan nodded encouragingly. Frances continued, her thoughts voiced for the first time. "To be recognised and rewarded for our loyalty is gratifying. To be awarded a formal place within the royal household creates great opportunities for my children. And peace of mind for me."

A stir in the room as the king entered, Prince James at his side. The Duke of York was a handsome man, with a fair countenance that opposed his brother's dark and grave expression.

Nan took Frances's arm as they stood from their curtseys. "Quickly. Before they become distracted by the gambling. Come. And then to Allen." She walked swiftly to the king and the Duke of York, who were already looking across the tables to Barbary. As they approached, the king turned, and a wide smile broke across his serious, dark face. For a moment, Frances recognized the boy in the man.

"Nan. And Frances. Two ladies I am most happy to see." He took both of their hands and drew them close, kissing each on the lips. Turning to his brother, he introduced them with a flourish.

"You remember Wilmot's widow, Nan, who saved so many after Edgehill and stayed true to us throughout our exile. And Nall Apsley's wife, Frances. She kept me company in Barnstaple when I was a lad and cared for our mother when Minette was born in Exeter."

The Duke of York bowed and graciously kissed their hands. "In that case, I share the love my brother has for you already," he replied. "For without your husband's care, he may not have escaped, and without your protection, Minette may not have survived. Both are too dreadful to contemplate."

He was charming, for sure. And maintained a roving eye. Frances was already aware of the appraisal accompanying his words. She could manage this.

"My thanks, Your Royal Highness," she replied. "But I only did what any other woman would do to care for an expectant mother and a helpless child."

King Charles puffed his cheeks and blew a sigh. "Something you may want to consider, James, in light of your own situation."

The prince contemplated the immense silk bows attached to his shoes and shrugged. "These things will work themselves out."

"Not unless I am involved." The king turned to Nan and Frances. "Forgive us, ladies. A family matter."

As Frances was about to change the subject, Nan interrupted.

"If I may be so bold, Your Majesty," she said smoothly. "I have just left Battersey House, where Sir Edward is indisposed. He stays with us to recover his . . . equilibrium. I fear by the third of September he will either recuperate or die from a failure of his heart."

The king raised an eyebrow. "Nan, I am amazed at your ability to know the most intimate of personal details." He glanced quickly at James, who was now winking at Frances. "How much did he tell you?"

"Enough to know that your brother needs all the support he can get. And Sir Edward is vilified either way."

"It is a sorry situation." The king sighed. "But a contract that I feel strongly will be the best solution for James . . . and his family. Despite Hyde's disgust."

Frances had no idea where this conversation led. But true to Nan's counsel as they'd entered the Villiers apartments, she let her continue to lead.

"The duke will need a steady head around him and a dependable ally for the months ahead in his new arrangement," Nan mused. "Perhaps someone whom the queen, your mother, trusts too."

A light broke across the king's face, and once again a broad grin smoothed the deep worry lines at the side of his mouth. "Nan, I believe you are offering me a solution to ease my mind and smooth my brother's path."

Nan smiled. "Your Majesty."

In the pause that followed, Frances remained still, conscious of the king's gaze upon her and trying to ignore the Duke of York's outrageous flirting.

"Very well." The king turned to his brother. "James, you already have Nall in your cavalry. Now your new wife will enjoy the pleasure of Frances's guidance in her household. A stronger ally she could not wish for."

What just happened? Frances had no clue. But as the king and the Duke of York bowed to her and the duke gave her a lingering look of appreciation before they left, she disguised her surprise and assumed a courtier's expression of indifference.

Nan laughed and tucked her arm in Frances's. "Come, Cousin, this has already been a long evening. A glass of wine to restore ourselves and drink a toast to your future."

"My future? And what wife of the Duke of York?" Frances took two glasses from a passing page and handed one to Nan.

"In two days, Prince James, the Duke of York, the current heir to the king, marries his pregnant commoner mistress in secret and yet with the king's approval. Queen Henrietta returns from France in outrage. The mistress's father will face vilification and hatred, accusations of deliberately putting his daughter into play to further his own career. The baby is due in November and will be third in line to the throne of England."

Frances was determined not to break her composure. "And?" Truly, this restored court had started with an explosion. For a fleeting moment, she envied Luce her quiet country retirement.

Nan gave her a look of approval. "The mistress is Anne Hyde, Sir Edward's daughter. And you are now appointed to the duke's new wife's household." She raised her glass and toasted Frances. "Use every bit of skill and experience you have, Frances. The challenges will be great. And the rewards even greater."

Frances lifted her own glass. "This might be your finest moment, Nan. Not only do you save John from execution, you promote Allen and me to the royal household and set my family up with a lifetime's office." She gestured across the room, where Barbary now sat on the king's lap. "And you are in the middle of the Villiers circle as a friend and mentor to Barbary."

"Barbary has no need of a guide. But I will keep a close watch on her climb," Nan responded, "from a distance. I return to Ditchley, to my boys." She leaned forward and clasped Frances's hands. "You and Allen deserve this place, these positions, my dear. You have sacrificed much over the years. And now reap the rewards of loyalty."

A thrill passed through Frances. Finally, she could put the deprivation of the past behind her. A footman approached. "Lady Wilmot," he bowed. "Mrs Hutchinson has arrived and is waiting for you in the lobby."

"Thank you." Nan turned to Frances. "Are we ready for the reason we all came this evening? Please meet Luce and bring her here. I shall join you after I ensure Allen is distracting the king. Let us make our obeisance to Cousin Barbary, and then I can be gone."

A shadow crossed before them. James barred their way.

"Lady Wilmot," he bowed to her. "Lady Wilmot, my thanks again for your kindness in helping Sir Edward with his difficult choice."

Nan curtseyed. "My honour, sir."

"I am particularly grateful for your help with his daughter." James leaned forward and gestured Nan to tilt her head towards him.

"I fear there will be much outcry, and court will not be a welcoming place," he whispered loudly. Even from where she stood, Frances smelled the acrid scent of wine tainting his breath. "And so I have also appointed you to Mistress Anne's household. As of September 3, you will hold the senior honour of Lady of the Stole to the Duchess of York. We will need you at court, Lady Wilmot. We will need you at court."

42

Luce

Many lords also of the colonel's relations and acquaintance, out of kindness and gratitude (for there was not one of them whom he had not in his day more or less obliged), used very hearty endeavours for him. Yet Sir Allen Apsley's interest and most fervent endeavours for him was that which only turned the scales, and the colonel was not excepted in the act of oblivion to anything but offices.

Luce Hutchinson
Summer 1660

Luce removed her black velvet cloak and smoothed the panels of her crimson gown. She arranged the many rows of pearls caught in a fashionable knot at her bosom, for tonight she wore the residue of John's wealth like armour.

Only on this occasion could she see fit to wear the jewels. After this airing, she would arrange for them to be sold, for the king's fines had ravaged John's finances, and there was little left but Owthorpe's land and her few remaining jewels.

If she was predestined to eternal damnation as Salome, she may as well dress as Jezebel.

Frances appeared, beautiful in her court gown, a shimmering turquoise which fitted her perfectly. Already, an abyss yawned between their lives, and in this hour it widened a little more.

"Promise me we will not stay longer than courtesy requires." Luce was firm. "I owe Barbary my public gratitude, but no more."

"I promise," replied Frances. "And once you have done this duty, you and John are free to go home to Owthorpe."

Luce straightened her shoulders, walking away and holding out her arm to Frances. "Never to return to London again," she called over her shoulder. "So you had best plan on visiting us, for tonight is the last I will spend in this viper's nest of corrupt patronage."

"The patronage is what freed your husband, Luce," Frances reminded her. "So please be cautious with your criticism."

Luce shrugged and followed the footman up to the grand salon. A din greeted them, and she paused on the threshold for a moment, getting her bearings. As she became used to the room, she located Nan standing by a tall woman with a mass of auburn hair and a gown cut low. Taking a deep breath, she squared her shoulders, lifted her chin and summoned every dancing and deportment lesson she had ever resisted. If Barbary wished for homage, then she would give her a lesson in grace and arrogance. Slowly, she walked forward, conscious of the crowd parting to let her through, the fluttering fans exhaling whispers and giggles.

Give me strength, Mother, to deliver my thanks and leave without more ado.

Luce executed a perfect curtsey before Barbary, her muscles and mind returning to the lessons learned as a young girl in the Tower. Her father had insisted she know the protocols of behaviour. How ironic her learnings should serve a purpose today.

"Cousin." Barbary stretched out her hand to Luce. Nan and Frances stayed close by her side.

"Cousin," countered Luce. Her eye was caught by the shadow of a woman in an alcove at Barbary's right. She started and caught herself. Surely, this was her mother's ghost. Yet Lucy had never had this air of malevolence about her. The figure leaned forward, as if straining to hear their conversation.

"I would like to express my gratitude for your help in securing my husband's release," Luce continued, keeping her voice low and her dignity in control. She was her mother's daughter. And just as Lucy had braved the Villiers so long ago, so could she. "Without your help, he would surely have been a condemned man."

Barbary inclined her head and glanced at Nan. "Our cousin was most persuasive in her argument," she replied. "I would not have contemplated intervening if not for Lady Wilmot."

Luce glanced at the woman in the shadows again.

Come forth from the shadows. Show your face.

"Just Nan? I thought perhaps you had other considerations." Luce stared up at her cousin's beautiful face. Deception veiled her almond eyes.

"How so, Cousin?" Barbary's tone remained unchanged, but an imperceptible shift in her stature reminded Luce of a cat stilled at the sight of a sparrow.

"Family loyalty. Old debts," Luce replied.

Nan interjected swiftly, "Our family loyalty is unquestionable. And old debts have been struck from memory."

"Let me speak for myself, Nan."

"You already have, Luce." Nan turned to Barbary. "Please excuse our cousin, for the strain of the last months has been extreme."

Barbary raised an eyebrow. "I fear her thanks come with conditions."

"Do you demand the same?" Luce fired back.

"No conditions," smoothed Nan. "Simply an appreciation for your assistance, Barbary." She pinched Luce's arm and held her in a tight grip. "Luce is now leaving for the country. She and John retire to a quiet life and will not return to Whitehall."

"A wise move." Barbary dismissed Luce, though not without first appraising her appearance again. "You will find little use for those pearls among the swine, Cousin. You may want to pawn those before you leave. I can give you the name of a Jew in Cheapside who would give you a good price."

Nan pulled Luce's arm, forcing her to curtsey. By the time she stood again, Barbary had joined Ned and Allen.

"Leave. Now," Nan murmured. "You have done your duty." She handed Luce over to Frances and walked over to Barbary. The crowd flowed around them, and Luce was left alone with Frances.

The woman in the shadowed alcove stepped forward into the light. "What old debts, Luce? My granddaughter owes you nothing. What was between your mother and me was our business and no one else's."

"Aunt Barbara." Luce tipped her chin higher, her mother's presence at her shoulder. "That old jealousy remained yours, but the taint burdened all of us." She paused. "And yet—"

At her side, she felt Frances's eagerness to walk her away from confrontation. Luce ignored her. She would never have the chance to say these words again.

"And yet," she continued, "there is not one day in my life that I do not give thanks to God for your betrayal. That your envy severed my mother from this life of indolence and corruption, that your deception gave her the freedom to break from the yoke of royal patronage."

Frances took Luce's arm, but she shook it free. "Do not seek to muzzle me, Frances. Allen may have reconciled with our aunt. I never will."

331

"You will show respect." Aunt Barbara stepped forward, and Luce did the same.

"Because your granddaughter is the king's mistress?" Luce's voice was full of contempt.

"Luce," Frances whispered urgently. "Luce, please, you thanked Barbary. Leave now."

"More than his mistress," Aunt Barbara replied. "She carries the king's child."

"His bastard?" Luce shot back. "How like a Villiers to turn vice into victory."

Frances took her arm. "Come, Luce, I shall see you downstairs."

Luce shook herself free. "There is one more thing."

She pulled Theo's miniature from her pocket and pressed it into Aunt Barbara's hand.

"Take him back. He was never yours and never will be. He loved my mother and despised you. When he lay dying and alone, it was Lucy he called for, Lucy who was the last he saw on this earth. You may have won him through deceit. But you lost him to true love."

Aunt Barbara stood as if struck, her hand outstretched still, the miniature staring up at her.

"His likeness is with you. His heart is buried with my mother." Luce took Frances's arm and walked away.

"Please call for my carriage, Frances."

Behind Luce, in the old life, Nan's laughter rang out. How her cousin adjusted her course, how rapidly she absorbed herself into the Villiers's conversation, the king's orbit. Certainly a skill that was critical to navigate court intrigue. And one that Luce would rather die than learn herself.

Luce waited as Frances commanded a servant to secure a hackney. They stood to one side in the opulent vestibule, watching in silence as several more guests arrived, courtiers flocking to Barbary's rooms.

"I do not regret my words." Luce's anger had drained from her, leaving her spent. "I could thank Barbary for her help, but her grandmother is someone I can never forgive."

"You certainly did not hold back your words. You could have ruined everything, Luce. You still might. Do you really think Barbary will accept an insult to her grandmother such as that?" Frances reproached her.

"She will not care." Luce pulled her cloak closer. "Barbary thinks only of herself." She fumbled to push the tag over the button, but her fingers trembled.

Frances helped and stroked Luce's cheek. "You play with fire."

"Allen will douse it."

Frances laughed, shook her head. "You two. When you join forces, we all must take heed." She kissed Luce. "I know your mother suffered greatly. You honoured her memory while expressing your gratitude for Barbary's assistance. And now you can go home. You never have to see any of these people again."

Luce was curious. "Do you choose this life willingly, Frances?"

Frances thought for a moment. "This life has chosen me," she replied. "For I love your brother with all my heart and soul, and the king and court is his world. And if I am to survive and bring my children up in a place where they will thrive, then I embrace this life and all it could bring us."

A servant hovered by them. "Your carriage is here, Mrs. Hutchinson."

Frances indicated her thanks. "I'll walk with you. You are good to return to Holborn on your own?"

"This is my city, Frances. I have no fear of London or what it holds. Just a desire to leave it behind forever and retire to Owthorpe to share my future with my love. Just like you."

They embraced, and Frances tucked her arm in Luce's as they walked into the mellow September evening. The last of the sunset cast shadows across the pavements, and a lamplighter was about his job, illuminating the buildings. Frances stood by the carriage as Luce climbed up and settled into her seat by the window.

"God speed back to Owthorpe." Frances held Luce's hand. "And to the life you both desire with your children and land, and in the service of God."

Luce put a hand on the window opening and leaned forward to kiss Frances. "And God bless you for the love you have for my brother. Allen is fortunate to—"

"Mistress Hutchinson!" A shout from a large carriage that clattered to a halt next to them. The vehicle took up most of the street and was emblazoned with the Duke of Buckingham's crest. "Mistress Hutchinson! What a pleasant surprise, for I have a message for you." A man in a cascading blond periwig leaned from the window, waving a flagon of wine. "Your regicide husband escaped this time. But do not think he has been forgotten."

"The duke." Frances turned swiftly. Luce jerked back from the window as if a physical blow had landed on her.

Others arrived, men of the court who stood silently next to his coach. In the flare of the torches, the shadows leaping high across the walls, the whole scene took on the air of a masque. And yet this was no playacting.

"Apsley's sister. So clever and yet so stupid." Drink slurred the duke's speech. He fumbled with the door in his eagerness to get out. He stumbled and kicked a servant trying to pull down the steps. "Apsley's sister, our cousin, wife of the king-killer." He swayed forward. "Be on the alert, Cousin. The colonel may have tricked the king into showing him mercy this time. But other eyes are upon him. The king may forgive. But I will not forget. Do not think your husband can hide in his sorry little country manor. Owthorpe is it? Or Cowthorpe?" The duke lifted his head to the evening sky and bellowed like a bull. His friends collapsed in laughter and mooed and brayed, the street resounding with their derision.

"Seek solace in your herd, my lord," Luce shouted, her control snapping. "And find your like in sycophants and mindless toadies."

"Go home—now." Frances pushed Luce away from the window and called to the driver. "Take Mrs. Hutchinson to Bartlett's Buildings, and hurry."

The carriage lurched, and the last Luce saw of Frances was her blond hair shining in the lamplight as she followed George Villiers back into his cousin's apartments.

Taking a shuddering breath, she collapsed in the dark corner of the carriage and let the familiar streets fly past the leather-shuttered window.

Good-bye, London. Good-bye.

PART FIVE

1664
PEACE

43

Luce

After these troubles were over from without, the colonel lived with all imaginable retiredness at home, and, because his active spirit could not be idle nor very sordidly employed, took up his time in opening springs, and planting trees, and dressing his plantations; and these were his recreations, wherein he relieved many poor labourers when they wanted work, which was a very comfortable charity to them and their families.

Luce Hutchinson
Autumn 1663

Bent over the church gate like an aged parishioner, the ancient crab apple tree bore purple fruit bursting with summer's juice. Neither Luce's mother nor John let the tree be cut back, for they both loved its determination to push out apples every year despite its antiquity. This year was no different, although the fruit would be blown to the ground by morning, bruised and blackbird-pecked, wedged in gnarled roots. Behind the tree's laden branches, dark clouds piled up in the western sky over the Fosse Way, heralding the approaching storm.

Best hurry before she got caught in the rain and wind. Besides, she must share her news with John, a brief encounter in the church, woman to woman, passing on county rumours.

A flash rent the sky, and already the air tasted different, charged with distant lightning. On the rim of her hearing, vibrating in her bones, the first thunder rumbled across the valley.

Her mother had shared her love of the earth with John as they laid out the ponds and gardens of Owthorpe. Now, in its maturity, Luce could appreciate their vision for the beauty of this fertile land. Everywhere she turned, the landscape thrived under John's care and the legacy of her mother's sympathetic guidance.

Five years to the day since her mother's death, and Luce still left her favourite roses on the plain wooden table in the church. A scented memory of her mother's garden at the Tower unexpectedly arrived, and Luce smiled.

How lovely to be remembered in flowers. She paused at the herb plot planted by Lucy so many years ago and clipped soothing marshmallow and pungent thyme. John's summer cough plagued him, keeping him housebound since June. Another tincture tonight, to keep worse ills at bay.

As she hurried to the house, lightning forked across the dark sky and heavy raindrops spattered around her. The wind whirled her skirts around her legs, clutching her ankles and tumbling golden beech leaves across the yard.

Summer succumbed to autumn.

Letting herself into the quiet house, Luce left the herbs on the scrubbed kitchen table and sought John in the library to share her gossip. Here he spent his days, wrapped in his warmest jacket, reading all the daylight hours God gave him, teaching lessons to their younger children and conversing with the oldest. Tom and Bee especially enjoyed their father's company and discussed the scriptures with him each day, delighting in his wisdom. Another reason to rejoice in their exile, for truly if John still served in Parliament, he would have seldom been home.

John looked up from his book, as he always did. No matter how absorbed in his reading, he always paused at her step.

"A kestrel on the wings of the storm, my love." He smiled. "You look enchantingly windswept."

She smoothed her hair to no avail. "It is my state and my temperament," she replied. "For thunder echoes over the Fosse Way, and I fear over this land too."

John raised an eyebrow. "How dramatic. Have you heard news?"

Luce sat on the stool by his knee, where she could rest her head on his leg and be soothed by his calm hand stroking her brow. "More talk of the papists and another uprising against the king in the north."

"On good authority? These rumours swirl like leaves before the west wind, Luce."

She nodded. "Mrs Bennett was leaving the church as I entered. Her son told her of many strangers in Nottingham now, with scarlet ribbons on their hats and contempt for the locals."

John's hand continued its caress of her head, and her heart began to slow. "And the uprising?" he asked quietly.

"Failed as soon as it began. The Duke of Buckingham personally ordered the execution of the leaders and showed no mercy in their pleas.

But rumours abound of more behind them, from Yorkshire to Leeds." She tried to ignore the sickness in her stomach at his name.

"A distance from Owthorpe," John soothed. "And a lifetime from us." She believed his words and grew tranquil.

They came for John just after seven that evening, black riders sweeping out of the storm, hammering on the door, demanding entry. Commanded by one Coronet Atkinson, who strode into the hall with his soldiers at his heels, leather coats dark with storm water.

So this is the moment Buckingham promised. Three years of peace shredded in a thunderclap.

His London threat scarred Luce's memory. Words kept from John. Her gift of tranquility to her husband. And foreboding to herself.

"Come with us. Now." The soldier looked around the hall. "And we search the house."

"What means this?" John stood tall, his ague forgotten. "Show me your warrant."

"I do not need to."

John folded his arms. He no longer carried a sword, but he still possessed an authority honed by years of combat. Luce remained at his side. Next to her, Tom watched closely, determined to defend his father. In his early twenties, he reminded her of a young Allen. And now she knew why.

The defining moment. She recalled her own father's collapse, when the roles were upturned and the young protected the old. Her son's steadfastness consoled her. John's constitution was fragile.

Holding out his hand, John insisted again the warrant be produced. "I will not accompany you without verifying your authority."

Coronet Atkinson thrust a paper forward.

Lifting a lantern, John read the words aloud. Luce took Tom's hand. Bee put her arms around the younger children.

To Coronet Atkinson

You are hereby required, to repair to the house of John Hutchinson, Esq., at Owthorpe with a party of horse and him to seize and bring forthwith to Newark, and to search said house of what arms you can find, and bring them away also.

"On whose authorization?" John demanded. "This says nothing."

"Francis Leke. Deputy lieutenant. And justice of the peace." Atkinson spun around to his men. "Search!"

"You'll find nothing but our birding guns," Tom called after them. "And I would thank you kindly to leave those in place in the kitchen. We have to eat."

The soldier ignored him. "Bring your horse round," he commanded John. "We leave for Newark as soon as the house is emptied."

"We have no horses here." Luce refused to let John go, not at this time of night into the teeth of the storm, into the darkness. "My husband has been too ill to ride these past months, and we cannot afford the cost of keeping them. Please stay, warm yourselves by the fire and you can escort Colonel Hutchinson in the morning." Anything to delay them, to find a way to divert their mission. Her pride recoiled at the thought of offering hospitality to these rude men, but she could not let John disappear into the darkness.

"You." Atkinson gestured to Tom. "Go to a neighbour. Get a horse. Now."

Tom stood uncertainly, looking to his father for guidance.

"The way to Newark is challenging at night," John's tone remained reasonable, amiable even. "And it is near twenty miles to reach the town from here. Surely you would rather rest and leave at first light."

Atkinson ignored him, and a dread came upon Luce. "Get a horse from your neighbour," he shouted at Tom. "And return immediately."

With a final look at his father, Tom pulled his cloak from the peg on the wall and ran outside.

"Where are you taking my husband? He is weak, ill. You endanger his life by travelling through the storm," Luce pleaded, but as his men re-entered the hall, Atkinson's burly shoulders hunched against her.

"Muskets? Arms?" he barked.

They shook their heads. "The lad spoke the truth," replied one of them. "Just birding guns in the kitchen. We let them be."

"Go follow him. Ensure he brings a horse. We ride tonight."

"Please." Luce choked back tears. "Please, my husband's health is frail—"

"Not my concern, Mrs. Hutchinson. Get his coat and hat." Atkinson faced John. "Say your good-byes. It is a long road ahead."

She knew then she was beaten.

John held his arms out, and their children ran to him, and with muffled cries they clutched him tightly, calling to him in a piteous way, kissing his cheeks and hands. He soothed his family with a whispered blessing, one by one, until only Luce remained. He took her face between his palms, held her close to him.

"This will be resolved, and speedily," he said. "We have endured much worse, my love. They have no cause, not even one shred of evidence to link me to any uprising. I will be home in a few days."

"We will be strong and wait here for you." He must not see her fears. "But please have a care to stay dry, and do not sleep in damp clothes."

What a silly statement. Surely she could give him more than a childlike admonishment as he left.

He smiled and kissed her sweetly, deeply.

"I will obey as if both you and your mother are watching over me," he said, his eyes crinkling in the corners. "Now stay alert for any message that may come." His voice grew serious, and in an undertone he whispered, "If I urge you to reach Nan or Allen, do so immediately."

Atkinson's voice disturbed their quietness. "Your horse is here. We are leaving."

"I'm coming with you," Tom's voice echoed across the hall from where he stood in the doorway, dripping with rain, his hair plastered to his head. Luce had never been more proud of her son.

"You do not need to," John protested.

Tom smiled, and yet his eyes were piercing in the darkness. "I want to."

Atkinson shrugged. "I have no warrant for you, lad."

"You need not arrest me to keep me with him," Tom replied. "I have a steady mare, Father, and I shall ride at your side. If we must go, let us travel now so we may return all the sooner."

John kissed her again and pulled his hat over his brow, turning up his collar. Briefly, she glimpsed the young man who had first intrigued her when they met in the shadow of the moon at Richmond.

And then they took him.

By early morning, the storm had blown itself out, and as the silvery light of dawn crept across the soaked fields, she could only pray John had reached shelter. She could think of no reason for his sudden capture, no rhyme behind this surprise arrest. Luce faced the truth of her fears. Hate carried no logic.

Throughout her sleepless night, Buckingham's words seared her brain. She had convinced herself John was forgotten.

But others remembered.

Someone still knew where the regicide lived.

They took him on the Sabbath.

God, were you sending a sign?

On Tuesday, with no news arriving, she dispatched a messenger to Newark with fresh linens and food and medicine.

By return, Tom sent word John was to be interviewed by the Duke of Newcastle.

On Saturday, her nerves stretched to a point where she could barely breathe, Tom arrived at the house. She flew out to the yard upon hearing a horse, disregarding shawl and coif. Tom jumped down from the mare and patted her neck, tossing reins to the steward.

"You felt safe to leave your father?" Luce asked breathlessly, gripping his arm in her haste to find out John's condition. "His health, how is he? Is he taking his medicines?"

"He insisted I return home. And you know how obstinate he can be." Tom smiled, his eyes red-rimmed with exhaustion, stubble shadowing his chin. "I'm starving, and we can sit while I tell you the news. Bring Bee; she should hear too."

In the comfort of the warm kitchen, Luce and Bee sat at the familiar old table while Tom tore at a chicken breast and hunks of bread and cheese.

"Father is in good spirits," he confirmed between mouthfuls. "And although angry at his treatment at the Newark inn, he kept his temper and did not cause trouble." Tom chewed thoughtfully. "Well, except for when he hit the guard on the head with a candlestick."

Luce and Bee gasped. "What?"

"The man took father's horse with the intent of coming here and stealing our bird guns. He'd heard from Atkinson's men they'd left them here. Father put a stop to his plans."

"Tom, please, what of his charges, and where is he being held?" Did Tom think this a game?

"No charges," he said succinctly, taking a deep draught of the ale. "He's at the Talbot Inn. Mean accommodation, but at least not a prison. We went to see the Duke of Newcastle. He assured us no grounds exist for the charges."

Luce dropped her head with relief and rubbed her face with her hands. "Truly, we must give thanks to our Lord," she said. "For he has protected John once again."

"Amen," replied Tom and Bee.

"Will father come home now?" asked Bee. She put her arm around Luce, her young strength reassuring.

"Undoubtedly." Tom drained his tankard. "He told me to wait here, for he would join us in a day or two. The Duke of Newcastle just needed to finish his report back to Buckingham."

Luce froze. "Buckingham?"

Tom nodded. "Yes, it was he who brought the charges against Father. Newcastle showed me the letter himself. *'Imprison him upon suspicion of his role in the Northern Plot,'* it read. *'And make a full report of your findings.'*"

"And Newcastle makes his report now?"

"Yes. And he assured us he found no cause to connect Father with the plot. He claims complete satisfaction of his innocence and has dismissed the guard. He is free to leave for home tomorrow."

"And Buckingham?" Luce squeezed her hands so tightly her nails cut into her palms. She welcomed the pain making this nightmare conversation real. "What does he write to Buckingham?"

"A full exoneration." Tom turned to Luce with a big smile. "Is there any apple pie?"

And yet John did not return the next day, nor the following. Luce tried desperately to sustain the children's spirits, to keep the servants busy. All thankless tasks, for everyone's mind fixed on John and his safety.

"I do not know why the delay." Tom twisted between anger and fear, his calm demeanour crumbling under the weight of time passing. "He insisted I return here, prepare for his homecoming."

Luce rubbed his arm, trying to calm her boy. "Are you sure there is nothing you have forgotten to tell us of the interview?" she asked again. "The Duke of Newcastle was positive he had no grounds to hold John?"

"Positive." Tom was adamant. "He needed to make his report to Buckingham, and upon its receipt, release Father."

"Something has gone amiss," Luce fretted. "Something must be holding him up." She walked to the tall windows again, where night's black curtain imprisoned her sight. "Oh God, please bring him home, I implore you."

She turned to her son. "Tom, you will ride in haste to Ditchley tomorrow with this news. Nan will know how to help us. She will know."

Later, when the fire had died and everyone retired to bed, she sat alone. John's precious wall clock struck the hour of midnight, a clear, high chime piercing the darkness. Another sound crept into her consciousness, a creaking and crunching. A coach? Surely no travellers were abroad this late.

Luce jumped up, her Bible falling to the floor from her lap, and struggling with the stiff locks, she flung open the front door.

A shower of rain flew in on a gust of wind, and the air was fresh and clean from the west. Ragged clouds parted to reveal a mantle of shining stars, and in the dim light, a black coach with a single driver trundled along the driveway beneath John's tall beech trees. Guards rode front and rear.

Praise God, praise God above, for John was coming home.

As the coach turned into the yard, she ran to the edge of the path.

"John," she called. "My love, my love, you are home!"

The door remained closed. And these riders. Not soldiers, but the men of neighbours, friends. A wonderful homecoming.

Hurry, so I can warm you by the fire, hold your hands in mine.

"My love?" she asked. "My love?"

The door opened, and John climbed out slowly, stiffly, and limped towards her. The men remained on their mounts.

"John?" A tiny frisson shivered on the back of her neck.

Her husband pulled her into his arms. His clothes smelled sour; his beard was untrimmed. And his voice, when he finally spoke, was hoarse.

"We are only stopping briefly. The coach turned over and broke. It needs repair tonight, and in the morning, at first light, we travel on to London. The guards accompany me. The investigation continues at Whitehall."

"What? How can this be?" He made no sense. "What happened to the duke's promise?"

John glanced around. "We can talk inside. Buckingham insists I am to be kept a close prisoner. I could not write to tell you, for I was denied pen, ink or paper. The duke showed me Buckingham's response to his findings. He wrote *'that though I could not make it out as yet, I hope I should bring Mr. Hutchinson into the plot.'* He seeks more evidence of my alleged implication."

"That's right." Coronet Atkinson stepped forward. "We are taking Colonel Hutchinson to London. As a courtesy from the Duke of Newcastle, he is not under guard, but accompanied by men volunteered by your neighbours. Our destination is the Crown Inn in Holborn. From there, we await further command."

Luce tried to gather her thoughts, tried to make sense of what to do next. She silently pleaded with John, her eyes searching his for direction. He was silent.

Buckingham. And so he forces a return to London.
I brought this upon us. I cannot stay here while he is taken from me.
I must be with him.

"Then we travel with you," Bee said clearly and confidently. "You and mother, me and Tom. We travel with you, Father, for it is not your destiny to be on this journey alone."

Luce turned at her daughter's words and bit back her denial. Bee and Tom stood arm in arm, united in their determination. And who knew better than she how to fight with a brother at her side.

Luce's heart broke at the crying of the young ones as they again said good-bye to their father. Standing in the hall, she thought a swift departure best, promising an early return. But when the servants lined up and a piteous wailing set forth from the cook, Luce could not pretend a simple farewell.

John spread his arms wide, and the children rushed into them. "My darlings, I am but gone for a short while, and your mother and brother and sister accompany me on this business. We are gone for but a brief while." He met Luce's gaze steadily above their youngest's bowed head. "Susan will take great care of you, as she always has. Now behave as the sensible children I know you are, and place your trust in God to protect me and look after you. Say your prayers daily, and above all be obedient and kind to each other."

Luce stifled a sob, for John's parting words sounded so final. "I can't believe this," she wept. "Why now, why are they pursuing us now?"

John took her in his arms and whispered against her hair. "Hush, my love, for you will frighten them with your tears. Be strong, be strong. Trust in the Lord. He will care for us."

She counted a few breaths and steadied herself. Leaving her children and accompanying him tore her in two.

"Stay," he said. "I would not think less of you."

Luce scrubbed the tears from her cheeks. "No. I must come. The children will be safe in Susan's care. And as soon as we arrive in London, we seek out Allen."

John kissed her. "Then say good-bye to the little ones, dearest, and let us leave quickly." Bee came with Luce's cloak, and he helped her fasten it. "We must show strength and prove my innocence."

The coach waited outside, an ugly black vehicle Luce hated for its mission. Reluctant to take another step, she then lifted her head, determined not to let her children see her fright, and climbed in. Bee and Tom waited inside, faces solemn.

"We are all together," said Tom. "And together we are the Hutchinsons on our way to London. They cannot separate us, nor make us cower before them."

Over Tom's brave words, the driver gave a great shout. The horses strained forward, and the wheels crunched on the gravel. As Luce looked out, the servants lined up solemnly on the doorstep of John's beautifully designed home. She whispered good-bye to this manor she loved, to the now-tall trees blazing a golden flame, to the solid church tower protecting her mother and lost children.

Tom reached across and took her hand, his clasp firm and comforting.

Good-bye. We return soon. All of us.

Home.

The convoy made good time along the Fosse Way and over to the Great North Road. The strange atmosphere of travelling as captives along the familiar route to their London home was enhanced by the guard. These men

348

knew John, and treated them with great courtesy and deference. The journey assumed a dreamlike quality. Fear hovered on the edge of restless nights, but their days were brightened by John's optimism.

Her husband insisted on referring to their passage as an outing, one planned all along to take Luce, Tom and Bee to London. He sang songs, he read aloud from his book of devotions, and he created the most dreadful riddles Luce had ever heard.

By the time the houses became more plentiful, and London's orchards and allotments crowded the roadside, even Luce had convinced herself their trip would be short and the misunderstanding resolved.

The coach slowed as they approached the city, for the way was busy, and with their outriders they took up a wide swath of road. Gradually, the coach inched through to Holborn, and Luce recognised the streets of their old home.

"Our tenants will not want to leave," John observed. "We will find lodgings once we reach the Crown Inn."

Luce swallowed her worry. Their means were limited, and they could not afford to rent expensive rooms.

"Do not be concerned," John continued. "We shall find suitable accommodations as soon as we arrive."

"Perhaps Allen can help," Luce ventured.

John's mouth tightened. "We can manage. I would not bring him into this confusion."

The coach pulled into the courtyard of the stage post.

"The Crown. The Crown." shouted the driver.

Cornet Atkinson flung open the coach door.

"Colonel Hutchinson," he commanded, "come with me. Mrs. Hutchinson, remain here and seek a room for yourselves."

Dazed by the bustling yard, Luce questioned his words.

"Why? Why are you separating us?" she asked. "You said we would wait here at the Crown."

Atkinson grabbed John's arm and half dragged him from the coach, over Tom's loud protests

"You can wait wherever you like, Mrs. Hutchinson," he said. "My duty is done with you." The soldier marched John to a saddled horse, four guards attending. His final words were shouted over his shoulder. "My orders were to convey Colonel Hutchinson here by any means. And escort him to the Tower of London."

44

Frances

Embracing Luce felt as though she held a fragile bird in her hands. Frances's sister-in-law bore a brittle quality. God only knew from where she mustered her courage. As Luce withdrew from Frances's arms, her eyes glowed in the depressing inn chamber, and Frances realised a fierce fire inside sustained her.

"We came as soon as we could." Frances drew her gloves off and gingerly placed them on the bed. The tattered blanket looked none too clean, and on a second thought, she picked them up again. "Allen and I now reside at Richmond Palace, and I'm so sorry days passed before the messenger found us."

"No matter, you are here now," replied Luce. As usual, she was in a state of some dishevelment, her fingers covered in ink stains. "I am thankful for your company, and for Allen going directly to the Tower with Tom and Bee."

Mother Mary, how serious could this be?

"And you are still refused access to John?"

"We all are. I am hoping Allen will convince the guards to admit him."

Frances concealed her shock. Such close arrest signified a higher level of security than she had anticipated.

"How long do you lodge here?" Frances looked around. How desperate their circumstance, how quickly John's fortune was ravaged by Parliament's fines and banishment. For three adults, the room was pitifully cramped. Overlooking the yard, the small chamber was filled with the constant rumbling of coaches and the calls of the carriers. She suspected the sound did not abate much at night.

"Until they discharge John." Luce turned from the window, where she had rushed at the latest noisy arrival. "Frances, they will release him soon, won't they?"

"I do not know," Frances replied honestly, for she would treat Luce as she would want to be spoken to herself. "Allen and I will do everything to secure John's release as quickly as we can."

Footfalls in the corridor outside, and they looked to the door as it rattled open.

"Allen!" Luce flew into her brother's arms. "Allen, did you see him?"

"Hush." He held his sister close, his eyes meeting Frances's over her dishevelled hair. He shook his head slightly. "Not yet, but soon."

"Uncle Allen insisted we be admitted," Tom continued from behind him. "But even the use of the king's name held no sway with the guard. Father is under close arrest on the Duke of Buckingham's orders, and the only way we can see him is with a written warrant."

"We can't even get food or clothing to him," Bee said angrily, and Frances caught a glimpse of her grandmother in her spirit. "But we will, Mother, we will."

Frances drew Allen to one side. She needed to hear his true opinion. "Bee, take your mother down to the parlour and see she has something to eat. You too, Tom. You all look exhausted. We'll join you there in a few minutes."

Tom took his mother's arm while Bee smoothed Luce's hair and brushed out the creases on her skirt.

As soon as they left, Allen took a great shuddering sigh.

Frances touched his arm. "It's bad, isn't it?"

"Yes. I couldn't get close to him. There is no chance to enter his cell without a warrant."

"Can you get one?"

"Yes. With some time and persuasion." Allen glanced at the miserable chamber. "Dear God, we have to get them out of here. I wouldn't house a dog in this pit."

"New lodgings can be found. But until we know John's fate, we don't know where would suit." Frances's mind jumped ahead. If John's prison remained the Tower, Luce would need to care for him daily.

She stopped herself. Luce and Allen knew. They'd grown up in the Tower.

Allen broke into her thoughts. "I did acquire a piece of information from a guard. Not much, but interesting."

"And?"

"Tonight they are taking John to Whitehall for questioning. If we can get a sense of the charges and what they intend to do with John, I can ask Ned to verify the duke's role in this. And perhaps we can persuade Sir

352

Edward Hyde to intervene. You've done so much for his daughter. As has Nan."

"I will use any goodwill I can muster. Whitehall, then."

Frances concealed herself in the shadowed embrasure adjacent to Secretary Bennet's chambers, her heart thudding. Ever since Allen had discovered the secretary of state intended to personally interview John, she had searched for ways to secure an audience.

She'd met with no success.

This was going to be more difficult than she'd anticipated. Not only was Bennet the king's new favourite, he and Hyde despised each other, and there was no advantage to Frances's relationship with Sir Edward or his daughter. And Bennet enjoyed Barbary Villiers's lavish patronage, making Hyde despise him even more. Sir Edward seemed to be losing his grip on power. In the three years since Frances had arrived at court, she had finely honed her political navigation skills, and she could smell a dying favourite.

This called for more devious methods to ascertain John's future, and while Allen waited by the Whitehall steps to watch for his arrival, she secreted herself in a small chamber adjacent to Bennet's rooms. The palace was hushed, for it was almost midnight, and no one sought to question a well-dressed lady slipping through the shadows to the chambers of the highest in the land. No doubt an assignation, for half the court indulged in clandestine affairs.

Thanks be to God her doubt of Allen's faithfulness had long passed. And with Nan's exalted position in the duchess's retinue, no whiff of the old gossip trailed around her now.

Marching footsteps alerted her to John's coming, and she shrank farther into the shadows. She'd found a spot where a chink of masonry exposed a passage to the secretary's chamber, an old part of Henry Tudor's palace overlooked during a renovation. Secretary Bennet came into view, a tall, handsome man with the distinctive black plaster dressing over the bridge of his nose, evidence of a careless moment during the war. Even at a distance, he commanded an intimidating presence, and she feared for John's interrogation.

Her hand flew to her mouth to stifle a gasp as John appeared. His clothes hung on his thin frame, and although tidy, his lustrous hair lay limply on his shoulders. As he walked forward, his usual grace hampered by a hesitant step, Frances swallowed the anger that rose in her throat.

Mother Mary, please do not let torture have injured him. Or she would kill the tormentors herself.

The guards forced John to stand before Bennet, who lounged in a wide armchair behind his desk. He swayed slightly on his feet but looked straight ahead and did not relax his stance. Frances could only imagine the effort it cost him.

Pulling a document before him and dipping his quill in the well, Bennet barked his first question. "Where have you lived these past four or five months?"

John's voice was quiet but steady. "Constantly at home, at my own house in Nottinghamshire."

Bennett did not look up. Nor did he write a word. "What company resorted to your house?"

"I have been ill. Not even my nearest relations, for my wife has been nursing me, and I have no need of other company."

Bennet scratched on the parchment and dipped his quill again. "Let me put this another way, Colonel Hutchinson. What company have you frequented?"

John held his ground. "None, for I have not stirred from my home these past six months."

Frances willed him to keep his temper, for this rude conversation was the sort to always aggravate John's decorum.

"Hmm." Bennet sniffed. "A godly man such as you? Where did you attend church to hear divine service or common prayer, sir? I heard you encourage sermons from those who are against the king, that you host preachers who pray for the king's demise."

"Not true." John's voice became steely. Frances put her hand over her mouth. "I told you, I have not stirred out of my own house."

Bennet threw his pen down in exasperation. "How did you then, for your soul's comfort, Colonel Hutchinson?"

"Sir, I hope you leave me to account between God and my own soul," John replied firmly.

Bennet scratched a signature and dusted sand over the parchment. He did not look up again. "Return to the Tower. Your answers are clear."

John stood stock-still. "I was told I would have an audience with the king. You have done nothing to give me hope I may be heard."

"You have just been heard. And you say nothing." Bennet's chair scraped on the flagstones. He gestured to the guards. "Remove him."

"I am forgiven by the Act," John persisted. "I demand a fair hearing, for the king knows directly from Lady Wilmot, Lord Grandison, Sir Edward Villiers how I have followed my conscience."

Good, John. Invoke the names of those who saved you before.

Bennet glanced at him.

"I hear your conscience leads you in a direction antagonistic to the king, Colonel Hutchinson," he said contemptuously. "Try pleading forgiveness to the Duke of Buckingham, when a dozen reputable men swear of your involvement in the Northern Plot and he has the authority of the king to pursue you. Do not be hasty to talk of your fine friends. Invoke their help and I will tear apart their certificate of lies in a single action. And send them to join you in your current accommodation while we investigate them too."

John bowed his head, and Frances gripped the masonry tightly to prevent herself from crying out.

"Return him to the Tower immediately," Bennet ordered. "And double the guard."

Allen poured himself a glass of French brandy and tossed the liquor down his throat in one gulp.

"This is all Bennet asked of him? Dear God, the man gave him no chance to speak." He refilled his glass, the decanter standing full on the sideboard in their apartments. Frances knew the signs. His anxious humour sought familiar refuge in drink.

"Yes. I'm certain. The interview was no more than a quarter of an hour."

"A travesty," Allen burst out. "After all this time, after all our work with the Commons and the Lords and the damned certificate, and Hyde's bribes and Barbary's gifts, we are nowhere." He drank again and threw the glass across the room, where it shattered upon the fireplace. Without even glancing up, Allen drew another one from the shelf and filled it again.

"Allen," Frances began.

"A damn travesty," he shouted. He was lost to her. "Buckingham is unrelenting in his revenge. The king hides behind him, encourages him on this mission in private, I am sure. And John is not going to fight this. I can feel it in my bones." He threw the second glass after the first and grabbed the decanter by the neck, swigging back another great gulp of brandy.

"We have to keep sharp," she continued. "There must be a way forward."

Allen swayed and lifted the decanter before Frances adroitly twisted it from his hand. "Come, my love." She led him to the bed, and he followed her, as so many times before. The storms were brief, followed by an exhaustion leaving him insensible. "The first matter is to secure a pass for Luce, Tom and Bee, so they can visit John and bring him comfort. We will talk to Sir Edward in the morning. Secretary Bennet may have the ascendancy, but Sir Edward still has the power."

He slumped on the bed. She drew off his boots and loosened his jacket before lying down beside him and folding him in her arms. He fell into a deep sleep. A tear rolled into the creases at the corner of his eye, worn by years of outdoor soldiering and rough sleeping.

Frances's own tears flowed then, as she wept for these damaged men and their deep scars of war.

45

Luce

At the last, Sir Allen Apsley procured an order that she might visit him, but they limited it that it must not be but in the presence of his keeper. He was kept close prisoner, and had no air allowed him but a pair of leads over his chamber, which were so high and cold he had no benefit by them; and every night he had three doors shut upon him, and a sentinel at the outmost. His chamber was a room where it is said the two young princes, King Edward the Fifth and his brother, were murthered in former days, and the room that led to it was a dark great room that had no window in it, where the portcullis to one of the inward Tower gates was drawn up and let down, under which there sat every night a court of guard.

Luce Hutchinson
Spring 1664

The Tower hunkered before Luce as she crested Tower Hill, the moat as fetid as ever, the massive stone walls defying entry. In the centre of the Liberty, the keep stood impassively, and no amount of colourful pennants or golden weathervanes softened the stone pile. The White Tower had survived the centuries as testament to the unyielding and brutal character of England's kings.

She and Allen reined their horses by the All Hallows church and wordlessly surveyed their former home. Leaving noisy Holborn, riding down bustling Cheapside, even approaching Tower Hill, Luce's spirits remained buoyant, for today she was to see John.

Until this moment. Until she stood before the most wicked prison in the world, the most vile of gaols, the destroyer of men.

Her birthplace.

The prison she and Allen had dwelled within for more than ten years.

Privileged children of the governor. Taught to serve the king. And where her educated, questioning mind had first doubted these beliefs.

The prison that now confined her heart, the man who fought for her conscience and his own.

"Nothing has altered," Allen wondered. "I have not returned in thirty years, and yet this view is as if I were still a boy running home from Merchant Taylors' after lessons."

"Did you really expect it to?" asked Luce. "These places do not change, only the prisoners differ."

Allen kept his gaze on the complex. He searched the towers, the imposing walls, his eyes moving from north to south until finally his gaze rested on the cluster of houses hard up against the inner curtain wall. "Home."

"Once, a long time ago," replied Luce. "We are long gone."

"Our father lies here." Allen gestured at the church of St. Peter ad Vincula.

"Only his earthly remains. His spirit watches over us from heaven." She needed to shake Allen from his sorrow. Frances had warned his melancholy still lurked within, particularly in moments of great stress. "Come. I fear our pass could be cancelled at any time. We must seek John. And if we are permitted, we will visit our father's grave and walk past our old home."

She urged on her horse, and Allen fell in behind her on the familiar path to the Byward Gate. The usual crush of hawkers and food vendors lined the muddy track, selling overpriced food and threadbare secondhand blankets. When the families of prisoners realised the extent of their loved ones' deprivation, these crooks fetched a great price for a hunk of maggoty beef or a louse-ridden shawl purchased under duress. Cold comfort indeed.

Together, they returned to the Tower of London.

Not the Bloody Tower. Please God, don't let John be held within the Bloody Tower.

Her memory returned to the stories of the two boy princes, the substance of nightmare in her childhood. Did their sweet innocence haunt the walls of John's cell as they had troubled her dreams?

Luce's stomach twisted as she and Allen were escorted by two warders along the cobblestones of the inner ward. How often she ran and played and walked these lanes with her mother, skipping while holding her hand, defying the terror surrounding her. There was her old house, gables peeping over the daunting wall. How often the sight reassured her, knowing inside her father would be sitting at his accounts, a ready smile and a broad lap ready for her to clamber up to as he smoothed the hair of his favourite child.

358

Home.

Adjacent to the Bloody Tower. Only her mother's garden separating the two.

Allen looked at her. "Ready?" His episode had passed; his eyes were clear. His determination drove her forward.

"Ready," she replied. "They don't know who they are dealing with, do they?"

Allen shook his head. "The Apsleys return to the Tower. We outdid it once, Luce. We'll defeat it again."

They turned by the portcullis and stopped at the entrance of the Bloody Tower. Her instinct had been right. Just before they entered the narrow doorway, Luce stole a glimpse of the garden to the west. The sassafras trees had grown tall, and still a rose clambered over the gate, November-bare now, but evidence of her mother's plantings. She took a deep breath, steeling her courage, and edged her way up the winding staircase.

He was in the same room where the young princes had been murdered.

To the front, a dark chamber with the mechanism of the portcullis. She recalled how it had frightened her, groaning like a tortured Catholic when cranked. Three massive oak doors rimmed with iron and bearing huge locks imprisoned her love, and when the guard finally opened the last, she was so overwrought she could only burst into tears and run into John's arms.

While he soothed her, she became aware of the terrible plight of his condition. Thinner than she had ever seen him, his beautiful golden-brown hair was shorn to his neck.

"Lice," he smiled ruefully. "Easier to maintain." His filthy shirt clung to his body, and he wore every piece of clothing she knew of, one on top of the other. Her tears turned to anger, and a great rage surged as she turned to the nearest guard.

"Fetch Governor Robinson," she commanded. The guard protested, and she cut him off. "Now!"

The guard saluted and ran from the room.

Allen clasped John in an embrace and then held him to look at him, hands on each arm. "You look terrible, my friend."

"So would even you, Brother," John shot back. "At least I can have the excuse that my barber has been detained." He tugged at Allen's wig. "What's this?"

"Frances insists I wear it," Allen mumbled. "It's the court fashion."

"Remind me to order one," replied John, still eyeing Allen suspiciously. "In ginger."

Luce paced the room, no more than four strides in each direction. Two tiny leads opened above their heads, casting the only light into the gloom. A stub of candle squatted on a rough plank table, which had a small three-legged stool tucked below. A straw mattress on the floor completed the furnishings. A small fireplace, no more than twelve inches wide, held ashes long dead.

"We are sending money weekly to pay for your keep and food." Luce turned to John. "My darling, do you receive nothing?"

John shook his head and broke into a paroxysm of coughing. Luce clasped him to her, his thin chest racked with pain under her hands. He took a while to recover.

The guard re-entered the room. "Governor Robinson is not available," he said. "But if you and Sir Allen would care to call upon him on your departure, he would be delighted to welcome you to the Queen's House."

Luce and Allen exchanged a quick glance.

"We will attend him there," confirmed Allen. "Now leave us."

"We are to guard Colonel Hutchinson at all times," the guard protested.

"He's not going anywhere," said Allen. "Give us some time with my brother."

The guard refused to move. "The Duke of Buckingham's orders, sir. Three-deep watching him and close arrest. No paper, pen nor ink. And guards at all times with visitors."

"In that case, stand in the corridor, man, and turn your back." Allen took a step towards the guard, and he quickly retreated.

Luce pulled John into her arms again, comforting him as if he were a child.

"My darling, we will get you released. We will remove you from this dreadful place." She held him and rocked him and smoothed his cropped hair, wondering at the lightness of his bones and how long his chest would survive the cold and damp.

And if the ghosts still came at night.

Luce quickly helped John remove his filthy clothing, and she and Allen took a cloth and wiped his body. She swallowed her tears as she ran her hands over his thin frame, his ribs bumping under her fingers. Pulling clean garments from the pack, they dressed John as if he were helpless as a babe, for in truth he stood and let them care for him, his eyes fixed on the windows above their heads.

Next she pulled forth bread and a roast chicken and sat him down on the stool, cautiously feeding him a mouthful at a time. Her experience from the war reminded her a starving man's stomach would reject a sudden feast. Allen held the wine pouch to John's mouth and carefully helped him take a few sips.

The guard looked back once or twice and then resumed his stance, his back to the room.

With a little colour in his cheeks, John revived.

"How are your words, Luce?" he asked.

"What do you mean?"

Glancing to make sure the guard's back was still to them, John quickly withdrew a sheet of crumpled parchment from underneath the ragged mattress.

"How?" whispered Luce. "When you are denied even writing instruments?"

He smiled. "Even in the king's prison, we have our friends, my love. A warden served under me in Nottingham. Although he cannot provide me overt care, he was able to smuggle in pen and paper." John handed the document to Luce. "Here. Take this and use it against Governor Robinson to shout aloud the plight of all his prisoners. My body may be incarcerated, but they will never silence our voices. This is a full account of his corruption and wretched treatment of his guards and his prisoners. Publish it so all might know the rough justice innocent men are served."

Luce quickly hid the document inside her bodice, her heart alight with John's inspirational words. This she could understand. This was a battle she could win. "We will always fight for freedom and against oppression, my love. We will ensure you are heard."

After they bade good-bye, promising to return on the morrow now they were permitted access, Allen and Luce stood at the door of the Bloody Tower. To the left was the exit of the Tower complex, and a return to freedom. Ahead, the wall of their mother's garden led to the Queen's House.

They made their decision.

361

Together, they walked towards the timbered houses embedded in the ancient walls.

"I will insist to Governor Robinson John receive the food and kindling we are paying for." Luce looked straight ahead, for she did not want to see the execution block site on Tower Green. She refused to even consider this in John's future.

"Without hesitation," agreed Allen. "The man is a crook and a scoundrel. I had heard before he lines his own pockets at the expense of his guards and prisoners. Now we have proof. Do not show him John's letter, for we must smuggle his note from here and into the hands of a printer."

The last sassafras leaves clung to the cobbles; the trees grown full height now.

"Sir Walter Raleigh brought these as saplings from his voyage to El Dorado." A childhood memory of her mother collecting the precious bark for medicine returned to Luce. "I remember Mother speaking of his experiments in medicine and alchemy when she first lived here."

"Truly, her stillroom remedies saved so many prisoners from death," Allen responded as they walked up to the door of the house, a red-painted ornate piece set within the well-maintained front of the building. Fresh paint, polished glass and black iron well-rubbed and oiled spoke to money lavished on the property. The bones of the house stood as Luce remembered, but it was tricked out in fresh designs, no doubt.

"A bit different from our days here," muttered Allen, scowling as he hammered on the heavy wood.

Luce agreed. Nigh on derelict by the time they left, their father's debts and illness had forced them to chop paneling for fires and remove into one room to save on expense. "I would not have recognised the house," she replied. "I remember a dark and fearful place, and only our mother's presence providing comfort in those last years."

A servant eyed them. "Yes?"

Allen pushed his way past the man, and Luce followed. "Sir Allen Apsley for Governor Robinson," he said.

Familiarity assailed them. There were the stairs ahead, where the boys used to slide on the banisters. To the right, her father's offices, where all the duties of the Tower were managed, and a constant stream of visitors wore the floor smooth. A tread still marked where boots pummelled the wooden boards.

362

She looked at Allen and nodded upstairs. Creaking and footsteps indicated the governor was obviously walking about in his own private quarters.

"Governor Robinson," Allen shouted. "A word with you, sir."

The steps hesitated, and then a footfall on the stairs.

A portly, short man descended. Perspiring heavily even on this cold November day, he greeted them. "Thank you for attending me here," he wheezed. "I was engaged, otherwise I would have met you at Colonel Hutchinson's."

"Let me get straight to the point," Allen looked at him with disgust. "Mrs. Hutchinson has made several large payments to you to provide for her husband's maintenance here. It appears that not only have none of these needs been met, there is no sign that any money is put towards his comfort."

"Well, I am sure I will have to look into that charge," Governor Robinson blustered. "You understand, sir, I am responsible for the maintenance of many hundreds of prisoners and keepers here within the Tower. If one payment should go astray—"

"More than one, sir," Luce said. "For I have on good authority not one prisoner under your jurisdiction gets the care he is entitled to."

"Entitled?" The man's voice rose. "I beg to differ, dear lady. Anyone entering these walls leaves entitlement at the door."

"That is not the case," Luce shot back. "And you know it well. The governor is responsible for the security of the prisoners. And he is also responsible for the health and welfare of them, and to deny them the comfort of medicine, food and kindling is downright cruelty." Out of the corner of her eye, she noticed that Allen had wandered towards the back of the hall, where she could just glimpse a long table and several chairs. It was the room her parents had loved to enjoy, an elegant parlour for receiving family and friends.

"That may be your assumption, Mrs. Hutchinson, but not mine." Robinson puffed himself up. "I can certainly investigate your claim that money received for the care of your husband may not have reached him, but I cannot promise more."

"Oh, but you will do both." Allen's voice cut across the chamber. Even from where Luce stood, she recognised the tension in his body. "I have evidence to print and circulate that you are stealing money from the prisoners, are not paying the wardens and are using both for your own means. Correct this immediately, else I will report you directly to the king, and you will be stripped of your position here."

Robinson swallowed, his cheeks even redder under Allen's warning. "You threaten me, sir? You have no grounds."

"I have plenty," replied Allen. "My father ran the Tower for thirteen years. And during his time here, no one went hungry, no one went without medicine, and no one was subjected to the cruel treatment you have made a way of life." He beckoned Robinson and Luce over to his side, and she wondered at the excitement in his voice. "I am completely familiar with the inner workings of this facility. And for the privilege of me teaching you how to behave as a true Governor of the Tower," and here Allen laid his hand on his sword, "you will thank me for not reporting you to the king."

Robinson took out a large handkerchief and mopped his brow. "I would appreciate you not making a report, sir."

Allen stepped from the doorway, revealing the room beyond,

Luce gasped. A life-size, full-length portrait hung above the fireplace mantel. There stood her mother, painted in the most beautiful dress of tawny and russet, her sweet eyes gazing down upon her with love. And by her side, a small child, standing on a chair as if his mother had just popped him there to pose, a bunch of red cherries clasped in his little hands. The detail was exquisite, so lifelike Lucy could have stepped from the frame and embraced Luce, pulling her into the familiar warmth of her arms.

"Mother," she said, in wonder. "And you, Allen?"

Allen's face softened. "Yes. It's the portrait, the one she told us Father had commissioned when we first moved here."

And the one she left behind all those years ago.

Luce did not hesitate. John may have been the collector. But she still recalled Nan's wisdom on the value of these fine portraits.

She wheeled round to Robinson. "Time for this to be returned to its rightful owner. You will deliver our painting to my brother's apartments at Whitehall immediately. And I expect Colonel Hutchinson to have food, fresh linens, medicine and a substantial fire by the time we return tomorrow morning."

46

Frances

Frances surveyed the sitting chamber of their Whitehall apartments, satisfied she overlooked not one detail for her guest. Sir Edward was her sole source of information on John's future, and after almost six months, still he maintained secrecy. At tonight's dinner in honour of her patron's birthday, she resolved to secure the truth.

How would Nan have handled him? Flattery and attention, no doubt. Nan's absence from court troubled Frances. She fervently wished she would return. But once she'd appeared at Anne Hyde's side after the public wedding, endorsing the marriage with the Wilmot blessing, she'd left for Ditchley announcing family commitments. And did not return.

Nan, you always know where you are supposed to be. And where you should steer clear.

The Duchess of York's generosity reflected in Frances's beautiful home. The room glowed a welcome with fresh candles in every sconce. Colorful stencils of fruits, flowers and birds graced the highest reaches, and a collection of tapestries filled three of the four walls. The fireplace surround gleamed with a costly golden finish. Above, in a place of honour, hung the portrait of Lucy and Allen.

Frances smiled at her mother-in-law. "You neither expected nor desired to return to Whitehall, I know," she murmured. "But your son is so proud of his achievements he wanted you to share the honour with him."

Thank you for loving him.

"I do, come what may," replied Frances, and then she laughed, shaking herself from her fancies. She was as bad as Nan, who had confided she also talked to her portraits. There were real conversations to be had tonight, with Sir Edward and the Duke of York. And John's future rested upon them.

"Sir Edward is here." Allen strode into the room. "We should talk to him now, before he is distracted by the wonderful dinner you have planned."

"Agreed. Let me try securing his confidence. He is always more amenable to a female touch."

Allen nodded. "And you have certainly won his heart with your care for his daughter and grandchild. Do as you think best." He caught her hand and pulled it quickly to his mouth, kissing the delicate skin on the inside of her wrist, the sensual touch sending a shiver through her. After all these years, he still could make her tremble. "I love you."

She kissed him fully on the lips. "And I you, my love," she replied. "Always and forever."

"Ah, what a charming scene," Hyde's deep growl rumbled across the room. He imperiously waved away their servant. "Two happily married lovebirds and a relationship I will take credit for healing. It does my heart good in this court of loose morals and looser loyalties to see my relatives demonstrate upright and honest love."

Frances took his hand and curtseyed. "Sir Edward. Such a pleasure to have you join us tonight. To dine *en famile* is a rare pleasure these days. And wishing you a twelve-month of health and happiness."

Hyde nodded vigourously. "How time is swiftly moving. I was just writing to the king that I have not had a chance to speak to him for a year." He set himself down on the bench by the fireplace with a groan. "Now that might be a slight exaggeration, but to require him to attend to anything but pleasure is a fool's job, for sure. And one I grow weary of."

"The king spends much time at the mews with Buckingham," observed Allen, handing Sir Edward a glass of wine. "He is always in his company."

Taking a claret for herself, Frances joined Sir Edward. "It must be most frustrating, and difficult to get your business done, when the king is so easily distracted by pleasure." She laid her hand briefly on his arm. "And I know how tirelessly you work to keep the country's affairs foremost."

Hyde nodded. "It is not a simple thing. Especially when the Villiers woman takes pleasure in distracting the king's attention at every turn." He smiled at Frances, and the lines of weariness lifted. "But I must thank you, my dear, for all you have done for my daughter and the duke. Their household runs smoothly and is a delightful home for my grandchildren. I know the peace is because of your consistent oversight. You must tell me how I can repay you for your kindness."

"Serving your daughter is my pleasure, Sir Edward." Frances glanced at Allen. "I am greatly fond of the duchess. And Isabella and Franny are delighted to be playmates to little Mary. We are all very happy, as if one family."

"Very good. Very good." Sir Edward looked at Allen from under his thick brows. "I have recommended some additional duties for you. The duke requires surveillance work; you could assist with this in your position as justice in Norfolk."

"I would be honoured to lend my services." Allen bowed. "Please let me know how I may help."

"Come to my offices tomorrow at five," replied Sir Edward. "I have drawn up a certificate to pay you an advance of two thousand pounds for your troubles. We can discuss the need then."

"As you wish." Allen glanced back at Frances. "You are most generous."

Frances refilled Hyde's glass and stood. "I will call for dinner to be served." As if an afterthought, she hesitated. "Sir Edward, there is one question I have,"

"Of course, my dear. What do you ask?"

"John Hutchinson." She continued quickly, before he could stop her. "He's been housed in the Tower for six months now, with no hearing and no sign of one forthcoming. Surely you appreciate a man's rights under *habeas corpus*. His wife has pleaded with a number of Privy Council members, to no avail. Can you tell me of his fate?"

Clarendon sighed and rearranged his bulk on the bench. "He is a thorn in my side. And one I wish I could remove permanently, to be honest." He glanced at Allen. "My pardon, Nall, for I know there is much love between you and Luce."

"Will he remain in the Tower, then, my lord?" Frances asked.

Mother Mary, please prepare me for the worst.

"I have authorised him to be transported to Tangier." Hyde shifted on the bench and looked around the room as a dog sniffs for its dinner. "A thousand miles away in a north African colony should keep him quiet. He is the most recalcitrant of all of those excluded from the Act, and frankly, I must set an example of him." He looked at Allen. "I can't help Luce is your sister, Nall; our family ties have let me be too lenient for too long. Buckingham is out for his blood, and if I show mercy now, he will take mine too. He has no love for me and seeks to undermine my influence with the king."

Frances leaned forward, trying to understand his reasoning. "Why, Sir Edward? What has caused him this unrelenting persecution of John?"

Sir Edward raised his eyes to Lucy's portrait. "Your parents knew his father well. They received great rewards from him; our families were close."

Allen followed his gaze. "When we supported the king."

"The duke never knew his father. He was assassinated when he was but a baby," Sir Edward continued. "He was brought up by the old king, who never recovered the grief at losing his beloved favourite."

"He thought of the royal princes as his brothers. They were treated no differently. Even now Buckingham takes liberties with the king that no other man would dare." Allen reached for Frances's hand. "He avenges the king's death as if it were his own father's. Powerless to punish the assassin who ended his life, he pursues those who killed the king."

Sir Edward nodded. "And there you have the truth. Buckingham is warped with revenge and seeks to destroy any living conspirators in the king's execution. And he may not stop with just those who signed the death warrant."

Frances squeezed Allen's hand, warning him to remain silent. "Does that include Nan?" she asked. "Is Buckingham out to destroy her too? He always was jealous of Henry Wilmot. Her name on John's certificate of pardon must have provoked his ire."

Hyde nodded. "You are very astute, my dear. And why I urged her to return to Ditchley and remain there after this latest uprising. Buckingham is intent on linking John Hutchinson to the uprising to justify his persecution of him. Her presence at court was a constant reminder to Buckingham of his failure in bringing to justice and executing one of the most visible regicides."

And so they were on their own. As she and Allen had been before, survivors of the war's battles. Now they must negotiate for John's life too. While all those around them turned against them.

"Tangier is a heinous punishment, my lord," Allen's calm tone broke through her thoughts. "If banishment is indeed to be his sentence, perhaps you can delay for a few months. My brother-in-law is a signer on many of my business affairs, and if he is to be exiled, I must get my papers in order before his departure."

Frances marvelled at Allen's casualness. She knew he was burning inside.

"Not an unreasonable request, and I understand your concern," replied Hyde. "I can arrange a deferral. Remind me again when I see you tomorrow, and I'll delay his transportation for three months."

"Three months." Allen paced before the fireplace, the flames leaping as he stoked the fire alive. The wall clock struck midnight as Hyde's carriage clattered outside the window and faded away.

"Tangier," exclaimed Frances. "That will kill John. And Luce."

"We will not let him be transported there, we will not." Allen paced more until Frances caught his hand and pulled him on the bench next to her.

"We have faced worse, my love," she said. "Remember during the war, when we were in Barnstaple, surrounded by Fairfax's troops, no way out but to surrender. And even then we found a way to leave, saving your men and our pride."

"Are we prepared to leave all this?" Allen waved at their room, the wealth surrounding them. "For if we rescue John, we could be branded traitors with him."

"In the beat of my heart," retorted Frances.

"You have all you desire, which we sacrificed so much for."

"And does this really matter when John is in mortal danger, Luce and their children's future threatened with obliteration?" Anger propelled Frances to her feet. "This is all just earthly trappings, meaningless fool's gold. I enjoy our rewards, Allen. But I could throw them all away tomorrow. Our brother's life is at stake. Your sister's safety under siege."

"And just as we fought before—"

"—so we fight again, my love."

47

Luce

The greatness of his mind was not broken by the feebleness of his constitution, nor by the barbarous inhumanity of his jailers, which he received with disdain, and laughed at them, but lost not anger on them.

Luce Hutchinson
Summer 1664

Luce stretched her fingers, cramped from frantic writing since the first weak light had infused her dingy room. She must capture the words filling her mind, ideas born of John's travails, brought alive by the fervour of his own pamphlets and letters.

John's inspiration came from a complete acceptance of his fate, an absolute conviction he would not change one thing about his past, no matter how many times the devil tempted him to renege his integrity.

She must remember this. Her ideology had prompted his decision that winter's night in 1649. His conscience had ratified it. From these terrible days of captivity re-emerged the symbiosis of their beliefs. No longer was he angry at her deception. No more did she feel guilt at her role in the execution.

The clock of St. Dunstan's chimed eleven. Another morning spent in worthwhile writing, and she still had time on her way to the Tower to stop at the bookseller in St. Paul's to arrange a reprint.

"Do not interfere this time, Luce," John's mild tone softened his admonishment. "Do not think to forge my words or signature. Write only your words, and do not put them in my mouth. My future is in the Lord's hands now. The God looking over me at Owthorpe is the same God offering protection in Tangier. Where my body eventually lies will not influence where my soul rises to heaven."

She caught his hand and knelt beside him, for he was weak today and could not rise from his mattress. The Bloody Tower was slowly, inexorably sapping the life from him.

"Do not speak of dying, John, or exile, I implore you."

"My death is only a release of these earthly bonds, for I look to my eternal rest with God, not this temporary abode on earth."

Allen crouched next to them so his words could not be overheard by the guard. They were still restricted in their privacy with John.

"Frances and I have pled with the king's brother for mercy," he whispered, "for Buckingham prevents us from speaking with the king. In all honesty, John, you may still be in prison for some time. But there are rumours you will remain in England. Frances is convinced that instead of Tangier, you will be sent to the Isle of Man."

"An exile commuted? And still a lifetime in prison?" Luce despaired. Already, their family was scattered between Owthorpe and London, her lodgings and the Tower. "How can I live by you and raise our children? We have little money and no prospects of more, John."

"Hush, my love, we will find an arrangement." John smoothed her hair and drew her into his arms. She still could not get accustomed to his thin frame, but his chin resting on the top of her head was dear and familiar.

"John's right. First, we must secure his safety here in England. I'll leave you both for now," said Allen, standing. "I am back to Whitehall to see if I can find out any more information. Buckingham still seeks final proof of John's role in the uprising. But be prepared for a sudden move. John's presence is too visible in the Tower, and if transportation is controversial, then a remote prison in England will be the answer."

"I am ready." John's eyes shone, catching what little light flowed in from the high leads. A tiny patch of blue reminded Luce of the passing of time. Summer was once more here.

"Perhaps Allen can secure a prison where you are not confined, my love," she said. "Where there is land to walk and a fresh breeze to return colour to your cheeks."

Allen briefly touched John's shoulder before he left. "Keep your faith, Brother. I am not giving up."

After a while, Luce lay down with John on the old mattress on the floor, whispering stories of Owthorpe and his gardens and how his beloved beech trees grew this past spring, as she'd witnessed on her recent visit. With these images on her lips, she drifted into a quiet sleep with John in her arms.

Tangier was deemed too divisive to Parliament for a man of John's character. Still, he had his supporters, those in Parliament who questioned Buckingham's motive but were not brave enough to challenge his rule. And yet the Isle of Man was considered insufficient in its security to hold such a dangerous state prisoner. Luce scoffed at the reasons. John only spoke the truth so many dared not utter. What security other than muffling his words could be enforced?

When the news came of his destination, no warning preceded. That night she left the Tower like any other. Only later did a messenger arrive at her lodgings to inform Luce of her husband's transportation to Sandown Castle in Kent on the morning tide.

Sending an urgent note to Allen to look out for their possessions, and gathering all the coin they possessed, Luce, Bee and Tom hurried to the Tower wharf.

"Colonel Hutchinson. Where is he?" Luce urgently questioned a guard.

"Gone, ma'am. Gravesend. And from there to Sandown." The man, old enough to be her father, looked at her with sympathy in his eyes. "You can still catch up. The tide don't turn for another hour."

"Thank you," Luce replied.

"God bless him, ma'am. Colonel Hutchinson changed our conditions here. If not for him and his news sheets, we would still not be paid."

The guard's words gave her strength. There was a purpose to their journey again. John would not be spirited into a secret prison.

They hailed a packet boat travelling downriver and, clinging to the sides, shot the bridge and left the Tower behind. Once out of the city, the river flowed smooth and silky, assisting John's voyage on the ebbing tide to the estuary and coastal marsh flats.

He's slipping away.

She ignored the devil's whisper and prayed instead. Her children's faces were resolute. Thank God for their strength.

Sandown Castle stood on the bleak Kent coast, a tumbledown defence fort from the days when King Harry had fought the French for Calais and Queen Bess challenged the great Spanish Armada. No more than a five-sided gun tower, with round walls to deflect cannonball and its feet anchored in the Narrow Sea, the castle looked impossibly habitable. Luce, Bee and Tom wearily stumbled over the rough hillocks to the damaged castle gate.

And were immediately refused entry.

"Ain't providing for no family calls." The guard stood adamant. "No visitors here. We only got two prisoners. It's a bloody nuisance to man a guard. Go back to Deal." He slammed the iron gate, throwing a series of bolts. And then only nature's silence, great torrents of seawater foaming around the castle's feet, the screaming of gulls rending thick spray-filled air.

"They intend to break our spirits," Luce raged. "They know not our character."

Bee nodded. "We will find lodgings in Deal. A walk along the shore will not keep us from Father."

As they turned south along a narrow path at the ocean edge, the waning light caught the steeple of a church tower and a cluster of houses about a mile away. A small pier jutted out into the water.

"Let us find an inn, eat and rest," said Tom. "There is no more to be done tonight. We know Father is here, and we will return in the morning."

Deal boasted a few streets of higgledy-piggledy cottages and a dozen inns. Judging by the number of sailors swaying through the alleys, these were the main attraction in the town. Stopping at the Anchor, which appeared the most respectable of the wharf-side inns, Tom settled Luce and Bee into a corner of the smoky tap room and ordered hot food and ale. The landlord came over and served them himself.

"Mrs. Hutchinson?" he whispered. His rough red face reflected the firelight, and his whiskers created a halo around his chin.

She looked at Tom, who nodded reassuringly.

"Jim Sibley. My brother served under your husband in Nottingham," the man continued. "Never was there a kinder, more generous colonel. He saved my Jack's life once when he would have been left for dead in a skirmish. My deepest thanks, ma'am."

"Thank you, my friend." Luce's eyes filled with tears; she could not stop herself. "My husband distinguished not between sides if a man's life was in peril once a battle was over."

The landlord bowed his head. "Thanks be to God." He looked over at Tom. "I hear you have need for lodging. In the attic, I have a simple but clean room. My wife and I would be honoured if you would stop here with us until you know your husband's situation."

Luce smiled at him gratefully. "Mr Sibley, your offer is most kind. We would be very appreciative of your hospitality. Thank you."

Within a week, Luce had managed to secure rooms with Mr Sibley's cousin. At least now she maintained a base from which to care for John. She sent Tom back to London to advise Allen of their situation, and on to Owthorpe to see to the younger children. With Bee at her side, she set about their new routine. And through sheer persistence of arriving at the wretched castle entrance every morning and refusing to leave until darkness approached, she finally broke down the guards' resistance.

The first day they were permitted to visit John, she cried aloud at the horror of his situation. No more than a corridor, his room consisted of a cold square of stone with five different doorways and no shutters to deter the constant wind on this forlorn coast. No bed, no furniture nor firewood, no table on which to eat.

"All can be had for a fee, Mrs. Hutchinson." The captain of the guard waved a filthy hand at John's lodging. "Pay me and you can have anything brought in for your husband."

And so back to Deal again, where the local merchants hiked their price when they knew she had no other choice but to buy their miserable goods.

At great expense, Luce arranged for furnishings to be brought to the terrible chamber and paid for a workman to create boards to keep the worst of the weather from blowing into the room. Although summer was upon them, terrible fogs stole into the damp ruins each night, and at high tide waves crashed at the base of the tower, just feet below John's room. As the weeks progressed, he developed a ceaseless cough, and she worried at the depth of the phlegm in his chest. Each day she scrubbed the mould from his blankets, despairing he would ever be dry and warm again.

Come soon, Allen, come and help me, please. I know the king and the duke keep you by their side, I know you have royal duties, but my husband is dying, and I need you here.

Finally, in July Allen arrived, bringing with him chests of warm blankets, medicines from Johanna and a pass for John to walk outside, secured by Frances. He brought news from Tom at Owthorpe, that their lands were in good hands, their younger children safe in Susan's care. And with the arrival of his brother-in-law and best friend, John began to rally, for with the good food and medicines, gradually he regained his strength.

Allen stayed for almost a month. On the day John rose from his bed and, leaning on Allen's arm, took his first tentative steps to the outside, Luce wept.

"I fear you would beat me in a horse race today, my brother," John joked. "But I would still give you a head start, just to make you feel better."

"And I would go at half-pace so you could keep up," teased Allen. He put his arm around John's waist and steadied him as he stood at the edge of the stony shore, both of them facing the sparkling sea.

"Thank you, Allen." John's voice fought the gusting wind, and the cry of the seagulls drowned his next words. Allen embraced her husband and released him to stand tall next to him. The two men Luce loved most in the world stood side by side in silence, shoulders touching, lost in each other's memories.

Thus they came together in adversity, as they always did.

Allen left the next day, promising to send news from Whitehall as soon as he could. "Keep him outside as much as you can, Luce," he said. "The fresh air and exercise is best for a man of his choler. Do not let him rot inside that hellhole."

She nodded. "Thank you, Allen. And thank Frances for us too. I know she takes a risk in these requests for John. It is not easy to be the sister-in-law of a prisoner of state."

Allen smiled. "You know Frances. She thrives in a challenge." He kissed Luce and held her close. "I will see you again soon, Sister. We are at Richmond through the summer now. I will be able to return before we move back to Whitehall. Do not despair, for we are out of the Tower, and John is stable and on England's soil. We will prevail."

Through the warm August days, John loved to walk along the beach with Bee at his side, and at low tide they would hunt for shells, bringing the prettiest back to his room. Always a collector, John spent his days sorting and laying out cockleshells, heaps of blue, black and purple treasures that gleamed like opals and onyx.

"See, Luce," he said. "Even in these most humble of places, God creates riches."

He read his Bible daily and chided Luce out of her sorrows. "God has granted me peace," he said. "And if I never read another book again but the Bible, my heart is content."

"Your library at Owthorpe waits for you, John," she said. "And your gardens."

"I think I will return one day," he replied. "For God is benevolent in his mercy, and I travel there each night in my dreams."

"Tom writes the harvest is good this year," she said. "And asks I return to pay the servants and take part in the bringing in."

"And so you should, my dear," John replied. "For they have worked hard for us. It is only fitting you should be there to thank them on my behalf." He picked up a piece of paper and handed it to her. "And while you are there," he continued, "please walk to the fishponds and see how my design for a new bridge and plantings will fit. I think I have the proportions correct, but I need you and Tom to pace it correctly. We should drain more of the land and create an additional pond to stock us for the winter."

"You do think of Owthorpe all the time," she mused. "You are never far from your home, are you, John?"

He smiled. "My love, to not think of Owthorpe would be to not think of my life. The two are inseparable. We have been so happy there, and we will be again."

He kissed her and caressed her cheek, smoothing away a tear. "Why do you weep, my love?"

She struggled with words, for she had none.

"Go and carry my dreams with you, and return to me soon with the news of home I long to hear. That is the best gift you could give me."

Her time at Owthorpe passed quickly, for Tom's sure hand guided the harvest, and John's loyal tenants knew the routine of old. She stayed long enough to pay them and attend the festival at the end of the gleaning. Her children bravely told her to return to their father, for his needs were greater than theirs. And, of course, she surveyed the fishponds and confirmed John's designs for expansion. She warned Tom this winter there would be work aplenty on his plans. Her son flourished under John's trust, and revenues began to flow from the land again.

Perhaps this double life could work after all. She said as much to Nan as she called in at Ditchley on her return to Sandown. Nan had gathered her into her arms and whispered encouragement, telling her to stay strong. As Luce surveyed the beautiful grounds, the mellow old house, and the riches of Nan's land and possessions, she took heart in her cousin's ability to endure great adversity. If Nan Wilmot could navigate the rough waters of marriage to Cromwell's hated enemy, Luce could conquer her own fears for the future.

Time to plan their life until they could return to Owthorpe. Perhaps she should bring the children to Deal, for surely their company would hearten John in his isolation.

In London, she stopped with Allen and Frances at their apartments in Whitehall, but despite their hospitality, she refused to linger more than a night. After hearing of her plans to move the children to Deal, Allen decided to travel with Luce to help find a suitable home, settle her new life. As they rode the five days to the remote Kent coast, they made plans for Luce's future.

On the sixth day, they rode the last mile to Sandown.

"We will rent a decent house here in Deal, where you can be comfortable and make a home for Bee and the other children." Allen's decisiveness cheered her greatly. "I have the means, Luce, for the duke has made me a rich man. We will furnish it well, and make sure you have every comfort. Tom can run Owthorpe now; he is experienced in the management of the land, and it is time he took on the responsibility."

"You make it sound so simple." Luce smiled at her brother. "We must get used to this new life, I suppose. And yet I fear that Buckingham still plans to send John to Tangier, and that is why he is by the sea."

Allen shook his head. "Frances and I have determined there is no danger of John being transported. Buckingham is distracted with pursuing Sir Edward now, eager to topple him from power. Nan is continuing secret discussions with Barbary to judge the king's mood. Gradually, John will fade from active memory. And when the time is right, we will bring him home."

"Our lives became complicated, didn't they, Allen?" Luce caught his hand. "And yet our love for each other endures."

377

"Always, Sister, always," he replied. "Deeper and stronger than ever. You know my heart is fully yours."

"And mine yours," she said. "If I am ever not a liability."

Allen reached and clasped her hand. "You will always be my little sister. Which means you are always a nuisance. But I still love you." He turned on his saddle, the fresh wind catching his hair, still the boy she remembered, the big brother she adored. "In John's honour, race you along the beach to the castle. I'll give you a ten-count start!"

"I can't ride as fast as you. And I'm afraid of falling."

"You were never afraid before, Luce. Not when we were in the Tower, not when the bailiffs came knocking, not when Leventhorpe Francke was so terrible to our mother." Allen gathered his reins. "Do not let fear become your prison, Sister!"

Luce urged her horse forward. She leaned over its strong neck, and the pounding hooves and sharp sea breeze brought her more alive than in months. Allen's horse was gaining on her, she could hear its breath, and she pressed hers forward faster, gripping tightly on. With a cry of triumph, she reached the castle walls and wheeled around.

"I won! I reclaim John's honour!" She jumped down and tied the reins to the hitching post, flushed and breathless, laughing at Allen's scowl. "Come, he will be so proud to hear that I recovered his pride and beat you!!"

"Next time, five count," he scolded, love in his voice. "You rode like the wind, Luce."

They laughed and entered the prison arm in arm.

And stopped when they reached John's room

Empty.

Except for Bee, who sat on a stool by the window, her hands sorting John's collection, her head bent over her task. In the set of her shoulders, Luce knew.

Bee turned at their footsteps.

"He's gone," whispered Luce.

Tears running down her cheeks, Bee nodded.

She choked on her words, picked up a shell. "Two days ago. He fell into a deep sleep, and upon waking, although most weakened, he gave Allen his blessing."

Allen gave a great sob, his anguish drowning the wild waters below.

Bee took a deep, shuddering breath. "His last words were for you, Mother. He said you would be so surprised." She choked again before her words burst forth in a torrent of tears. "So surprised that he would leave while you were away. His face became so calm, speaking of you. He died in complete peace."

Luce could not move, would not speak. For to acknowledge Bee's words would be to accept the truth of her loss.

Bee reached onto the tray and pulled forth an object. "And he left this for you. He told me you would know what this meant."

She placed the fragile last gift from John in Luce's palm.

A delicate golden starfish.

A star.

Destiny.

48

Nan

Nan caressed the spines of the books in John's library. So many volumes, so lovingly worn. She perceived the empty space above the fireplace and the blank wall opposite the window. The ghosts of paintings remained in nail holes in the plaster. Signs of better times.

"Did John purchase all these books?' she asked. "There must be over a thousand volumes here."

By the window, staring out across the flat fields to a distant hill, Luce stood etched against the cold northern light.

"Some were his father's," she murmured. "But many he acquired." She tilted her head slightly, as if listening to a voice no other could hear. "When we first married, he gave up a position in the Star Chamber in favour of being tutored in the philosophies contained within this library. He always preferred the company of words."

"And you," added Frances from her place by the fire. She'd ordered the logs lit and wine and cake brought to the library upon their return from the funeral. "You were his words and his world, Luce."

"His world. Allen has taken the children for a long walk through the woods to the ponds," Luce mused. "John would have enjoyed being with them. Owthorpe is his world. But no more."

Nan joined her at the window. "John is everywhere you turn, my darling. In the sky, the water, the land and this beautiful house he built for all of you. He is home and at peace now—"

"With Mother."

"With Lucy." Nan glanced at Frances, motioned her to come close. "They are in heaven. And we are left on this earth to carry on their legacy."

Frances brought a glass of wine to both of them. The house was cold, and the church colder. Frances raised an eyebrow, and Nan lifted her goblet slightly, a message between them conveyed and accepted.

"When Allen and I were in exile, and knew not where our next meal would come from, I did not think times could ever be good again," Frances began. "And yet, through the challenges, I always believed I would survive somehow, and my children would give me purpose to continue."

Luce remained silent but sipped her wine, the warm red Madeira raising a slight flush in her pale cheeks.

"And when Henry died, and I knew not if I could hold Ditchley for even one more day, my boys' future was my solace," Nan continued. She turned as if examining John's books, glancing at Frances again.

"And now my daughters are brought up in the royal household, and Allen holds court positions to keep us in comfort for the rest of our lives," Frances said. "My dream for them came true."

Luce turned to the window again. Her eyes reflected the pale blue evening sky, her face thin and cheeks hollowed.

"My boys are my life," agreed Nan. "Now Allen has formally presented Johnny to the king, he is invited to join the court on his return from his grand tour."

"You both have high ambitions." Luce turned from her contemplation. "I do not wish the same for my children. The wicked life of court is one they will never know. They must stay here in the country and enjoy godly lives, content with their education and books and love of family."

Nan drifted over to the other side of the fireplace, where more bookshelves lined the alcove. The light grew dim here, and she bent to examine the volumes stacked in the dark corner.

"More books, Luce? And yet these look handwritten." Nan opened one. Line upon line of clear, tightly penned writing filled the pages.

Luce broke from her reverie.

"These are not to be read." She wrested the notebook from Nan's hands.

"They are yours?" Frances joined them and pulled another volume from the shelf. Nan did the same.

Luce let forth a cry and reached for them. "These are private diaries. My words. My life. My sorrows." She seized the books from Frances and Nan and stood defiantly in front of the shelves.

"John's words. John's life. And John's happiness," Nan shot back.

Luce's head jolted as if slapped.

"These are your children's legacy, Sister." Frances reached past Luce and pulled another handful of small leather-bound volumes from the shelf.

"Their father lives in each of these books. Would you deny them knowledge of the man you love so much?"

At Frances's words, Luce dropped her hands, her face crumpling.

"He is lost to me. He is gone. Gone."

Nan drew Luce into her arms, encouraging her cousin's sorrowful keening, the balm of tears.

"He is with you, now and always. His words are your words, and yours are his." Nan stroked Luce's thin back. "Take your notebooks and diaries, his letters, your thoughts, Luce, and write. Write as you never have before. Write the story of his life, of yours, of all of our lives."

Nan gently turned Luce and smoothed away her tears, lifting her head so she gazed out beyond the clear glass to John's beloved land.

Frances joined them. "Write for your children, so they may know the man he was and how his courage and conscience transformed a country."

They linked arms around each other's waists. Beyond the verdant green pastures of John's beloved land, Luce's children darted from the copse, fleet figures running towards them, the west wind at their backs. Allen followed, dogs at his heels, a man walking alone.

Frances raised her hand as Allen drew close to the house. He waved in return, the grief on his face fleetingly lifted before he dropped his hand and walked on.

"Go to him," Nan said quietly. Frances's place was with the living. "Go to Allen and bring him the comfort only you can."

Frances nodded and wiped her own eyes. Kissing Luce on the cheek, she paused. "John's legacy is yours to honour, Luce. Uphold his integrity, his beliefs. You can speak for the voiceless women of this land."

She left and moments later ran across the grass to Allen. He stood still as Frances embraced him, drawing his head to her shoulder, wrapping her arms around him, two figures standing as one against the wide October skies.

Luce's weeping quietened. Within Nan's arms, she ceased trembling, became still.

A hawk hovered over the Fosse Way and circled higher and higher until it vanished in the heavens.

Nan released Luce from her embrace. "Our husbands died for England's future. Their blood nourishes her recovery. And as women we can also restore our nation's health." She must break through Luce's grief,

382

ignite the fire that always sustained her. "We have no role in politics. We depend on the men who sit on the throne and in Parliament. But we have power. And it lies in our ability to influence from the shadows and shine light to diminish the old darkness. We must ensure England never turns against herself this way again."

Luce nodded, standing on her own now, her eyes on the far distant horizon, the ridge of the thoroughfare between London and Nottingham.

"I cannot conceal the facts of our cause," she said.

"You must not lie," Nan spoke fiercely in her response. "But in doing so, your words will be controversial, even dangerous."

"I must write the truth as I know it to be."

"Yes." Nan clasped her cousin's hands. "For the sake of healing, speak honestly from your heart. And when you have written your memories of John's life, entrust me with their safekeeping. I will protect them from John's enemies. And I promise your children will know the cause you fought for, and the enduring grand passion which gave them life."

"Memories," repeated Luce. "A memoir. Of the life of Colonel John Hutchinson. Of my love." She took the notebooks and gathered them to her breast. "This is my destiny. For you, for my children, for England."

Author's Note

Frances

Sir Allen Apsley and his enterprising wife, Frances Petre Apsley, remained at court, where they continued to enjoy the patronage of the Duke of York. When King Charles died with no issue and James became king, Allen and Frances's daughter "Franny," Frances, later Lady Bathurst, became maid of honour to James II's daughters, Mary and Anne. Mary succeeded her father during the "Glorious Revolution," putting a Protestant firmly on the throne. Franny maintained a deep friendship with the future Queen Mary throughout her life, and Allen and Frances were the beneficiaries of a long and profitable employment in the household of the duke.

Allen and Frances are buried next to each other, not far from Edward Hyde and Barbara Villiers in Westminster Abbey. Their direct descendent, the 9th Earl Bathurst, maintains the secondary title of 8th Baron Apsley. The beloved portrait of Lucy and Allen remains in the family in a place of honour.

Nan

Anne Wilmot, Dowager Countess of Rochester, lived well into her eighties and continued her ingenious scheming for the rest of her life. After negotiating and securing the extremely advantageous marriage of Frank's child, her grandson Edward Lee, to Charlotte Fitzroy, the illegitimate and highly loved daughter of Charles II and Barbara Villiers, she then attended to the rise of her beloved son John Wilmot. The 2nd Earl of Rochester replaced Buckingham in the king's affections and remains famous today for his scandalous wit, charm, lethal charisma and vulgar yet brilliant poetry. As she nursed him through his early and painful death, Nan's plaintive letters to Johanna St.John begging for curatives are heartbreaking.

Luce

Luce Hutchinson retired to Owthorpe after John's death, where she began writing an account of her husband's life for the benefit of her children, composed poetry, wrote significant theological tracts and lived on the fringe of the burgeoning early modern women's literary movement. Her

385

extraordinary poem *Order and Disorder* is considered by many to be equal to Milton's *Paradise Lost.*

Dangerous to publish in her own time because of its controversial content, Luce entrusted the finished memoirs manuscript and her notebooks to Nan, where they were discovered upon her death in the late 1680s. Luce's eyewitness account of the English Civil War was published by her great-grandson Julius Hutchinson as *Memoirs of the Life of Colonel Hutchinson* in 1806 and has been in print ever since. Her writing is now considered one of the foremost examples of seventeenth-century women's literature and a fascinating insight into England's Civil War.

Although Owthorpe House has long vanished, St. Margaret's church remains, and within lie Lucy, John and Luce, forever together and memorialised by Luce's words.

Made in the USA
Coppell, TX
23 October 2020

40122277R00225